SHADOWS

OF

PECAN

HOLLOW

SHADOWS
OF
PECAN
HOLLOW

A Novel

CAROLINE FROST

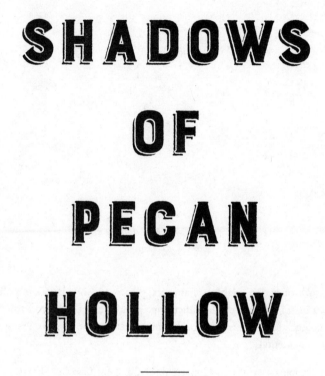

WILLIAM MORROW
An Imprint of HarperCollins*Publishers*

SHADOWS OF PECAN HOLLOW. Copyright © 2022 by Caroline Frost. All rights reserved. Printed in the United States of America. No part of this book may be used or reproduced in any manner whatsoever without written permission except in the case of brief quotations embodied in critical articles and reviews. For information, address HarperCollins Publishers, 195 Broadway, New York, NY 10007.

HarperCollins books may be purchased for educational, business, or sales promotional use. For information, please email the Special Markets Department at SPsales@harpercollins.com.

FIRST EDITION

Designed by Nancy Singer

Library of Congress Cataloging-in-Publication Data has been applied for.

ISBN 978-0-06-306534-5

22 23 24 25 26 LSC 10 9 8 7 6 5 4 3 2 1

for Jake

SHADOWS

OF

PECAN

HOLLOW

PROLOGUE

ROUND TOP, TX, 1976

The young woman awoke to the sound of scissors. She blinked the haze out of her eyes, rolled over the tangled sheets to greet him. She was nineteen or so, but the crease between her brows and the wear on her skin hinted at a life not lived but endured.

He sat naked beneath the window, a stack of newspapers beside him, cutting. The light dripped down his slick black hair and pooled on his shoulders, the tops of his knees, but his face, which was bent toward his work, was only shadow.

"Morning," she said, her voice dry as sand. She groped the nightstand for something wet and drank the rest of a warm Dr Pepper from who-knows-when. "What's that? Did they see us?"

He continued to pump the scissors, long and heavy ones with black handles, and sniffed.

"You shoulda put ice on that," he said.

She cupped her cheek, which was hot and swollen as a late summer plum. If she flicked it, she thought, it would split from eye to ear.

"It doesn't hurt," she said.

"Well, it should," he said. "The fuck is wrong with you." He'd given the

bruise to her yesterday, when she had rushed the getaway and stalled out. A sucker punch to the side of the head.

He arranged the cut pieces in front of him, flipped them over, and brushed glue along the backs. The fumes snaked across the room to her, a smell she had always liked. As he worked, a gold medallion necklace, one he'd lifted off a guy passed out behind a club, swung and tapped against his chest.

"If they got eyes on us, we should take off. Hang out in Louisiana for a bit," she said. He paid her no mind. He was always tempting the law and the day would come he'd get them both locked up. This life was mean. The late nights, the constant running, and the sickening fear of getting caught. It was too mean, even for her, but she hadn't figured out a way to lose the life and keep the man.

She sat up, gathered the motel sheet around her, and wrapped herself up next to him. He smelled like their violent tumble from hours ago, hadn't showered. That was a good sign; when he showered, it usually meant he was going somewhere she wasn't welcome. But he was cold this morning. She couldn't stand when he was cold. Angry, fine. But cold she could not bear and would do anything to bring him back around.

He leaned away, shrugged her off. She began to pulse behind the eyeballs, something awful rolling up inside her.

"You wanna know if they saw us?" he asked. He put aside the scissors and glued the last of the papers to a card stock backing, then gave it to her. There was a tight arrangement of articles and a blurry picture below the headline TEXACO TWOSOME CAUGHT ON CAMERA. In the image, two masked figures are driving away in a Mustang. One drags his leg out the open passenger door. The driver faces forward, her eyes reflected in the rearview mirror, her dark hair whipping behind her. "They saw us, but they'll remember you."

She wanted to end it all right there. Beg him to give up the life and settle down somewhere, change their names, get a dog. They could build something, maybe, instead of tearing off with other people's things.

It didn't matter what she wanted, though.

He peeled the sheet away from her, snapped it up in the air, and lay it over the floor beneath the window. Her skin goosed at the sudden cold.

The sun bounced off the blade of the open scissors in front of her. With two quick curls of his fingers, he gestured for her to hand them over. She picked them up and noted the heft in her palm, the metal smell.

"Kneel down," he said, and she lowered herself at his feet. He gestured again, reaching out. She put the handle in his palm but didn't let go of the blades. He yanked them out of her grasp and gathered her long hair in his hands. Burying his face into it, he inhaled. Then he sheared the hair away from her scalp, one section at a time.

PART I

CHAPTER ONE

PECAN HOLLOW, TX, 1990

CICADAS RATTLED THE PECAN TREES OVER THE LISTING RANCH house where Kit Walker assessed her opponent, a mass of blackberry brambles. Their vicious tendrils snaked around the back porch, pried up floorboards, and wove between balusters, rendering the back door, now fully obscured by the fearsome thicket, defunct. She sluiced the sweat off her arms and rubbed her palms down the front of her jeans. She could have done this in January, when the scarlet canes had lost their leaves and the crowns would be easy to spot and remove by the fibrous roots. In January, there was no nuclear sun, no cloying humid air thick with the smells of manure and hot grass. January would have been better.

Although Kit was not one to brood, today a memory perched on her shoulder, taunting and elusive, a spectral crow that flapped out of sight each time she turned her head. It was a far-off thing, long for-gotten, dismissed, or buried. Kit had survived by keeping a keen and suspicious eye on the present—planning was pointless, regret even more so. No patience for mystery, she dealt in concretes. Could she touch it, swing it, scrub it, crush it? Could she put it in her mouth and taste it? Track it down and skin it? Unless it was in her hands or on her back, unless it had a color or made a sound, she wanted no part.

She pulled a few luscious black fruits clustered on the vine and ate them, juicy sweet and staining.

Compact and mule-strong, her jaw-length hair chopped in a careless arc around her face, Kit looked like an Aztec warrior. Her cheekbones high and sharp, narrow eyes that cut left and right, always scanning. Her skin was an earthy tapestry of marks. Burns and scrapes of wet red if they were fresh, pale pink and cruddy with scab if they were healing; nicks on all her knuckles; a crooked scar under her eye, like a wink. She plucked the machete from the soft pile of dirt into which she'd plunged it and began to hack. A pair of tit birds darted from their hidden nest, but she carried on. As she ran her blade, choppily at first, then in a long X formation, her mind went clear. The machete an extension of her arms, she sank into the feeling of destroying something that didn't belong. Splinters and twigs sprayed around her, clung to her T-shirt, planted themselves in the layers of her self-cut hair.

The tinny clang of the phone sounded from the kitchen. She rarely got calls and resented the interruption. *Let it ring,* she thought and carried on, slashing doggedly. It pestered, ten, eleven times before it stopped. She hacked a great hole in the brush and peeled much of it away from the wall and onto a growing pile of tinder. The finer work of detangling the vines from the balusters she'd save for Charlie, who had more patience for little things. When she began to choke on the soupy air, wet and warm, she took one last slice, staked her machete in the ground, and walked around front for a gulp of water.

She exhaled in the cool of the house, a once-white clapboard two-story built imperfectly, but strong, by its first owners in the teens. The interior was shabby but inviting, designed for guests, with wide doorways and halls, big picture windows, a dine-in kitchen that peeked into the formal dining room. Though Kit had lived there for fourteen years, it still had the air of being someone else's home. She had neither the desire nor the means to make her mark on the place and had been content to live among the floral walls, fabrics, and other grandmotherly things.

She doused a kitchen rag under the tap and ran it behind her neck, down her back, over her collarbone and stood in front of a dust-heavy tabletop fan. She'd drunk two tall glasses of water, felt her belly swell, when the phone started up again. It was a curse, this phone, a shackle. The school had required her to include a phone number when she enrolled Charlie, years ago, and she regretted it every time they called her. She had never gotten used to the idea that people should know where you were at any moment, be able to reach you on a whim. She was about to pick it up and slam it right back into its cradle until, remembering Charlie, she picked up.

She unhooked the pale blue receiver from its mount on the wall. A woman cleared her throat on the other end.

"Miz Walker? This is Lorraine Fowler," said the principal of Charlie's school, her voice dull and detached. Kit girded herself for whatever infraction Charlie had committed and the inconvenience it was likely to cause her. Fowler waited for a reply, a slight asthmatic whistle as she breathed. "Miz Walker, you're gon wanna come down here and pick up Charlie. There's been an incident."

"An incident?" Kit asked. "Is she okay?" Charlie had been called down to the office before but it was usually truancy or mouthing off to teachers. The only other time they had called it an "incident" was when Charlie was suspended for whispering hateful things into a classmate's ear, things which neither party would divulge. The boy had been so affected they sent him home to recover. The suspension had lasted a week, which suited Charlie just fine and had been a real hardship for Kit, as her daughter had been ornery and fickle company in the year since she started puberty.

"Oh, she's alright," Fowler said. "Just go on ahead and come down here now, we can sort out the details in my office. Mmkay?"

Kit looked at the clock above the stove. Quarter past 9:00 a.m. and she had to be at work at 10:00.

"Shit."

Ms. Fowler grumbled her displeasure and cleared her throat. "We'll be seeing you real soon, then."

Kit didn't like when Charlie got in trouble. It wasn't so much the acting out—for Kit had been far worse by comparison—it was the consequences. Trouble meant scrutiny, meetings, making nice with other parents. She liked a quiet life where her business was no one's but her own.

She started walking toward the door and the phone began to ring again, with the same incessant urgency. If it was Fowler, she could wait fifteen minutes until Kit got to school. As she opened the screen door she heard the answering machine—an old refurbished one only Charlie knew how to use—beep and clatter into motion. Kit was too far gone to hear who had called, and too annoyed to linger and listen.

KIT TOOK A SEAT IN the waiting room of the principal's office at Pecan Hollow Middle School, the walls around her papered with announcements and cheery art projects. It smelled like fifty years of pencil shavings and paste. She felt partly responsible for her daughter's troubles, because in the almost fourteen years they had lived together in Pecan Hollow, she had never found them a place in the community. She sometimes wished she knew how to be a part of something, but it was so much easier to keep to herself. She didn't get any of it. The rules, the manners, the tacit agreements. All she could manage was the little world she had created, just her and Charlie.

Principal Fowler, dressed in beige from head to shoe, her faded chestnut hair teased and sprayed into a wiggy-looking bob, opened her door and dealt a hot stare.

"Miz Walker, you wanna go and warsh up?" She had a way of asking questions that sounded like commands.

Kit had not, until just now, noticed the spatter of violent purple staining her arms and clothes and, she imagined, her face.

"I'd just as soon get to it," Kit said.

Principal Fowler looked like she would just as soon get to it, too. She motioned for Kit to come in.

Charlie sat glowering in the corner of the cramped office, her long hair spilling over her back in coarse waves. Like her mother's, her shoulders were set close to her ears, as if always ready to dodge a hit. She was too tall for the stool she was sitting on, knees up by her chest. Seemed not too long ago that Kit could hold her, propped on her hip. Now Charlie stood an inch taller than her mother. Kit squared herself to Fowler's desk and folded her arms.

"Is someone gonna tell me what this is all about?" she said.

Fowler sat down and steepled her fingers. She looked at Charlie then back at Kit and sighed a shallow, tired sigh.

"Miz Walker, I called you here today because Charlie stuck a sharp pencil in her classmate's cheek. The point went clean through." She pantomimed the pencil with her finger against her face and made a pop sound with her lips. "Practically skewered her like a shish kebab."

"Jesus Christ," Kit said.

"Miz Walker, *please*," said Fowler, pursed and scolding. "*Language*."

"Is this true, Charlie?" Kit asked.

Charlie nodded without making eye contact.

"Well, that's just— Why would you—" Kit stammered, embarrassed to be caught off guard like this in front of an audience. "Who was it got stuck?"

"Leigh Prentiss. You know, Sugar Faye's girl," Fowler said. Leigh was Sugar Faye's fifth child and only daughter, and she had been coddled her whole life like she was the last child on Earth. Kit would never hear the end of it from Sugar Faye.

Her first impulse was to march the girl out of there and put her somewhere she couldn't make trouble. But Charlie looked so melancholy and far away. Kit reached out to stroke her daughter's hair but ended up squeezing the back of her neck until she jerked away. With Kit, tender feelings rarely led to tender actions.

"I didn't mean to," Charlie mumbled. "It just happened."

"Well, that doesn't add up," Kit said. "What did Leigh do to make you stick her?"

"Can't say, won't snitch," Charlie said resolutely. Kit couldn't argue with that on principle, but she also didn't think Charlie should take the fall if she wasn't the only one to blame.

"We don't know yet what could have provoked such . . . savage action," Fowler answered. Kit took umbrage at the word *savage* and gathered it was not a slip of the tongue. Fowler went on. "I can't imagine this came out of nowhere, but Leigh couldn't tell us her side of the story because, well, she had a pencil sticking out of her face. She's with Dr. Metzger being fixed up as we speak. We'll need to meet with you and Leigh's folks and see if we can't put together what happened. Till then, Miz Walker, you're gonna have to take Charlie home and keep her there till after the year-end tests. She can come back in two weeks or so when school is over to make up her tests—which I will proctor myself."

"She's out for the rest of school?" Kit said. "No, no, that's not gonna work."

"I can't have her poking holes in my students, provoked or not."

Kit gnashed a protest between her teeth. These days, anytime Charlie was home alone, she'd wander off without telling Kit where she'd gone. Kit would fret until Charlie sailed through the door like she'd done nothing wrong.

Fowler leaned in and lowered her voice.

"Miz Walker, ever think maybe Charlotte needs a man in the house?" She looked down her nose at Kit. "I don't know what kind of home you run, but kids need discipline. Especially teenage girls."

Anger boiled over Kit's chest and behind her ears and clouded up her eyes. She jutted out her chin and set her knuckles on the yellowing varnished desk.

"I really don't care for your opinion on how I run my home." She swallowed a mouthful of expletives and stalked out, grabbing Charlie by the fist. In the hallway, Charlie yanked her hand away and barreled ahead of her mother and out the double doors that opened onto the parking lot. Kit let her go and leaned against a wall. Kit turned around to face the wall and stared at a bulletin board of planetary systems in gaudy glitter and neon paint. She would never be the mother who stayed up late gluing shit to colored paper, who enjoyed brushing her daughter's hair shiny or packing little sandwiches cut just so and sealing the brown bag with a sticker. It all seemed so false and fussy. And yet she pitied the girl for being stuck with a mother like her. She pinched one corner of the bulletin backing between stained finger and thumb and peeled it away, exposing the pocked corkboard underneath. Without checking to see if anyone was around she ripped the whole thing off and walked out the doors.

CHAPTER TWO

THE OLD BROWN PICKUP RUMBLED DOWN THE ROAD, KICKING UP
dust that billowed and fanned out with the southerly wind. Kit
gunned it over the train tracks to catch some air, one of the few ways
folks got their kicks around here. Jumping the tracks and shooting
bottles for skeet, watching garbage burn in massive pyres and drinking a case by the creek until they puked or passed out or both. Usually
Charlie would hoot and make Kit turn around for another go, and
again and again, laughing and jumping at the right moment so that
they were, for a moment, suspended in air. But today she was slit-eyed
and sullen.

Kit's feelings pinballed from a salty anger that her daughter had
gotten herself in trouble, to a guilty knowing that she had done
worse in her day, to a darker, unsettled feeling she couldn't quite
place. Absently, she floated a hand over and rested it on the seat
behind her daughter, not touching, but near. She couldn't read this
girl, who looked blankly at the road ahead. Until lately, she had always known what Charlie felt as if the feelings were her own. She
felt it in the fibers of her muscle. Over the past year her daughter
had drifted, her behavior unpredictable, her moods illegible. The
stitches that had held them together were frayed, splitting with each
big fight.

If only Charlie knew how lucky she was. A home, a nice school, a room of her own. And yet wasn't the point to bring her up so she would never know the alternative? Had Kit chosen differently they could be living on the move. No address, just a different motel every week when they could afford it, crashing at shelters when they couldn't. The musty couches, the sleeping bag cramps. Cheap food that didn't spoil, washing the same pair of underwear every night and wearing them damp or just going without. The aching teeth, the shoes that pinched, the constant, scraping hunger. And yet she had protected Charlie from her past, as if even knowing about it could harm her daughter.

Charlie slipped off her boot and punched the radio on with her toe. It was tuned to an oldies station, clearest they could get at forty miles from Houston. The Bee Gees were on, kind of gasping like someone had grabbed onto their nuts. Those wobbling, tortured sounds were the soundtrack of that winter Kit spent with the Crowders or Crowleys, Crow-something. The memory of her foster mother, an average-bodied woman with great flaps that hung from her arms, serving her four children from a steaming saucepan something warm and good. Chicken and dumplings, maybe. Kit watched as she ladled it out, dividing it evenly between the four bowls, adding some here, taking away there, so that every child got an equally full bowl except Kit. Hers gaped open and empty in front of her.

The kids were increasingly older than her by about a year, and freckles pocked their faces like a disease. She watched them eat, blowing each bite and burning their mouths anyway. She pulled a slice of bread from its sleeve and folded it over and ate it like it was a sandwich and not just a bare fragment of a meal. When it was clear she would not be served, she slid off the chair—she was small enough that her feet did not touch the floor—and went to the kitchen. Bracing her feet against the base of the refrigerator, she threw herself back to open the door. She gathered everything she could hold in her arms and had a feast of her own making in the dark of the pantry, a killing of condiments, leftovers in aluminum foil, a black banana. That family had not been cruel to her, had not beaten or punished her, like others had. But the pain of being overlooked hurt more than any whipping.

As they drove off the farm road onto the rutty dirt path toward home, the *whoop whoop* of a siren nearly stopped Kit's heart. She cursed, slowed, and stopped. After all these years, she was still jumpy around police.

"Do you think Leigh's parents called the cops?" Charlie asked, looking more thrilled than worried.

"Don't be dramatic. It's nothing," Kit snapped, though she wondered the same.

Kit glanced at the rearview mirror and relaxed a little. It was only Caleb. She noticed the purple stippling on her face and licked her thumb and rubbed at the spots on her cheeks, but the stain had set. She gave up and watched him, half-wary, half-curious. As Officer Caleb Nabors walked toward the truck, he smoothed back the ridges of his hair, which would have been wavy if he didn't keep it so impeccably trim, and repositioned his hat. He centered his belt buckle, straightened his gig line, and gave a final inspection of his uniform before presenting himself at her window.

She hooked a muscular arm over the door and met his eyes with a look intended to cut him off at the pass.

"Listen, I don't see the point of all this," she belted out at him. "Nobody knows what happened. It's just a schoolyard tussle."

"Afternoon, Kit," he said and tipped the brim of his hat.

She humored him with a slight nod.

"Kit, did you know your gas cap was missing?" He seemed, just then, to have manufactured a reason for stopping her. She breathed deeper into her lungs as she shook off her earlier concerns that he'd heard, that she'd have someone more imposing to reckon with than Mrs. Fowler.

"Yeah, so? Is there a law against missing gas caps or something?"

"Oh, uh, come to think of it?" He laughed, unnerved, and rubbed the back of his neck. "I guess not, it's just it might be dangerous was all I was thinking." Kit took no pleasure in witnessing him flounder. As if seized by a fresh idea, he snapped his fingers and tried another angle, ducked his head to window level.

"What's this you say about a schoolyard tussle?" he asked casually.

"It's nothing. Forget it," Kit said.

"Anything I could help with?" Though Kit was never fully free of suspicion, he had a friendly air.

"I stabbed a girl in the face," Charlie interjected with a proud half smile. "It was self-defense."

Kit muzzled her daughter with the palm of her hand.

"Can you shut your mouth and let me handle this please?"

Charlie pulled away. "What, you want me to lie to a cop then? Jesus!"

Caleb whistled without concealing his horror at this confession. He tipped his hat back to wipe his brow. "Sounds like you can handle yourself, little lady."

"Listen, I gotta go. We done here?" Kit had already shifted into gear.

He chuckled self-consciously, taking a step back from the door, and opened his mouth as if to speak a thousand words. Then he leaned in just slightly and she could smell his good soap and the Juicy Fruit on his breath.

"Y'all coming to the cookout Friday?" he asked. "Pastor Tom's cousin is smoking a hundred pounds of brisket for eighteen hours or something."

Kit shifted in her seat, itching to leave and wishing she were the kind of woman who wanted to stay. "I don't think so," she said, and as he held his smile against the disappointment, she was sorry to let him down.

"Suit yourself, ladies," he said, tipped his hat, and turned around.

As Caleb walked away, Kit recalled the smooth, even curve of his nails, so clean underneath. She glanced at her own—one thumbnail blackish, split down the middle, the rest ragged from gnawing and cruddy underneath—and curled them into her palm. Kit did not like the feeling she got from Caleb. She knew he had a thing for her; that had been clear for a long time. Most guys would hoot from afar or try to hustle her. They were easy to blow off because she knew what she was dealing with—blunt, horny, shallow. But with Caleb she had this horrible sense that he wanted her in a different way. In a *for keeps* way. He was too sensitive, and backed off at the slightest rebuff, but he was patient. He had never given up trying as long as she had known him. Once or twice a year he'd ask her somewhere—trail rides, bonfires, church functions—in his Caleb way, both gentlemanly and shy. When he approached her, she felt nervous and conflicted. She didn't deserve the attention of someone so kind and plainspoken, so different from Manny. What was love if it wasn't violent and confusing, if you weren't a slave to it? She couldn't begin to see how she and Caleb would work together, but his interest reminded her of how lonely she was.

She remembered what it felt like to want someone, to settle into him, thread his legs with her own. The long mornings with their noses overlapped, passing the same sweet humid air between them. If only she could keep the parts she liked and trim away the rest, she might think about loving a man again. A swell of pain rose up from her ribs and into her throat. Her eyes wet, her neck flushed. *Nope,* she thought. She willed away her feelings, a little trick she'd devised as a girl, and felt the sadness fade into a sinking numbness, her merciful retreat. Her arms stiffened at the wheel and she drove ahead as Charlie stared out the window, far away.

Kit was late for work but she needed gas. She coasted up to the filling station and parked under the red and blue flat top, always in front and closest to the road, never boxed in, and squirted some gas in the tank and another gallon or so in a greasy red portable just in case.

She hadn't racked up much good fortune in these places and avoided them when she could.

Charlie lay across the bench seat and pressed her bare feet to the passenger window.

"I'm going inside to pay," Kit said.

"You could offer me something to eat," Charlie said. "I'm frickin' *starving*."

Ah, she's hungry, Kit thought, though she knew food could only go so far in easing Charlie's chronic bitchiness.

"I'd take one of those roller dogs, if it's nice and hot," Charlie said. "I can pay for it."

"With what money?" Kit said.

"I don't know," Charlie said, instantly sour. "I thought I should at least offer but now I take it back. Christ." She stretched her legs up to the ceiling and pushed its dented surface up so it made a *wonk* and let it *dunk* back into place. She was tall for her age, a leggier, browner version of her mother, more loosely put together, and she moved like there was plenty of space between her bones. Her fierce dark brows nearly grew together, giving her a permanently intense expression. She hung her head, her blanket of hair over the edge of the driver's seat, and scowled.

"What. Are. You. Staring. At?" Charlie sassed, as if Kit were some ogling creep.

Kit wanted to ignore her daughter, or fight her, or scream at her. But she knew she had to be the parent, and that didn't come naturally to her. She had to think before she spoke and decided to take a direct approach.

"Look, kid," she said. "I'm just standing here wondering why you stabbed a girl in the face."

Charlie shook her head and looked out the window, neither guilt nor care upon her face. "I can't explain," she said nonchalantly. "It just happened."

"Did she say anything? Was she pushing you around?"

Charlie slammed the dash. "What does it matter? God, Mom!" she yelled. "I did it, it's over."

Kit knew she had to leave it there or risk making things worse between them. From the look in Charlie's eyes, a smoldering determination, she knew she couldn't pry any more from her if she had a crowbar.

"What the hell am I going to do with you if you're not in school?" Kit said, not so much to Charlie but to herself.

"Well, I guess you'll have to figure that out," Charlie mumbled. Kit breathed and stretched an angry knot between her shoulder blades.

"All right, as soon as we get something to eat you're coming with me to Doc's," Kit said. She walked away a little looser for having made a decision and, in case her meaning had been lost, shouted over her shoulder, "I'm putting your ass to work."

AS SOON AS SHE WALKED inside the cramped quick mart, an internal countdown gave Kit a minute or less before she would need to bolt out of there. She could reason all she wanted that she was safe, but she still spooked at gas stations. She grabbed a gas cap, two oily dogs hot off the rollers, and a package of Fig Newtons, and went up to pay for them along with her fuel. The cashier, skinny and ball-eyed, put down his jerky to chew her a "Howdy do."

"Hi, Kenny." She lay her money on the counter and looked out the glass door at the truck, rehearsing her exit.

"Ain't Charlie s'pose to be in school?" he said and sorted her change, and by the way he played it real casual she could guess that he had heard about Charlie and Leigh. And if he knew it, soon everybody would know.

"Not today, Kenny," she said, rubbing the fat of her earlobe. Suddenly, it felt like the temperature rose by twenty degrees. "Can you hurry please? I'm late for work."

"I just run out of pennies, hang on," he said and stood up to fish around in his pockets. "It's just three cents I owe you. Should be able to dig it up if ya just gimme a minute."

A dark feeling came over her. The gasoline fumes, the scrape and *ting* of the cash register, the subtle flicker of fluorescent light. Her heart beat high in her chest and she began to sweat. She took the food and the change he'd laid down, shouldered the door open, and hustled back to the truck.

CHAPTER THREE

KIT AND CHARLIE STAMPED THE DUST OFF THEIR BOOTS ON THE cheery welcome mat and stepped inside Pecan Hollow Veterinary Clinic, where Kit had worked odd jobs since Charlie was a baby. The front office was about two hundred feet square, cluttered with plants and paperwork and nearly every inch of wall space tacked with pictures of Doc Robichaux's patients. Lame horses, mangy dogs, coyote-bitten goats, and hen-pecked chicks, many accompanied by thank-you letters from their owners. The office adjoined a much larger space used for exams, surgeries, and when the time came, euthanasia. Out back, she had a couple of acres with eight stalls, a riding ring, and a barn for hay, feed, and equipment storage.

Animals were as important as people at her clinic. Doc stood just over five feet tall with natural, springy brown curls around a cheerful, chubby face. Though heavy, she was also very nimble and stronger than the average man. In vet school, she had been known for tearing a phone book in half for free drinks. Known to no one by her full name, Clothilde Hélène Robichaux, Doc called herself a Creole from West Baton Rouge. Why exactly she ended up in Pecan Hollow of all places was unknown. According to her own account, it was divine intervention. Having recently graduated, Doc had asked the powers that be to lead her where she was most needed. She had taken I-10 across the Texas border with nothing but her degree, her car, and the gas that was in it. The tank had gone empty just outside Pecan Hollow and she had pushed the car a half mile until she made it into town and, seeing her prayer answered, there she stayed.

Kit liked to think Doc was a runaway, like her. The people of Pecan Hollow, of course, had spun their own mythology about Doc. There were rumors she had been sent away after a woman she had spurned called up her family in a rage and told them the shameful truth about their Clothilde. Kit didn't put much stock in the rumors since any woman over thirty who hadn't found a man was deemed a lesbian, but neither did she dismiss them. It simply wasn't her business.

"You're later than late!" Doc said and pointed to the Felix clock with its wagging tail. Half past eleven. Dorelle Chapman, a tall, thin woman with sun-dried skin and a beautician's cap over her hair, waited at the counter to pick up her cat. When she saw Kit, she scowled like she'd tasted something nasty and shook her head. Kit could imagine Mrs. Chapman biting her tongue so she didn't say what was really on her mind. *You're a better woman than me, Doc, I wouldn't trust her for a second. Uh-uh. I just hope you don't let her touch the money, now. You can be a good Christian without being stupid.* Kit scowled right back.

"Sorry, it was Charlie's school," Kit said to Doc. "I'll stay as long as you need me." Kit hated being late, not because Doc would be mad, but because she didn't like to take advantage of Doc's kindness. She owed her boss more than she wanted to admit. Doc had always given her steady work and time off for Charlie whenever she needed it. She had given her a job when most people in town wouldn't leave her, an interloping brown girl, alone with their wallets. Some thought she was a grifter, others just didn't like the look of her, most were mad she didn't attend church. The summer after Charlie was born, Kit ran out of money. She spent what little she earned from odd jobs on the mortgage and the rest went to diapers. She got so hard up one month, she hunted squirrels and nutria, lived on meat, mostly, boiled pasta, and what little she could glean from the garden. Hunting to eat wasn't so bad, and

Charlie was content to feed from her breast, but she lived in fear of losing the house. She couldn't bear to ask anyone in town for help. And though the temptation was always there, she was determined not to steal. More than once she had pushed a cart through the aisles of the market, with Charlie in the basket, taking food off the shelf—a box of cereal, a gallon of milk, cans of soup, and bottles of Coke—and thought how easy it would be to slip a few things into her backpack, to push the cart to the register, and once all the food had been tallied pretend like she had forgotten her money and go home, her backpack full of food. Then one day she saw a Help Wanted sign at the feed store and went to the vet with Charlie in arm. She told Doc she had no experience and would have to bring her daughter, but would work harder than anyone else. Doc had hired her on the spot.

Kit and Charlie washed up while Doc tended to Mrs. Chapman. She handed a sedated tomcat wrapped in a towel over to its owner, who wiped her nose with a tissue.

"There now, not to cry, Miz Chap. He's got time yet. We'll keep him real comfortable and you just spoil him rotten, okay?" Doc stuffed another tissue in Mrs. Chapman's pocket as she cradled the drowsy tabby like an infant. She reached into her purse, but Doc stopped her.

"Don't be silly, sha. This is no time to worry yourself with that. I'll send you a little invoice and you just take your time. Oh, one more thing." She rummaged through a drawer and pulled out a pungent sachet tied with a crimson ribbon and a chicken bone. "Just a little charm for you. Put it under your pillow before you go to bed. Light a candle and pray to Saint Lazarus."

Mrs. Chapman opened her mouth as if to protest.

"Ba-ba-ba-ba! Just trust me now," Doc said and shooed her away gently. She waited for her to leave before formally greeting Charlie.

"Hello, Charlie! How do, how do?" She slapped her palms and rubbed them together like she was warming them.

"I'm in trouble, so Kit's forcing me to work," Charlie announced, a touch defiant.

"That's good medicine for bad behavior—you're very welcome here!" Doc tucked one thick leg behind the other in a curtsy and bowed her head.

Charlie giggled. Doc turned to Kit.

"Could you have a conversation with Warbucks and see if he'll agree to try on some new shoes today? I am having the damnedest time with him." A dimpled smile broke across her broad face. "Pretty please?"

Kit wouldn't admit it out loud, but it felt good to make Doc happy. She nodded and clucked Charlie toward the door. "Come on."

THE STABLE WAS OUT BACK, a dusty riding ring, and a pasture thick with dandelion and buttercup. As if on cue, a swaggering buckskin stallion stepped out from behind the building into full view. He had strong legs and a shaggy black mane, his neck arched as if he was posing. He snorted and whickered a taunt.

Kit approached him and he waited, still but tense, then pivoted on his back legs, shying playfully away from her. She eased toward where he had stopped to mock-nibble a clump of ragweed and hid the halter behind her back. He kept eating, even until she was one long step away from him. When she tried to drop the lead rope over his neck, he snorted and lunged diagonally away from her, bucking gleefully. Kit slung the halter down and walked away from it. Charlie straddled an overturned barrel, laughing.

"Man," she said, "your attitude sucks."

"Excuse me?" Kit took a step toward Charlie, head cocked.

"Why would he want to stop what he's doing and hang out with you? You're all wound up." She swizzled her finger in the air like a spring. "You can't care so much about catching him."

At that Charlie took a coarse bouquet of alfalfa, stuffed it in her back pocket, and slung the halter over her shoulder. She walked to the center of the ring so he could see her and bent down to tie her shoe, the alfalfa wagging like a tail. She picked up a dirty water bucket and dumped it out, then walked into the stall, never once looking in his direction. There she began to fluff the sawdust, refresh his water, and scooped molasses oats in his feed bucket. Warbucks watched for a minute, then, with no self-consciousness, walked in the stall and nudged Charlie in the small of her back. She ignored him. He nudged harder, almost knocking her forward. She turned and scrubbed his blaze with her knuckles. She held a halter under his nose and let him sniff it and grip it with his rubbery lips, then slipped it over his head and fastened it loosely behind the jaw. She handed the lead rope to Kit.

Kit watched with a mixture of appreciation and resentment. She hated how easily Charlie drew Warbucks in and how smug she looked. Kit winced on the inside to be shown up by her daughter, whom she had worked so hard to shield from her weaknesses. In truth, she had never been comfortable around horses. A decade of working around them had not made it any easier. She could ride a little, had had to over the years, but not for pleasure. Maybe it was because there was no controlling a horse—you had to relate to it. Maybe it was the fear in them, the twitchy ears, the panicked eyes, the tremble under the skin, the unpredictable switch and sway of those deadly haunches. Maybe it wasn't their fear, but her own.

"That's good, Charlie," Kit said casually, careful not to give herself away. "Looks like you just found yourself a job. From now on you're in charge of the stable." She handed Charlie a shit-covered shovel. "You clean out the stalls and find me when you're done."

Doc stood by the sink washing, foamy up to her elbows. She whistled "Camptown Races" and stamped a wide, Birkenstocked foot in time, one of many things she did that made Kit mental. She turned and smiled at Kit.

"Charlie sure is gettin' tall. Taller'n you by the looks of it. How old is she now, fifteen?"

"Thirteen," Kit said. Doc whistled.

"Hoo-wee! What have you been feeding her? Can you get me some?" Doc wheezed out a laugh. More seriously, she said, "It's too bad, though. I wish they could stay kids a little longer. Seems like they see too much before they're ready." Kit met her gentle, olive eyes for a second.

"What about you?" Doc asked. "What were you like at her age?"

Kit bristled at the probe.

She looked out the window at her daughter, whose long legs and slender build belonged to the girl's father. She moved like water. Like him, too, she had drills for eyes. Kit, by contrast, was built for work. She was low to the ground, her muscles tensely strung around a solid frame. She was not pretty, but she didn't mind the way she looked, her clear skin the warm brown of pecans. She was grateful to be small-chested and had never worn a bra; nothing on her body hindered free movement.

"A foot shorter, a hair meaner, and a lot dumber," she said, hoping to water down Doc's need to pry.

Doc chuckled and shook her head. "Must have been pretty rough, Walker, whatever it was."

She could feel the question hiding in her tone. *Where you come from, Walker? What happened to you?* This wasn't the first time Doc had wondered about her. She had been the subject of plenty of speculation among the people in town when she first arrived. Some said she was the bastard granddaughter of Aunt Eleanor. Others said she had been a prostitute and not to trust her around their husbands. Kit didn't know what she could tell Doc that wouldn't spark more questions. Easier to shut her down.

"Don't bother, old woman. Nothing to tell."

"*Bon!*" Doc laughed, rinsed and dried her baseball mitt hands. "You're as thorny as a thistle, but you're good inside. I see you there, Walker."

Kit's skin goosed at her sincerity. "You mind your business and

I'll return the favor," she said. Doc shut up, but her silence was as conspicuous as a horn.

OUTSIDE, CHARLIE SHOVELED MANURE INTO a wheelbarrow, stopping liberally to rest and turn sunward. Out of school, she felt loose and free. The confines of the classroom, its garish decorations and fluorescent lighting, made her dizzy. Twenty kids to a class, the stupid chatter, the teacher calling for attention. The best part of school was the fifty-minute period of enforced silence during an exam.

She heaved the shovel into the soft pile and leveraged its handle over her thigh, then swung and deposited her load. She had not meant to stab the stupid bitch. Put her in her place, yes. Pierce her cheek with a number 2? No, that had been an accident, though she still thought Leigh Prentiss had had it coming. A lifetime of teasing had given Charlie a thick hide, or so she liked to think. But she wasn't normally one of those kids that fought for attention. If anything, she had tried to lay low. Growing up in Pecan Hollow, with a batshit mom and no dad, was bad enough, but being that way and not attending church made people suspicious. The town was full of characters, but most went to church, every Sunday, whether the sun shone or rain fell. It was the only requirement of country living.

Trouble started when Charlie caught Leigh copying off her test. Cheating in and of itself didn't bother Charlie—it was the hypocrisy. Leigh was supposed to be a big Christian, and to prove it, she carried the Good Book, with its ruffled and monogrammed Bible cozy, hugged to her chest like a teddy bear. While Charlie was trying to take the test, the girl kept leaning in, closer and closer. Charlie hissed a warning, but Leigh looked at her primly and jotted down an answer, then leaned in again for another look. She backed away from the tickle of Leigh's frizzy hair, and smelled a waft of her cat breath.

Something about the stink pushed her over the edge. She went hot with claustrophobic anger and jabbed left to push the girl away. There was a hollow pop and Leigh's eyes widened, her brows arched high on her forehead, lips forming an O. Charlie left the pencil in her cheek and laughed out of shock, focusing on the strange expression and not the horrible thing she had done. Once the teacher, Mrs. Blaine, saw what had happened, she came running and flapped her hands a bit before sending a student to fetch the nurse. She looked around and asked who had done this. Leigh, mute from shock, pointed a pudgy, shaking finger at Charlie.

She was sorry to have hurt Leigh. If she had been thinking clearly, instead of jabbing her, she would have leaned over and whispered, "I just wrote down all the wrong answers," to fuck with her. Or, to be more to the point, Charlie might have said, "Brush your fucking teeth, you cheating stink-mouth bitch."

Their classmates had encircled Leigh, who was screaming and bleeding, and Charlie was stung with jealousy. She couldn't help wishing for some of that concern given so easily to Leigh. She thought of the times when she had been pushed around by kids in the hall, how the other kids turned away, how the teachers pretended not to see. Earlier that spring, she had tried out for the track team and had cleared a set of hurdles as part of the agility test. When she came around the bend for the second set, Nancy Sprenger, who was a few paces ahead of her, dropped a hurdle right in her path. Charlie tripped and went sprawling forward. She lay there reeling from the pain in her nose, blood in her mouth, on her face, in her hair. The top layer of skin on her hands had been sanded off on the dirt track. She could tell by the way people covered their mouths and looked at each other that they'd seen what happened. The coach had jogged over and slapped her on the back.

"You're good, right?" she had said. "How about you go on and hit the showers?" She hadn't offered Charlie a hand, or sent her to the nurse. Just had everyone take an easy lap and carried on with tryouts. Charlie held her palms to the light. The scars had faded almost completely, as if it had never happened. Some might say she was lucky, but she wanted something to show for her pain.

She lifted the wheelbarrow and guided it to a steaming compost pile of manure and kitchen scraps, grass clippings and old *Times-Picayune*s that Doc had delivered special. For twenty minutes she mucked the stalls and dumped the manure, running through a cycle of getting angry and cooling off. Just as she finished her fourth stall, someone cleared his throat behind her. A guy with a straw hat and no shirt leaned on the fence a few feet away. He smiled at her.

She brandished her shit-covered shovel at him. "What do you want?"

He tipped his hat up to reveal more of his face. He looked high school aged, was linebacker fat—chubby but with lots of muscle and thick bone underneath—and led with his chin. "Well, I sure don't want a busted face," he said, holding up a hand to block her.

"Put that shovel down, man. Goddamn."

She kept the shovel where it was.

"What are you doing looking at me like that?" she scolded.

He laughed. "You just looked so happy with your face turned up at the sun, I was just wondering what you were thinking about."

"I was thinking about how I punched a hole through some girl's cheek with a pencil." She felt a satisfaction that this was, in fact, what she had been thinking about and hoped to impress on him that she was not to be messed with.

"You're serious, aren't you?" he said, looking delighted. Charlie planted the shovel at her side.

"Daaamn," he drawled. "Well, I guess she must have deserved it."

"Yeah," Charlie said. "She did. She was all up in my business. Kinda like you are now."

The boy laughed again, unaffected in a way that irked Charlie. "Okay, I can take a hint. Not welcome. I'll be on my way." He waved goodbye and walked away.

Charlie felt a tug and was sorry to see him go. "Wait, what's your name, perv?"

"I'm Jim Dirkin, but they call me Dirk." He waited for her to offer her name, but she hesitated. "You're Charlie, right? Kit Walker's kid?"

Charlie tensed, expecting him to tease her. She nodded, not convinced a latent attack wouldn't follow.

"Cool. I'm surprised we never met till now," he said. "I like to know the misfits."

She didn't know what that meant exactly, but she had a feeling it meant "wild things." She liked that.

"She *is* kind of creepy though, your mom."

There it is, Charlie thought.

He went on. "I never seen such a dark look. It's too bad, because she could be pretty if she didn't always look like she wanted to kill you. You could, too."

Charlie flushed, embarrassed and disappointed.

"Please don't talk about my mom and me being pretty in the same breath."

"You don't have many friends, do you?" he said.

"I don't care to have any," she said, her arms basted across her chest.

"Well, that's silly. Everyone needs a friend. I'll be your friend if you like." Now she felt embarrassed for him. He was so out there with his feelings, just open for attack.

"I don't even know what the fuck to say to that," she said.

Dirk kind of sighed and splayed his hands out like he'd done what he could.

"I'll leave you to it, Charlie," he said. "Looks like you got work to do." He turned and disappeared behind a bend in the road. She felt stupid, like she'd said too much and too little at the same time.

Just then she heard her mother behind her.

"Who was that?"

Charlie got flustered. Her thoughts tumbled around, and her embarrassment was beginning to show on her face. But she didn't want to let it show. She took hold of the shovel as if to anchor herself and mumbled over her shoulder.

"Just some asshole."

KIT AND CHARLIE CAME HOME from Doc's hungry and tired. Kit opened a can of franks and beans, dumped it in a pot, and struck a match to light the hiss of gas below it. She unscrewed a jar of pickles to eat while supper warmed up. The two leaned against the kitchen sink, passing the jar back and forth, content to snack in silence. The troubles of the day had retreated with the heat, and what remained was the subdued peace of a hard day's work and nothing left to say.

Kit fished out the last pickle and thought back to Caleb. He really did seem to always be around her. She admitted he was a man who looked good to her. The cream of his skin and his even build suggested a life clean from too much drink and drugs and other things that wore on a body. He was meant for something better, she guessed, than being loyal shepherd to this town of thankless and errant sheep. She remembered seeing him one winter bringing a drunk to the Truxtop for a hot cup of coffee and pie. Caleb sat with the old man and let him talk nonsense while he sobered up. At the time, she had thought him foolish, knowing the drunk might never remember the gesture. It wouldn't stop him from drinking; if anything, he might take advantage of the kindness. She was reluctant to admit Caleb's willingness to sit with a stranger might be admirable; it was harder still to admit that she might want him to sit across from her, nodding and listening and caring about what she had to say.

Just then, Kit heard the sound of a big-ass engine growling up toward her house, and Charlie hollered from the living room, "Incoming!"

She went to the window and saw the Prentisses' black Suburban parked askew. The passenger door swung open and Sugar Faye slipped out. She smoothed her skirt and staked one stilettoed foot in front of the other across the drive and up the steps. Leigh climbed out the backseat and followed her mother, an ice cream Drumstick in hand. Kit went to the door.

"Yew-hew!" Sugar called out over her furious knocking. Kit readied herself for a talking-to and opened the door. Sugar looked like she had left the house fully made up but had gotten stuck in a windstorm, the big golden pouf of her hair mussed on one side, a little mascara under her eyes. She wore a spring-green dress, belted at the waist, a thin black line between the masses of her bust and hips. Her lace slip peeked out below her hem. Leigh, whose cheek was padded with gauze, hovered behind her, picking peanuts off the chocolate cap of her Drumstick and tossing them aside.

Sugar Faye shifted slightly, protectively, in front of her daughter.

"Listen, Kit, I got a bone to pick with you," Sugar Faye said in a tone that was both indignant and vulnerable. "We just left the emergency room." She paused for Kit, who had nothing, at that moment, to say. "To patch up her cheek? After Charlie . . . maimed it?"

Kit nodded. She wished Sugar would just come out and say what she had to say.

"Right," Kit said. "How's she doing?"

"Well, how would you feel?" Sugar snapped.

"Iff ackffley not vat bad," Leigh piped up. "I got ife keem." She held up the melting cone like a torch.

"I just had to pick up a little treat for the patient. Idn't dat right, baby?" Sugar said, squeezing Leigh's hand so hard the girl let out a cottony "Ffftop!" and tugged her hand back.

Sugar continued, "She was *so brave* when they were stitching her up, and I was crying like I was the one in pain—but it does hurt when our babies are suffering, it hurts more for us than them, duddn't it? Like a dull knife to your gut? Duddn't it, though?" And as she talked about it her eyes flashed with angry tears that spoke all the bitter words her lips could not utter.

Kit raked back thick handfuls of her short hair, wiped the sweat off her neck with the collar of her shirt. She knew she should apologize for what Charlie had done. At least she was imaginative enough to put herself in Sugar's shoes and knew that if it had been Charlie with the hole-punched face there would have been hell to pay. Kit was in the unexpected position of feeling sorry for Sugar Faye. She took for granted that she could always turn to violence. If all she could do was blink away her tears and make subtle hints and rub the shine off her pearl earring like Sugar was doing now, she would have given up long ago.

Sugar Faye pulled a little jade tube from the purse hanging from her elbow, took the cap off, and applied her pink lipstick. Kit watched the ritual with interest, how she traced her thinner top lip in an M shape twice, going a little outside the natural line of her lip, then she dragged the lipstick from one corner of her full bottom lip to center and again on the other side and fish-smacked her lips. The most striking thing was how she managed to continue talking during the whole procedure.

"Of course I'll always love my baby no matter how she looks," Sugar said with a hand over her heart, "but lord, look at this!" She peeled back the bandage on Leigh's face to reveal what was, in Kit's opinion, a minor puncture wound with some light swelling.

Sugar took a tissue from her glossy black purse and mashed it between her lips, bizarrely removing half of the shimmery pink she had just applied. "I've been trying to understand what God wanted for us here, because you know I do trust he has a plan for us, and I know I have suffered from vanity, but is it so bad to miss the face she had?" At this, Sugar pried open her compact to vet her work.

"'On't you ffink I'm fftill pwetty?" Leigh said.

"Hush it, now, Mama's talking," Sugar said with a bit more bass than before. She retied Leigh's oversize bow, a fresh green that matched Sugar's dress, at the top of Leigh's head. "How's Charlie then?" Sugar dragged her teeth over her pretty painted lower lip. Boy, did she look pissed. She was gonna keep Kit here until she got what she wanted and the more she wanted it, the less Kit was willing to let it go. "She must be feeling awful guilty, huh?"

"She's . . . a little shook up, I guess," Kit said.

This seemed to push Sugar within about two high-heeled paces of the edge of sanity. She forced a little hyperventilated laugh, shook her head, and blinked.

"You know, Kit, Miz Fowler said the silliest thing after all this happened. She said to me, 'Sugar, it would be within your rights to *press charges* against the Walkers.'" She eyed Kit for a reaction. "Can you believe that? And I just said, 'Kit is a personal friend of mine, and I'm not gonna do any such thing when we can handle things civilly. Between us.'"

Kit wasn't going to beg her off, but she had no power, no money. She had to find a way to blow the smoke off Sugar without directly admitting blame. She crossed her bare arms and pinned her hands tight beneath them.

"I was thinking I could come by, do some work for you maybe. I noticed you had a bunch of brush out by your gate. I could clear it." It was as close to sorry as she was gonna get.

Sugar looked at her in a tired-of-caring sort of way.

"Aren't you sweet," she said, like she was pondering stronger words. "You know? I got my four boys, and Rob, too. I'm positively drowning in helping hands. We are all set," she said and wheeled around on one tiny, pointed heel, and as she did her blond curls swung away from a mottled brown stain on her shoulder where she'd held her bleeding, sobbing girl.

Kit felt sorry for the first time since she'd gotten the call this morning. Sugar wasn't all bad. She was vain and selfish, but she had a good heart. She was good to her kids, helped people out. There was an elderly woman in town named Nell Clover who had outlived her husband and both her grown children. Nell had devoted herself to taking care of them through their various illnesses, and by the time the last one died, there was no money left for her. Sugar had been the first one to start a fundraiser in church, and before long she had extended Nell an open invitation to stay in her decked-out garage. Over the years, Kit had even wondered about being friends with Sugar, like those unlikely pairings of species, a golden retriever and a bobcat. It wouldn't have taken much effort on Kit's part. But Sugar's eagerness, her chattiness, her beauty, even her generosity, had all been too much. Trying to be friends with her was like driving a Mack truck through a pinhole.

She willed herself to apologize, to throw Sugar a rope.

"Hey, Sugar?" she said and heard the strain, like even her vocal cords weren't used to making nice. Sugar broke stride ever so slightly, just enough that Kit knew she'd heard her. Then she loaded Leigh into their massive Suburban and drove away.

CHAPTER FOUR

FORT BEND COUNTY CORRECTIONAL

MANNY SAT QUIETLY AS HE WAITED FOR THE CALL. HIS BEDSHEETS were folded square, the toilet buffed to a brilliant shine. He looked around the chilly cell with appreciation, holding only the borrowed Bible—he would take nothing with him but the clothes he'd worn when he arrived. Narrow, efficient, hard. This place had been a crucible for his transformation. Once, he had been lazy, indulgent, distractible. Gone now were his vanity and pride, the rage, the bluster. He had given in too easily to the whims of his loins, that barking urge that compelled him to plow the nearest piece of flesh. He had even done men, in the early days of his term. Terrific come, he remembered with a hot shudder, then clocked his head on the cinder block behind him. *Steady.* Though it had taken many years, he was now well liked by the inmates. As hardened as everyone tried to be, he had learned their needs—for friendship, for touch, for someone to hold their secrets.

Perhaps he had not given Kit credit for keeping him company. He had never done well on his own, and yet he was bored by others, repulsed. How the loneliness had crept in and reached down his throat and gagged him. He'd known this feeling before, it was the oldest one. The sound of no one there. The cool of no one's touch. He'd felt it in the corner of his treeless yard, where his mother would send him for being too loud, or for creeping around. He'd sit in the scant shade of a ragged bird of paradise until he blistered, wishing her dead. He'd felt it in the room he shared with his brother, he alone in his bed while his mother, smelling of rum, would slip in next to Leo and make the covers move. To his face she called Manny an angel, her Baby Blue, but in the night she passed him over. He had used his eyes as a weapon against the loneliness, tricked the teachers into loving him, made fake friends, but the feeling followed him still. From the tennis clubs to strip clubs, it crept along, cautious and hungry at his heels, as he held hearts and broke them, as women woke up from a dream to find that he, and their money, had disappeared.

As he got older and more skilled at outwitting the loneliness, he'd enjoy long stretches of snag-free cons. He'd start to have kinder opinions of people; even as he was slipping the diamond from a woman's finger, he'd wish her well. *They're only things,* he'd tell himself. But the lonesome feeling gained on him, gulping and smacking, and the longer he'd enjoy some peace, the more brutal the blow when the feeling returned.

And then came Kit.

Like him, she was angry and lonesome, misunderstood. And she scared him, that fiercest glint when her eyes narrowed and stared straight through him. Still, he knew she loved him. Sweet words were not her way. Her staying with him, watching all he did, that's how he knew.

I trust you was what he'd understood when she stopped sleeping with a shiv. And when he finally took her in his bed, her teeth in his flesh had done the talking for her. *You're all I need,* she had said without saying a word.

He supposed part of what he loved about her was that she was capable of leaving, hurting him, that wildness he had seen so early on, had felt under his skin like the itch of a poisonous plant. Something pitiless and feral. It thrilled him, stirred up a feeling in him he had never felt for anyone: respect. Having Kit in his life all those years, someone to look after and think about, someone he wanted to please, had warmed him over. Because of her, the heart he'd left for dead had stirred and coughed back to life. Even the sex was secondary; it was that this creature was the one person on the planet he understood. He had finally found his kind.

And she had just driven away. All that time, he just hadn't thought about it ending. Certainly not like that. Not with her leaving him. In his fucking Mustang.

ON HIS FIRST DAY IN prison, they stripped, probed, and penetrated, doused him in chemical cleaner, sheared his beautiful hair. Within hours, he had committed an infraction—so minor, a nothing little comment about the children of one of the guards—that landed him in solitary confinement. He had retched at its smell, sharp with aged and layered human mess. They had not told him how long he would be there, so the time stretched out like one long horrific night. When the hallucinations came, it was a comfort, because at least he wasn't alone.

By the time he left solitary what turned out to be a week later, he had broken two fingers and stripped his nails and cracked his skull. He had spilled his own fluids, of every sort, and the stench had become a part of him, unscrubbable, a permanent stain. And in and out of solitary he went. It had come as a great shock that there was no way to predict or avoid what would get him in trouble. Charm, manipulation, cunning were of little use to him among the inmate brutes and the sadists that guarded them.

His great revelation had come during a particularly long stretch in the hole—such a fitting name, a dark, empty, swallowing thing. As usual, they hadn't informed him how long he would be there, another form of torture, so it could have been three months or six, he couldn't be sure. He could only describe it as the sensation of melting under immense and excruciating heat, where the thing that was melting was not the body, but the self. He felt himself melt, then boil, then evaporate, then vanish. And in the stillness, he sensed the awesome presence of God. It was a feeling of being held and accepted just as he was, and from nothing, he rematerialized, he was reborn.

From then on, Manny knew that he was not merely a son of God, but His right hand, the doer of deeds on His behalf.

The waiting was over. Now, he was coming for her.

He was ready.

The buzzer sounded and the steel gate opened, gnashing on its rails.

MANNY STEPPED OUTSIDE THE PRISON walls and took a moment to savor his freedom. It was overcast and humid. In a lookout thirty feet overhead, an armed guard hocked a gobbet from deep in his throat. Manny squinted up at him and smiled, saluted. The guard spat and it splatted an arm's length from where Manny stood. His younger self might have let the gesture spoil his day, but today he filled his lungs and merely felt grateful to be here.

A two-tone gray-and-black Cadillac blaring Guns N' Roses pulled up on the wrong side of the road. A long, panty-hosed leg kicked open the door and Red unfolded herself from the driver's seat. "Well, heyyyy! Am I late? I am, aren't I? I swear to you I left the house early, I promise you I did. Sometimes I think the clock is playing tricks on me. But that's not important, look at you! You're so skeeeny!"

He smiled, let her talk herself out. Her round parts had withered some with time. Her spandex tank and skirt were the tired pastels of too many washings, and when she embraced him he smelled dental decay, heard the rattle of pleurisy in her lungs. She needed a shower more than he did. Still, he was pleased to see her. He had phoned her a handful of times while he was inside. Red was his only friend, and he had known he might need to call on her when the time came.

THEY HAD SCARCELY LEFT THE penitentiary grounds when Red slapped her hands to the wheel and ogled him. She twisted a knob on the radio to lower the volume.

"All right, spill it," she said, her face pregnant with anticipation. "Did you let them F you in the fuckin' B?"

Manny smiled and ignored the prompt, preferring to gaze at the blur of trees and stacks of clouds above them, feel the speed of the car charging down the highway, like flying. It was all so magnificent. God's glory, a welcome. He rolled the window halfway down and closed his eyes against the wind.

"You *did*, you dirty boy," she said, maddeningly satisfied. "What did you think? Not bad, right? Not my thing personally, but I hear it's sensational if you've got a prostate. Y'know, I think all you guys would be effin' each other if you weren't so dang insecure. That's just my opinion, but *tell me*, now that you've had a taste? I bet you had a ball—" She slapped him in the chest. "*Ball!*" she said loudly and laughed a little too hard at the accidental pun. Manny thought she seemed wired, maybe had a little toot before picking him up. He had seen her deteriorate over her infrequent visits, and the organized professional he had known was now little more than a junkie whore.

"I'm on a different path now," Manny said calmly. "I've found the Bible."

Red raised her eyebrows and puckered her mouth mockingly. He had damaged her pride by not playing along with the sordid inquiry. She lit a cigarette and turned the volume back up, some moody pop song that bored him.

"Okay, Father Manny," she mumbled. "Good for fuckin' you."

Red kept her mouth shut, a rarity, the rest of the trip. When the

Cadillac arrived at her weathered little bungalow, she muscled open her front door and pushed aside a pile of unopened mail, pocketed her keys. The once tidy home had the look of a flophouse, more litter was visible than floor. On the coffee table, a scattering of needles, cigarette butts, cracked eye shadow pucks, a clear plastic bottle filled with liquor or piss or lemon Squirt. There was a humid, cheesy smell about the place. Manny opened a window.

"Oh my word, is it that bad in here?" She fished a book of matches from her waistband, struck one on the sole of her shoe, and blew out the flame. As she waved the smoke around, her breasts bobbed together, but Manny felt only disgust.

"I'm so embarrassed," she said. "You know in the good old days, I had a maid come twice a week to clean up after my sloppy ass." She flicked her teeth with a long nail. "I guess I've let things go a bit. You always did like things just so, didn't you? I just don't know how you made it in prison, must have been— Well, I don't even want to imagine, but it must have been awful. I bet you're happier'n a bird dog to be out of there. Whew! Let's toast to that!" She unhooked her bra, a graying lacy thing, and let it slither out her sleeve. She lifted an open bottle of Southern Comfort and poured the auburn liquid into a coffee mug, passing it to Manny.

He sniffed, grimaced, set it down on the windowsill. "I don't mess around with this anymore," he said. Red clicked her tongue and shook her head, a little venom in her eyes. "The tables have turned, haven't they? Well, here's to freedom." She tipped up the bottle of SoCo, sending the fruity syrup down her throat.

"Looks like you've hit some hard times, Miss Red," Manny said. "Why didn't you mention it to me?"

Red laughed. "You know? I never did need a pimp before. Small town men were just kinda docile, easy to manage. Everyone had a wife, everyone cared if their wife found out. They never got rough with me, never anything I couldn't handle. I don't know what changed." She trailed off and headed for the front door with a manic thrust. "What am I doing complaining to the man who just spent the eighties in prison? You hungry? I'm hungry. Man alive, I could eat a bear right now. Let's go out."

Manny took her by the shoulders and felt bones that were very close to the skin. "You still have running water?"

She nodded. "You have to ask?"

"Okay, go clean yourself up," he said. Truth was, he couldn't stand the smell of her.

"Me clean up? You're the one fresh out of the pokey!"

"I was thinking I'd fix us some supper," he said.

"Honey, I don't have shit to eat. I was thinking we could go sneak into a Sizzler or something."

"I learned to cook in there. You'd be surprised what I can do with a can of meat and some ketchup." He grinned and flashed his million-dollar blues. He knew the power of that simple, winning act of charm, the look that made people see possibility where there wasn't any, that made them lower their defenses when they shouldn't.

Red nibbled her chapped and flaking lip. "You're not gonna fleece me, are ya?"

"I'm hurt you'd even mention it," Manny said.

She laughed herself into a coughing fit and skittered out of the room. "Okay, you win! I'm gonna wash the scum off me," she said over her shoulder, "but I'll always be a dirty whore!"

Manny found a packet of dried onion and a can of olives in the cupboard, a tube of Jimmy Dean sausage in the freezer behind a berg of frost, and some white rice in a take-out container in the fridge. He spooned some cloudy bacon fat from a can under the sink into a hot pan and sizzled the onion. Then he added chopped olives, browned the sausage, dumped in the rice, and wet it all with a splash of water. He put a lid on it and turned the heat down low.

While he waited for the thing to cook, Manny observed the chaos of memorabilia on Red's fridge, photos of babies grown into kids and all the way to adulthood, blond, sunburnt, cheerful. Primitive drawings. Birth announcements and Christmas cards. He was amused by these strange artifacts from a world far away from his.

One note buried among them stuck out. The letter was written on yellowing paper and unsigned, but he recognized the handwriting immediately, large and careful, like that of a child who is learning her alphabet. He plucked it from its smiling rooster magnet.

> *Dear Red,*
>   *I found my aunt.*
>   *Thought you should know.*
>   *Dont come looking.*
>   *Just wanted to tell you I made it out and Im okay.*
>   *Hope you are too.*

Her aunt. He remembered her spinning the tale on the spot, with her dirty face and the dribble coming out of her nose, and that he had been sure she was bluffing. He'd gone along with the story and even taken her to the edge of that town, whatever it was, certain that she was trying to make him think she had somewhere to go where people were waiting for her. But the aunt really existed, and now it seemed the girl had picked up the scent she had been following all those years before. He was lost in a rare slurry of insecurity. All that time they were together, had she just been waiting for her moment to escape? He lost his bearings as the kitchen swayed around him, and he lowered himself into a nearby chair, buried his face in his hands. No, that girl had worshipped him, had put herself in danger for him. There had been plenty of opportunities for her to leave, and she was more than capable. He had never kept her in a cage.

He slipped the letter in the folds of his near-empty wallet. If Red was in touch with Kit, she'd know where to find her.

TWENTY MINUTES LATER, RED APPEARED in a bathrobe with a towel on her head, looking just as terrible as before, but wet.

"Guess they shut off the gas, cause that water was cold as a witch's titty," she said and wiggled a pinkie in her ear. "Ooh, heyy, that smells good, Merlin. What kinda magic you making?"

Manny had accidentally let the bottom layer scorch while he snooped but it didn't matter. Junkies weren't choosy. He piled the prison cell hash in a bowl and sprinkled some salt over the top.

"Voilà," he said. Red threw him a coy look and dug in.

"Oh my . . . *God.* OhmyGod." Her eyes rolled back and she pressed both hands on the table. "Oh, Manny, honey, darling. There are not enough blow jobs in the world to thank you for this." She stamped her heel like she was killing a cockroach. "I'm not kidding, I will fuck you into an early grave, I swear I will."

"There *is* one way you can thank me," he said, cocking his head.

"Anything you want, baby. I'm yours," she said through a mouth-ful of rice, parting her robe and shimmying her still buoyant breasts. "Name it."

Manny wiped his mouth and folded the napkin across his lap, then leveled his eyes on Red. "I need you to help me find Kit."

She stopped chewing and went still. "Sorry, I don't know where she is, Manny." She held up both hands. "Haven't seen her. Hide nor hair, Manny, I swear."

"You don't need to lie," he said. "I saw the letter."

Red folded her arms over her chest and shook her head like there were flies in her face. "No, no, no. I don't know shit, the letter just showed up one day, *ages* ago. She didn't say where, and she never wrote again."

"Look," Manny said, trying to keep his voice tame. "I'm not gonna hurt her, I just miss her. That's all. I don't blame her for leaving me, I don't blame her for any of it. I'm the one who needs to apologize. I can't live knowing how I hurt her, so I need to see her. Can you understand that?"

Red was crying now. With shaking hands she held a cigarette to her lips and searched the room for a light. Manny went to the stove and turned on an electric burner.

"Here's the thing," he said, the rage moving him to hasty words. He was trying to be cool, but nothing got under his skin like being misunderstood. "I ask for one thing, *one thing* so I can get on with my life. You let me in and now I know where your sisters live and all their little progeny and now I may have to tell them why you never show up for Christmas. And you know that's not all I'll do, but I'm hoping it won't have to get that far, okay?"

Red's face was dripping with tears and snot. "That's evil, Manny. I knew you were a sonofabitch, but I didn't think you'd be that cruel to old Red." She started to look around the room, and Manny suspected she was searching for a weapon.

"It's in the letter," Red said. "She found her aunt. She told me once, but I can't remember the name of that town she lives in. Armadillo Bend or some shit, okay?"

He pressed his foot against the chair she was sitting on and sent her flying back, whacking her head against the floor. Her bathrobe flew open, and she snaked around, emaciated, pathetic. She rasped out some cries. Then she pushed herself up, drew her chair up to the table, and sat back down.

"Lord help me," she said, all tearful, and he knew she'd come around. "It's Pecan fuckin' Hollow. And that's all I know, motherfucker," she said. "Godfuckingdamn."

Thank you. He slipped a fresh cigarette from the pack on the table and went to the stove. By now, the coil glowed orange. He lit the cigarette on the burner and crossed the kitchen to where she sat. "You made me the bad guy," he said, holding the hot end toward a sore on her wrist. She yanked the arm back. "I'm not the bad guy, I'm trying to do the right thing. I'm right with the Lord and I have to get right with Kit." He slipped the cigarette between her lips, then thumbed the storm of bruising and track marks in the crook of her elbow. She whimpered, and glared at him in helpless rage.

"You're the bad guy," he said. "Not me."

CHAPTER FIVE

MANNY THANKED THE BUS DRIVER AND STEPPED ONTO THE STICKY
asphalt of the bus stop in Pecan Hollow. He was close. But first, he
would need to eat to quell this screaming hunger. He inhaled the
unctuous odor of deep-fried potatoes and crossed the main road to
the diner. In prison, nearly fourteen years of insipid slop had passed
through his system, bland calories all bearing the same undertone
of tin and rancid fat. And there was never enough.

Inside the diner, Manny scanned the room, taking account of every person in there. It was a habit he'd picked up from robbing gas
stations, because every person was a variable, and he needed to know
who was there, where they were, and what they were doing. To his
left, at nine o'clock, sat a middle-aged Mexican couple, hunched over
matching plates of eggs. Immigrants, maybe. Trouble-avoidant. At
one o'clock, a portly trucker picked his teeth, his plate wiped clean,
while a redheaded waitress warmed up his coffee. Women screamed;
truckers tackled; the elderly were usually meek, but some had nothing
to lose and would take risks. Directly to his right, a milquetoast man
of forty laid down a fiver and sorted his change by category. He was
the type to soil his pants silently and call the cops.

Dead ahead, a homely girl in her mid-twenties cleared away some
dishes. As she ran her rag up and down the counter, her waist-long
braid, loosely bound, hung over her shoulder and swayed. She had a

faintly inbred look to her, poor teeth, a soft chin, and her hair nearly matched the putty color of her skin. He sat down right in front of her.

When she looked at him, her eyes darted away as if he were hot to touch.

"Hello, there, little lady." He let his words unfurl like a spool of velvet. She did not look up, but the skin around her collarbone flushed pink in splotches. He cocked his head to meet her eyes and she acquiesced. He had not lost his touch.

"Can I help you?" she gasped, but it sounded more like "Kah-hehpye?"

"What's your name, sweets?" he asked. She looked down at the nameplate pinned to her breast. He smiled.

"*Sandy*," he said, clasping her hand between his before laying it back on the counter. "Howdy, I'm Manny. Now, I'm awful hungry."

She slid a menu toward him and continued to wipe down the same clean spot, the blotches on her chest now more defined.

"Let's see here," he said, surveying the menu. "Well, it all sounds so good, how am I gonna pick just one thing?" As he looked from Sandy's braless breasts to the menu, he felt the shimmer of his appetites, electric with wanting. He deepened his breath and slammed his knee firmly up against the counter.

"You okay?" she asked, sweet with concern.

"About to be," he said, and pushed the menu back to her. "I'll have one of everything, please."

She stalled, confused, and waited to hear more. "Everything?"

"First meal in fourteen years," he said with a wink. "I told you I was hungry."

She started slowly for the kitchen and turned around at the swinging doors. "I don't mean to pry, mister, but how are you gonna pay for all that?"

Manny smiled, slipped a gold link bracelet from his pocket, and coiled it on the counter. He hadn't stolen but merely recovered it from a woman's purse, which had fallen on the floor of the bus while she was sleeping. Sandy draped it over her wrist. She pursed her mouth into a white line while she deliberated, then disappeared into the kitchen. When she returned, she had frosted pink color on her lips and had smoothed back her hair.

"My boss says he'll take it," she said.

A young man with an apron around his waist and a rag slung over his shoulder slammed his hand on the bell and barked, "Order up!" Sandy startled, scurried away, and disappeared between the swinging doors of the kitchen.

Manny was irritated at the manager for interrupting what seemed to be a promising conversation. He was starving, too, and could scarcely wait the fifteen minutes or more for the food to come. There was a thin newspaper left behind by a customer on the seat next to him. He picked it up and tried to read the headline, but he was too distracted. Although he had fantasized for years about what he would do, he found that the closer he got to her, being here where she'd been living, it was as though the slate were clean. He had so many questions he needed answered. But you couldn't put pressure on Kit like that. You had to go slow, give her nothing to push against. He knew how to handle her.

A dusty-looking cowboy ambled in and swung his hips into the first booth by the door. He looked like a real shitkicker. A horrible thought crossed Manny's mind as it occurred to him that she might have been with someone other than him. After all this time, had she given up waiting for him and caved? If she had, she never would have stayed with anyone, but maybe she'd shuffled through a lot of them, searching, always searching for a substitute for her one and only. Her Manny.

He seethed at the thought. As he looked down he realized he had shredded the newspaper into a feathery mess.

Just then, a cook, two waitresses, and Sandy brought out trays of bacon, sausage, pancakes and waffles, a half dozen sandwiches, sides of cornbread, beans, and rice, migas and chilaquiles, roast beef and gravy, pies, cakes, and pralines. They spread the plates out and covered the entire counter. Sandy looked as proud as if she had made the food herself. He put a napkin in his lap and said a prayer of thanks. Manny took exactly one bite of each of over fifty dishes. When he was finished, he wiped his lips, folded his napkin, and tucked it under his plate.

"Miss Sandy, how old are you?"

"Twenty-five next month."

"Oh, you're just a little baby," he said. "You wouldn't know my friend then."

"Maybe I will, who is it?"

"A girl I used to know. Strong legs, little titties, kinda looks like a pretty boy. At least, she used to. She could be a big fatty now, for all I know." Sandy giggled, exposing crooked front teeth, and covered her mouth.

"I don't know, doesn't ring a bell just yet," she said. "What was her name?"

"Kit," he said.

"Well, *sure*! I know Kit!" she said, a little loudly, excited to have made a connection.

"You know her?" Manny asked. There was a rush of heat and he nearly lost his breath.

"Yeah, of course, everyone knows everyone around here. What about you? Just passing through, or . . . ?" He was so swept away by the good news that her innuendo took a moment to sink in. She could be helpful, this one. He'd indulge her.

Manny slid his hand next to Sandy's and rubbed her pinkie with his. "Do you know where she lives, sweetheart?"

Sandy pulled her hand back self-consciously and looked down, smiling. "She lives just down the road—I can show you, if you like."

A calm befell him. "No, darlin', just point me in the right direction. I'll find my way."

She looked disappointed as she walked around the counter and led him to the window. "Just down that road a mile or so. Little white farmhouse, chicken coop in the yard. Can't miss it."

"I hope I'll be seeing you soon," he said and dusted her marshmallow soft hand with his lips. "It's always good to have a friend in town."

CHAPTER SIX

KIT STOOD AT THE KITCHEN COUNTER, STAPLING SOME CHICKEN wire to a wooden frame. A raccoon had muscled loose the henhouse door, and while it hadn't hurt the chickens, all the eggs were gone. Charlie sat cross-legged in an antique chair by the window, filing the knees of her jeans until they frayed. Kit had already yelled at her for ruining perfectly good pants and said that she would have to pay for the next pair herself, but today she let it be. Charlie had been surprisingly helpful at the vet's, and the hard work had seemed to chill her out a bit. Kit was enjoying the little stretch of ceasefire between them, certain it would be brief.

"Who's that man?" Charlie called from her perch at the window.

Kit went to the window, but whoever it was stood out of view. She hoped it wasn't some fallout from the pencil incident. Sugar Faye's husband worked in oil and probably had a hotshot lawyer in Houston that could take her for every cent, but that didn't seem like Sugar's style. It was more likely she'd bring over some guilt cookies and try again to get Kit to atone.

Kit was trying to decide which was worse when she heard the man's footsteps on the creaky stairs and a knockety knock at the door.

OUTSIDE THE HOUSE, MANNY POPPED a lemon candy he'd taken from the diner and crushed it between his teeth. He buffed his dusty boots

on his calves and tucked in his shirt. It was fortunate he had been able
to satisfy his hunger and clear his head with the long walk. It helped
to settle the urges, the pesky lashes of desire. He had longed for her
in prison, and defiled her in many ways, for which he had repented.
Even now, he thought he could smell her, woodsy and bitter, gamy . . .
But he was a godlier man, cleansed and polished to a comely glow.
The canopy of pecan trees rustled above him, filtering the last of the
light of day, and he felt just fine as he ascended the front steps and
knocked. The day had come, and he was ready for her.

KIT OPENED THE DOOR A crack to see who had come to bother her.
There was a man standing there, tall and fit, but she couldn't make out
his face. The western sun hung low and lit him in silhouette from behind. Was it a drifter looking for work? She felt above the doorframe
to make sure her gun was there if she needed it, and it was. Cool and
loaded.

"What do you want, mister?" she said, her voice husky and bored.
She heard him chuckle softly and clear his throat. She bristled at the
sound but couldn't place it. She flipped on the porch light.

"Hello, Kit," he said.

Before her brain could register, her nerves fired all at once on
high voltage. There stood Manny. Older, his physique severe and
sinewy, handsome as ever. Blue eyes glinted under smiling lids. He
wore a checked button-down and old jeans with the waist cinched to
keep them up. The same clothes he wore on that last day. Kit realized
she had stopped breathing and inhaled fast. She said nothing, for no
words came to mind. Only a violent clash of fear and longing. In one
vessel were all the qualities she had loved: the confidence, the caring,
the crisp attention that made her feel singular in a room, when all
she'd ever felt was invisible. Yet she could not forget he was all she
hated, too. He was calculating, selfish, and he had a capacity to de-
ceive like no one she had ever met.

Manny's expression was soft, gentle. "Forgive me for popping up like this . . ." His voice trailed, but his gaze stayed with Kit, steady and probing. "I only just got let out and had to come see you," he said. His eyes dropped, and with his middle finger he strummed the mesh on the screen door between them. "I won't stay long, just hoped you'd allow me to say a few things one of these days when you're ready. I've had a lot on my mind. I'll be staying at the Big Sky Motel off the interstate, not five miles away. I won't call on you again, but if you'd like to talk you can find me there. I live honestly now, Kit." He seemed to be waiting for a response, but what could she offer? She could scarcely trust her senses that it was really him, let alone make sense of the information. It felt as though the walls around her had become brittle and thin, that the whole house could fold in on her. Whatever sense of safety she had scraped together over the years vanished.

He cocked his head and a dark wing of hair swept over one eye. He tucked it behind his right ear. "You don't have to fret, Kitty," he said and smiled with sympathetic, upturned brows. "Though I won't blame you if you do."

Her body was frozen, but her mind roiled like a thousand rats. She couldn't make sense of this Manny. How neatly she had tucked him away in a box and left him, untouched, except when he emerged in her dreams. She remembered the article she'd read, how he'd taken the blame for their crimes. Did he think that had settled the score? How would he collect the debt? And what did he really want from her? A cold sweat slicked across her forehead and the back of her neck as she thought of Charlie.

"You're gonna have to get on out of here" was all she could say and she toed the door shut with her boot, locked it twice.

"Fair enough, Kit," he called out. "You know where to find me." Then he turned and left, scuffing his boots in the oyster shell driveway, humming a gospel hymn.

"WHO WAS THAT?" CHARLIE'S VOICE sounded sweet, but taunting.

I have no idea. Kit knew she seemed shaken. She searched for words but hadn't the means to form a sentence, no less lie convincingly. She filled a glass with water from the tap, the tinge of sulfur from their well strangely soothing.

"Used to be a friend." It was the best she could do for now. She hoped it would satisfy Charlie at least until she could think of something more convincing.

"You don't have any friends," Charlie said, arms folded, looking like she smelled a story. She wasn't going to let this go.

"He's not a nice man," Kit added, falsely absorbed in a scab on her elbow.

Charlie laughed. "Seemed pretty fuckin' nice to me."

"Hey, you don't talk like that in this house!" Kit's voice got shrill. She wasn't ready to discuss this.

"Okay, I'll talk like that out there." Charlie barged through the screen door and stood outside, shouting, "He seems pretty fuckin' nice to me!"

In a few swift steps, Kit bounded through the door and tackled her daughter to the grass, fists pinned at her ears.

"Girl, you listen here. Keep away from that man. Do you understand?" Charlie glared back at Kit, her features hard and defiant, but her eyes wavered. She pushed Kit off and ran inside.

Kit sat on the steps, unsteady with fright. A crowd of emotions barged in at once. Regret for getting physical with Charlie, terror that Manny was back, bewilderment at how different he seemed . . . kind, almost, and humbled. She was pissed that she had been caught off guard. Ashamed at realizing that beneath it all, a part of her was happy to see him, as if her heart had forgotten all the rest. Standing there in her home, between her daughter and Manny, she had felt ready to burst, like every thought or worry from Charlie's entire life wedged itself into that moment. She tried to numb out but couldn't pull the plug on her feelings.

Kit quaked. She dashed around back, grabbed the machete, and tore into the tangle of blackberry vines at the door. There was no way to push the feelings away, so she brought them down on the brambles. Long, vicious slashes in quick succession, sections broke off and flew around her. Each time her blade made contact she yelled savagely, like her voice could do the cutting, on and on until her muscles turned to mush. She collapsed on a litter of thorns, blind to her surroundings, breathless.

The memories, long sequestered, emerged like bees dispatched from a shaken hive, one, two at a time, then several more until the whole swarm was upon her.

PART II

CHAPTER SEVEN

HEMPSTEAD, TEXAS, 1970

THE GIRL COULDN'T RISK BEING SEEN ON THE OPEN COUNTRY ROAD, so she crossed the tree-heavy pastures and threaded the fences that divided them, spring-loaded grasshoppers bouncing away from her ankles. All around her, cicadas thrummed in harsh staccato, sounding like hard rain on a tin roof. Woozy with lack of food and drink, she swayed and propped herself against a young pecan tree until her blood made its slow crawl back to her brain. She knew now not to ignore the rattle of true hunger and pushed steadily through the grass toward the gas station sign in the distance. Forced to approach the road to get to the station's entrance—and, she hoped, food—she heard the rumble of an eastbound car. When she saw it was police, she squatted low, head tucked, arms hugging her bony shins. Her heartbeat slowed and her mind stilled, and she stayed this way long after the car had passed.

Someone like her wouldn't last long on the lam. She could hear the crackly APB now: *Unaccompanied minor, says she's thirteen years of age but doesn't look more'n ten, possibly of Mexican descent, possibly in need of medical attention. All units be advised.* Like most kids, she had picked up the lingo from watching *Dragnet;* unlike most kids, she had also learned it from the backseats of cop cars. Every other time she had tried to escape her foster homes, she had been caught. Not today. Today she was going to meet Eleanor.

The girl had first heard of her great-aunt Eleanor a few months ago when one of the social workers, a perpetually stressed, coffee-scented woman named Barb, had mentioned to her foster parents, the Machers, that she had just found a note in her case file about a relative, her birth mother's aunt, named Eleanor, who lived in a town called Pecan Hollow. Barb said they had tried to reach her when Kit was an infant, but for some reason or another, it hadn't worked out. The girl had tried to punch the social worker for not telling her sooner, as if she hadn't been wishing for something like this her entire life.

The Machers had had to hold her down and nearly stuffed a chill pill between her clenched teeth. If the girl had been a gentler child, if she had asked nicely, maybe she could have gotten more information out of the beleaguered and cross social worker. But by the time she finally settled herself down, Barb was packing her bag to go. The girl had begged the social worker to put her in touch with the aunt, a phone number, a last name, but she sighed and shrugged, and though Barb said she would look into it, Kit knew from the look in her eyes, like she had already moved on to her next appointment, that this woman would do no such thing. She trudged out of the house, her monstrous briefcase slapping against her calf.

Why the great-aunt hadn't claimed her, the girl didn't know. Sometimes she got angry at Eleanor, thinking of the bastards and idiots she'd been entrusted to, people who oughtn't be allowed to care for animals let alone children. She worried if she found Aunt Eleanor, she might be so wicked to her aunt that she'd get kicked out before she had a chance to prove she was worth keeping. She supposed it was an awful lot of trouble to take in a child. But now that she was thirteen she could help take care of her aunt. Sometimes she let herself look forward to the day they would meet. Maybe

Eleanor flicked her earlobe when she was nervous, too. Maybe she also hated candy. Maybe, for once, the girl could see her features in someone else's face.

BY THE TIME SHE REACHED the filling station, it had been a day and a half since her last meal, and she trembled with hunger. She kept cover behind a staked panel of particleboard that read DIRT FOR SALE and watched. A guy with gray skin and suspenders sat behind the counter, smoking and chatting with a local, while a city man in a maroon suit stood in line, jittering with impatience and too much caffeine. Outside, a glossy station wagon refueled, a friendly looking dad with bushy sideburns manning the pump. Three kids, covered in snacks, chattered and tugged at each other in the wayback, while their pretty mom with Patty Duke hair stood outside the car stretching her legs. At once frightened and rapt, the girl watched them as if they were a strange species. They had the most beautiful, peachy skin, smooth and even, like it was painted on. No spider veins or sores, no bruising or eczemic flaking, no dimpled flab. Nothing like the decaying people she had known.

Mom strutted around behind Dad, laced her fingers in front of his soft paunch, and squeezed. Dad turned quickly and scooped Mom up and she laughed, the kids joining her with peals of mock disgust. The girl felt flush on her cheeks and neck, a deep throbbing in her chest. She turned away, confused, the brief spell of wonderment eclipsed by such longing.

The diesel engine started and the wagon lumbered onto the feeder road and disappeared on the horizon. The girl sat and sobbed, overcome by the beauty of what she'd seen and a searing bitterness that she would never know it from the inside. Though it had been just seconds, she despaired to see the family go. She reached in her pocket for the note, the only possession she had ever cared about. Folded in quarters and protected by a sandwich baggie, it gave her a prick of something sweet and tender just from being touched. Though she opened it only rarely, she knew its message by heart and chanted it like the rosary.

Sensing self-pity, she withdrew her hand and scrubbed away the tears with her sleeve. *Quit, now. Quit your bawling.* A numbness spread from her belly outward, until she felt only a faint buzzing, an airiness more tolerable than the shock of emotion from before. She thumbed her eye sockets until she saw spots and refocused on her plan.

If she could get enough to eat and sock some food away in her backpack, she might just make it to Pecan Hollow. Squatting there, watchful and still, she waited until the customers left and the cashier had gone to the bathroom. She dashed inside, snatched a bag of sunflower seeds and one of pork rinds and stuffed them into her tucked-in shirt. She could hear the lazy stutter of urine and made a run for drinks. An icy lemony soda and a bottle of Coke. When the faucet began to run, she snagged another bag of pork rinds for good measure and headed for the door, high on the promise of a solid meal.

Just then, the animal rumble of a Mustang approached, and the car idled and then stopped. The girl huddled behind the magazine display and peeked out, eyes fixed on the man who got out of the black car. He was unlike anyone she had ever seen, more action hero than man. He was strong and wore clothes meant to be noticed. A tight patterned shirt unbuttoned to the middle of his smooth chest, slim jeans that flared at the bottom and swung when he walked. She marveled at the creamy brown leather of his skin, the molded cut of his muscles, the slick, dark hair that flipped out at the nape of his neck. The foster fathers had been fleshy and sedentary or cigarette-skinny and nervous. This man moved surely, fluidly, like a hunter. The icy crackle of his blue eyes seemed to produce a light of their own.

The doorknob to the bathroom turned and snapped her attention back to escape.

She hustled outside and around the corner, narrowly eluding detection by the cashier. She was in range of the man with the Mustang, whose back was turned only briefly to select his fuel. Flush against the building, she froze and scanned the terrain for others. When she looked back, the man was gone.

She had to move now. Shirt stuffed, drinks in hands, she shuffled toward her spot behind the sign as quietly as she could without crinkling her spoils. As she passed the Mustang, she saw on the dash a white paper fast-food bag, its top folded neatly like that of a fresh order. Her stomach began to grind, and she knew if she had a chance at nabbing it she would have to act fast. The driver's-side window was two-thirds down. She looked around—still no one—and ran. The handle wouldn't budge, so she one-armed the drinks, hoisted herself halfway through the window, and grabbed the bag. She could smell the starchy French fries, the beef patty, the tang of mustard. Wriggling back, she clamped the bag tight between her teeth, feet groping for the pavement.

"Hey! What do you think you're doing there?" someone said behind her. The cashier, she thought. She would need to let go of everything and run if she was going to get away. She dropped the drinks and pushed back, the bags of crushed pork rinds and sunflower seeds now slipping out of her shirt, the drive-thru bag still in her mouth. A strong arm belted her waist and lifted her high.

She flailed, kicking and cussing between bared teeth, never letting go of the bag. His grip tightened, and he clutched her close. She writhed and clawed, taking skin and hair. He managed to pin her arms down so that she could only thrash like a fish until at last her strength waned and she stopped, panting and twitchy.

"Everything okay, mister?" an older voice said.

"She's all right, just a little lost, I think," said the man, who was holding her like a bundle of loose sticks, and he turned so that she was face-to-face with the cashier. If that was the cashier, then who had caught her? She looked down and determined that the arms around her were those of the Mustang's owner. Her heart sank as she felt the concrete strength in his grip and realized she might not get out of this. She began to worry about the next placement and hoped to death they just sent her to juvie.

"I'll make sure she gets home," the man said, his voice smooth and near.

"Okay, well, I don't ask questions and I don't want no trouble," the cashier said and wiped his forehead with a yellow chamois. "If you're gonna call the authorities, make sure you do it somewhere else. People don't like to see cop cars. They'll just go to the station across the road and keep going there."

"Understood, sir. Thank you much. I'll take care of it."

The cashier, agitated now by his own discourse, went on, "Won't matter how much I lower my prices, and I do have a bottom line, mind you. My prices are fair but I do have a bottom line. But the minute someone sees trouble they pay a premium to stay out of it—"

"We'd better mosey then, mister," the man said, marking the end of the conversation with a hard smile.

The cashier finally took his cue and walked away, muttering and dabbing at his neck with the chamois. The action-hero man opened the passenger door and set the girl down. She could run now, but she was too feeble to go very far. If they were sending her back she would like to eat first. She opened the bag, which she had managed to keep between her teeth through it all, but except for a wad of greasy wrapping papers, a fries carton, and a handful of unused condiments, it was empty. Too weak to scream or cry, now mourning the lost bags of rinds and seeds outside the car, she collapsed on the seat. With quivering hands, she attempted to open a packet of mayonnaise.

"Sweetheart," the man said. "You're starving."

She could not even muster the strength to look at him and was so fatigued she took pleasure in not moving for a moment. The man smelled of lemon drops and bread. Even he made her hungry. She closed her eyes. Something touched her lips. A straw.

"Drink, now," he said.

She sipped. Cherry cola. Caramel sweetness, effervescent and chilled. She sputtered, coughed, and drank again, stronger already as the sugar slid into her bloodstream.

"This'll hold you until we get you some real food."

He got in the driver's seat, keyed the ignition, and squealed into a sharp turn.

"You know, if you were so hungry," he said, and looked at her like he was trying to figure her out, "all you had to do was ask."

CHAPTER EIGHT

THE GIRL WORRIED HER EARLOBE WITH HER THUMB IN THE brightly lit café as they waited for lunch. The effect of the sugar had crested and was now fading, soon to drop her like a junk car from a crane. He had ordered a feast, the promise of which, coupled with the time it took to arrive, had her both anxious and flaccid in an attempt to conserve energy.

Not accustomed to such generosity, she tried to assess the extent to which he was fucking with her. She had seen the faces of snaggle-toothed boys and girls pasted to telephone poles, heard the safety mantras in school. On the surface, she was not in a favorable situation, yet it seemed less worrisome than many others she had known. It was difficult to see this man as a real threat. He had been friendly on the drive over here, though she'd been too tired to answer him back or say anything for herself. Maybe it was the way he had brushed the crumbs off her seat before she sat down; or how he decrusted the ketchup bottle with a damp napkin. How bad could he be if he tended to such details? He looked at her now in an unfamiliar way, searching and curious. She scorched under the light of his attention.

Just as the girl was about to crunch on another packet of sugar, the waitress brought a large tray of burgers, fries, and sodas. She transferred them to the table, one by one. The girl, who seconds before had felt nothing but the dry hollow of deep hunger, sprang to life with appetite. She reached for the oozing cheeseburger in front of her, but the man swiftly pinned her hand to the table. The perfect aroma wafted around, torturing her. She nearly passed out with disappointment.

"I know you're hungry, but let's be civil and introduce ourselves, little miss." He released her hand. "I'm Manny Romero. What's your name?"

"My name?" she said, searching for an answer. The policeman who had found her as an infant had supposedly named her Katherine, but the only time she heard her name spoken was when a teacher called roll or a social worker handed her off to a new foster family. It was official and girlie and nothing to do with her. The Machers had called her Bug, and the other families had put their own spins on her name, all of which she hated. It struck her, now, as a chance to give herself something more fitting. Nothing came to mind. The silence began to embarrass her.

"Well, you must be called something," Manny said, rolling the teal cuffs of his sleeves to his elbows. She stared at the meat of his forearms, wondering what it must feel like to be that strong. "If you don't tell me, I'll have to name you myself."

Then, it came to her. A name she had heard at school, maybe. Whose she couldn't recall. Short and sharp, neither male nor female. Easy to say, easy to forget. She reached out her grubby hand, and he shook it.

"I'm Kit."

"Good to know you, Kit," he said, with a smile that softened the hunch in her shoulders. Kit. She could live with that. He released her hand and gestured to the gorgeous burger, with its butter-glossed bun.

"Eat, eat!"

Kit ate faster than she could swallow but forced it down anyway, desperate to be sated, tearful, a puppy at the teat. Crisp lettuce, creamy mayo, juicy rich burger, and fluffy bun to bind it all. She took a dozen fries, dragged them through ketchup and stuffed them in her mouth. Salty, golden—the best single mouthful she had ever known. She ate it all and thumbed the plate until it shone. She drank her Coke in long draws, sip-gulp-breathe, sip-gulp-breathe, and watched the level drop below the ice until she could hear the sputter of her straw taking in air around the last drops of drink.

With every vital swallow, she felt herself take shape. It was only now she had the wherewithal to look at the man sitting across from her with any attention. Taut oiled skin stretched over beautiful bones, straight sepia-edged teeth, minky brows pinched in amusement above eyes that burned blue. The whole arrangement of his features was so perfectly harmonious, she wished she could stop time and study them, run her fingers over their contours, commit them to memory.

Manny salt-and-peppered his ketchup and dipped a runt fry. "So, are you gonna tell me who you're running from?"

Here we go, she thought. Kit reflexively looked out the window. A westbound eighteen-wheeler might do if she needed a quick getaway. Stow away in the back of the cab while the driver wasn't looking. Hot day, windows were open. Trouble was, he'd probably overshoot Pecan Hollow. Better to get there on foot as planned. The big variable was Manny, and his agenda, if he had one, was unclear. Would he let her go or try to turn her in?

"Actually, I'm going somewhere," she said. She had to make him think there was someone waiting for her, that she would be missed. "I have to meet my aunt. I was supposed to meet up with her but stopped for food, and that's when you found me." She cringed at the lameness of the lie.

"What about your parents? Anyone I can call?" More questions she couldn't answer.

"No," she said, gauging his interest. She couldn't tell yet if he was being helpful or trying to suss her out. Maybe he was the type to hold her for ransom. She nearly laughed at the thought of a moneyed couple pacing the halls of their fancy upholstered home, anxious to bring their darling girl home. "Just my aunt. She'll be wondering where I am, but you shouldn't call her or you'll worry her even more."

Manny looked at her suspiciously but said nothing more.

The waitress dropped off the check and a monstrous, oozing banana split with two spoons.

At the sight of it, Kit grew damp and queasy. Unaccustomed to the richness of the meal, her stomach revolted. She wiggled out of the booth and broke for the bathroom, slopping the floor with her sick on the way. Bent over the toilet, she vomited lavishly, what must have seemed like an improbable amount coming from such a small person. She looked at the mess she had made and peeped, "It's all wasted." She felt ashamed to see the splatter of her insides on the toilet bowl, the floor, her shoes.

Manny touched her back. He must have followed her in. She tensed against it, half expecting him to shove her head in the water. But he held his warm, broad hand against her like a compress, and it dawned on her that he was not mad, he was there to comfort her. Her cries slowed, her breath settled. He brushed the tangled dark hair away from her face and dabbed her chin with a coarse paper towel.

"I've seen roadkill looked better than you." He was teasing, intimately. She didn't smile back but felt less afraid. It sounded like he cared.

A woman who had been standing at the mirror cleared her throat pointedly. In one hand, she held a wand of lip gloss; with the other, she pinched her nostrils. "I'm sorry, but that is just nasty," she said.

Manny pivoted on his knee in her direction, his head cocked. "That isn't very nice, is it? She's just a little kid." Was he standing up for her? Kit burned with a feeling that made her forget about the nausea and the mess and all of it.

"I guess so." The woman, deep in her thirties, had rouged her cheeks so it looked like she'd been whacked on either side of her face with a stick. "You're not supposed to be in here, mister," she said. She bit a glittered nail and smiled. "I should scream."

Kit didn't like the empty way she was making a threat, her lips pouty, like those of a child.

"Why don't you be a sweetie and go scream for a mop and some rags?" he said to the woman.

She inserted the wand into its slim bottle, twirled it closed, and dropped it in her purse. Every gesture performed slowly, as if for an audience. She pressed her sticky lips together and walked toward the door, where she paused as if thinking of something to say, then closed the door behind her.

"Ya fuckin' slut," he added under his breath. Kit startled at the nastiness of what he said. The comment seemed so unlike the rest of what she'd experienced with this man, she wondered if she had heard him wrong.

"Let's get you cleaned up," he said, kindly now; he lowered the toilet cover with a square of paper and flushed. "Don't mind her."

Kit nodded, shelving the flash of ugliness he'd just shown her. She wiped the tears and snot from her face and sniffed, detecting a pungent combination of vomit and body odor. She pinned her elbows to her ribs and hoped he couldn't smell her, too.

"Will you come with me?" he asked.

She was so used to being bossed around or yelled at or physically handled, his asking struck her as a great kindness, and she did not refuse. She took his outstretched hand, a catcher's mitt that enveloped hers, never minding the mess they were leaving behind, and followed him out of the bathroom.

ALTHOUGH THE TRIP WAS SHORT, Kit fought to stay awake in the Mustang, its throaty engine and bumpy ride like a lullaby. She noted the easy landmark of the towering cartoon Road Runner which stood above the diner. She tracked their course, noting turns, exit signs, and any resources that would help her out should she need to take off on her own. They pulled up to a motel, a horizontal roadway inn with an empty kidney-shaped pool and a half dozen trucks in the lot.

Manny killed the engine and they got out. Kit trudged up the coarse, gravel-inlaid stairs and followed Manny along the flickering outdoor corridor into a chilly room.

"Home sweet home," he said, cheerful and a touch expectant, as if he hoped she would like it.

"You live here?" she asked, taking in the thick turquoise curtains, the frayed brocade bedspreads, the brass hanging lamp. It was beautiful.

"Well, I roam a bit, I guess. Never did stay in one place too long."

"Me neither," she said, turning the dial on the space-age TV set.

"You're welcome to stay here until the morning, if you like." He adjusted the air conditioner, beads of humidity gathered around its vents. "No pressure, I just thought you looked pretty beat. I suppose I can take you to your aunt tomorrow."

She tensed at the prospect of staying in his space, this man whom she'd just met, who seemed too good to be true. She had visions of being whacked across the head and thrown into the trunk of a car, dumped in an alley, or a lake. But she just didn't get that feeling from Manny. He had left his wallet and keys on the table, right by the door. Who did that? She could just snatch it and run away. He was nice, she thought, not the type. And besides, she was so tired, she couldn't imagine another night sleeping in the grass, the sound of insects crawling, the swish of coyotes nearby, the incessant threat of being seen and found and taken away.

"You can sleep by the door if it makes you more comfortable," he said, as if reading her mind. "I'll be on the floor by the bathroom. The bed's too lumpy for me anyhow," he said. With the fingers of both hands, he raked his long hair back and there it stayed, glued by she didn't know what—wax, gel, its own grime.

Suddenly aware of an urgent need to pee, she went wordlessly to the toilet, embarrassed to admit the errand. She shut the door and relieved herself as she always did—as fast as possible, never knowing when someone would bust in and hijack the bathroom. When she flushed, the paper took a slow orbit around the bowl, but the toilet didn't empty. She staved off panic at the thought—of what, she wasn't sure. Him seeing her waste? She had already puked and nearly passed out. What did she care? He was no one to her. Still, there was no way she was leaving her stuff in there. She jiggled the toilet handle, then lifted the heavy lid with a scraping echo, as on a tomb. She fished around for the loose chain at the bottom of the tank and reattached it to the lever that lifted the plug. Outside, Manny was whistling some chirpy ditty. She made sure the door was locked and tested the flush. The toilet gurgled, swished, and swallowed every unwanted trace of her.

Crisis resolved, she inspected Manny's things: razor and shaving foam on the sink, a fresh tube of toothpaste and a pink toothbrush, three thin towels folded neatly in a stack, a damp washrag hanging to dry on the side of the tub. Tidy as a church. No sour stench of many bodies, no furry grout. No goopy hair products and makeup clutter and loaded litter box wedged by the tub. She ran a finger along the smooth, shiny lip of the sink.

She sighed a little resting sigh.

For the first time since she left the Machers, she saw her reflection in the mirror.

"Wretched," she whispered. She had heard a social worker describe her once this way. Dark eyes, in color and regard, tangled hair to her shoulders that would be inches longer if she'd kept it brushed (never owned a brush, wouldn't use it if she had), dirt stenciled along her hairline and jaw, sooty smudges under her nostrils. Under her eye, a raw scar, kinky from her uneven stitches. She took off her shirt, her flat chest ashy blue against the dirty tan of her neck and arms. Skinny, ribby, with a belly slightly bulging. *Wretched* summed it up.

"You look like a boy," she said as a matter of fact. Her expression had the vulnerability of someone who is trying hard to be invulnerable.

A rap at the door. Kit dropped to the ground and covered herself with her shirt.

"Jesus H.!"

"Easy," he said without opening the door, "just making sure you didn't fall in. Make yourself at home. I'm gonna run get you a change of clothes."

"Fine," she called out, hoping to sound indifferent, though she was relieved she'd have the chance to bathe alone. She listened for the click of the door, the thud of his boots on the stairs, the rowdy start of the Mustang. It wasn't until the sound of the engine had faded that she turned on the faucet, stripped to her underpants, and sat in the tub as the water crept up over her till she was submerged in warmth. With a clean washrag and a honey-colored puck of soap, she scrubbed her skin pink and prickly, washed her hair and rinsed until it squeaked when she dragged her fingers through it, tugging at the snarls. She drained the murky pond and refilled with fresh water, just for the pleasure of it, but not before rechecking the lock on the door and bending the razor blade into a makeshift weapon, just in case.

She wondered if the Machers were sweating that they'd lost her again, if they'd see punishment, or if someone would just cross them off some master list of eligible foster parents. Paul and Fran Macher were different from her other families. They had vanity tans and co-ordinating billowy caftans and sometimes walked around au naturel. They had spent their savings traveling to Woodstock the year before and were desperate to tell you all about it. They were people who believed they deserved nice things but never seemed to work hard enough to have their own.

Paul was often involved in sensational "business strategies" that required him to purchase some volume of inventory (at a deep discount), which he was never able to turn around. He would disappear at odd hours and return bleary-eyed and morose, at which point it was wise to avoid him. Fran stayed mostly at home. She did psychic readings for old women she met in the market, women who wanted to speak to their dead husbands or children or pets. Her favorite pastime was sunning herself on a towel on their little patch of grass, anointing herself with baby oil.

The first time Kit had tried to run off, maybe a month before, she had gone three days without eating before she passed out in a cluster of bluebonnets. She had awoken in a shower curtain hospital cubicle, a bag of cold fluid dripping into her arm. She'd detubed herself and staggered toward the lit red exit sign at the end of the hall. She'd made it as far as the elevator before being escorted back to the holding area where the other, mostly Spanish-speaking, patients sat awaiting treatment.

Kit spent the night there on a cot among the sounds of the ill, in and out of sleep, and in the morning her social worker showed up none too glad to see her. She lay on the backseat of the woman's sedan as they drove back to her foster home, a prefab box house in a subdivision forty miles west of Houston, indistinct from the other homes on Pine Oak Terrace except for a collection of hanging stained glass in the windows. Peacocks, mermaids, and various scenes of psychedelia. Inside, it was a nauseating mix of pea-soup shag carpeting, wood veneer paneled walls, and an ozone of cigarettes and hairspray.

The tired rep from social services left Kit just inside the door with a final warning. Fran was away at a seminar for Gifted Persons, which left punishment to Paul, historically avoidant of conflict or even really acknowledging Kit's presence. That day he beaned her square in the face with a dictionary, still wrapped in its plastic, that they had won in a sweepstakes.

The impact split her cheek like a dropped tomato. He swooned when she bled so hard it inked the front of her shirt. Her face felt hot and numb.

"Shit, sorry—I didn't think it would hit you." He floundered with a dishrag, dabbing it in the area of her face but not daring to touch her. "Should we get you to a doctor?"

"I'm not going back to the hospital. It's fine," she said, the blood pooling in the little reservoir at the base of her throat. Seeing the horrified look on Paul's toast-colored face, she decided to push it further.

She found a sewing kit in the laundry room and returned to Paul, who was seated and bent over at the waist, drawing slow breaths. She pulled up a chair next to him, threaded a needle, and stitched up her cheek right there at the kitchen table. Her eyes watered reflexively, but it did not hurt.

"What the shit is wrong with you?" he said and stumbled to the bathroom.

She relished twisting the knife to his weakness. Maybe it was a fucked-up thing to do, but this toughness was the only thing she liked about herself, the only scrap of leverage she had. It was more than toughness, though. For as long as she could remember, when her body was injured, it failed to register pain. So, Kit had to learn to look for signs of damage since she couldn't feel them. But it wasn't that she felt nothing—she could feel temperature, pressure, tingling, moisture. And she was hypersensitive to touch. If someone got near her, her skin goosed and she could feel their body heat. On the rare occasion someone had tried to touch her affectionately, it burned.

A doctor had checked her out once after she had gone to school with a broken left arm and didn't realize it until she tried to pick up her book bag and it fell to the floor. The doctor kind of scratched his head and said, "I knew you people were tough but I've never seen anything like this." His best guess at why she hadn't felt the break had been nerve damage. Then he put a cast on her and signed her discharge papers.

A pretty resident who had been standing in the room lingered after the doctor left. She told Kit's foster parents to leave the room and asked Kit questions like "Have you been hit?" and "How often?" and "Who takes care of you when you need help?" The resident said she had a hunch that this condition, this numbness, may have been on account of all the bad stuff Kit had been through, that she should see a psychologist to know for sure. She said the same thing to the parents and even wrote down the name of a psychologist in Houston, but they never followed through. They didn't have time or money to shuttle her to Houston just to talk to a shrink. Not that Kit was eager to get to the bottom of it either. She didn't see the use in fixing it—to do what? Make her feel pain again? She hoped it never went away, this special power.

MANNY KNUCKLED "SHAVE AND A HAIRCUT" on the bathroom door and hung the shopping bag on the knob.

"Just a few things for you when you're ready," he said and turned on the television. Sounded like news. Artillery shells, chaos, the rhythmic *thwack* of helicopter blades, the war that had been dragging on as long as she had been alive. She felt sorry for those people getting shot and captured, their villages torched. She had never understood why the Americans were even in Vietnam.

She slipped out her pruned hand and hooked the bag's handle with a finger while clutching a towel at her throat with the other, then shut and locked the door again. The fact he had gotten her clothes at all was beyond expectation; nevertheless, she hoped he had not bought her some girlie nonsense for which she had no use. She was relieved to see inside the bag some T-shirts, striped and plain, some shorts, a pack of underwear, and a simple pair of blue jeans. She poked her legs into the denim, kicking a little to work her toes through the holes, and tugged a shirt over her wet head. She stepped out into the room.

"This'll be fine," she said with a cautious glance toward Manny. "Thank you."

"They look big, but the lady said they would shrink in the laundry." He must have seen the stiff denim gaping at her waist and piling up at the tops of her feet. Kit couldn't be sure, but from the way he leaned forward and smiled, eyebrows high and hopeful, it seemed that he wanted her to like them.

"Never had these before," she said.

"What, jeans?" he said.

"New clothes."

When he looked at her, so interested and kind, Kit wished she had not revealed this to him. She thought it best to share as little as possible. Manny reached toward her and she took a two-step back.

He showed her his palms. "Sorry about that. Okay, no sudden moves. Can I get these for you?" He gestured toward the price tags dangling from the collar and belt loop.

She stayed put and removed the tags herself with two swift yanks.

"Roll up the ankles for now. We can find a place to wash them tomorrow."

She folded the cuffs twice over. "On our way to my aunt's house?"

"You betcha."

MANNY LAID A BLANKET ON the floor and stretched out alongside the bed, fully dressed, his jean jacket draped across his chest. He fell asleep quickly and easily just moments after the lights went out. Kit stayed up for an hour or more to make sure he was asleep, and after running her escape route in her head until it felt automatic, until she felt that the risk was manageable enough, she finally succumbed to the exhaustion of the day, razor-blade shiv in hand.

CHAPTER NINE

THE NEXT DAY, KIT AWOKE TO THE CHUGGING AND HUM OF THE AIR conditioner and a bar of light across her eyes from the gap in the curtains. By some miracle, she had slept all night without waking. As she pushed herself to sit up in bed, she wondered again if the Machers had sent anyone to look for her, or even noticed she was missing. She slid onto the tufted carpet and went to see if Manny was still sleeping. But the space between the bed and the bathroom was empty, the blanket squarely folded and pillow back in its place on the bed. Kit scanned for traces of him, anxious for a sign that he hadn't left her.

She looked in the bathroom, but his things were gone. Panic inched up her chest and into her throat. She pulled out some drawers and found a King James Bible and a matchbook. Pressing down a swell of panic, she checked the closet again and swatted the wire hangers in furious protest. Then she noticed a length of black cloth on a high shelf underneath a spare pillow. Balancing on the chair, she strained to reach a corner of the fabric. The chair tipped and gave her the extra quarter inch she needed to reveal the objects underneath: a Remington 12-gauge and a box of shells. The gun's oily barrel gleamed. Her breath came back. He would not have left his gun behind. There was no money in the bathroom, but she did find Manny's toiletry bag, neatly zipped and hanging from a hook on the door, hidden from view in her initial desperate search. She slid her arm under the bed and collected an origami five-dollar bill and a couple of nickels.

Kit was hungry again and decided to return to the café where Manny had taken her last night. She walked out of the room, leaving a slip of paper in the door to keep it from latching. The sun shone more gently than it had the previous days. A cooled breeze tossed her hair around and tickled her cheeks as she followed the route they had taken the night before in reverse: right turn onto the feeder road for about a half mile, then another right at the Denny's onto the big road and keep walking toward the cartoon Road Runner.

She had nearly reached the café when she saw a coyote hesitating at the shoulder of the road. It looked around, not noticing Kit, and took a tentative step forward, then recoiled as a car sped past. She wondered what the animal was doing out in the middle of the day. When there were no cars visible, the coyote ventured to the middle of the asphalt, pausing there before looking back and continuing on her way.

Up from a dip in the road, an eighteen-wheeler appeared. Even Kit hadn't heard it coming with the wind blowing. The truck didn't brake or honk. Maybe he didn't see her, maybe it wouldn't have mattered. It charged a straight course and clipped the coyote on her hip, sending her spinning through the air. Kit gasped. The coyote skidded and rolled and came to a stop on the opposite shoulder of the main road. She was still moving slightly but could not get up to walk. Then she lifted her head in the direction she'd come from, whining metallically like a stopping train. She seemed to be calling for something. She dropped back on the road, having exhausted all her strength. Her belly heaved rapidly and then stopped altogether.

Kit approached, a sickly flutter in her gut.

From the culvert, she heard a raspy chorus of yips. She followed the sound and found four coyote pups. One was licking himself. Two nipped and tumbled with each other. The last whimpered as he struggled to climb the steep ditch up to the road to follow his mother. Kit gripped the one climbing toward the road by his scruff and pulled him to her chest. She scratched his head and he nipped at her playfully, his new teeth sharp. She stroked the down on his belly, and the pup slowly relaxed in her arms. She couldn't believe how trusting he was.

Kit began to fret, unsure what to do about the motherless pups. She felt faint. She wanted to scoop them all up, put them in a pouch, and keep them near. Bottle-feed them in her lap (they would fight each other for the bottle) until they were drowsy; bring squirrels as soon as they were hungry for meat. But where would they stay? She didn't even know where she would be tonight, what she would eat. She couldn't save them all. The pup in her arms wriggled and mewed, then dozed off in the crook of her elbow. She closed her eyes and bowed her head, waiting for the guilt to pass.

"YOU CAN'T HAVE THAT THING in here," the middle-aged waitress said, looking down through her glasses at Kit and the wriggling pup that pawed at her chest.

"His mama's dead," she said and pointed to the lump on the road.

The waitress—Maude, according to her nameplate—squinted and shaded her eyes, then looked back at the two of them, deciding what to do. She glanced at the register, where the balding manager in a green vest stood pecking at a calculator.

"As long as it's quiet y'all can stay, but once it starts yapping you're out of here."

Kit nodded.

"And I swear to Jesus if he makes a doody I will pick you both up by the scruff and toss you out myself." Maude touched her bouffant as if to make sure nothing had mussed it during the excitement. "Now what can I getcha, sweetheart?"

With the pup nestled between her thighs, snuffling and whimpering from time to time but keeping quiet enough, Kit sawed into a stack of pancakes half a foot tall, buttered and syruped to saturation.

She alternated bites of bacon and cakes and then got wise and tucked a piece of bacon between each pancake and the next.

"I think I remember you from yesterday," Maude said, sliding in the booth across from her and placing the bill on the table. "You look like you haven't had a bite in days."

"I'm just built like this," Kit said through a sticky mouthful. The waitress looked her over then down at the pup. He was beginning to wiggle and yip. Kit figured he was hungry. She took a strawful of milk like a dropper, her thumb over one end, and fed the coyote. He lapped it up and chomped at the end of the straw, massaging his gums.

"See, he's quiet now. He just needed something to eat."

Maude didn't look convinced. Kit wadded forkfuls of pancakes and finished the last of her bacon, determined to get her meal before something went wrong.

"You know, sweetie, you can't keep a wild animal like that. He's cute now but he'll turn on you soon enough. When I was your age, I used to rescue every one of God's creatures that passed through our yard." The waitress held out her forearms and rotated them to show the scant design of scars, thin and pearly. "Some friendlier than others, but most of 'em died anyway, and it broke my heart in two every single time. I think maybe they would have been better off just fending for themselves, letting nature decide what became of them instead of me."

Kit couldn't respond; all she could think was it couldn't be wrong to love a thing. It couldn't.

"So, where's your daddy?"

Kit shrugged, amused by the thought of Manny being her daddy.

"You don't know?" Maude said gravely. "Well, that's not good."

Seeing the alarmed look on the waitress's face, Kit said, "I mean he just went to pick up some stuff for me. He'll be right back."

Kit started to worry about Manny again. Where had he gone, and why not tell her he was leaving? It bothered her to feel tethered to someone she didn't even know. For now, she just needed to keep the waitress from raising flags.

"I almost forgot—he asked me to order him some pecan pie and a glass of milk." She checked her cash and looked at the total on the bill, already more than she had brought with her. The waitress sucked her teeth skeptically, stood up, and turned on the heels of her white sneakers toward the kitchen.

Just as Kit was about to slip under the table and take off for the motel, she heard boots scuff up to the table and a voice say, "You ate without me?"

Kit looked up to see Manny, smiling, cool as a mint. It took all her strength to hide how relieved she was to see him.

"She was real hungry, sir," Maude said, accusation on her brow, as she walked toward them with the pie and a frothy glass of milk.

"You're telling me!" Manny ribbed Kit and winked at the waitress. "She's eating me out of house and home."

Maude shifted her weight onto one hip and crossed her arms, evaluating the pair. Kit looked down at the pup and wished the waitress would take her skeptical eyebrows and go away.

"Who's this little fella?" Manny said, scratching the pup under the chin. "Is he for me?"

Another waitress swept past Maude and handed her a tray full of dirty dishes. "Can you finish busing six for me, hon?" the waitress said, then whispered, "I gotta run for a *maxi pad*."

Maude's new burden seemed to take precedence, and she left the two with an updated check and a pair of green and red peppermints. "Y'all take care, now, hear?"

Kit sighed and pulled the kicking pup under her chin. "Where were you?" she asked.

"Why, did you miss me?" he asked. She looked up quickly and met his smiling eyes, so blue against his dark lashes.

"No," she said. "I was just making sure I still had a ride to my aunt's."

"Cute little guy," he said. "I don't know shit about animals—you got plans to take care of him?"

"I'm thinking about it."

"You think your *aunt* will be all right with him?" He said *aunt* like she was a fictional character.

"I don't know . . . probably not. The waitress said they turn mean when they grow up."

"Huh," he said, finishing off the last sticky bite of pie. He wiped his mouth with a napkin. "You can't deny an animal its nature."

THEY WALKED BACK TO THE motel in silence, the noon sun high and hot. The coyote followed them in short sprints, stopping after each run to gnaw an itch, bite at a flower, or sit down to rest. When they approached the carcass of the pup's mother, Kit scooped him up and held him to her chest. When he thrashed and cried against her arms, she felt ill thinking that he had recognized his mother's passing scent, was trying to get back to her.

"Look, no pressure," Manny said. "But do you want another day to think about what you're gonna do with the pup? I don't have to be anywhere—why don't you sleep on it and I can still take you where you need to go tomorrow. He seems awful sweet on you."

She said nothing at first, then nodded, relieved, yet burdened with the thought of making a decision at all. When they got back to the room, she made a bed for the pup in the bathtub with a pillow and filled a clean ashtray with water for him to drink.

"I gotta step out again for a few hours. You gonna be okay?" Manny tossed the remote on the bed. "Nothing on but soaps, I don't think. Sorry."

She rolled the pup on his back and scratched his chin. "We'll be fine."

THAT NIGHT, ALONE IN THE motel room, Kit lay awake with thoughts of the other coyotes in the ditch. They must be starving by now, she figured, imagining them climbing out of their den, stumbling up the bank to the road, following the scent of their mother. The pup had been whining intermittently all night, hungry, thirsty, lonesome; she wanted to hold him and feed him something warm and sweet, would tap her vein to nourish him if she thought that would help. But she knew she wasn't enough, and every sound he uttered ratcheted up her guilt, made her feel selfish for trying to keep something she couldn't care for. All she had ever known were people who'd taken her in and realized she was too much. But then, how could she expect complete strangers to take care of her when her own mother hadn't wanted her? She remembered hearing about how some animal mothers, when they would smell something wrong with one of their young, maybe weakness, or poor constitution, would eat the weaklings; others would simply leave them to predators and the elements. When she heard this, she couldn't help but think that her mother must have sensed something with Kit, a congenital wrong that no amount of love could right.

She thought she had been loved once. There had been a family, the Foyts, she lived with when she was seven. They seemed perfect. Little house with a yard, a ten-year-old boy named Teddy and three-year-old girl they called Shel. Miss Rhonda, the mother, worked during the day, but at night, after bathtime, she would scruffle Kit's hair with a towel, comb the "rats" out, and braid it tightly. She'd read stories to her, as many as Kit wanted, and perform a different voice for each character. Kit had loved those nights, when Miss Rhonda would tell her about her days growing up on a farm in Oklahoma, how her parents were "Bible Thumpers" and how she'd run away as soon as she was old enough to work on her own. Kit just listened, mute, because she was afraid if she opened her mouth she would tell Miss Rhonda how stupid she had been for leaving a perfectly good family. Kit would never say anything to make her cross. Miss Rhonda hugged her, good, long, tight hugs that felt like sugar to Kit. None of the other parents had hugged her, hardly anyone at all, and Kit got to where she needed a hug as soon as she got home.

A few months into her stay, Mr. Foyt left with all his clothes and never came back. To keep the family afloat, Miss Rhonda took an extra job. When she came home, she would kick open the door, drop the keys and her purse on the floor, and disappear into her room to sleep until her next shift. Kit never saw Miss Rhonda cry about her husband, but after he left, she lost her sweetness and stopped spending time with Kit. The loss of Miss Rhonda's affection was devastating.

Kit missed Miss Rhonda so much she stopped sleeping at night and could scarcely keep herself awake during the day. The school nurse diagnosed Kit with mono and ordered her home from school. She lay on her mattress for a week, too tired and too sad to move. It was as if a horse had rolled onto her and died. She would have rather been a wild child, eating garbage and hunting ugly animals no one would miss. Even if it meant she'd die young, of hunger or violently by the tooth of some near-city predator, she'd take that any day over the feeling of being ignored.

One day, while Kit was still in bed, a social worker came and explained that Mrs. Foyt was no longer able to take care of her. Her hurt bloomed anew at the thought of leaving. She wrapped her arms around her shins and pressed her eyes to her knees until she saw bright white and yellow splashes and the heaviness and the heartache dimmed to a bearable numbness, and for the first time, Kit discovered how to kill her feelings. How sweet it was to master this one, small slice of her life. How powerful she felt.

The social worker waited in the car while Miss Rhonda helped Kit pack up her things, which were few, and saw her out. She hugged Kit goodbye, but by this point Kit had detached. She couldn't want Miss Rhonda anymore. As they drove away, she watched the house shrink in the distance, swallowed up by the pretty trees lining the streets.

IT HURT TO THINK OF Miss Rhonda and the little taste of loving that was given and taken so abruptly. As she lay there in the motel, the pup whining and clicking at the tub, Kit pushed at her eyes and swallowed the ice cube sadness in her throat. She was embarrassed to think how much she had relied on Miss Rhonda, hadn't even seen the end coming. Maybe that was when she'd learned that being loved was a fairy tale, and the best she could hope for was making it on her own.

Kit left the bed, slipped on her jeans, and cracked the bathroom door. The coyote pup had finally passed out, kicked a limp hind leg in his sleep. She lifted him by the loose sleeve of skin at the back of his neck, held him at her belly with one hand, and tucked her shirt into her pants with the other, making a little pouch. As quietly as she could, she carried the chair to the closet, pulled the shotgun from the shelf, and stuffed four shells in her pockets. She knew how to kill a thing, how to follow the creature as it moved with the barrel of her gun, take aim, and pull for a clean, quick death. A shotgun like this had more recoil, so she'd have to hold it tight against her shoulder, and even then, she knew it would knock her back a step or two.

She walked the quarter mile up the road and took a grim survey of the surroundings. The mother's carcass lay where it had landed, no doubt riddled with nascent maggots and rot, but there were only two pups left and no sign of the third. Most likely he had become a meal for some passing hawk. *My babies,* she thought, and again she wanted to scoop them up and lay them on soft bedding and give them everything they needed. She choked on her tears and lay the pup she'd been holding with the others. The numbing washed over her, a tingle at her cheeks that sank and spread outward, fanning across her body and through her organs until the suffocating sadness seemed locked behind some door, the chinks stuffed tight.

She stood up, gun raised, and aimed at the silver mass nestled among the weeds. She realized she must look deranged out here on the highway, holding a loaded weapon at a litter of pups.

She heard someone walk up behind her.

She whipped around and saw Manny, just a few feet away, aiming a revolver at her. She froze. She could try to get a shot off, but the gun was so heavy. She'd be dead before she could even take aim. She squeezed her eyes shut.

"Use that and you'll blast them to tatters," he said.

Her heart was pumping so fast she could barely understand him. When he started walking toward her, she heaved the shotgun to her shoulder. Manny was not afraid. "Don't shoot me now," he said, easily disarmed her, and laid her weapon in the grass. "We've only just begun."

He passed the revolver to Kit and clasped her hands between his, warming them. She suddenly felt the weight of her feet on the ground, could hear the breath move through her, and on her skin, the cool of deep night. She felt less alone, that there was one other soul in this world that saw things as she did.

"Here," he said, "I'll hold it steady, you fire."

With that she steered the gun toward the pup she had carried with her all day, the one she'd so hoped to save. She'd take him first, because he was the hardest, and because she didn't want him to be the last of his kin to go. He had curled up on top of the head of his sister and slept, little belly rising and falling with his breath.

She said no goodbye. She squeezed the trigger, but it wasn't enough to fire. Her eyes shut and she felt Manny gently correct her aim. She pulled as hard as she could and felt the gun swing up and back in recoil, steadied by Manny's sure grip. The crack of gunfire sang in her ears well after the shot went off. She heard the other pups react, harsh squeals of fright and confusion, and quickly took aim and fired twice, this time eyes open to make sure she did it right.

THE NEXT MORNING, THEY PACKED up the few things they had. Manny tossed his bag on the backseat of the Mustang and lay the shotgun on the floor.

"Off to Auntie Eleanor, right?" He looked to her for confirmation, and she nodded and stared out the window, squirmy under his gaze.

He fished a map out of the glove compartment and made a show of unfolding and refolding the edges around the route to Pecan Hollow.

"Let's see, okay, here we are right now just outside Navasota." He tapped their location on the map. "So, where's this Aunt Ellie supposed to be?" he asked. She pointed to the town in tiny print.

"Okay then, vámonos," he said and eased the car into gear.

She felt heavy from last night. She knew she had done right by those pups. Killing them had been an act of mercy. No food, no mother to look after them. Nothing good ahead of them, she thought. They would have died anyway, from hunger or from predators. She had been driven by a sense of duty. But even the act of justifying her choice struck her as wrong. Now guilt and sadness crept in, almost imperceptibly, an odorless poison. She wondered what Manny thought of her and was still trying to figure out why he had helped her finish them off. Maybe he had been punishing her, rubbing her face in the mess of her own decision. It didn't seem like him, but then, who was he after all? He seemed friendly, caring in the little ways he would think of her. He gave her space, but she never felt ignored. He seemed interested, curious, and yet he was patient enough to let her be known at her own pace.

THE HUMID AIR, HOT ALREADY, rolled over her like nausea. She debated what her next move was going to be. On the one hand, she was getting close to what she thought she had always wanted. Family. A home. How many times had she daydreamed about what it would be like to wake up knowing she'd never have to leave, never want to. That something deeper kept her there, not an arbitrary placement by an overworked system, but something connected to who she was, in her blood. Still, Eleanor was no one to her, not yet. They were kin, but that hadn't been enough for her aunt to take her when she was a newborn. Why did she think her aunt would want her now?

Manny rolled onto the shoulder of the road and slowed to a stop.

Kit looked around. To their right, a horse farm for sale; to their left, cars speeding past on the interstate.

"Hey, can you listen here?" He rapped her on the head with his knuckle. "I need to tell you something important."

She looked at him out of the side of her eye.

"Last night, the coyote pups," he said.

She had hoped they wouldn't have to talk about this.

"That was pretty messed up, don't you think?" he asked.

"I don't know," she said, focused on a crack in the windshield the size of a bullet hole. A grasshopper bounded through her window and landed on her, its claws clinging to her skin through her T-shirt. Manny reached over and flicked the insect from her shoulder back through the window.

"Well, I think it must have taken guts."

She exhaled a little breath she had been holding.

"You see, the point is"—he turned toward her—"you are special. I suspected it when I first caught you swiping my lunch like a little bandit. You have a wildness about you. Not that shallow, anxious thing most people have. You're strong, Kit. You're fearless. You can do things others can't."

Special. This sounded like a good thing, but she couldn't make sense of how it had anything to do with her. It felt strange to hear him talking about her with enthusiasm. She only vaguely had a concept of herself at all. Life had been a series of capture, punishment, and escape. If anything, she had always been punished for being herself— for being a leech, a reject, for taking up space. She wasn't special. She wasn't anybody. She was formless, liquid, slipping out of sight or absorbing into her background. She was wretched.

"You wouldn't think it, but we're the same." He went on, "I've been alone all my life, and so have you. Don't you feel a bit . . . different than other people?"

Something tweaked inside her. A lump formed in her throat.

"I think I found you for a reason. Do you understand?"

She looked down at her lap and took a few steadying breaths. His words were sweet beyond anything she had dared hope for. This swelling warmth, this desire to please, this urge to be a part of something important. It felt like the answer to everything. She didn't need some old aunt who hadn't bothered to look for her, who probably didn't even want her. She needed a friend.

Kit got out of the car and kicked through the high grasses and sat on a salt lick by a feed trough. Horses had come here to eat, but not in a long time. Grass had reclaimed the places worn by many hooves; the lumps of manure turned to powder underfoot. Carefully, she pulled the baggie from her pocket and removed the note inside. Kit read to herself the pretty cursive, carefully drawn.

Take this child and care for her. She will be something.

She folded the note, bagged it, and replaced it in her pocket. In a bashful voice, she said aloud, "She will be something . . . special."

She got back in the car, and with all the courage she could summon, she spoke, nearly faint with the stress of asking for something she wanted so dearly.

"Could I just stay with you instead?" She forced herself to look at him. He smiled.

"Kiddo, that's what I was getting at," he said, and he held out his hand. She high-fived him as hard as she could, splitting with joy.

Manny put his arm across the seat back and one-handed the car to merge with the fleet of vehicles speeding away, his tires kicking up gravel and smoke.

CHAPTER TEN

IT WASN'T LONG INTO THEIR DRIVE BEFORE KIT BEGAN HAVING SEC-
ond thoughts. He was nice to her, sure, but what would a whole life
with Manny look like? Was it just going to be the two of them all
the time? Did he have family? Friends? What was she going to do
all day? Not that she had ever liked school, but it had been a place
to escape the foster homes and get a good meal. Sometimes she even
learned something. Would Manny even know to put her in a school
somewhere?

Manny slapped the seat back so loud she jumped.

"We should celebrate this new partnership," he said. "Where
should we go, Kitty Cat? Somewhere fun? We could drive to San
Antonio and have enchiladas on the River Walk . . . we could go tub-
ing at Schlitterbahn? Anything you want."

"I don't know where those places are," she said. She was feeling
guilty for thinking about leaving him, but eventually she would need
to figure out a backup plan in case things didn't work out. "You pick."

"Come on, this is your chance!" he said. "Okay, look, how about I
surprise you?"

A surprise. Another thing no one had ever done for her. She pic-
tured the props of a surprise as she understood it: balloons and a cake,
a bike. She could stay around for this.

Within an hour she started seeing signs for a place called Galveston. Clues that they were entering a different climate started to
appear. Bushy oleanders lined the esplanade between several lanes
of traffic on Interstate 45, wind whipping them around, scattering
across the windshield blossoms of white and apricot. The sticky, salty
air a coating on her skin. Gulls appeared, cutting through the sky, settling on billboards and dropping guano. Then the highway took them
across a great causeway that stretched over miles of marsh and water
rippling below. The bridge swept them up, high above the waves. She
felt dizzy looking out over the expanse but could not take her eyes
away. She saw little splashes bloom at intervals. Fish? Dolphins? She
couldn't imagine what wonders teemed beneath the surface.

"Is that the ocean?" she asked.

"Not exactly. That's a big waterway. We'll be at the coast in a few
minutes. Don't tell me you've never seen the Gulf of Mexico before."

She shook her head.

"Goddamn." He clicked his tongue.

The causeway spat them out onto Galveston Island, and they
pulled up to a single stoplight at the coastline, the entire Gulf spread
out, waves tumbling toward them. Manny took a right onto a narrow
highway. To their left was a long gray beach and a line of cars and a
broad boardwalk between the two. Traffic immediately slowed down
as people looked for parking and took in the sights.

As they rolled down Seawall Boulevard, Kit observed the little
scenes like a comic strip. Surfers undressed behind their cars, peeled
wet suits to their waists. Sunburnt children sat in open trunks, legs
dangling, sucking on Popsicles or scraping black gobs of tar off their
feet with shells. A man smeared oil all over his wife's freckled and
rounded back, her bathing suit straps fallen to each side. A Jeep full
of shirtless young men cruised to the sounds of the Beach Boys, hung
their arms out the windows, and a group of beautiful girls in rainbow
bikinis swanned by on roller skates.

Manny U-turned and parked along the boardwalk.

"Hey, I'm just gonna grab us some treats," he said and pointed to a pretty, darkly tanned woman in cut-off shorts and a crocheted bikini top standing under an umbrella. Kit looked back at him and then to the ocean, which looked bigger now, menacing. "You scoot down to the beach, splash in the waves. I'll be right back." Then he removed his shirt, folded it neatly, and lay it on the front seat. He walked away, his strong back catching the warm tint of the sun. Kit considered waiting in the car until they could go down together, but she didn't want him to think she was afraid.

She found a set of steps and made her way along the craggy seawall to the sand. Blue crabs scuttled sidewise into rock crevices, flies swarmed a putrid fish that was tangled in strands of net.

Kit was overheating in her new blue jeans. She sat down and yanked off her shoes and socks and rolled her cuffs up to her knees. The sand was not loose and gritty like she had imagined, but fine and wet, more like concrete before it has cured. There was a powerful smell, of salt, fish, and minerals. She approached the water, sharp bits of shell underfoot, and squatted near the slow, lapping tide. She watched the exchange of sea and land, waves slurping up sand and drawing it back, then spitting out shells, plants, replacing some of the sand it had taken.

"Why don't you go in?" Manny said, his voice pushed back by the wind. She turned around and saw him standing there with a bright yellow towel over his shoulder and in his hands, two dripping ice cream cones.

She took one of the cones and licked up the layer of soft, sweet melt. "Thanks," she said. "Where'd you get that towel?" she asked.

"Oh, I made a friend up there." He winked. "She thought you were cute. I told her you'd never been to the beach before, so this is all her treat." Kit looked at the woman under the umbrella. Her shorts were cut so high Kit could see her butt folds. The woman turned and waved and smiled a big, white smile at Manny. Kit was suspicious at the idea of perfect strangers giving her things for no reason, but then Manny had been a stranger not that long ago, and here they were.

When Kit had finished the last of her ice cream, Manny took her by the hand and led her to the water. She leaned back. "I'm not too good at swimming," she said. She flashed to Paul Macher chucking her into the public pool, the water up her nose, down her throat. How she'd flailed and tried to scream but the water had overcome her and she sank, thrashing, and watched the distorted shapes of people passing by without looking. How someone's dad had picked her up and laid her on her back at Paul's feet and pumped her chest till she spewed pool water, her lungs on fire, and how Paul had teased her afterward, to keep things light, to downplay how he'd almost killed her.

"I won't let you go," Manny said. He picked her up and rested her on his hip like a much smaller child. She held tight to his neck and tried to look brave, but every muscle in her body was tense. She was ashamed she hadn't learned to swim and hoped Manny wasn't going to test her. Manny waded into the bath-warm waters until they were in up to her chest and they bobbed up and down with the gentle current. The salt piqued her pores and tingled in her cuts. She loosened her arms around his neck and closed her eyes.

"Okay, now, I'm gonna teach you to float," he said, peeling her hands away from his neck. "You're gonna have to lean back and hold most of your breath in your lungs so you stay on top of the water. Take little bitty sips of air and let them out just as small." Kit did as he said, lowering her head into the warm water, but held tight to his hands. She felt her rear end sinking and pulling her down. It scared her. When she tried to sit up her head dunked below the surface and she took in a great gulp of brine. Manny lifted her, sputtering and coughing, and whacked her on the back. "Strike one, let's try that again," he said.

"I'm not ready," Kit said through the matted hair over her face. She was out of breath and the waves were getting bigger.

"You can't wait for ready, kiddo," Manny said. "You can do this. Be cool, okay? Now, let's go."

She didn't like being rushed, but Manny talked to her like he believed in her. She held tight to his hand and stretched herself out, straighter this time, and kept her lungs mostly full. The salty water lapped in her ears and stung her eyes. She could feel the great movement of the ocean all around her and Manny's hand in hers. The water was perilously close to her lips, to filling her lungs and pulling her under, but knowing he was there was enough.

On their way back to the seawall, big, gelatinous blobs splayed out on the sand, clear and glassy. She found a strange blue and purple one that was filled with air, a liver-shaped bubble. She poked it with a stick.

"That's a man-o-war," Manny said, squatting down next to her. "Hell of a wallop. They'll sting you after they're dead, too." He stood up, swept the sand off his calves, and walked toward the stairs.

Can't sting me, she said to herself and poked it with her bare finger.

They changed in little huts on the boardwalk. Kit struggled with the heavy, wet jeans and was glad for the new clothes Manny had brought, a plain white T-shirt and a green pair of shorts. They walked north along the seawall for a half hour, the breeze coming off the waves too loud to make talk practical. The sun had dropped behind the island, casting a nectarine glow over the Gulf.

Back at the car, Manny suggested they get something to eat. Kit was grateful she didn't have to ask him for food. He chose a restaurant with a giant, lifelike crab on the roof. Inside there were white tablecloths and the waiters wore black. Kit tugged on Manny's hand to leave, afraid they would get kicked out, but he strode ahead and asked for a table with a view. The maître d' looked circumspect but escorted them to a table near the windows.

"Put your napkin in your lap," Manny whispered, and Kit opened the ironed cloth and spread it across her legs. She could feel the sand gathered around her toes and ignored an impulse to pull off her boot and dump it on the floor.

They ate a feast of chilled crab claws, fried oysters, and shrimp rémoulade. Kit had never seen these foods before, let alone tasted them. She was shocked and delighted by the perfect morsels of crab, the oysters, briny and creamy within the cornmeal crust, the plump pink shrimp in their tangy sauce. Kit was so giddy she forgot to worry about how expensive the meal was, even after Manny ordered a banana dessert prepared tableside and set aflame. When the waiter went for the check, Manny folded his napkin, took her hand, and led her quietly out the door.

The sidewalks were full of people, some strolling, others—saddled with wet towels, beach chairs, and umbrellas—returning to their cars. Kit hoped Manny would explain to her what just happened, but he only pushed on ahead. She had to jog to keep up.

"Hey," she said. "Hey, Manny, wait up." She dodged left and right to avoid running into people walking in the opposite direction. "Are we gonna get in trouble for that?"

"Trouble? Why should we get in trouble?" he said over his shoulder, not stopping.

Kit said nothing and jogged behind him. It was one thing to steal out of necessity, but the meal they had eaten was lavish. They could have had McDonald's for under a dollar. This was stealing for the fun of it. The way he made a show of picking the nicest table and ordering like a king somehow made it extra deviant.

"Look," Manny said. "I worked in a restaurant once, and you know, they comp people all the time. Crazy thing is, they give free meals to people who need it the least. Politicians, celebrities, power players, what have you. The way I figure, if those people get a free meal, why shouldn't I?"

Kit didn't have a ready response to his logic, nor did she have any moral ground to stand on, considering that they had met when she was trying to steal his lunch.

Manny finally slowed down to a pace Kit could match. They strolled up the boardwalk and came across a long pier with a wooden souvenir shop called Murdoch's Bathhouse. The building was long and narrow, and she could see all the way to the back. Inside, it was a treasure box. Hanging on the ceiling and walls, stacked on shelves, and dangling from displays were dried starfish and seahorses, painted sand dollars, jewelry made of shells of every color, papier-mâché parrots on perches, ships floating in glass bottles, pastel-colored T-shirts with silly slogans, key rings, magnets, and statuettes. There were saltwater taffies and pralines in a long glass display, lollipops the size of plates.

Kit wanted to touch each thing. She could spend a year in this place.

Manny clucked at her. "Hey, let me get you a little something to mark the moment," he said. "Anything strike your fancy?"

There was a display table in front of her with a rack of ornaments made of pink shells. She pointed to a tiny hanging chandelier, no bigger than her hand.

"What is it?" she asked.

"I don't know, it's pretty though, isn't it?"

"Sure is," she said.

"Take it," he said.

"Take it?" She knew what he meant, but she was feeling guilty about the big dinner they'd eaten without paying.

"I don't have any money for that."

"Didn't you just see a thousand little shells like that on the beach? It's fine, just take it. Think how happy it will make you. They won't miss a thing."

She looked up and down the boardwalk. People passed by in twos and threes. There were too many people.

"No," she said. "I'll get caught."

"Suit yourself," he said with a slash of bitterness that surprised Kit and walked off in the direction of the car. It stung to see him pivot so harshly away, and she was angry at him for setting her up like this. She didn't need the damn shells. Why risk getting caught now after they'd already skipped out on the dinner bill? Why would he push their luck? She was starting to think ripping people off was more than just a prank to him. Maybe this was how he rolled. Maybe it was a test, to see if she could keep up with him, and it all came down to this sixty-cent trinket. It had been a near-perfect day: she'd dipped in the ocean for the first time, floated on her own, eaten like a queen. All her life people had treated her like she was less than nothing. With Manny she felt important, prized even. What was a little petty theft in exchange for the world? She knew in that moment she wanted to stay with Manny, and if stealing was the price, she would pay it gladly. She brushed past the display without looking at it, hooked the chandelier with her pinkie, and sprinted back to the car.

CHAPTER ELEVEN

KIT STAYED WITH MANNY FROM THAT POINT ON. FOR SEVERAL months, Kit worried the Machers or child welfare had put out pictures of her and that she would get snatched up and taken from Manny. She had nightmares about it and one night woke up heart pounding, clinging to him like a tree frog, though she had started the night in her own bed.

But no one came for her. And after some time, she took for granted the life she had with Manny. He told her she was free to leave whenever she wanted, but she had no desire. They moved from motel to motel, using a different alias at each new place. Their dark hair and nut-brown skin made it easy for anyone who noticed to accept them as father and daughter.

In the early days, they did whatever they wanted. When there was money, they slept in the dark, cool box of the motel until he woke up. When the money ran out, they would sleep in the car, he keeled back in the driver's seat, she tucked into the den of the trunk, which he left propped up with two cans of refried beans. He said if anyone tried to kidnap her the cans would fall and the racket would wake him up, and somehow she found that comforting. They played cards, snuck into the movies, stole quarters at the arcade and played all day and into the night. He taught her how to drink whiskey neat and how to roll a smoke with one hand. If anyone saw them and asked why she wasn't in school, they said she had terrible cramps. That shut people up real quick.

On the best days, he would ask her to help him score.

"You're my lucky rabbit's foot," he'd say. "I ought to wear you around my neck." How rich she felt when he put his faith in her.

The first time he took her out, he stopped a homely woman in a blousy, flowered dress and moccasins at the grocery store and doffed his hat.

"Excuse me, ma'am," he said, soaking her in the blue of his eyes. "My girl here wants to make chocolate chip cookies, and I just wouldn't know where to begin. Can you help us out?"

She brushed her feathered hair away from her neck and took a fluttering look at him.

"Well, that's easy," she said, gesturing down the aisle. "Baking supplies are just right over here, but . . . no offense, isn't this a mother's job?" Her tone was not suspicious, but hopeful.

"Her mother? Well, she's not around anymore," he said, with lowered voice and a sad smile, in a way that suggested her mother had left them. When the woman heard Kit was a motherless child and he a brave father, doing his best to raise a daughter on his own, she seemed to take them up as a personal mission. A jealousy billowed up and Kit held him by the wrist, tight as she could, to feel his pulse against her palm.

The woman clasped her hands below her chin, moved by her own generosity. "I'm gonna fix you right up," she said, taking Kit by the hand. "Y'all follow me."

She led them to the baking section and scrutinized each product, making sure he got the best deal on flour and the right kind of chocolate. While she was absorbed in the task of her random act of kindness, he slipped his hand inside her plush suede purse, deft as a lover. Kit couldn't believe the things women kept in their purses: huge sums of loose cash, diamond earrings, salad dressing. One woman had had a little pouch filled with a couple dozen teeth Kit hoped belonged to her children. Manny thanked the woman with a humble, honeyed kindness, and she sashayed away, looking like she'd just been told a juicy secret.

Kit had a hard time shaking the feeling that she would get caught, and sometimes she felt bad for the people they stole from. Usually it was people with plenty of money, but sometimes Manny picked someone just because they looked gullible. When she voiced her concern that they should focus on wealthy targets and leave regular folks alone, Manny reasoned that they weren't being violent, and most of the time he was making the women feel so good about themselves, they wouldn't even know they'd been robbed. It wasn't worth it to argue with him. Depending on his mood, he would either dismiss her or be offended.

She often worried he might get rid of her. None of the foster families had kept her more than a year, and she had developed a sense for when she was on her way out. She was getting that sense with Manny. He wasn't making as much eye contact, and he seemed to find fault with every little thing she did. Even when she was easy and played along, even when she did everything right, she still got the feeling he was fed up with her. She had never tried to stay with the foster families—they had never given her much reason to—but with Manny she was determined. She wondered if maybe he didn't want her to play along. Maybe he needed her to be more active, aggressive even. He had called her special that day on the way to Pecan Hollow. So she tried to imagine how she could live up to that, how she could contribute and earn her keep. Finally, after about a year of doing things his way, she came up with her own plan.

She told it to him one day as they were sitting at a drive-in, waiting for the show to start. They were there to see *Five Easy Pieces* for the seventh time. Manny knew certain scenes by heart, and he would laugh his ass off every time Jack Nicholson told the waitress to hold the chicken salad between her knees. "There's something about that guy," he said, shaking his head. "He just does it for me."

She was so nervous to tell him about her scheme, she hadn't touched her popcorn. When the previews started up, she knew she only had a few minutes to deliver the pitch before he would be absorbed in the movie.

"Hey, Manny," she said. "I think I have an idea."

"Oh yeah?" Manny mumbled through a handful of popcorn. His attention was focused on the screen. She'd have to be quick and convincing.

"Yeah, I think I thought of a way to make us some money."

Manny looked at her, a half smile brightening his face. He was giving her an opening.

"Okay, so, it's still a little rough," she said. His eyes, so bright and direct, made her stammer. "I—I don't know . . ."

Manny looked intensely at her. "Don't humble yourself," he said. "You know. Now say it."

Kit took a deep breath and shook out her trembling hands.

"Okay, so, I think we should go to Houston for this one. Find a grocery store near one of the oil money neighborhoods. We find a Mercedes or a Jaguar or something and wait for the owner to come back. Just as they're backing out, I get hit."

"You get what?" he said, turning toward her. Now she had him. She had never been this direct with him before, going for what she wanted.

"I get hit. I throw myself behind the car and get hit. Not too bad, but bad enough that there's blood or scrapes or something they can see."

"This is *wild*, Kitty Cat," he said, thumbing the stubble on his chin like he was thinking it all over, then waved at her to keep going. "But I'll save my questions for the end. Go on."

She was doing her best to act cool, but she could feel the blood in her cheeks and the nerves in her voice.

"I figure most decent people will get out and try to help," she said. "That's when you slip in and grab whatever they left behind. Handgun, jewelry. If there's a purse, take some money, but leave the bag."

He nodded as he considered her plan.

"I like your thinking, Kitty Cat. Rich people never know how much money they have on them," he said, rubbing his hands together. "What next?"

Encouraged by his reaction, Kit stopped hedging and carried on more confidently.

"Right, so you take what you can from the car. While you're in there, I'm talking to the person who hit me. I make them feel sorry for me and try to guilt them into giving me money for the damage. They cough up a few hundred bucks thinking they got off easy, and you get to carry me off looking like a hero." Her heart thumped and she was grinning with pride.

The opening credits began to roll, and Manny didn't even notice.

"Okay," he said. "But I can't have you injured for real. How can we be so sure they don't take you out seriously?"

"It's not a problem. I don't get hurt."

Manny laughed and stuck his hand into the bag of popcorn. "I know you're a tough little bitch, but what the hell do you mean you 'don't get hurt'?" He looked skeptical.

She had not specifically told him about her condition before; she hardly understood it herself and was worried he might think she was some kind of mutant. But he would need to know if she was going to convince him to try the con.

"Ever since I was little and something happens to me, like I break a finger in a car door or something, it doesn't hurt. I can tell something's wrong, but I don't feel the pain."

Manny seemed to be mulling the implications of this new development.

"You can't feel pain," he said. The movie had begun, but instead of tuning in, he cranked up the window to block out the sound. Then he pulled out a lighter and held it out for her.

Thinking he wanted a smoke, Kit fished a cigarette from its pack on the dash and handed it to Manny. He stuck it behind his ear.

"Give me your finger," he said.

Kit understood now that he didn't believe her. She hadn't expected him to ask for proof, and she felt uneasy that he would be willing to risk hurting her if she was lying. But she wanted a chance to run this game so he could see she was worth keeping around. She took the lighter from him and flicked it aflame. She hesitated, her heartbeat quickened. Though she knew she would not feel the burn, she had never tried to do herself harm. The light winked in the reflection of Manny's eyes and his smile egged her on. She sucked in a breath and split the flame with her finger.

"Hot *damn*, little sister!" Manny said.

Kit glanced at him and kept her finger there until it blistered and she could smell her skin.

He slapped his thigh and laughed out loud.

"Kitty Cat, you are bad to the bone!" He removed the plastic top from his soda and plunged her finger into the icy drink.

Kit smiled, relieved that she seemed to have won him over. "Can we try it out tomorrow?"

"I can hardly wait," he said, and rolled the window back down.

KIT'S IDEA TURNED OUT TO be a cash cow. Except for a few tweaks, they followed her plan and it worked every time. Kit even got into the theatrics of it, and the more she could play the part, the less guilty she felt about ripping these people off when they'd done nothing wrong.

"I'm so clumsy," Kit would say. And of course, the woman (women usually had more stuff to steal in the car), feeling terrible, would be moved by this and correct her. "No, sweetie, *I'm clumsy*. You poor thang." They would ask where it hurt and Kit would point a shaking finger to the point of impact, which often had scrapes and emergent bruising. "I'll be okay, though, I really have to go." Kit would try to stand up and collapse. The woman would shriek and fuss over her, then Kit would grasp the fine silk blouse, look up into the woman's eyes, and deliver the lines Manny had written for her.

"Please, ma'am, I'm so worried about my daddy, if he has to stay home and take care of me, he'll lose his job. And he won't be able to pay our bills. Can you help us? Please, don't tell him I asked you, he's too proud." Some seemed to feel real compassion for Kit; others acted like they wanted to make the problem go away. But Kit and Manny always got paid.

Then Manny would show up, horrified. "My baby, what happened?" he'd moan. The woman would be emptying out her purse to help the poor family. Manny would refuse, at first, then Kit would take the money and thank them kindly. One man wrote a thousand-dollar check made out to cash. Even if they could only do it every month or so to give Kit time to heal, the game was a jackpot. Better than the money, though, was the way Manny carried her away and spoiled her afterward. Sweets, movies, roller rinks. One time he had even taken her to a nice hotel, the kind with room service and fresh flowers in the lobby.

SHE HELD HIS ATTENTION FOR another year or so running these cons before he started drifting. As Kit got older, Manny seemed less interested in taking her to work. She was growing, and when she looked in the mirror, her features seemed all out of whack. Her nose spread out, her face grew round and made her narrow eyes look piggish. Maybe she wasn't as useful if she wasn't cute. The less he took her out, the more she worried she would wake up one morning and he'd be gone.

But it wasn't just that he didn't take her out. He was acting bad, too. Sometimes he went to the bars and came back with loud women who would burst through the door, laughing out smoke and grabbing him by the crotch. It made her furious to see him drunk or high and distracted while she had waited all night, counting the water stains on the ceiling and biting her toenails to the quick. Manny and his guest would go at each other with her in the room, so Kit would have to slink out with a blanket and stew in the parking lot or by the pool, if there happened to be one.

ONE WOMAN, KIT HAD LIKED. Her name was Red.

They were staying at a motel outside a tiny town called Harper, Texas. The motel looked nice on the outside, with its striking A-frame registration building, but inside the rooms there was a loud odor of must and armpits. Kit had been hanging around all day watching the tube and picking at her nails, just waiting for Manny to get home. He dragged Red through the door around eleven without introducing her and disappeared into the bathroom. It seemed like he was in a mood. The shower shrieked on and steam seeped out the bottom of the door.

Red was stirring to look at. Long legged, all done up, in high-waisted jeans with fringed holes in the butt cheeks, a peasant blouse that showed her midriff, high-heeled cowgirl boots, her blond hair teased and piled on top of her head like a drawstring purse. Kit thought it must take a lot of work to look like that.

The woman eyed her surroundings and landed on Kit. "Well, heyyyy, how arrre yew?" she said as if they had known each other all their lives. "I'm Red. It's Winifred, actually, but, Lord, who goes by Winifred, can you imagine? What's your name?"

She couldn't hide a smile. "I'm Kit."

"Kit! I *love* that! Three letters, just like me. How fun. I love names."

Kit sized up the newcomer, completely unprepared for this level of pep.

"You like my outfit?" Red posed, hands on hips, weight shifted hard to the left. "It's new. I gotta stay fresh or the boys'll get bored and the cops'll get wise. Not like they don't know me already but anytime there's a newbie they haul me in and I gotta go through the whole shebang like it's my first bust. And it's just tiresome at this point, you know, we—the cops and me—we got a gentlemen's agreement that they let me work my territory and I throw them a freebie from time to time—very clean, very private, no issues whatsoever—and we all live together in peace."

Kit fidgeted with her jeans, unsure how to talk to this person.

Red fished a frosty Dr Pepper from the ice bucket and pulled the tab with some difficulty. "These nails, I swear, they are barely worth it but you know it's all part of the fantasy, right? You wouldn't think it, but at heart I'm a very practical girl—it's true! Don't look at me like that. Underneath the glamour I'm a sneakers and capris kinda girl."

"How long have you known Manny?" Kit asked.

"Manny, oh boy, couple years now, whenever he comes through town we do a job or two. He's a piece of work. He'd steal a walker from an old lady. No scruples, none whatsoever. But I don't judge, not me—uh-uh, no way, I seen ministers and doctors and husbands do stuff—well, I won't even start, but let's just say, between you and me, let's just say this: the better they try to look on the outside, the more nasty shit they got going on in their hearts. And that's a fact. And I might be a dropout, but I seen everything you could see and that's worth something, don't you think?"

"Is he"—Kit paused halfway through a question that only had one answer she wanted to hear—"Are you together?"

At this, Red cackled and coughed, and Kit could smell menthols on her breath. "Aw, that's the sweetest thing I ever heard. I mean, he is a fine specimen, and in another life, I would absolutely fuck him, but no, we're business associates."

"What do you mean by that?" Kit asked, jealous to learn she wasn't Manny's only partner.

"Well," Red said, looking toward the bathroom. "I guess it's okay to tell you. You're cool, right?" Kit nodded. She didn't volunteer that Manny had Kit stealing for him, too. "For example," Red said, leaning in and lowering her voice. "Big shot in a Caddy pulls up, maybe didn't wake up this morning looking for a date, but I walk by and . . ." She drags her fingertips from her head to her hips and back again. "Well he didn't see *me* when he woke up this morning. So, he pulls up and winks and I lean through the window and compliment him on his big car and his big hat and what else is big in there, if you know what I mean. Ninety percent of what I do is flattery. And all the while, Manny is popping the trunk and takes whatever he can get. He's very smooth."

"What if you get caught?"

"Well, if they catch you, it's not like they can call the cops because I'd just rat on 'em, but the problem is they won't be paying for sex anytime soon, not from me! Can't hardly blame him, though, can you?"

"You're a whore?" Kit said. She realized the idiocy of this question only after it came out of her mouth.

Red set to laughing again, holding her crotch with one hand, waving off Kit with the other. "I can't! Stop it! I'm gonna wet myself!"

She waddled to the bathroom with her knees pinched and left the door open, laughing out bursts of urine while Manny showered on. She poked the shower curtain violently.

"Where'd you get this girl? She's a stitch!"

"I told you, didn't I? She's my niece," Manny said, his voice muted from the steam and rush of water.

"Niece, huh?" She flushed the toilet and arranged some fallen strands of hair around her face and pouted at her reflection. "Who are your parents? How come he never mentioned you before? I have five sisters, well, four, actually, God bless her, Linda's with the Lord, she drowned in a creek when we were all teenagers, drinking and cuttin' up and being stupid. That's why I don't drink anymore on principle. Keeps me sharp anyway, and you gotta be sharp to stay in this business, I'm not joking. Razor sharp." She drew a long, magenta nail across her throat. "Especially when you're a free agent like me. You gotta be smarter than the streets."

That was the first thing Red said that made any sense.

She washed up, came back to the bedroom, and lit a cigarette.

"So, did you get your period yet? First kiss? Tell me everything."

Kit could not begin to address these questions, aloud or even to herself. Her cheeks and chest fired up and she found her glass of water on the table and drank it all down as a distraction. She was almost fifteen, and the dreaded Change was happening. For a few months, her chest had burned and prickled, and there'd been a marrow-deep pulsing in her thighs and knees. She was stretching and warping and growing dark hair everywhere. She looked and felt like a werewolf.

"Aw, sweetheart," Red said, and bit her knuckle in regret. "I didn't mean to embarrass you with my big mouth. But you don't need to be ashamed of those things, not at all." She squatted and dropped her weight on her high heels, wobbling a bit, probing Kit with eyes encumbered by long nights and heavy mascara. "I bet it's not so easy to be you right now. I remember what that feels like. Everything's confusing, no one hardly talks to you straight. Even with all those women in the family I still didn't understand sex until I was plumb in the middle of it."

Kit could see straight down the front of Red's shirt, crowded by her breasts, full and tan, like two buns, risen, baked, and buttered. Breasts, and all they brought with them, were a beautiful but unwanted burden Kit was not ready to carry. Even though it embarrassed her, it was nice to be spoken to this way, like these matters of the body weren't so frightful. It stirred up a desire for a female friend. A sister, maybe. Someone she could talk to about things that were too private for Manny.

Red pulled a pen out of her purse and found a square of rolling paper on the table where Kit sat. "Let's make a deal," Red said, and scribbled something on the translucent swatch. "You have a question, I'll answer it best I can." She held out the note, her nails lengthening her fingers by a solid inch. "This is me. You call or swing by whenever you need to. Wait, strike that. I work ten at night till three in the morning, so don't come knocking till after noon. I gotta get my blowie sleep." Then she winked. Kit smiled and folded the note into her pocket. She considered the offer seriously, brightened by the possibility of confiding in someone. Red smiled, her lipstick faded now so you could see the true outline of her lips. Thin, younger in their natural state. Kit did not know if she could follow through but was comforted to know she had the option.

Manny came out of the bathroom in a puff of steam, hair combed back, wearing a blue satin button-down, bell-bottom jeans, and a huge oval belt buckle studded with gemstones. Kit noticed the wrinkled bend in the leather four notches away from where Manny had fastened it and imagined the fat cat rancher he must have stolen it from. Could he have slipped it off undetected? She was glad she hadn't voiced this thought aloud when she realized the man must have been naked when they stole his belt.

"My father always told me no good ever came of two women alone in a room together," Manny said. "What are you two conspiring about?" His attempt at humor didn't quite conceal a strain of jealousy. He looked at Red stretched out on the bed like she shouldn't be there.

"You're not gonna make me party alone, are you?" he said.

Red rolled her eyes. "I came to work. You wanna get loaded, fine, but don't drag me into it. I aim to get paid today." At this she pulled a tiny emery board out of her clamshell purse and began to file away an invisible snag. Manny sat on the bed across from Kit's seat at the table.

"How about you, Kitty Cat? Wanna try something fun?"

She didn't like his tone. He seemed different, like he was on another plane shouting through an opening. She shook her head.

Red reached over and slapped him on the hand. "Leave her alone, you! She's just a kid."

Manny snatched Red's hand and twisted it around her back. She winced, unafraid and not struggling. He huffed at her ear, as if holding back some bigger action he must have known the situation did not call for.

She broke free and clasped her purse shut. "I'm calling it off. You're too high, and I'm not in the mood anymore." She turned to

Kit. "Sorry, sweetie. Gotta fly." She took a Dr Pepper on her way out and hooked the door shut behind her with the toe of her boot.

Gelled strands of Manny's hair had fallen into his face. "I don't know what crawled up her butt," he said. Kit hated the way his eyes lost focus when he was high.

"I thought she was nice," Kit said.

"She's a slut, don't forget it," he said. "I work with her because she's good. She's smart and determined and I like that. But don't you listen to her. I won't have you ending up sucking some good ol' boy's willy for scratch."

Even though she had liked Red, Kit was relieved to hear him insult her. Kit knew she had no rights to Manny, but she had felt something for him, a fever she couldn't name. Sometimes she fell asleep in a chair in front of the television and felt him slip his fingers under her ribs and the pits of her knees and carry her like a treasured thing to her bed. There was a loosey buzz, like a wind fluttering the down on her skin; an urge to press against him, to clamp down so hard she left a mark where her arms had been.

She would be fifteen soon and had felt the warm coils of her own desire, especially in the twilight before she woke up each day, but there was nowhere to put it, no one to fumble around with to sharpen the blade of her wanting. Real sex, the actual mechanics of it, seemed so base and humiliating, something people did out of weakness. She had the unfortunate memory of having walked in on the Machers one time, Fran bent over the bed, Paul heaving himself into her rippling, sunburnt behind. The room had smelled of incense and deli meat, and she could hear the frantic flapping of his balls. If that was sex, she was happy to abstain.

ON KIT'S FIFTEENTH BIRTHDAY, MANNY was sleeping off a rough night with the curtains closed when she got the idea to take the Mustang for a ride. They had had a fight the previous night, the worst they'd ever had. Kit had been up all night worried, not knowing where he had gone or whether he would be back. When he scuffed through the door looking churlish and hungover around seven in the morning, he offered no apology. He just sloughed off his shirt and collapsed on the bed. Before he fell asleep he told her he had been drinking and had taken a swipe at a cop outside an icehouse in Houston. They had locked him up and would have pressed charges, but he recognized a dealer in the holding cell with him and told the cops all about the operation the dealer was running. They set Manny free without any trouble, but Kit was furious that he would put them in jeopardy like that. He had taught her precision and planning would keep them safe. They could not afford to be careless.

Kit squeezed him to test how heavily he was sleeping. He would be down until after noon at least. She pocketed the keys and slipped out the door, shutting it softly behind her. When the engine started, she marveled at how different it felt to sit in the driver's seat alone, her whole body connecting to the power of the engine. She practiced coordinating the clutch and shifting the gears as Manny had taught her. After stalling out a couple of times, she synchronized the clutch and accelerator smoothly and drove in first gear, getting used to the feel of the road. Even at ten miles an hour, the ride was thrilling. A semitruck throttled past, its horn screaming. She swerved onto the shoulder and cursed at the driver ten different ways. When her heart found its rhythm again, she eased back onto the open road and worked her way up to third gear on a long stretch of bare asphalt. The farther she got from the adobe motel, the looser the grip of Manny's influence. The heaviness of his moods and the sting of his criticisms billowed up and disappeared like the dust behind her. When she approached the feeder road to I-10, a massive freeway that stretched from Florida to the California coast, she braked and idled.

To be alone, fully in charge of herself, had not appealed to her since meeting Manny, but here, on the crest of a hill under a bald blue sky, she felt high with possibility. It occurred to her that she was old enough to get a paying job, to work for her money for once. Manny's everyday opportunism wasn't doing it for her anymore, and she didn't like the way she felt when they went back to wherever they were staying and Manny dumped out their spoils on the bedspread, sorting through other people's things. She could wait tables or even find work on a ranch somewhere, maybe near Austin, where the air was dry and there was a big public swimming hole with clear natural springs.

From between the seats she fished out a couple of quarters and a dime. She took the next exit and parked the car at a rest stop where there were bathrooms, a water fountain, and a pay phone. She fed a quarter through the slot and dialed zero.

"What city please?" the operator said with practiced sweetness.

"Pecan Hollow."

"What's the name, dear?"

"I just have a first name. Eleanor."

"Let's see here . . . Eleanor, huh . . . ? Just give me a minute, please. I'm gonna see what I can do." The operator grunted, and it was several minutes before she spoke again.

"Miss, you still there?"

Kit cleared her throat. "Yes."

"Lucky for you there's only a few hundred people in Pecan Hollow. I have two Eleanors here, is it Roark or Weber?"

"I don't know. Can I have both? Addresses, too, please." She used a pen attached to a string that was hanging from the phone book to write the information down, right above an ad for Derby Debris Disposal.

Then she heard the velvet call of Manny's voice in her head. *Where you off to, Kitty Cat?* He would look for her. He would look and he would find her because he was the only person on the planet who gave a damn about her. And how could she leave, really? It was true, he had been good to her. There was no reason to run except that deep inside she knew she was not free. That had always been the choice, between freedom and belonging. He had saved her life, and she belonged to him.

An old man with a new cowboy hat and slacks up to his rib cage stood there waiting patiently for the phone, a thin newspaper held to his chest. She hung up and tore out the directory page with the numbers and addresses, which she stuffed in her pocket.

She turned the Mustang around on the empty road and drove back to the motel absently, as if on rails.

When she pulled up to the parking spot outside their room, Manny stood there waiting like a soldier, arms folded, feet spread. She wanted him not to be mad, to hold her and tell her how much he'd missed her, how she'd worried him so. Never to leave. But he didn't look likely to do any of those things, so she had to play it cool, not revealing where she had been or how close she had come to leaving him. She got out of the car, not acknowledging him. As she passed, she tossed him the keys and said, "Happy fucking birthday to me."

She went inside and flicked on the television, flopped down on the bed. Manny followed her in and turned it off.

"Dadgummit, you're ready," Manny said, his smile broad and proud.

Kit was hesitant to ask. She didn't like being prompted like this, but neither could she let it go. Was it a new con? A special trip? He seemed weirdly happy, but knowing Manny, it could be a trick.

"All right," she said. "Ready for what?"

"Come with me to work today, and you'll find out."

CHAPTER TWELVE

MANNY PULLED UP TO A PUMP AT AN EMPTY FILLING STATION ABOUT halfway between the tiny towns of Yoakum and Cuero. Gasoline fumes swirled through the open windows, noisy buzzards circled overhead. There was an attached convenience store, with its shiny red Coca-Cola refrigerator, padlocked ice machine emblazoned with large, frozen red letters I C E across the front, and a coin-operated Creamsicle machine. Kit had been chewing her dry tongue since they'd left the motel and would have enjoyed something cold and sweet right about now.

"I'm thirsty," she said.

"It's just nerves," Manny said. "Okay, look," he told her and pointed to a teenage clerk, acne pebbling his cheekbones, who sat tipped back in his chair. He was so absorbed in his nudie magazine that he did not appear to notice the two drive up.

"This is what you call a perfect mark," Manny said. "The guy in there, he's a good target. He's distracted. Look at his eyes, see how red they are? Pretty sure he's stoned. Not banking on it, but if he is, he'll be slow and confused. Not likely to fight back. Did you see the register when we drove up? Slightly open. He's lazy, he doesn't like to unlock it every time. Not sure how much is in there, but it's the end of the day. I'm bettin' the till is as full as it'll ever be."

Kit tried to play it cool but was bursting with questions.

"What will you be doing?" she asked. "Do I go in with you?"

"I will be working my powers of persuasion," he said, and began to drive around the back of the store. "And you're driving getaway." He backed in, parked in an oily loading zone, and turned toward her. "Here's what you need to know: park out of sight and pointed in the direction we want to head. See here, we're facing southwest so we can cut across the lot to the main road and scoot onto Route 77. Keep the engine running; and accelerate smoothly—don't gun it like an idiot. You don't save any time by doing that, and you lose control of your vehicle. You have enough power to get where you need to go without burning up my tires and running us off the road. Besides, you go too fast and you'll look suspicious. Just keep cool, Kitty Cat."

"Keep cool," she repeated, feeling hot around the neck and arm-pits. "What do we do if he's got a gun?"

"He won't. Trust me, I'm a student of human nature. Whoever his boss is would never take the chance. Better to lose a couple grand than risk this kid shooting himself or someone else."

Her heart kicked at her rib cage like it was trying to bust out.

"Don't worry," Manny said, gathering the strands of his dark hair into a short ponytail. "I always win."

He rapped his knuckles against the dash. "Well?"

Had she looked him in the eyes he would have seen how happy she was. "Why the hell not?" she said. Manny patted her on the knee, got out of the car, turned, and rested his arms in the window. She slid over and adjusted the seat and mirrors.

"Now remember, keep it running and be cool. I'll be back before you know it." He turned toward the station, and as he walked away she saw the gun tucked between his waistband and the small of his back. From his back pocket, he pulled what looked like a green sock and worked it over his head. He turned around and winked through the ski mask, then disappeared around the whitewashed corner of the building.

She gripped the wheel to keep from trembling. The gun, the mask, the getaway. It was all new and terrifying. Had he been doing holdups all along and just now asked her to join? Hadn't he trusted her enough before? She smacked both cheeks with her hands, then rehearsed the escape to focus her attention. Her eyes never left the corner where she had last seen him, where she willed him to return each passing moment. Every car that whipped by made her jump. She had expected shouting, screams, but all she could hear were the baritone idling of the engine and the sound of her own shallow breath. As much as she wanted to keep cool, she could only imagine the worst, the image of Manny with a handful of cash and a crisp bullet hole in the center of his forehead.

And then he was jogging toward her, a brown bag, neatly folded, in hand. Even with his mask on, he looked happy. In a few strides he slipped in beside her. She was so relieved she wanted to cry.

"You're on," he said. "No rush." She eased her foot on the gas as she released the clutch, going slowly like he had said, scanned the road ahead for oncoming traffic. Then she heard a cowbell and a door clanging shut.

"Shhhh," he said in response to her startling. A heavyset man in an orange hunting shirt and reflective sunglasses appeared at the rear entrance of the station.

"Who's he?" she asked, slamming the gas. She let go the clutch too quickly and they lurched and stalled out.

"Hey!" the man said. "I called the cops! Y'all stop or I'm ohn hafta shootcha."

Kit could scarcely breathe and felt prickly all over. This was the closest she had come to getting caught since the day Manny picked her up. The man raised a pistol from a straight arm and squinted.

"What's he doing?" Kit said, her heart tearing around her chest. "Is he gonna shoot?"

"Easy does it," Manny said, and when his hand grazed her neck it was cool and steady. She popped the gear into neutral, restarted the car, and engaged the clutch. The man released a round high over their heads.

"Jesus Christ," she yelled, ducking her head out of sight.

"Hot dog! He's not fuckin' around. Okay, stay low," Manny said and slid down in the seat. He was grinning, like this was fun for him. "And don't worry. He wants to be a hero, but he's scareder than you are."

She took a large breath to calm her nerves, then, peering over the dash, shifted into first and swapped the clutch for the gas. They coasted forward and she repeated for second gear, then third, slipping easily down the path she had planned. Another round went off and when she looked in her rearview the man had dropped the gun to his side. Once they were on 77, she finally exhaled.

"Holy shit," she said.

Manny was laughing. "Slow down, sister."

The speedometer read 95 miles per hour. She downshifted to 65 and cruised in the direction of the motel, large with pride and feeling something like a woman.

Manny yoked his arm across her shoulders, fingers grazing her collarbone. His touch felt new and so did she. She felt like his partner, no longer his pet. Before, her feelings for him had confused her, but now, as calmly as she had handled the car, she reached up and worked her fingers between his. The beastly power of the engine beneath her, the expanse of the road ahead, she owned this moment and everything in it.

"Oh, shit, I almost forgot," said Manny. He pulled from his waistband an icy, dripping bottle of Coke. He pressed the yellow callus of his thumb against the cap until it slid off. He wiped it dry with his shirttail, then passed it to her, and beaming, she grasped the bottle like a trophy.

THE SUN WAS SLUNG LOW on the horizon, wrapped in gauzy clouds of sherbet. Kit was squinting to read the backlit exit sign when Manny signaled to get off the highway. As she parked in the spot closest to their motel room, she was already looking forward to debriefing the run, going over every moment, fine-tuning their approach. Manny walked around front and opened her door. She thought he was being chivalrous, something he only ever did when someone else was watching. She didn't need special treatment, but she didn't hate it either. Today, at least, she'd earned it.

Manny motioned with a flick of his fingers for her to get out, like sweeping crumbs. "You can leave it running," he said. "I got somewhere to be."

Kit was puzzled. She shut off the engine and got out of the car. She was a foot shorter than him, and she hated that she would never be big enough to meet him eye to eye. How could he take her seriously when he was looking down on her?

"Somewhere to be? Don't you want to celebrate?"

Manny said nothing and dropped into the driver's seat. All the levity of moments before stalled and sank. Kit felt thirteen again.

"Where are you going?" She was ashamed to hear the whine of disappointment in her voice. Manny looked to be elsewhere.

"I'll be back before morning, probably." He shifted the seat back, checked the mirror, and tongued a lemon drop from a little metal canister. "Don't wait up."

Kit reeled at the chill of his casual shift away from her; how could he leave her after the day they'd had? Who would he rather be with? Had she done something wrong? The rejection smacked her like a toxin, noxious and systemic. The sun disappeared, and in an instant, the glow of moments before became the faded purples and grays of an old bruise. Manny restarted the engine and a musk of gasoline and motor oil surrounded them. He tipped his cowboy hat.

The rage set in like a centrifuge, spinning hot blood outward to Kit's extremities. Before she knew what she was doing, she had swung through the open window and punched him in the nose. He hunkered down, and she opened the door and grabbed him by the collar of his shirt. He pushed her skidding onto her ass, but she was up and lunging for him before he'd even gotten out of the car. He swiped, she dodged and then kneed him in the groin, and he crumpled to the pavement moaning. She kicked him in the ribs and soft organs, screaming on impact. How could he build her up, let her feel big and important and strong, when he was just going to toss her aside? Even now, she was incapable of revealing the words she wanted to say. *What about me?*

Manny got to his feet and folded Kit over his shoulder as she thrashed, nearly bringing them both to the ground. He kicked the motel door in and slammed her down on the bed, pinning her at the wrists and thighs like an insect. His face, studded with sweat and grit, hovered an inch from hers. Kit felt equally compelled to kill him and to surrender. His expression moved from confusion to outrage, and finally something Kit couldn't place but recognized deep in her core. Her whole body pounded like the beckoning beat of a drum, and she knew the feeling now, a feeling familiar as her shadow: hunger. Active hunger. The hollowness, the wanting, the urge to stuff. Tired of never having enough, she wanted everything right now, all of him and all at once.

He kissed her, sucked her lip between his teeth and bit until it bled; she pushed her tongue into his warm, lemony mouth. Manny skinned her tank top over her head and went for her jeans, but she kneed him into the dresser, furious. He rebounded and snagged a thick handful of her hair, lifting her off the bed, pinning her to the wall.

"You think you want this," he said, gruff in her ear. "But once we start—"

"I know," she said, but all she knew was that loving him like this was what it would take to keep him.

"You have no idea. You have no fucking clue," he said. There was a bitterness, maybe fear, in his voice that startled her. But everything had already changed. There was no returning to before. The way he looked at her now, desperate and scared, was worth the innocence lost. Someone who needed her that much would never leave.

THEN THEY WERE IN IT, the meat of it all. Pushing, mashing, their skins and smells, a blind and vicious grasping, lungs outstretched, muscles hot and wrapped around each other. Kit felt like she was fighting for her life. Her body was responding, like it knew something she didn't, but her heart was confused. She kept looking for the blue of his eyes, as if they would guide her through the shadows, but he was somewhere she could not follow. She hated him for going away, even now, and dug her nails into the back of his neck as hard as she could. For a moment, quick and sweet, she found him. He saw her there and seemed to her alert, the wrinkles around his eyes smoothed as he caught his breath. She wanted to cry for the relief, to stop and be wrapped in his arms. But soon he was lost again and the light in his eyes went out, so swiftly she questioned whether she had imagined it. What followed was both intense and unconscious, a thrashing dream that seemed to go on for hours and when it was suddenly over, she lay there soaked in sweat, wondering what had happened.

Manny rolled away from her, farther than she liked, and slept and she was alone with the sounds. The toilet running, cattle groaning in the distance, someone scooping ice from the dispenser one floor down. The shame seeped in like car sickness and she crossed the room to hang her head in the toilet just in case. She drooled into the bowl, didn't vomit but wished she could. Then she dressed and left Manny facedown and huffing in heavy sleep.

It was late and more lonesome than usual with the new moon void of light. She pushed a quarter into the pay phone on the sidewalk by their motel and called the number Red had left her. The phone rang so long she was about to hang up when Red picked up sounding groggy.

"Uh-huh? What-what's wrong?" she said, her voice muffled like she was talking through her pillow. "Who died?"

"Hey, Red, did I wake you?" Kit said.

"Oh, is that you, Kit?" Red said, extra sweet. "Honey, you can wake me up anytime. What's shakin'?"

"I guess I just had a question about . . . what you do, and stuff."

She could hear Red sniff and sit up in bed.

"You wanna know about fuckin'?" Red said in a voice that was soft and alert.

Kit squeezed her eyes shut. "Yes," she whispered.

"Well, shit, baby, where do I begin?" Red cackled and there was a click and the rush of air as she lit a cigarette.

"First off, do not let him come inside you," she said through a breath of smoke. "He's gonna want to. *Don't* let him. Put it in your mouth, put it in your butt, I don't give a damn. But do not. Let him. Put it up your chacha."

Kit laughed a little. She tried to remember if he had, through the haze of the last few hours. There had been something warm and sticky on her stomach after he rolled off of her that smelled of starch.

"I just don't want to do it wrong," Kit said.

Red exhaled into the phone so Kit got an earful of static. She held the receiver away from her ear.

"Baby, baby, lookee here. Pleasing men is as easy as putting on lipstick. Nothin' to it. You got to worry about getting your *own* goodies." Kit didn't follow.

"You find your magic button yet?" Red said. "Little sweet spot at the top of your pussy?" Kit cringed and nodded as if Red could see her. "You get you some canola oil and some Barry White and play with that fucker till you arch your back and dig holes in the bed with your toes and your limbs feel like rubber that's been sitting in the sun. Everyone knows how to screw, but you gotta find that good feeling for yourself. Cause no man in Texas knows how to give it to you if you don't tell him first. And I should know," Red said, thumbing her lighter for a fresh one. "Cause, baby, I fucked 'em all."

Kit's heart cooled. Red made it sound so simple, but she was describing something completely different from what Kit was doing with Manny. Maybe that's how it was when sex was your business. She hoped one day to feel as relaxed and amused as Red.

Normally, Kit could at least fake nonchalance, but tonight with Manny she was totally lost. This new thing they were doing had her confused and needing him more than she ever had before. It felt like so much more was on the line. She had thought that by having sex with him she could keep him close; it had felt like a kind of power. But the power had wavered, even as he moved on top of her, and dissolved the moment he was done, and when he had rolled to the far edge of the bed, she could see this power had only been an illusion.

"Whaddya say, hon?" Red asked. "Does that help?"

"You bet," said Kit, and she hung up the phone, went back to the room, and crawled into bed.

ONCE THEIR RELATIONSHIP TURNED PHYSICAL, some opening between them, some space that let her know she was Kit and he was Manny and that she had existed before and would exist beyond, sealed shut. She was a grafted limb, the broken part of her fused to the broken part of him. His wishes became hers, her desires to fulfill his. There was nothing she could not endure, nothing but losing him.

She renewed her wish that being lovers, or whatever they were, would bring him closer to her, but it seemed to drive him into a kind of episodic madness. He would swing from one extreme to the other, one moment burying his nose in her pits to drink the smell of her and the next locking her in the bathroom all night after he had drawn her a bath and she hadn't thanked him. After sex he would call her a Jezebel, sulk, and get drunk. He was always quitting her, shutting her out and vowing that it would be just business from there on out. Each time it stung more than the last, even though he always came around. Since it was her body he couldn't leave, she was glad to offer it up to him, as long as he would keep coming back to her. She learned the mechanics of his moods, when to lay low, when to be bold or pull away to draw him near. She got by on a reservoir of good times together, like swimming the warm, muddy waters of the Brazos, or eating breakfast for dinner and sneaking into a double feature, or best of all, when they were working.

They ran all the regular cons, picked pockets and purses, shoplifted and swindled, but nothing worked him up like the thrill of an armed robbery. The formula had worked every time: always off the interstate, at the end of the day so the till was full, far enough from a police station that they would have plenty of time to get out before the law came. As long as they stuck to the plan, they would never get caught. "Taxes are for suckers," Manny said one time when Kit asked him what it was like to have a job. Working for wages, giving the government a cut of your earnings, clocking in and out. He said all that was akin to slavery. Kit didn't like when he ranted. It made him seem smaller, the way he thought about normal things like working for a living. She would have rather heard him say the truth, that he knew it was bad to steal but he did it for fun. Kit's truth was that she stole to make Manny happy.

The price for the good times was always the same. When a job was done the cocksure invincibility of the robbery left him rabid for her. With Manny, it was wild and angry, competitive. She was a gladiator, clashing and lunging and fighting to stay in the game just a little longer. Kit's strength was no match for Manny's, but she was slippery and able to distract and evade his grasp. They fought and strangled each other, punching, and fucking and heaving desperately until they collapsed and he slept like an infant while she roamed the room, shaking the fight from her bones.

KIT WAS SLOW TO MATURE, and it plagued her to look so much younger than she felt. Manny said it was poor nutrition that kept her scrawny, that she'd never have a figure. But by the time she was eighteen, Kit had finally grown into her limbs and filled out the seat of her jeans. She kept her hair waist-length and loved to feel it swish behind her. Around this time, she noticed men noticing her. She felt their eyes shadow her as she walked. She'd scowl, or spit on the ground at their feet, but sometimes, if the man was handsome, or seemed like he would be kind, in a small, quiet place she let herself enjoy the attention.

Manny bloodied a lot of noses over Kit, but increasingly, he took out his jealousy on her. One night they were smoking outside a bar and a young man with aviators on his head and rings on every finger grabbed her between the ass cheeks. Manny tackled the guy into a pile of garbage bags. The guy still had a lit cigarette in his mouth, and Manny took it and put it out in the guy's ear, then kicked him in the spleen.

That night he was on top of her, his face all crumpled.

"Why do you have to egg them on?" he said, veins snaking across his forehead. "You think you can do better than me?"

She was so stunned and confused, she didn't try to fight back when he held her neck down with the butt of his hand so hard she lost consciousness. He dunked her in a cold bath, and when she came to and looked in the mirror, the whites of her eyes bloomed red where the vessels had burst.

The next morning, he rolled toward her and tickled her nose with his fingertips like nothing had happened. She couldn't look him in the eyes. She missed the Manny she had first loved, strong and aloof and dripping with charm. These days, she never knew which Manny she would get. One minute he was cold and callous, the next, manic and deranged, or paranoid, brooding, possessive. Other days he was lusty and didn't want to leave the bed. It was easier to blame herself, for the way she looked and for letting Manny have sex with her. He had tried to stop, she reasoned, but she'd kept it going. She had wanted to keep him so bad she'd made a deal with the devil and lost.

ONE DAY IN APRIL WHEN she was nineteen, after a couple of profitable runs outside Austin, Kit was sitting cross-legged on the floor watching

TV when Manny brought home a newspaper. He slapped it into her lap and sat down next to her. He pointed to an article below the crease. POLICE LINK TEXACO ROBBERIES. The article said they'd noticed a pattern in three robberies in the Austin County area and were coordinating with police in neighboring counties to see if there were any more instances that would fit.

He pulled her face to his and kissed her, hard, like he was drinking her in. "We have a *trademark*," he said, a grin forming on his face. "They said we have style. People are starting to talk, calling us the Texaco Twosome. Here," he said, opening the paper to where the story continued and laying it out on the floor in front of her. "Get this. 'Police have identified several features common to all the robberies. There are two accomplices, one manning the getaway vehicle, the other holding the cashier at gunpoint while collecting the money. The ringleader is described as a tall, fit man in his thirties. Witnesses have remarked on his *cool demeanor* and *charming persona*.' One woman is quoted here as saying, 'I couldn't see his face, but I could tell he was a looker. Something about his eyes. You never did see something so blue.'" He slapped his thigh. "Ha! You hear that? We're famous! They love us."

She didn't see the upside of this turn of events. With the police now coordinating and sending word to the press, they'd surely be caught and thrown in jail. They'd go to separate prisons and she worried she might never see him again. She crumpled the paper and tossed it aside.

"How can you be happy about this?" she said. "Are you trying to get us locked up?"

Manny looked at her like she was insane and smoothed the wrinkles out of the newspaper. "We're not gonna get caught," he said, sullen. "I'm too smart for those country pigs. They talk a big talk but they ain't coordinating shit. They're telling the press cause they gotta make it look like they're doing something."

The more he talked, the angrier she got. Her throat was tight with all the words she wouldn't dare say to him. She turned away and pulled a loose string from the hem of the bedspread.

He flicked her hard on the back of her head. "Don't you turn away from me. We're supposed to be partners. You wanted in on what I was doing, and this is just part of the package."

A part of her melted at the word *partners*. It *was* what she had wanted, so much more than what she had thought possible for someone like her, a discarded girl with a made-up name. Manny had found her, given her a life, and taught her what he knew. She owed him. But she had too much to lose to get locked up on account of his vanity.

"If we get caught," she said, dead serious, "I'll never forgive you." For a tense moment, Manny merely looked at her, the way he sometimes did when he was provoked but did not want to be seen losing control. She waited to be hit, or shoved into the bedspread so hard she couldn't breathe. Instead, Manny picked himself up off the floor, took a shower, and didn't speak to her for a week. After that she was more careful with her opinions.

"CHEER UP, KITTY, WE'RE GOING for a ride," he said one morning after he'd decided to start speaking to her again. He stripped the sheets away from her.

"Where to now, then?" she said, hoping he would say they were heading somewhere far from Austin to wait out the hype around the Texaco Twosome. They had kept a low profile hiding out since the write-up in the paper, but she needed more distance between her and Austin County.

"Oh, just wait and see," he said as he folded one of his shirts into a perfect rectangle.

After they'd packed up their few things and eaten at a stand that served patty melts and fries and Cokes and nothing else, they headed south on Route 77 from Giddings down through Schulenburg, then cut southwest at Hallettsville. He was keeping a wide berth from Austin, at least. They had just passed through Yoakum when she thought she saw the filling station where Manny had taken her out for the first time. She wasn't sure why, but the sight of that place lodged a pit in her stomach. As they approached Cuero, Kit saw billboards leading up to a motel called Clifford's Hollywood Palace, each one boasting a different celebrity. Mae West folding forward, her bosom spilling out, *Come up and see me sometime, why dontcha?* Elvis mid-swivel, snarling, *Come on down, and thank you very much;* Little Richard crouching over a piano, black dash over his lip, a bird's nest on his head: *Good Golly! Come to Clifford's!* The closer they got, the edgier Manny seemed. His voice ran dry, and he ate his lemon drops by threes, like nuts.

The air was thick with rotten eggs. Kit pulled her T-shirt up to cover her nose and mouth.

"What the shit is that smell?" she asked.

Manny started looking for his exit and switched on his brights. "That's sulfur carried over from the oil field in Luling," he said. "That's the smell of money."

An hour and a half after they had left Giddings, Manny stopped the car under the porte cochere of the motel advertised on the billboards and led her inside. The reception office of Clifford's Hollywood Palace was the prettiest room she had ever seen, pretty enough to disperse the anxious feeling in her gut. The ceiling was painted gold, with a complicated chandelier dropping from its center. The carpet was primary red and hatched with marks from a recent cleaning. Three walls were mirrored, and Kit felt pleasantly disoriented seeing all these versions of herself. She followed the line of her profile, flat short forehead, broad nose, full lips, and a squared-off chin. Thick, haphazard braid that was so coarse it held itself together. The padding of puberty had melted away, and the contours of her face looked as if they had been carved and sanded out of soft wood. She didn't see a pretty girl, but she liked what she saw. She had a fighting face.

The receptionist looked like a bellboy in his cream suit with green velvet trim and brass buttons. He broke into a studied smile and spread his arms wide. "Welcome to Clifford's Famous Hollywood Palace. Here for a romantic getaway?"

"As a matter of fact," Manny said, hanging his arm on her shoulders, "it's our honeymoon."

Kit shifted slightly away from Manny. He had only ever presented her as his daughter. Why would he change the script now? She glanced over at him, and he seemed irritated, like she should just go with it. She forced a smile across her teeth.

After sizing Kit up briefly, the receptionist clapped.

"Congratulations, you two. I'll put you in the James Dean suite. Comes with a complimentary bottle of bubbly."

Manny bristled. "Uh-uh, no way, what else you got?"

The receptionist seemed to take this personally. He sucked in his cheeks and took a measured breath.

"We have several rooms," he said, running his finger down his list. "But I can assure you, the Dean is the best available."

Manny shook his head. He didn't like pushback.

"I don't want that room. James Dean was a fag and a loser, okay?" he said as if it were common knowledge. "What else you got?"

The receptionist pulled the ledger toward him and smirked. "Maybe you should ask *her* where she'd like to stay. James is very popular with the ladies."

Manny lunged over the counter and grabbed the receptionist by his velvet collar. The man shrieked and looked ready to cry. Manny leaned in. His hair had come out of its ponytail and brushed the receptionist's cheek.

"Why are you making this so hard for me?" Manny said.

Kit shrunk away from Manny's thin-skinned reaction. Once he had been slicker than oil; now he seemed a slave to his impulses. She wanted to peel out of there and find somewhere new to stay, but she knew she had to smooth things over and bring Manny back to Earth.

"I think what he's saying, sir," Kit said, "is that he wants a room with tits."

The guy rubbed his neck under the collar and chuckled nervously.

"Right," he said. "We should have something that fits that description."

She read the ledger upside down and fished a tenner out of Manny's pocket, slipping it to the receptionist.

"Dolly Parton's available. We'll take that one."

THE DOLLY PARTON ROOM FEATURED color TV; a deluxe, heart-shaped bathtub; and a life-size cardboard cutout of Dolly wearing a purple bell-bottom jumpsuit, her hair a regal sculpture of curls. She was rigged to a turntable, spinning to the song "Jolene." A purple sequined bedspread and matching curtains, plush lilac carpet that was thick and deep as grass.

Kit seesawed the boots off her bare feet, tossed them to the side, and wiggled her toes in the dense synthetic yarn. Manny locked and chained the door behind him and hoisted his duffel and her backpack onto the bed. He sat on the edge and the backpack slid down the sequins to the floor. He was unsettled. She felt she was in trouble for something. Could be he was still mad from their last fight, when she said she would never forgive him if they got caught. Sometimes he chewed on resentments for days before exploding at her, his argument so detailed there was no room for her to fight back. She went to the bathroom, removed the paper lid from a glass by the sink, and drank until she was full. Dolly stopped singing. Kit heard the TV turn on, change channels, and flare off in a crackle of static.

Then it was still, quieter than sleep. For a moment, she had a flash of walking out to find Manny on the carpet with a gun in his hand, the insides of his skull broadcast across the walls. She held her breath, turned the knob, and slowly opened the door.

Manny stood there very much alive and looking kind of smug, like he had won a game she hadn't known they were playing. He smiled, sly and amused, lip curled over good straight teeth, a fan of creases at the eyes. She relaxed when he smiled, always. He was holding something out to her, a ring perched like a hat on the tip of his little finger.

"I've been carrying this damn thing around with me for weeks, trying to figure out how I'm gonna ask you," he said and drew a halting breath. "It's strange, after all we've been through, to ask this of you. I never wanted to be married before. But it doesn't feel right anymore, us not being family in the eyes of the law."

Kit froze up, terrified of saying the wrong thing. He sank to one knee, and it struck her as so odd and upside down, she smiled. He tracked her closely, seemed to be searching her face for a sign. The ring looked pricey, a teardrop set high on a gold band. It caught the light and winked.

"Where did you steal that from?" she asked, edging away from the proposal like it was a snake.

"I didn't steal it," he said, looking hurt. "I bought it. Cash."

Maybe she should have jumped up and down and thrown herself into his arms, weeping *Yes! Yes! Of course, yes!* Forever was a good thing, wasn't it? Especially for someone like her? She should be grateful. She should do whatever it took to keep the good thing going. But everything about this setup rubbed her the wrong way. The fact that he was proposing after shunning her for a week; and that he had either thrown money away for a diamond or stolen one and lied about it. She could not understand him like this, below her, as if begging.

Then, to her horror, an involuntary snicker forced its way through her nose. His smile faded, eyes darted over her face in a silent rage. A sheen of sweat appeared above his lips, which had lost their lively curl and were pressed tight against each other. She looked away and locked eyes with Dolly, curvy and apple-cheeked, willing herself to be serious.

"Stupid fuckin' idea," he said, standing, and curled the ring into his fist.

"Wait, no, start over," Kit said. "I'm sorry." She had no plan for making this right; once he turned sour it was nearly impossible to bring him back.

"Don't you have to have a birth certificate to get married?" she asked. Reasoning with him was pointless, but she was frantic. "I don't have documents. We could never do it legit anyway, I don't think."

"It. Was. A. Stupid. Fuckin'. Idea." He pitched his voice in such a way that her eardrums chimed. "You're a child."

"I'm nineteen," she said, not sure why she was arguing.

"You're immature. I was trying to do you a favor, make you legitimate. I could have faked your documents, it would have been fine."

"I'm sorry. You just caught me off guard," she said, the worry making her sick in her throat. "Just let me think about it."

"You blew it, kitten. There's no do-overs with shit like this. Best you learn that sooner than later." He went to the purple toilet, lifted the lid with his toe, and dropped the ring into the water. "It's fine. It's just a fuckin' rock."

"You can't do that." She scrambled after him, reached into the water, and brushed against the diamond's beveled edge. He flushed. The ring nudged toward her fingertips and then slipped out of sight.

"No!"

He took the duffel with his clothes and his gun and started to leave. She was furious.

"You can't leave, you're being ridiculous," she yelled. She found an ashtray and flung it at his head. It spun past his cheek and dented the wall. "Get back here and talk to me like a man!"

He kept walking and opened the door. She threw herself into the door, crushing his hand. He winced, spread his fingers out, and then made a fist. She held her breath, waited for the hit, but he just walked out without a word, without looking at her at all. She chased him outside, jumped on his back, choked him in the crook of her arm. She could smell the grease in his hair, the smoke from his last cigarette. He slammed her back against the brick wall of the motel, and she dropped to the ground. Though her head spun, she could see well enough to watch him stuff his duffel through the back window of the Mustang and drive away.

She screamed but could not match the roar of the engine or the distance he had already covered. He had left before, just not like this. She knew she had humiliated him, touched something brittle at his very core. She had ruined everything. She gasped as her ribs curled in on her lungs. She could not breathe, felt she could die here in this deserted lot. She dropped her head, her hair drawing closed around her face. The numbing began, a softness in her lips, a fuzz that spread across her skin and into her bones. It was like static on the television after the screen went blank. The panic sounded a warning—*he's gone, he's gone, he's never coming back*—that was swiftly, mercifully silenced.

It had been so long since she numbed out she had forgotten how good it felt afterward, alert and relaxed, the pop of caffeine and the mellow of alcohol. She brushed the grit off her ass and went inside, reminding herself that he had never left for good. He'd be back. She was sure of it.

She went to the toilet to see if she could get the ring back. It had been heavy and small, maybe the force of the flush hadn't been enough to drag it all the way down. Maybe she could reach for it. She lifted the padded seat and straddled the bowl, snaked her hand into the hole and felt around with her fingers, careful not to knock the ring out of reach. She shifted and dropped her right shoulder to gain a few extra inches, resting her cheek against the lavender rim. She wiggled her fingers in tiny increments until at last she grazed the ring with her knuckle. Her fingers were bundled and couldn't grasp, so she pulled her hand back and reapproached to center the ring in the hole, then dragged it slowly with the tip of her middle finger. She pulled it out, dripping water in a trail across the floor, and ran it under the tap. She set it aside, washed her hands, and held the ring to the light.

"What a fuckin' drama queen," she said aloud. She didn't know about diamonds but it looked costly. She had a hard time believing he'd spent money on it and figured he must have lifted it off someone, some Houston socialite with skinny fingers. She put it on, held out her hand. It was beautiful in itself, twinkled against her skin, but she felt ridiculous wearing it. Impractical and uncomfortable. She tugged and screwed it over her knuckle and slipped it into the pocket of her backpack.

CHAPTER THIRTEEN

THE NEXT DAY KIT WOKE UP SPRAWLED ACROSS THE BED. SHE HAD wondered if Manny would have slipped in while she slept, as he sometimes had, or if he would roll in that evening smoking someone else's cigarettes, drunk and cranky. He'd been gone at least two days before, maybe three. She wasn't worried. She folded a stick of peppermint gum into her mouth, wiggled her feet into her boots, and took off for some food.

The receptionist directed her to a supermarket about two miles down the road, and she set to walking. She checked the pocket of her jeans and found about a hundred bucks from their last run. Manny was "treasurer" and always handled the money, but she had slipped a couple fifties before he took inventory. She often took a cut without his knowledge as a small tax for the risks she took for him.

She walked through the brightly lit aisles of the supermarket and filled her basket with all the food she knew he liked. Instant coffee, hickory meat sticks, Fritos, bean dip. After the cashier had rung up her items, she pocketed her change and walked the long stretch of highway back to the motel. She replayed his proposal over and over again, each time like a kick to the ribs. How could she have been so ungrateful, so stupid? He had bluffed about other things to get his way, but not this.

By the time she got back to the room, she found herself so hungry for Manny that she tore the room apart looking for some piece of him. But he hadn't stayed long enough to unpack. There was only an empty lemon drops tin, crushed underfoot. She picked it up and pried it open and smelled its citrusy dust, licked a little that had gathered in the seam, and cried. She wept over the days they had spent together, the things she had never told him. She wished she could cut him out of her, but he was now a vital organ and nothing else seemed to work right without him.

In her fit, she had torn the sliding closet door from its runners. Hanging from a hook inside the closet was her beat-up backpack, the one she'd had when Manny found her. In the outer pouch were the phone numbers and addresses she had saved, Red's and Eleanor's. Then she unzipped the main compartment and pulled out its precious contents: the pink shell souvenir from Galveston, the plastic baggie containing the note from her mother, and Manny's ring. She pressed the note to her cheek and tried to imagine her mother scribbling the instructions on the hood of a car, but all she saw were colorless geometric shapes. Then she held the tiny chandelier to the light and twirled it. Its strands of pink shells tinkled against each other and reminded her of the feeling that day, of hopeful surrender, that day she signed herself over to him. Last, she put the ring on her finger and held it out, felt its facets and smooth band and the claw that held the stone. He must have loved her when he picked it out, he must have wanted to keep her. That had been something, hadn't it?

She wiped her eyes and put the note back and zipped the pocket closed. She put Dolly in the closet and brought the slatted doors together, for it pained her to look at pretty things. People loved beauty. They couldn't help it. Kit was not beautiful, but she had, she thought, been loved. Despite all the wrong she had done, and wrong done to her, Manny had seen something in her. He had taken her along and shown her his trade. They had been partners, and she had carried her weight and then some. She should be grateful to have felt his love at all, but she wished she'd never met him, now that it was gone, and she was alone. Alone.

KIT RAN OUT OF FOOD a week after Manny left, and had given the rest of her money to the manager, who demanded payment for the room. She was still short but convinced him to let her stay another night on the promise that Manny would be back with money. By now she was reckoning with the fact that Manny was gone for good. It was only a matter of time before the manager unlocked the door and clipped the chain to shoo her out like the trash she was, always had been. Hours ago, she had finally summoned the will to leave the bed to pee and had worked through the steps she would take, movement by movement. She would crawl if she had to. But before she could pull the sheets away from her legs, her bladder had let go. There was so little urine, a bright pungent splash of it, that she rolled to the other side of the bed, grateful she would not have to get up after all.

She was just beginning to drift into sleep when the phone rang. The sound cut across the room and startled her. She froze and listened, wondering if she had conjured it. It rang again, echoing. She groped across the bed, pushed herself up, and reached out for the phone. She was so weak she dropped the receiver and collapsed back onto the bed, then, groping, she found the receiver again and raised it to her ear.

In the background there was a soupy noise of music and chatting and then someone cleared his throat and spoke.

"You're still there," he said. The relief swept her upright. She squeezed her eyes shut and bit the back of her hand. He couldn't know how much he'd hurt her. She closed her eyes to focus on his voice, which was heavy with whiskey.

"I knew it," he said, "I knew you'd wait for me." The sweet and slow of his voice dripped over her. She listened in a kind of rapture.

"I picked up a job in Oklahoma," he said. "Scored pretty big, you would have loved it."

She imagined him working without her or, worse, with someone else.

"You giving me the silent treatment?" he said, irritated already.

"All right," she said. "I'm here."

"Guess you might have wondered where I was," he said. *Wondered.* The word was cruel in its understatement.

"How much?" She had to keep her mind on numbers or she would crumble.

"Huh?"

"The job," she said. "How much?"

"Oh, enough," he said. "Doesn't matter. I'll be back tomorrow. I'll take you to dinner."

The anger came quickly, and she imagined all the ways she would show him he could never do that again. Every time she opened her mouth to speak, the only thing she wanted to do was scream, and so she imagined that, her dark and screaming mouth a cave, with bats and bees and fire and bile spilling out and swirling around him until there was nothing left of him but sparks and dust.

And yet, suffering wasn't meant to be seen. The most powerful thing she could do, the only way to hurt him, was to shrug and ignore him. She looked around the littered den she'd been living in and could see the suicidal state of her room like it belonged to somebody else. The few rays of light that eked between the curtains caught dust motes billowing.

It was a long, weary walk to the maid's closet down the hall, but when she got there, she was able to pick the lock and found a three-gallon tub of cheese puffs. She sat with it between her legs and ate them, one orange ball at a time until she felt her strength return, then she sucked and chewed the cheese paste off her fingers and rolled the housekeeping cart down the covered walkway to her room.

She stripped the sheets, sallow and rank, the pillows dappled with dried tears and drool, and made the bed like Manny had taught her, with hospital corners so tight you needed two strong hands to undo them. After dousing a rag in ammonia, she scrubbed every hard surface in the room until it shone. With a big canister of Comet, she scoured away the water lines, the copper sediment, even cleaned the inside of the toilet tank, until the muscles in her arm felt like custard and the tank was better than new. She vacuumed the plush lilac carpet and opened all the windows to air out the stench of her misery. She could smell the damp stink of her body now, felt her scalp crawl with grease, tongued the gluey surface of her teeth. She showered with the little free soaps and shampoos and brushed her teeth till they bled and carved the grit from under her nails.

She could hear the suede crooning of a Willie Nelson song from an open window and suddenly remembered Dolly. She found her leaning in the closet, still cheerful as the cherry on an ice cream sundae. She lashed Dolly back to her rigging on the turntable and positioned the stylus. It was a happy room again, its freshness and color restored. Just the act of cleaning had lifted her spirits so much that she wondered if she had done it sooner things wouldn't have gone so terribly south. She unscrewed a mini vodka she'd pocketed from the maid's closet and drank it like water. *I've been just fine without you*, she told herself. *Just fine*.

Then she lathered her hands and worked the diamond ring over her knuckle with soap. She rinsed it of suds and admired the stone, a perfect frozen teardrop. Its value pulsed in her palm. She could sell it for thousands or sew it in the lining of her backpack for a rainy day, a little windfall, something just for her. As she turned the ring over in her palm, she knew the money didn't matter. What she could not stomach was the thought that Manny would ever know how completely he had broken her by leaving, that she had gone after it and worn it like a comfort while he was gone. She pinched the golden band between two fingers, its facets spraying the room in tiny flecks of light, then dropped it in the toilet and flushed. This time, she did not go after it.

KIT AWOKE FROM DEEP, BLACK sleep to the sound of the Mustang grumbling up to the motel. She heard him take the stairs by twos and walk right up to the door and pause. A minute went by. Then three. Was he having second thoughts? Did he know she was listening? If he turned around, would she go after him? No, she vowed. She would never chase him again. Ten minutes went by and an ill feeling at the back of her throat told her he wasn't coming. All the flames and the bile and the bees gathered in her mouth and she threw off the sheets, launched for the door, swung it wide, and opened up her mouth to scream.

But she couldn't, because there was Manny ramming into her, into the place the scream would have been. He clamped his hands over her cheeks and ears and sucked her mouth till it felt like her tongue was coming away at its root. It happened so quickly her only reaction was to fight, and she clawed at his neck and kneed at his groin. She let out a muffled "get off of me" one word at a time when she could break the suction from his mouth and finally pushed him off and caught her breath, and he let her.

He returned to her at half speed, distant behind the eyes, but driven. He took her by the waist and carefully rolled down her jeans like a woman removed her stockings, lowered her to the bed, and lay over her, breathing into the mess of her dark hair. He moved on her slowly, rhythmically. He had never come at her like this before. Sex had always been war, never soft, but piercing. A test. Now, she found that she could feel everything so acutely, every subtle movement, until a warming pleasure crested, then swelled again and again, each peak warmer and fuller than the last, and each time she thought they were done, there would be more heat and she'd hold him deeper, wrapped around all of him. She was so lost in the softness of the feeling, like their very cells were mingling and melding together, that she did not think to look for the signs that it was time to pull him away. By the time she noticed, when he rolled his head back so far it disappeared behind his neck, and his moans turned into ragged little breaths, and he held her hips to his like he was punching through her, she knew he had already come inside her.

She remembered Red's warning. She had always been careful to pull him up and plant him in her mouth to finish, but tonight she wasn't thinking. She left him sleeping and drew a bath in the goofy heart-shaped tub. While waiting for the tub to fill, she scooped out the dollop he'd left in her, wiped it on a tissue, and tossed it in the purple wicker trash can. She lowered herself into near-scalding water, swished her fingers around again to flush out any residue. She recalled the grainy silhouettes of tadpoles she'd seen in a science textbook, imagined them swimming in formation out of her, tails flicking, and almost smiled. He was back. A giddy relief, a feeling so profound it was religious, opened her heart and her senses. The chlorinated smell rising up from the water, the drip drip from the faucet, the chill on the parts of her body—head, shoulders, knees—that weren't submerged. It was as if she were returning to the world after a long absence and everything was like new. She closed her eyes and rested her head against the plastic lip of the tub and breathed out.

CHAPTER FOURTEEN

IN THE MONTHS THAT FOLLOWED MANNY'S RETURN, KIT WAS ME-
ticulous about keeping him happy, doing nothing to risk losing him
again. They bounced from motel to motel, as usual, never long enough
to be remembered, and to Kit's relief, Manny hewed close to the
holdup rules they'd established. She wondered if he, too, had been
spooked by their separation.

One night, after an easy job looting a filling station that was
closed for the night, Manny suggested they hit the local icehouse to
get drunk and spend some of their winnings. Kit knew she should go
with him, but she had been exhausted lately, so tired she fell asleep in
the car. Manny let her out in front of the motel room, sour, but not so
bad that Kit felt she needed to rally.

That night, she dreamed she lay next to Manny in bed and felt a
stirring between them, like the surface of a lake being disturbed by a
turtle. Then she was attached to a balloon and it lifted her out of the
bed and through an open window, setting her down gently in a field
of soft grass. She felt relieved and peaceful.

When she woke up to a bright round moon between the parted
curtains, she knew that she was pregnant. There had been signs, of
course. Her period, which had never been regular, had stopped coming altogether. Strange, but not surprising. And she became more
fearful. Instead of picking fights with Manny, she shied away from

them. Her appetite was capricious, would rage like a squall then quit with no warning; after a few bites, she found whatever she was eating, no matter how much she had craved it, repulsive.

She swept her hands over her head to gather her hair into a bun when she felt the bristled, patchy surface of her skull. Only days ago, Manny had cut her hair after her picture had been published in a newspaper. He had made it seem like it was a practical measure, but it had felt more like a reprimand. She could have bleached her hair. Or worn a hat. He didn't have to shear her like a sheep. At least the swelling around her eye had settled, allowing the fading purples of her bruise to blend somewhat with the brown of her skin.

SHE PEED AND DRANK TWO glasses of water, desperately thirsty, then filled a third for her bedside. Now that she was up, she wouldn't go back to sleep for hours. Manny rolled over and wrapped the pillow across the back of his head to block out the moon and her noises.

Pregnancy did not seem like something that could happen to her. She knew for girls like her, poor, itinerant, and unfit, the only answer was to abort. But for weeks now, she had felt a sort of contentment, as if, wherever she went, she had been accompanied by a kind and quiet friend. She wanted someone to tell her what to do about it, but she couldn't tell Manny, not yet. Kit thought of Red, her warmth and how she had a way of talking about things, like she'd never been ashamed. The few times Kit had called Red, it was just to hear her shoot the shit, perhaps to feel less lonely. She could try calling, but it was late, and Red was more than likely working. Tonight she needed to see her in person.

There was plenty of time to get to Harper, the town where Red had been living the last time they saw each other. Manny would sleep late as long as she didn't wake him. She cranked up the AC and closed the gap in the curtains. She pulled on her jeans, tight now around her middle, and carried her shoes to the car. The Mustang would wake him for sure, so she put it in neutral and pushed it to the road before starting it up.

It took an hour flat to make it to Harper and she still had a couple of hours of darkness by her count. Kit walked the village's few gridded, empty streets, and it wasn't long before she found Red, not under a seedy bridge as she had imagined, but in a quaint commercial strip in the center of town. The antique streetlights were on and businesses—an optometrist, a notary public, a hair salon, and a church-run thrift shop—all closed for the night. Red sat on a bench, reading a book, as if waiting for the bus that would take her home. Kit brightened to see her but kept her distance and planned what to say before they met.

A pair of headlights rounded the corner and crawled slowly up the road. A souped-up sedan pulled up next to Kit, some slick Top 40 song thumping and quaking the half-down window.

A redheaded man with freckles on his bald spot craned across the passenger seat and looked Kit up and down.

"Hel-lo, princess," he said, eyes skipping with interest. "You're new."

She took note of a crushed forty of malt liquor in the gutter, a good enough weapon should the guy get out of line.

"Wallace, get your ass over here, you dog," Red yelled. "She's not for sale!"

"Well, shit, woman! What's she doing out here all alone at night?" He hung halfway out the driver's-side window, a little goofy to see Red. While he turned away, Kit plunged the broken bottle neck into a worn spot on his tire. He hadn't exactly crossed her, but she just didn't think guys like this should have an easy time of anything. Wallace was too pleased to see Red to notice the slow sinking of his car.

Red skittered over in her high-heeled boots, big hair bouncing out of time with her breasts. Her arms outstretched, she ran right up to Kit and hugged her hard.

"KEE-uht! I can't believe it's you. What are you doing here? Is everything okay? What happened to your hair?!"

"I'm all right, I just wanted to talk," Kit said, and scrubbed the back of her head with her knuckles. She felt silly for coming here in the dead of night, bothering Red at work.

"Okay, baby, hold tight. You wait right there." She held up a finger and slipped in the car. Leaning out the front window, she stage-whispered, "This won't take but a minute."

Kit turned around and walked the block. The waistband of her jeans chafed her hip bones, so she flicked the button through its hole to make room. In a few minutes, the car door opened and the sedan rolled away, back tire flubbing.

Red reapplied a slick of dark lipstick and fluffed her hair. "If I don't like a guy I charge him ten bucks a minute, so he tends to wrap up real quick." She looked around and hooked Kit by the arm. "Well, this is no place for a lady. Come on, my house is just down the road."

THE COMMERCIAL STRIP TURNED INTO a residential neighborhood of turn-of-the-century bungalows, all apparently built in the same batch, of the same blond brick with open porches and cut-glass details in the front windows. The yards were maintained modestly, dutifully trim but not embellished.

"Here we are, home sweet home," Red said as she fished her keys from her green lizard purse. The house looked similar to its neighbors except for its voluptuous landscaping and freshly painted green door. It sure didn't look like a home for hookers and bandits. It was a place for Thanksgiving dinners and tire swings, where ice cream trucks stopped in the summer, a place that twinkled with Christmas lights in December. It was a place where you could raise a child.

"Sure is nice to have company," Red said. "It's been years now, hasn't it? You were such a scrawny little thing last I saw you." She pinched a little roll on Kit's belly. "But you're all filled out now, aren't you?" Kit blushed. She had never even needed a bra, but now her breasts were heavy and tender.

"Well, tickled as I am to see you, it worries me a little. I mean, my lord, what's with the mysterious late-night visit?" She struggled to open the door, jimmying the lock.

"Yeah, sorry about that," Kit said. She chewed on her thumb, wishing the door would open already. "I need advice, I guess."

"You come to the right place then," Red told her. She pumped the key in the keyhole and turned it forcefully to the left while lifting up on the handle. The door finally gave way.

"I swear, I have to do something different to it every day. It's old and cranky—just like me. Ha!"

Kit relaxed at once inside the home. Donna Summer on the radio, roses in the air, everything lit in warm marigold, it was a real home. A signed ZZ Top poster hung above the fireplace; on every flat surface squatted a fluffy houseplant. On the coffee table, an unfinished puzzle, a sleeping tangle of Labrador puppies. She thought she could spend the rest of her life in a place like this. By comparison, the rotating string of motels were all different shades of shitty.

Red flopped onto the couch, unzipped her boots down the back, and rubbed her arches. "Something to drink?"

"Sure, I can get it, though," Kit said. "You look comfy."

"You are *sweet*. Kitchen's through the dining room." Red flopped back and lit a cigarette.

Kit found her way to the fridge, which was quilted with children's drawings addressed to *Aunt Winnie* and Christmas cards affixed with magnets and tape from what looked like Red's sisters' families. She grabbed a couple of cans and brought them back to the living room.

Red had taken off her bra and was sprawled on the couch. She reached out to take the soda.

Kit began to squirm under the weight of why she was here. She cracked open her drink, took a long, bracing gulp, and sat down.

"I'm pretty sure I'm pregnant," she said. She let the news hang, not even sure she wanted a reaction.

Red sat up. "Wow." She sandwiched her face between her palms.

"Wow, again. So, what do you need to hear right now, 'Congrats' or 'I'm so sorry'?"

"That's the thing, I don't know how I feel about it. I know I'm supposed to be freaked out, and maybe I am a little, but . . ." She needed to do something with her hands, something to focus on. She knelt on the floor in front of the coffee table and began moving the puzzle pieces. "Did it ever happen to you?" Kit asked.

Red started to feather Kit's hair with her fingers, running them from her hairline to the nape of her neck. At first Kit felt ants under her skin, her scalp aflame. Not wanting to offend Red, she held still. In time, she settled and she could almost remember the way she felt wedged into the V of Miss Rhonda's legs as she ran the brush in long, soothing strokes through her hair.

"I've been pregnant before, if that's what you mean," Red said.

"Oh," Kit said, suddenly sad.

"I was young, like you, and it would have meant giving up my career, moving home. I didn't see how it could work. Looking back, I was just scared."

"What was the . . . procedure like?"

Red looked off into the middle distance. She scrunched her face to the side, and two dimples Kit had never noticed appeared in her cheek. "Kinda lonesome," she finally said. "Painful. But you convince yourself of things that make it better. Just like getting a tooth pulled, some piece of your body that's not working for you. It's what you've gotta do to take care of yourself."

"Do you regret it?" Kit asked.

Red looked down and folded her hands in her lap. "Sweetheart, I got no time for regrets. They'll swallow you like a catfish in one big gulp if you wander near." She clutched Kit's shoulders and turned her. "Now, who's the father?"

Kit looked at her lap. She picked at a frayed cuff.

"Is it Manny?"

Kit met her eyes, an angry blush.

"Oh, honey. That's what I was afraid of." The dimples again. "Look, I know you're not his niece, okay? Don't worry about that. But you're gonna have to have a plan if you want to keep this baby. You can't raise it with him."

"I can't?" Kit felt stupid. Why was it so obvious? He had taken care of her when she was little, why not a child of his own?

Red reached out and touched Kit's bruised cheek. "No, honey, you can't."

"Now that it's here, it doesn't feel like a choice," Kit said. "It's happening."

"Honey, it *is* a choice. I want you to think real sober about it. The question you need to ask yourself is not whether you want a child but whether you want to be a *mother*."

Kit couldn't utter that she did not even know what it meant to be a mother, or even what it meant to have one.

"Having a child is one thing. They're cute, they kinda love you no matter what. But it's not just feeding them and making sure they don't fall in a creek. You have to be ready to do the work. You have to be there for them, for their little spirits, you know?"

Kit wanted something concrete. She felt lost.

"For example, your kid falls off a swing and starts crying. What do you do?"

Kit thought about it. *Tell him to stop crying before someone sees? Make him get back on the swing? Ignore him?* "I don't know," she said, and felt she might cry herself.

"Well, I don't know either, but I think you'd probably go give them a hug and hang with them until they felt better. Let 'em know you're there."

The pieces of the puzzle blurred together as Kit's eyes filled with tears. She forced a piece into a hole where it didn't fit. She yanked her head away from Red and swiped her arm across the table, scattering the pieces on the floor.

"Honey," Red said and reached for Kit.

Kit got up and stood in front of the window. She knew she didn't deserve this baby, but she couldn't just get rid of it, pretend it never existed. She couldn't leave Manny either. Who was to say he didn't want to be a father?

Red stayed quiet and gave her time.

"I'm telling him," Kit said. "Once I see how he reacts, I'll know what to do."

Red lit a cigarette and sucked so hard she nearly swallowed it. "I'm not one to tell another woman what to do," she said through a smoky exhale. "But, baby, you best have a plan before you walk through his door." She got up and stood next to Kit by the window, took her by the shoulders and touched her forehead to Kit's. "You know where to find me now. If you need anything at all—money, a place to stay, what have you—you call, okay?"

WHEN KIT RETURNED, IT WAS nearly seven in the morning and already heating up outside. She opened the door into the chilled, dark room. Manny lay on his side, facing away from her. She pulled off her jeans and lay next to him, studying the moles on his back.

"Where were you?" he mumbled without turning.

She paused, savoring the stillness of this side of the line she was about to cross. She bargained for more time before it all changed, because once she opened her mouth, the whole thing could fall apart. If she didn't speak up, maybe today could be one of the good ones. They could sneak into a movie and eat popcorn with extra butter, they could drive to an open field and shoot targets, or they could just stay in bed, watch TV all day, and forget to eat. She felt tearful as she thought about the last time she was happy with him. They had snuck into the tail end of a wedding and stolen an expensive camera that was hanging off a pew. When they pawned the camera Manny saved the film and developed it for her. Some of the pictures were junk, but there was one beautiful shot of the couple walking down the aisle. The groom was laughing at something the bride must have said and Kit could feel the love between them.

"You deaf or something?" Manny said. "Where the shit were you?"

Her dreams of a perfect day dissolved. This secret wouldn't keep.

"I'm pregnant, Manny."

The silence that followed was tense, almost solid matter. Kit couldn't manage a full breath.

"Whose is it?" he said, his voice dusty and cruel.

The insult hurt the way it was meant to. "It could only be yours," she said.

He stayed quiet and still did not turn to face her, nor did she reach out to him. The space between them widened.

"What do you think?" she asked, the slightest waver in her voice.

At this he turned over, propped up on his elbow. He was laughing, but the scorn blew her back like she'd opened a hot oven.

"What's to think about? You can't keep it, dummy." He tried to nudge her in the navel, but she swiftly blocked his hand. "It'll make you fat and awkward. You never get your shape back, you're never the same."

She shook her head. He wasn't taking her seriously. "I don't give a shit about getting fat."

Manny got up and ripped off the bedsheets.

Feeling exposed, she moved to the chair by the window and covered her lap with a pillow. "I could figure it out," she said, convincing no one.

"That's just the hormones talking," he said. He opened the door, shook out the sheets, and let in a steamy gust, a licorice smell of tar. "Besides, you haven't even asked me if I want a child."

"Do you?" she asked and it pained her to realize how much she wanted the answer to be yes.

Now he raised his voice, paced like he was lecturing.

"I'm sorry, I just didn't realize you were this naïve. How would we raise a kid like this, motel to motel, ripping people off to survive? You ever think about school? Hell no, kids are a fucking drag. You're not thinking straight."

She turned in her chair away from him, afraid he would see the disappointment on her face. She hated how much sense he was making, but the fact that he was so clear, so righteous about getting rid of the baby, made her feel like she had to argue in favor of keeping it. She knew she couldn't make the decision out of stubbornness, but she couldn't just go with what he was saying either. She could hear him resume his bed making as he snapped and draped the sheets over the bed, then tucked them in tight. He always seemed a touch calmer after the bed was made. He walked around and squatted in front of Kit.

"Don't think so hard, Kitty," he said, pinching his eyebrows together. "Once it's done with, you'll see I'm right."

He smoothed a wrinkle from the coverlet and sat across from her. He held her cheeks together between his warm hands. "I know a doctor. He's clean, he's good. He'll take care of you."

No, don't make me do it. Don't make me choose between you and the baby.

"What if I don't go?" she said.

Manny clasped his hands together as if he were crushing a small bird between them. She tensed and glanced at the door.

"You'll go," he said.

THE DOCTOR, A PALE-SKINNED MAN in his fifties, met them outside his trailer, which was parked a long way off the main road on an empty, overgrown lot. He wore overalls and had his stringy gray hair pulled into a loose ponytail. There were no outward signs of being a doctor, no scrubs or stethoscope or sterile white coat, nothing to balance the sketchiness of the setting.

He led them inside, and Kit saw the kitchen straight ahead, a medical cot and built-in benches to the right and a bed to the left. A pot of something boiled on the stove, lid jangling, and some instruments dried on a rack. An oxygen tank and IV pole by the bed, several cardboard boxes containing medical supplies stacked and half-open on the table. It was air-conditioned, at least.

Manny started up the stairs behind Kit.

"You're gonna have to wait outside," the doctor said.

"Hell no, I'm coming in," Manny said and tried to edge around him, but the doctor blocked the doorway.

"I don't think so," the doctor said, waving him off. "It's not sanitary, plus I only got so much room to maneuver."

"How do I know you're not gonna molest her in there?" Manny said, flushed around the collar.

The doctor shook his head wearily. "Look, man, I don't know what to tell you. Do you want this or not?"

Manny held up his hands and backed down the stairs.

"I'll be right outside. Just holler if he pulls a fast one on you," he said to Kit.

He sat on a rusty glider and clasped his hands. Kit thought he actually looked worried, which only made her angrier at him for forcing this on her. She considered whether this was, in fact, all his idea. He hadn't held a gun to her head, had he? It seemed true that once she ended the pregnancy, things could go back to normal. Manny would be happy, they'd carry on just the two of them, partners in crime. Until she got pregnant, she had only ever wanted to be with Manny. But now the balance was upset, now she had a little something separate, and she was beginning to want something beyond him. But the idea of walking out there and choosing the baby at the risk of losing him, the only person who ever loved her, it made her ill even to think about it.

The doctor closed the door and slid the lock, but she could still hear the tight creak of the glider, back and forth. *Squick, creee, squick, creee.*

"Here, have a seat," the doctor said, gesturing to the special medical cot that had stirrups for her feet.

She hoisted herself onto the cot, the sanitary paper crinkling and bunching underneath her.

"How old are you?" he said.

"Nineteen."

"Any health issues I should know about?"

"No, sir."

"Ever had an abortion?"

She shook her head no, cheeks hot, feeling shorter and shorter of breath.

Squick, creee, squick, creee.

He wrapped a Velcro cuff around her bicep and pumped.

"Looks good. Before we begin I'm gonna give you something for the pain."

"I won't be needing that," she said.

The doctor looked confused. "I'd feel better if you took it," he said. "Maybe I should walk you through the procedure—it's not just a Pap smear, you know."

"I have a high threshold," she said, wishing she could run out on all of this. The pressure of this decision, of pleasing Manny, the fear of what he would do if she didn't comply. The fantasy that he would want to raise a child with her, that they could be like that station-wagon family at the gas station all those years ago. All of it was clogged up in her throat. She began to sweat. She needed more time to think. If only she *could* feel the pain. She deserved to suffer for this.

Squick, creee.

The doctor tried to tourniquet her arm. She pushed him off.

"Look," she said and pulled a scalpel from the towel-lined tray he'd laid out. She jabbed the scalpel into the round muscle of her shoulder. There was pressure, but no pain. "See?" she said. The doctor gasped and pulled the scalpel away; the purple slit oozed blood that ran in a neat rivulet to the underside of her arm and fell with a *tap tap* on the waxy paper.

"What the shit, are you high?" The doctor dropped the blade in the sink with a clatter.

"I just don't want any fucking meds, okay?" she said.

The doctor's eyes stayed pinned wide open. He lifted his hands up like she held a gun at him.

"Okay, easy there," he said and slowly lowered his hands, still holding them out so she could see them. "I believe you. Look, I have to stitch up that wound, okay?" He glugged some alcohol over a cotton ball and swabbed the gaping cut, his hand shaking a little. Then he tore open a packet of sterile dressing and had her clamp it down with her thumb to stem the bleeding.

"You made your point, lady. You don't *need* meds. But it would make me feel better if you had some."

Kit shook her head.

"You're gonna have to explain why or I'm not doing anything."

Kit looked in her lap and sighed as she calmed a bit. "I just like to keep my wits about me."

The doctor dropped his shoulders and his head tipped back, like he couldn't believe what he was about to do. "All right, I get that," he said. "But if you want me to do this thing, you gotta settle down and keep your hands off my shit. Understood? Don't touch my surgical instruments."

Kit nodded.

A knock at the door made them both jump.

"What's going on in there, you two?" Manny said, his voice warped through the metal door. "I heard raised voices. Y'all trying to make me jealous?"

The doctor slid open the lock and cracked the door. "Just a few nerves, happens all the time. If you could just wait on the bench, we'll be done in about forty-five minutes."

Manny peered over the doctor's shoulder at Kit, who waved him off. He shrugged and the doctor closed the door. The doctor sewed up the wound in silence, and quickly. Then he taped the stitches and covered them with an innocuous beige Band-Aid. When he was done, he handed her a folded gown.

"Here," he said, his voice thin and wary. "I'm gonna steal away for a minute before we begin." The doctor went into the bathroom while she changed. She took off her clothes in the cramped living room, balled them up and shoved them in her backpack, then slipped her arms into the flimsy white smock.

She sat back on the cot and pulled her knees to her chest to still the violent beating of her heart. Of course she had to get rid of this baby. What kind of fucked-up mother would stab herself just to make a point? Maybe her own mother had been crazy, too, maybe it was a virus in the blood. Had her mother made it this far, to the verge of ending her? Had she wanted to be a mother and suddenly, when it was too late, changed her mind? Or maybe she had never wanted a baby in the first place but couldn't pay for the abortion. How many times had Kit wished she'd never been born and cursed her mother's foolishness? It wasn't fair that she had been burdened with the ability to create life, and to end it.

She remembered the last creatures she had killed, those squirmy little coyotes huddled in a ditch. The long, dark walk; the weight of the gun. With a few more months, they could have learned to hunt, fend for themselves, but they were too young and hadn't any sense. Hadn't any sense at all. Her heart ached to see them there, warm and sleepy, and she wished she could have scooped them all up under her shirt and let them live there like possum joeys until they were ready for the world. It had been so obvious at the time, why she had to kill them. It had felt like mercy. But then she remembered the mother coyote, how even as she lay crippled and dying on the asphalt, she had looked for her babies and cautioned them to safety. Then she imagined her little something asleep and tucked away between the layers on layers of her body, peaceful, protected. The image was so vivid, so comforting, the whole room seemed to warm and soften, the light turning peachy. And as clear as if it were written on her skin, she knew what she had to do. There would be no mercy kill.

The doctor knocked and cracked the door.

"You ready?" he asked.

Kit tucked the gown under her thighs. She glanced through a part in the curtains and saw Manny in profile on the glider. The creaking had stopped. He was eavesdropping.

"Listen here," she said, quiet but firm. "I want you to cut me, but leave the baby alone."

He looked at her like she'd just started speaking in tongues.

"*Now* what are you talking about?" he said.

"Quiet down," she hissed and grabbed him by the arm. "He's listening. Please, please be quiet and just hear me out. I want to keep the baby, but that guy can't know. Cut me and he'll see the bleeding. Nick me just inside, not too far."

He shook his head. "Lady, this ain't worth it. You don't want to go through with it, fine. But don't bring me into it. Your friend out there is scary as hell."

She squeezed his arm tighter, and he yanked it back. "But that's what I'm trying to say, if you don't do what he paid you to do, he'll beat both our asses. We gotta make it look like I had the thing done until I can figure out a plan. I need more time. You can give that to me, okay? Please."

Then he sighed a heavy sigh. After a minute or so, he said, "All right, look, I'll do it."

"Thank you," she said and pulled a fifty from her backpack. She slapped it in his hand. "That's all I got."

He looked at the bill in his palm and back at Kit, bewildered. He sighed again and gave the money back. "Keep it," he said, and turned to wash his hands.

She leaned back, then fit her heels in the stirrups and closed her eyes. She felt like she and her baby were hunkering down in a house in the middle of a hurricane. Outside, all hell had been unleashed, but inside they were cozy and safe together. Safe, at least, for now.

CHAPTER FIFTEEN

THERE WAS A PLUMP BOUQUET OF WHITE LILIES ON THE PILLOW when Kit awoke the next morning, not the kind sold from umbrellas staked outside cemeteries, but natural looking, like they'd been growing in someone's garden not long ago, damp and imperfect. Manny was in the shower. He came out of the bathroom scrubbing his hair dry with a hand towel.

"Happy Independence Day, Kitty Cat."

Kit felt motion sick, like the room was rocking, and her eyes struggled to latch on to him. She waited, sensing he had more to say.

"Bi-cen-fuckin-tennial is what it is, 1776 to 1976. That's a pretty goddamn auspicious date for a new start, don't you think?"

"What do you mean, 'new start'?" She was halfway toward puking. She could hold it off for now, but sooner or later she'd need to dash to the toilet.

"I've been thinking," he said and slipped into bed, nothing on, warm and damp against her. Nothing could stop this from feeling good. She sank into the rightness of their bodies next to each other. He nested his face between her cheek and shoulder and spoke to her there, muffled and slow.

"I'm sick of these dull, dusty highways. Let's head east. New Orleans, maybe? Miami?"

Kit pulled away a little. "What for?"

He didn't try to close the gap, but stayed sweet. "I know what you did yesterday was hard, and I want to make it up to you, I guess."

She tossed the lilies on the bedside table, and a couple of blossoms fell from their stems, leaving sprays of orange pollen on the carpet. "It's fine," she said, feeling dry and bruised. What she wouldn't give to get back to normal and level the ground between them. But the terrain had shifted and cracked open, a black and howling gash. She did not know how to forgive him for this.

He propped up on one elbow and looked at her with plotting eyes. "Listen, I been scoping out a job. No security cameras, pretty low-tech establishment with easy access and no barrier to the cash register. It'll be easy in and out, and we can use what we have to get to New Orleans, or wherever you want to go."

She couldn't deny the pull of erasing everything, starting over somewhere else, with him. Together.

He was looking at her now with the challenge of adventure, with a doting twinkle that felt like family. "What do you say, Ki' Cat?" he said and laid his palm open on the bed, as if inviting a bird to land. Knowing full well she was throwing herself across the chasm, she hooked her leg into his and rolled toward him, letting him wrap her in his arms. She rested there in numbing comfort, taking in the clean smell of lemons and fresh soap, almost forgetting yesterday.

He held her behind the neck with one hand and kissed her, then nibbled around her ear, brushed his cheek against her hair. She lay there, not giving back, but not pushing him away. She was stuck there wondering how she was going to leave the loving behind. She felt so different now, and yet he looked the same as always. It was as if she were changing around him, a fixed object in time and space. Maybe he had been twenty-five when she met him? She didn't trust herself to know. He had just been a grown-up. A guardian, maybe. Then, her partner. And now she didn't know what to call him.

He ran his other hand across her thigh, then up over her hip and rested on her stomach.

"You did the right thing, Kitty," he murmured in her ear, his breath hot. "This is how it's supposed to be, just us two."

She didn't want to be reminded of yesterday, of what he had asked her to do. She pushed his hand off her stomach and rolled away.

"I don't want to go out today," she said.

He seemed to tense up. "What are you talking about?"

"I'm not feeling so good," she said, bringing her knees to her chest. "I just want to stay here and sleep or something."

He was eyeing her, reading her. She could feel him turn hateful. Then he pushed her off the bed and onto the floor. She reached out to protect her belly and landed on her hands and knees. She teared up. It wasn't the fall, but the ugliness behind the push that hurt.

"Didn't you hear what I said? I *said* it was an easy run. I said we start fresh, go wherever you like. I thought you'd be grateful," he said, his outrage turning bitter.

Normally she would fight back, but she didn't want to take any risks. She stood up and got dressed, then she closed the bathroom door, turned on the fan, and threw up as quietly as she could. She brushed her teeth and rinsed her face, then went out and sat down on the bed next to Manny.

"I'm sorry," she said. "I'm feeling better now. Let's go do this thing."

Manny sat facing the window, a glass in one hand, a bottle in the other. In the time she had been in the bathroom, he had drunk the top three inches off a fifth of whiskey.

"As you wish, your fuckin' highness," he said, tucked the bottle under his arm, took his gun from the dresser, and went to the car.

Kit tipped her head to catch the wind as they sped down the interstate later that afternoon. It tugged at the skin on her cheeks, ruffled the short fur on her head, the freshness of the air a balm to the nausea that threatened with every bump to blow her cover. She hoped she could hold it in until Manny was gone. He couldn't know she was still carrying their child. *Her* child, she reminded herself. He had signed away his privileges the day he told her to get rid of it.

Manny tippled the whiskey and set the bottle back between his legs. Steppenwolf was on the radio, electric guitars grinding, vocals long and loud. He was edgy as hell. And drunk. And once he got this way, there was no way to manage him unless she could get him so wasted he passed out. They had a rule against drinking before work—his rule—but it would do no good to remind him of that now.

Kit angled her ear toward the wind to block out the music and Manny.

Up ahead, a veteran in jean shorts and a GI jacket waved a half dozen sparklers in each hand, hawking his scant assortment of fireworks. Even at this speed she could tell he was off, some distant scene rattling around in his body, jerking and weaving like he had extra joints.

"Look at that crazy motherfucker," Manny said, leaning on the horn. "Someone ought to put him out of his misery." The man shot up his middle finger, grabbed his crotch, and humped the air. Kit turned around as they sped past and watched him light a bottle rocket. It screamed and burned a brilliant red, spiraling toward them before bursting into a spray of crackling sparks.

They were passing a roadside joint called Stoker's BBQ when Manny took a hard right into its dirt parking lot. The rear tires skidded, and they fishtailed, sending up a cloud of dust. Manny laughed as he wrestled the car back in line, then braked to a sudden stop.

"I'm starving," he said. "What do you want?"

There was a long line of people waiting, sweating and chatting, some sipping icy beers or Cokes they'd pulled from an open cooler. To the left of the wooden structure, a thick column of smoke rose from an enormous, greasy smoker, which was tended by a burly pitmaster. A middle-aged woman wearing a kerchief around her hair took orders at one end of the building, and a plump teenage boy worked the pickup window at the other. Off the pickup area, there was a big covered lot with picnic tables that must have been twenty feet long. People ate elbow to elbow, hunkered over trays of brisket and sausage and ribs.

"You never eat before a job," she said.

"Look, I'm peckish," he said. "How am I gonna focus if my tummy's grumbling?" He ruffled her bristly hair and left her in the car. Kit didn't like the sudden change of plan, but maybe she could waylay him here long enough to spoil the job. Nothing about this seemed like a good idea to her.

WHEN HE HAD DISAPPEARED INTO the end of the order line, she closed her eyes and willed her stomach to settle. It was hot in the car now that they had stopped. The smells of leather and lemons bloomed in the confined space, and barbecued meat smoke seeped through the windows. She fumbled with the door until it swung open, lurched toward a nearby trash can, and vomited. She felt some relief and rested her head on her forearms, waiting for a second surge. She gagged, but nothing came.

"How far along are you, hon?" someone said. A woman with ebony skin and short shorts, a child of three wrapped around her leg, held out a cup of ice water. Kit took the water and drank it in small, cooling sips. "Thanks," she said to the woman. "Must have been something I ate."

The woman smiled sideways, like she didn't believe Kit. "I sure hope not," she said, pointing to the man tending the smoker. "That's my dad over there. People come from all over for his ribs. Wouldn't look good if they knew he had served up funky meat."

Kit didn't know why she had lied, but she wasn't in the habit of sharing secrets with strangers. She glanced at the line to see where Manny was, if he'd seen her.

"I haven't eaten here yet," she said. "I'm sure it's real good."

"It's not good, baby," the woman said, flicking the braids off her shoulder. "It's the best."

"Maya," the woman said, touching her chest, and pointed to the boy at her side. "This is baby Ray. Hey, we have some cold ginger ale in the back. You want some? It'll fix you right up."

Kit wanted to get back to the car before Manny noticed she was gone, but she was still queasy, and ginger ale might be just the thing to settle her stomach. She followed Maya around the back of the building to the open kitchen door. Boxes of straws and napkins outside on a pallet and crates of onions, lettuce, and potatoes blocked half of the short hallway that led into the kitchen. A loud fan mounted to the ceiling blew warm air inside. It was so dark compared to the outside that she couldn't see anything but Maya's pink tank top and the open order window ahead of her. Before her eyes could adjust, she heard someone speak. At first it was hard to hear over the fan, but a few steps further and she knew it was Manny, cool and creamy.

"Easy does it, now. I'm in charge. Keep your head level and your eyes down, if you please."

Kit blinked, shapes beginning to emerge from the dark room. Two figures by the window in the corner, one tall, the other short and plump. She could see Maya better now. She had stopped, behind a stack of crates, her son tucked behind her.

There was the sound of bubbling oil and the smell of something frying. Kit swallowed back a retch. A woman crying. Praying, maybe. Then Manny behind the woman, a gun held to her spine.

Not here, not now, Kit thought. She couldn't believe he had started something without telling her, completely off script, with all these people around. There must be two hundred witnesses, who knows how many of them were armed. If he didn't pull this off perfectly, it would be a bloodbath.

"That's my mama," Maya whispered.

Kit took Ray by the hand and spoke into Maya's ear. "Back out slowly, and get your boy far away from here." Maya clenched her eyes shut. She dipped down, scooped her boy up, backed toward the door, and disappeared.

Kit had to stop Manny. Maybe if she could talk him out of this, they could gag the lady and run out before anyone noticed. The counter was clear, for now, but wouldn't be for long. She walked up to Manny.

"What the fuck are you doing?" she hissed. Manny turned toward her but kept his gun aimed at Mrs. Stoker. "You start a job without telling me? I'm not even ready. The car is a hundred yards away, there's people all over the place. How are we gonna get out of here now?"

Manny was swaying, and he stank of whiskey.

He smiled and squinted at her. "Don't you tell me what to do."

There was an order of ribs piled like firewood on a paper-lined basket. He took one and ripped off a shred of meat with his teeth. "I own you. I make the calls and you follow." He pulled Mrs. Stoker's printed kerchief off her head, mussing her hair, and handed it to Kit. "Throw a little gag on her now, she's about to blow." Mrs. Stoker, looking ready to faint, lowered herself to the ground.

"Fuck, Manny," Kit said. She took the kerchief and squatted by the woman.

"Please, don't scream," she said to the crying woman, rolling up the kerchief. "I'm so sorry for the trouble. Listen to me: Maya and Ray are safe. You're gonna be okay, too, y'hear?" Mrs. Stoker wouldn't take her eyes off Manny's gun. Kit pushed the gag into the woman's mouth and tied it behind her head. She was hyperventilating, her hand clutched to her heart. Kit had never been so close to someone who knew they were being robbed. For the first time, she felt like a criminal.

There was a long prep counter, maybe fifteen feet of it, covered with cutting boards, knives, a half-sliced side of brisket, tubs of pickles and rounds of onions, a deep stockpot full of beans and another full of sauce. Next to it was a fry station with a basket full of dark, bubbling things, buoyant and smoking. Lying on the ground in front of it were two men, both bleeding from the head.

"Manny, what the fuck?" she said, pointing to the two men.

Manny made a face at Kit, mocking her outrage. "Manny, Manny—when the fuck you get so uptight about every goddamn thing. How am I supposed to rip this place off with two knife-wielding motherfuckers, huh?" He took a deep breath and let it out. "They're just knocked out, okay? Little pistol-whip is all."

What was this rampage? Because she hadn't wanted to work today? Had he heard her vomiting this morning and put it together? It was all spinning so wildly out of control. People were getting hurt, and if she wasn't careful someone could get killed.

Just then an older man with a swirly scar at his throat came up to the order window. Kit's stomach fell. Maya's mother had crumpled to the floor. Manny tossed the rib aside, wiped his hands and mouth, and appeared in the window.

"Pound of fatty brisket, side of slaw, side of pinto, extra sauce please and thank you," the man said.

"We'll have that right up for you," Manny said, side-eyeing the menu. "That'll be three seventy-five please."

"Where's Miz Stoker?" the man said, suspicious. "She always takes my order."

"Run off to the potty, sir. I'm just here to help."

The man with the scar cocked his head and looked at Manny. He made a visor of his hand and peered into the room. Kit couldn't tell if the cooks were visible from the window. She had to get Manny out of there before Maya came back with the police or worse, a bunch of men with guns.

"Say," the man said and pointed at the fry station. "Your hush puppies is burnin'." Manny smiled and went over to the smoking fryer. Kit tensed. For a moment she thought he might fling the boiling oil at the man. At this point, anything seemed possible. But he just lifted the basket out of the oil and dumped the blackened fritters into a nearby garbage can. The man with the scar shook his head and laid a five-dollar bill on the counter. Manny made change from the coins in the register and dropped them in the man's hand.

"Bone appa-teet!" he said. When the man with the scar had moved on to the pickup window, Kit grabbed Manny by the shirt.

"Listen to me now, I'm—"

He swiped at her with an open hand, but she ducked out of reach. "Quit distracting me," he said, so loud Kit worried people on the outside could hear him. "I'm trying to get us some scratch, okay? Here, watch the lady while I empty the till."

She gestured at her mouth that he should keep his voice down. Manny turned his back, gun lowered, and began filling a brown take-out bag with money.

"How long do you think before he realizes his food isn't coming, huh?" she said, gesturing toward the man at the pickup window. "I'm getting the car."

"Fine, okay, I'm done, get the fuckin' car," Manny said. He aimed his gun at the woman, who cowered and winced, then took another rib from the basket.

Kit looked out the order window to see if people knew what was happening. In the dining area, all was calm. People ate, talked. She lifted herself up, swung her legs through the window, and jogged to the Mustang. She started the car and drove, calmly as she could, down the dirt path that led to the back of the building. She stopped just short, then reached across and swung the door open for Manny, like always. If she carried on straight, there was a clear exit route that would put her right back on the freeway without having to drive past all the customers.

She pressed her forehead to the steering wheel. A month ago, she would have gone to jail for him without a second thought. That was when she was the one who just wanted someone to tell her what to do. Manny always said being scared was how we knew we were alive, but she was sick of being scared all the time. Why would she want to live like this, nothing earned, nothing granted, always bringing danger near?

As if searching for comfort, she held the little bump at her waist, tucked her fingers under her shirt and felt the warmth and the fullness. Her heart threatened to crack her ribs and she breathed again with purpose. Her nausea gone, she felt an electric surge of something she did not recognize. Strong and alert, a brilliant warmth flowed through her, and as she noticed the tears skating her jawline, she knew what to call it. It was love, elemental and transcendent.

Someone screamed and she looked above the dash. On the other side of the lot, Maya stood by the smoker with baby Ray in her arms, weeping. The pitmaster, her father, was gone. Maya must have told him. Kit's heart pounded; she scanned the area for him. There was a pickup truck under a tree a ways off from the pit, and the pitmaster was running from it, a long, black gun in his hand. A half dozen men leapt to their feet and ran for the smokehouse. She could not see inside for how dark it was, but she could hear a struggle.

"Get out here!" she hollered.

A shot fired off. She whipped around and saw the pitmaster, gun locked into his shoulder, aimed right at her. She ducked below the seat. Then Manny appeared in the doorway to her right, one arm locked around Mrs. Stoker's neck. In his other hand he held a pistol to her temple. The woman's mouth gaped as if she wanted to scream but couldn't. The pitmaster swung his gun and pointed it at Manny. He called out to his wife in a voice both desperate and enraged.

Whatever frayed ligaments had held Kit to Manny snapped, and before they could knit back together, she shifted the Mustang into gear. She looked back once, a glance in the rearview, the last thing she'd remember about Manny. The hate in his eyes when the woman slipped out of his grasp as four men tackled him to the ground.

She gunned it, her wheels churning up a blinding cloud of dust. She turned up the radio to block out the sound of Manny calling after her as she fishtailed out of the alley and onto the interstate. And when she hit the open road she said a prayer that was more a promise to herself, that no one would ever hurt her baby as long as she could spit and scratch.

CHAPTER SIXTEEN

IT MUST HAVE TAKEN AN HOUR OR SO OF BLIND, AIMLESS DRIVING before Kit's heart slowed and her hands stopped shaking, before she could think clearly enough to make a plan. The scene she had fled came back to her in bright flashes. Stoker pumping his legs to get to his wife; baby Ray grasping at the fringe on his mama's shorts; the barrel of a gun pointed straight at Kit. She exited the highway and found a hidden side street at the bottom of a double silo to get her bearings. She leaned across the seat, rummaged for a map of Texas in the glove box, and spread it on the dash. Her heart raced anew as she remembered the day Manny had nearly left her in Pecan Hollow, had pulled the Mustang to the side of the road, found the little town on the map, and promised he would take her there. She had visited the brink of freedom, sensed its promise and its ambiguities, and when he held her close and called her special, she had chosen him instead.

She unclenched her hands and smoothed the map again, resolving to keep Manny out of her head for now. Police were looking, she was sure of it, and they'd nab her if she wasn't swift and careful. She would need the car to get to Pecan Hollow, but she couldn't keep it once she got there. It took her a few minutes of squinting at the worn and wrinkled map to find the town's name in the smallest font, not sixty miles from where she was now. She made sure no one was milling around and swapped out the plates for a spare set Manny had

lifted off a Buick near Dallas. Then she started up the car for the last
time, returned to the highway, and headed to Pecan Hollow.

When she was within ten miles of Eleanor's town she started
looking for a place to hide the car. Most of the fields around there
were no good—too well kept and flat. But a few miles out she found a
small, dumpy lot with a broken wire fence and a faded FOR SALE sign.
She drove through the opening and, seeing no house and no animals
that would bring a person around anytime soon, rolled through the
high grasses toward an old barn. Though many of its heavy timbers
were missing, it would provide good cover as long as no one came
inside. She parked the Mustang under the hay-strewn loft and tossed
the keys on the seat. She wiped down the surfaces for prints, pulled
her backpack from the trunk, and took to the road on foot.

Kit followed the crumpled map to Pecan Hollow, the rumbling
engine echoing in her head like a song she couldn't shake. The sun
behind her, she kicked through high grass instead of walking on the
road because of how fast the cars were speeding by. She trudged across
soppy ditches and muddy cow paths, stopped from time to time to
slap fire ants from her ankles or pull up a sock that had slipped and
gathered at the toe of her boot. In about two hours she found the
point where the highway broke off to the farm road that led to town.

Without the map, she might have missed the sign, which was
blocked by a bigger sign that read HUNT RIDGE HILLS. Then she recognized this place as the turnoff where she and Manny had stopped
and nearly gone to Pecan Hollow. The grasshopper clinging to her
shirt, the old salt lick. She clapped her hands over her eyes and there
was a woeful sinking at her middle. Weary of walking, weary of the
dull ache in her heart, she wished for sleep and amnesia and oblivion.
Then a car sped past and its wind wrapped around her, bringing her
to fresh alertness.

You're too close to stop now, she thought.

She looked around to make sure she was on the right path. Where
the old horse ranch had been, there was now a housing development

fronted by a kelly green lake and a great spewing fountain. The spray drifted over on a gust and wet her skin, and she remembered how long it had been since she'd had anything to drink. She was hungry and the inside of her mouth was sticky and hot. She was used to going without, fasting when there wasn't food enough, skipping out on water in favor of beer or Cokes. But now that there was someone else to look after, she couldn't afford to neglect herself anymore. She began to wonder, was her baby thirsty, too? The idea of denying her baby food and water threw her into a panic. She broke into a run. The running made her feel afraid, like something was chasing her, and her legs pumped faster, her toes just skimming the loose dirt road. Everything dry and dusty. She hated herself for not loading her backpack before she left that morning, for the fifty convenience stores she'd passed on her way over here. She looked around as she ran, but all she saw were trees and fences and the long asphalt road in front of her.

Finally, she spotted a hose looped around the base of a tree in a great orchard, dribbling into the tree's roots. She cut across a culvert and ducked under the fence. Then she lay on her side so the hose didn't lose pressure and held the metal valve to her lips and drank. The water was warm and slippery, and she cried for joy and closed her eyes.

When she'd drunk till the water sloshed in her stomach, and she felt like she'd eaten a big meal, she let the water trickle over her head and scrubbed the bristle where her long hair had been. She found a bandanna in her backpack, draped it over her head, and tied it behind her neck.

Her map wasn't detailed enough to show these country roads. She knew she couldn't be far but wasn't sure how to figure out which place was Eleanor's, if she even lived there at all. That would be her luck, wouldn't it? To come this far and find out the woman had moved or died, or never existed at all. She fished out the page on which she had written two addresses in that phone booth, years ago, and looked for an address along the fence line.

Up ahead she saw a young woman on horseback with a yearling on a lead. The woman had a full face of makeup and thick ginger curls clawed up into a bushy ponytail, and a white western shirt tucked into jeans. Kit could see the woman had clocked her, even at a distance, from the way she straightened her posture and kept her eyes fixed. Kit guessed she'd be wondering what this brown-skinned, roughed-up girl was doing roaming these roads on foot. She might think she was up to no good. She might call the cops. Neither spoke until the woman was a horse's length from Kit. She pulled back on the reins and murmured to the young horse behind her to stop.

"You lost or something?" she said to Kit, her tone circumspect but not unkind.

Kit was a little stunned to be speaking with someone after the day she had had and tried to assume an air of calm.

"I'm looking for Miss Eleanor," she said, hoping the waver in her voice hadn't traveled. "Do you know which house is hers?" Kit found the phone book page in her pocket and unfolded it, showing it to the woman. "I have her address here but I don't see any numbers on the houses." The woman squinted down at her like she was trying to figure her out.

"She's an old relative of mine," Kit added.

"An old relative?" the woman repeated, then seemed to reflect on this. "Why you on foot? Your car break down?"

"Yeah," Kit said. "A ways back, I left it in the shop. Anyways, she's expecting me but I can't find her place. Can you point me in the right direction?"

"I don't know," the woman said.

"You don't know where her house is?" Kit asked.

The woman shook her head. "I don't know if I should tell you."

A panicked anger welled up in Kit that she knew would not do her any good. She could tell the woman she was pregnant and hungry and had been walking for hours, but she had learned from Manny the more desperate she seemed, the less people wanted to help. Most people wanted to help if they thought you were like them but had hit a little hard, but resolvable, luck. If they felt pressured, or manipulated, they would balk. Kit took a breath and let it out and held out her hand to the horse. The chestnut-colored mare nuzzled her hand and lipped it as if searching for a treat. Its breath was hot and damp, and there was grassy green foam at the corners of its mouth.

"Sorry, my name's Kit," she said, choosing not to press her luck. "If you see Eleanor, you let her know I'm on my way. I'm sure I'll find it before long. Appreciate your stopping." She held up a friendly hand and continued walking. She hadn't gotten far when the woman shouted at her.

"Keep going straight till you get to the T. Turn right and it's the first place on your left. Little white house with a chicken coop."

Kit turned around and waved. "Real nice of you," she shouted back.

IN A FEW MINUTES KIT arrived at a faded white house on a three-acre parcel. A split-rail fence, badly in need of repair, enclosed the overgrown yard in which bug-eaten zucchini, melons, beans, tomatoes, and lettuces grew at random. A cube of chicken wire filled with straw and a large crate housed a cheerful crew of orange chickens, which were scattered around, burbling, debugging the lawn. Something about the peacefulness of the scene frightened Kit, as if she might at any moment see Manny ambling toward her, with sweet words in his mouth and a gun in his hand. But as she drove away, she had seen those men tackle him. He was drunk and outnumbered and she'd taken the car. There had been nowhere for him to go, nowhere but down. Her heart thumped around and her lips began to buzz.

"Shhhhhh," she said aloud. The sound merged with the rustling trees. *I'm safe*, she thought. *No*—we *are safe*. She calmed and focused on the cast-iron knocker in front of her.

Before she even lifted her hand, an elderly white woman with a nest of rusty silver hair, twisted and pinned on top of her head, answered the door.

"I heard you walk up," the woman said, casual and curious. "How may I help you?"

"Are you Eleanor?"

"I am she," Eleanor said, quizzically.

This woman seemed the right age, but her oatmeal-colored skin gave Kit pause. She had always imagined her mother's family looked like her. Kit turned to leave.

"Sorry, I think I got the wrong Eleanor."

"I'm the only one in town, dear," the old woman called out. "The other one is dead, so you might as well talk to me." She hung there in the doorway scouring Kit from head to toe with her gaze.

Kit didn't know what to say; her tongue felt as thick as foam. She was afraid of finding out that she had come all this way for nothing. If the other Eleanor was her aunt, then her only known family was dead and she was back at the start. This woman sure didn't look like a relation, but she had an inviting sort of presence.

"All right then," Kit said.

Eleanor chewed on the corner of her mouth. "Won't you come in?" She shuffled in her quilted polyester housecoat to the kitchen table and pulled out a chair. Kit followed her inside.

"Sit, sit," Eleanor told her, continuing to look her over, with a dozen wrinkles gathered like bunting between her pinched, penciled-in brows. "Well, there's not much can be said on an empty stomach. Let's eat, shall we?"

She pulled a jar of pimento cheese and a loaf of white bread from the refrigerator and made a thick sandwich for Kit. Kit took it and ate it in four bites and washed it down with a cold bottle of Dr Pepper. She belched and Eleanor laughed, her hand cupped at her mouth.

"I know who you are," Eleanor said, looking down at her hands and fiddling with a cuticle.

Kit held her breath. She fixed her attention on the oiled skin of the table, its scent of orange peel, its grain whorled and mysterious. She could sense Eleanor start and stop, as if unsure of how to tell the story she'd begun.

"They came to me, when you were still a baby," Eleanor finally said. "And they asked me—well, if I could raise you. But I couldn't, not then. I had lost my Emily that year. She was only nineteen but she got cancer in her bones, and it went everywhere, and fast. The doctors couldn't do a thing, and I was angry. I was older and widowed, too tired to raise a child alone." She bowed her head and shook it ever so slightly. "Or so it seemed at the time. Several months later I got to feeling better. I went to the county to see if you still needed someone. They said the nice family you'd been living with wanted to adopt you. At the time I thought you'd be better off with a young family than with an old woman living alone." She began to cry, the tears leaving tracks in the powder on her sunken cheeks.

Kit felt heavy; her thoughts lumbered around drunkenly. She remembered Miss Rhonda, the smell of shampoo as she brushed and brushed her hair. To think that at one time there was a family who was interested in adopting her—and ultimately chose not to—was almost as rending as to learn now that Eleanor had passed her up, too. There was music, very faint, coming from an upstairs room. It sounded like three-piece suits and forced wartime gaiety.

"That nice family gave me up," Kit said, a hollow around her middle filling with a flicker of something that burned. "I was all alone. I wasn't safe at all."

Eleanor wept into her fist now.

"I can't believe you didn't try to meet me," Kit said. "It would have cost you nothing. But for me . . ." Kit trailed off and tried to swallow the pain that was wedged in her throat. "It would have changed everything. To know I had family, that I mattered to someone."

Eleanor nodded her head as Kit spoke, and her eyes were wild, like she was sorting through every moment of the last two decades trying to find a sliver of meaning.

"At the time, I don't know, it just seemed like more than I could bear." She squinted hard, a new crop of tears. "I am so ashamed, but you deserve the truth. I didn't want to think of what could have happened to you. It was easier not to think about it."

Kit had come to expect rejection, but most of the people in her life had been shitty in general. What really stung was that Eleanor seemed decent and kind. How was she supposed to get over the fact that someone as nice as Eleanor had just turned her back on her?

Kit tugged at her earlobe.

"But I did wonder, time to time, how you were doing. I imagined your family had found a nice school for you in Houston, that you were awful smart and maybe a little impetuous like the women in our family." She dabbed her face and reached out her hand, but Kit drew hers back. It was insulting, the thought of Eleanor telling herself lies so she didn't feel guilty, lies that kept her from trying harder to find Kit.

"I beg your mercy, dear."

Kit swayed in her chair, woozy with it all. It was too much for one day. If she didn't keep moving, she feared she would sink into the mire of it, the black sludge of anger at everyone for letting her down, the shame of being unwanted, regret she didn't leave Manny sooner, regret she left him at all. If she didn't keep moving, she thought, she might never get up again. Kit did not know what to do with Eleanor's tears and hospitality and the sickening news that she had known about Kit but declined to take her in, that there had been a family who had wanted to adopt her. What had happened to that family? Had they, too, given her back when they realized how defective she was? How could Kit stay here and not hate Eleanor for what she'd failed to do? The questions, and the feelings that came with them, swelled in a panic, then slipped away, like passengers swarming to the high point of a sinking ship that finally, quietly submerges.

"I'm sorry to have bothered you," Kit said, her voice cool. She stood, tucked her chair under the table, and hoisted her backpack on her shoulders.

Eleanor looked stricken. She made no move, only watched as Kit left and let the screen door clap behind her. *Too little, too late*, Kit repeated to herself, and she marched away. Eleanor hadn't even gone after her. Again. A trio of hens skittered out of her path.

She was halfway to the cattle guard when something thumped her between the shoulder blades. She stumbled forward and spun around.

"The fuck!" Kit shouted, searching for the thing that had hit her. It was an orange, split and seeping juice.

Eleanor marched down the steps in her house slippers.

"Now listen here, girl," she said, shaking her finger at Kit. "I don't know how you appeared here out of thin air and why you have barely more than the shirt on your back. But I'm not letting you walk away. You can't have come all this way to leave now. I don't know what all's happened to you . . ." More tears. Kit wished for her not to cry. "Well, dammit," Eleanor said. "What's it gonna be?"

Kit toed divots in the dirt. Maybe the Mustang hadn't been found yet, maybe she could drive to Mexico and learn Spanish and raise her baby near the beach somewhere. Or peel off to New Orleans, like Manny had suggested. Things were crooked there, he'd told her, freaks like them would blend. A swell of nausea rose to her throat and she remembered, again, that she could not afford to keep her pride.

"I'm going to have a baby," she said. "I need somewhere to stay for a bit."

"A baby?" Eleanor said. Her fingers fanned open and she looked at Kit's belly, as if she very much wanted to caress it, but instead she fingered the collar of her housecoat. "That's . . . just wonderful, dear! Of course you can stay here. As long as you need." She nudged a tear from the corner of her eye. "I feel a bit sheepish to ask you this, dear," she said and held a trembling hand to her breast. "But, can you remind me of your name?"

Kit shook Eleanor's hand, which was stronger than it looked. "Call me Kit."

Eleanor kept hold of her hand, then drew her toward the front door.

"Kit, why don't I show you around the house."

Kit followed Eleanor back inside. It had been ages since she had been in a home since none of her foster assignments had been a home to her. Looking around properly now, she saw that the place was shabby, but tidy. It felt like a set from a 1940s movie. Florals everywhere, on wallpaper, drapes, and upholstery; cross-stitch pillows and lace draped over the chairbacks.

Eleanor pointed to a few framed photos clustered on the wall above a dresser in the living room.

"Here," she said to Kit. "Who do you think that is?"

In an oval brass frame, a young woman dressed in a fringed flapper dress kicked a long leg high by her ear. Her eyes were defiant, the little black heart of her lips pursed in direct provocation.

"I was a dancer, not very good, but well loved by the gentlemen."

Kit smiled.

"Not *that* kind of a dancer, of course," Eleanor said, hand over heart. "But I was pretty wild; I was lucky to be young in the twenties. Being a woman was just beginning to get interesting."

"Is that your husband?" Kit pointed to a photo of Eleanor in a white skirt suit and a tall, Nordic-looking man in his army best, clutching each other in front of a waterfall, soaking wet.

"My Amos," she said, her voice catching on the sound of his name. "That's us on our wedding day in 'thirty-nine, a few months before he shipped off to France. I was an ancient bride, nearly forty, but we had Emily a year later, my little wartime miracle. Am I boring you with all this?"

"No, no, please. Tell me," Kit said. "I never knew anything about my family."

Eleanor's eyes fogged up again. She cleared her throat. "I'll tell you anything you want to know, dear."

Kit squinted at the next photo, a tiny daguerreotype of a man and a woman in shabby Victorian dress. The man looked too small for his suit, but the woman had a proud beauty, and her cheekbones, high and round, looked like Kit's. To see herself in another's face gave Kit a shock, an alertness. She leaned in, studying this woman, overwhelmed.

"What's her name?" Kit asked.

"Her name was Charlotte. That's my mother—your great-grandmother."

Tears rose to Kit's eyes. She sniffed and blotted her face with her T-shirt.

Eleanor let out a sympathetic laugh. "Oh, dear, oh my goodness, I hope those tears are happy."

Kit's throat was all closed up. She blinked and forced half a smile to show that she was all right.

"And that grumpy fella is your great-grandfather Patrick. Believe it or not, that's their wedding day, November first, 1899. I was born in 1900," she said proudly. "That was the year of the great Galveston hurricane. It killed thousands, bodies floating everywhere, just awful. But somehow, we survived. They said I came out during the eerie silence in the eye of the storm. My mother would say it was because God wanted to hear me cry, but that's a load of bullshit, don't you think? She always insisted my being born in a church, alive and well, in a deadly storm, should have made a believer out of me. But I had never had the imagination to rely on the promise of something I couldn't experience for myself. I go to church to keep social, of course, but no one could convince me that there is anything other than this. Right here, right now."

Kit listened and nodded. She liked the way Eleanor told stories and the music in her voice, the way it swept you along, dipping here, rising there. Kit's voice was raspy and low, a stiff broom on a hard wood floor. There was no music in it.

"So," Kit said. "How is it we're related then?"

Eleanor paused and looked serious, as if removed from the pleasures of her storytelling to a more sober world.

"My only sister, Ruth, was your grandmother."

"My grandmother," Kit repeated.

"Marie's mother, bless her heart."

Kit braced herself against the wall. *Marie.* Her mother's name. It sounded like an exhale in her mind. "Marie? Is she still alive?"

Eleanor shook her head. "I wish I knew. Your mother was always wandering, never checking in. As a child she was disobedient, brilliant, stormy. Taught herself to read before she was five but wouldn't read nothing but comics. She could have been something."

Kit's skin goosed at the phrasing and she remembered her mother's note. *She will be something.* Was that a refrain her mother had been told often? What had she been thinking when she had written it? Eleanor carried on. It seemed like she hadn't spoken or maybe even thought of her niece in a long time.

"She was stuck being raised by your granddaddy, poor thing. Honestly, I feel sorry for the both of them. Lloyd was an old cattleman, as dry and dusty as they come."

"Cattle?" Kit asked. She imagined a great sweeping ranch like the ones she had driven past, with their grand limestone entrances and pastures that seemed to stretch out forever.

"Oh, yes, he bred the last of the longhorns. They were a wild breed, you know, left behind after the Spanish came and ravaged the land and everyone in it. The cattle that remained had to adapt or die. You couldn't kill a longhorn if you tried—heat, pests, disease, predators. They survived it all. That was a long time ago now. They've gone out of fashion because they don't fatten up like the new hybrids do, and because of the spread of their horns, you can't pack them into cattle cars. People need their beef, I suppose."

Kit could scarcely believe these were her people. She strained to imagine herself growing up in a home like that, among beautiful animals, a place with history and purpose, but the girl in her mind had someone else's face.

"Lloyd was a marvelous breeder but he couldn't adapt. Or wouldn't." Eleanor was quiet for a moment. Her eyes switched back and forth as if she were replaying a scene in her mind.

"He was a drinker before the bust, but after? He pretty much pickled himself. Stuck there in that easy chair with a glass in one hand and a ciggie in the other, one leg crossed over the other like it was glued there. I'd go visit and bring food and try to be a good influence on Marie, but boy she wasn't having any of it. She was a cold mystery, your mother. Wither you with a look. Reckless, always sneaking out, running with boys, more a danger to others than to herself, though. Selfish as the devil. I suppose she had to be, after what Ruthie did."

"What do you mean?" Kit asked, feeling like she might not want to hear any more.

"Ruth took her own life," Eleanor said, with a sigh. "Young. I've never met anyone so disappointed in the world. I think she had Marie hoping a child would make her want to live for something. Marie must have been seven or eight when her mother died. Lloyd went broke trying to sell cattle nobody wanted, and then his wife killed herself, and Marie was stuck with him, a failed businessman and a widower. He didn't know how to braid a girl's hair or talk to her about love, and I can't imagine he was any good at helping her understand what had happened to her mother. She got the hell out of there as soon as it was legal."

Kit stayed silent. A great, heavy sadness rolled through her. Was misery her only link to these people? What good could this unborn child know with these genes? Was she condemned to a pained existence like all those who came before her? Kit was terrified of passing down this family gloom.

She closed her eyes and imagined the life inside her. A glowing, orange being, a beating heart. She exhaled. There was a subtle shift within, like the baby was changing position, then a settling. Had she imagined it? But it had been as real as a smile, there one moment, gone the next, leaving only a happy feeling behind. The child, she realized, had chosen to move and seek comfort. True, the little one was a part of her, and made of her, but it was also separate from her, capable, even now, of choice. Her fears receded, and what remained was love. Maybe the world was shit, maybe she couldn't count on anyone, even family. She couldn't change her blood, or her upbringing, or any of the things she had done, but she knew in her heart she would do whatever she could to bring this baby happiness.

CHAPTER SEVENTEEN

WHEN KIT WOKE UP IN A WOODEN TWIN BED WITH WESTERN CHINTZ sheets, she wondered for a minute what motel room she was in and how she'd gotten there. Out of habit, she rolled over and extended her leg to hook over Manny's and nearly slipped out of bed. She could hear chickens grazing outside the window. When she opened her eyes, she saw curtains that matched the sheets she was tangled in. A belly flop feeling hit her as she remembered peeling away without him, the murder in his eyes. Ditching the Mustang once she'd covered enough ground, walking, then running, in a daze before arriving, finally, in Pecan Hollow. She had betrayed him, left him alone to pay for their crimes. He would be outraged, even vengeful. Maybe she deserved to be locked up as much as he did, but it wasn't just about her now.

After the belly flop, relief. Days ago, the idea of leaving Manny had seemed impossible. He had been the clever one, always holding the cards. Even after she decided to leave, she hadn't known how to put a plan into action. There was life with Manny, and beyond that, nothingness. But a plan had unfolded for her. Manny's terrible idea to hold up the BBQ joint had created an opening for her to see him more clearly, as violent and selfish and a threat. And although he had for so long carried her heart in his hands, she had answered the call to something more powerful than her fear of leaving him. Something holy glimmered in her heart. She rested her hand below her belly button and closed her eyes. She repeated her vow to protect her child and whispered a reassurance to them both. *We are safe, little one.*

She lay there long enough to notice the light change around her. The hurt she had felt yesterday on learning that Eleanor could have saved her and didn't was not so heavy as it had been. She was here, at last, with Eleanor, and yet she didn't feel like family, and sure didn't look it either.

Smells of breakfast—hot coffee, sweet baked things, and hickory—lured Kit from the comfort of the bed. She pulled on her jeans and went downstairs, bashful at the intimacy of having slept in this stranger's home. Eleanor stood at the stove, poking a panful of bacon with a fork. Behind her, the table was set for two and already covered in breakfast enough for six—a pitcher of orange juice, a basket of biscuits, butter and jam, sausages and eggs, sunny-side up.

"Sorry, you expecting company?" Kit said and glanced out the window.

"Oh! You're up," Eleanor said. "I hope I didn't wake you. You need your rest, much more than you think. Here." She pulled out a chair for Kit. "Get started without me—I'm putting the last crisp on the bacon, but you might as well dig in while the rest of it's hot!"

"I don't feel right letting you wait on me, ma'am," Kit said, with manners she had rarely been called upon to use.

"Bullshit! For God's sakes, child, you're pregnant, you've been on the road, just set there like I said and let me take care of you."

"At least let me—"

Eleanor shushed her and held the plate of foaming, popping bacon in front of her.

"Subject closed," she said. "Here, take all you can eat. I'm not supposed to touch the stuff." She looked sad, briefly, then held up a finger, remembering something, set the bacon on the table. Kit took a clawful and dropped it on her plate. Eleanor was bent over the sink, drinking out of the faucet.

"Forgot to take my little pill," she said, then turned off the faucet and sat down at the table. Some water had run down her neck and chest, and she wiped it away.

Kit ate as her aunt monitored her every bite, head rising ever so slightly in sync with Kit's fork.

"Is it good?" she asked.

Kit sighed and nodded. It was quite possibly the most elegant, perfectly tuned meal she had ever had. She paused a moment to remember the taste of the biscuit, soft and steaming, with its butter and juicy jam, blackberry maybe. It was heaven in her mouth. Kit was not prone to noticing the nuances of food—she ate, felt better, moved on—but this meal begged for attention. Even the butter was perfect, sweet and bright with salt, just soft enough to spread.

"How did you do this? It's normal food, but it's so, so much better."

"I have this theory," Eleanor said. "If you pay attention, you can tell what a thing is supposed to be—like its destiny, I suppose." She reached into a wire basket of motley eggs, cocoa and cream, speckled and faintest blue. "So, this egg here, it's very particular. And if you heat it too fast, or don't give it enough fat to keep it from sticking, if you undermine it in any way, you prevent it from becoming wonderful. Even if it's good, or very good, you've shortchanged it. I suppose I don't see the point in messing with an egg if I can't help it achieve greatness."

"I would never give so much thought to an egg," Kit said, buffing the yolk off her plate with a bit of biscuit, "but I'm sure as shit glad you do."

Eleanor went over to the sink and plugged it up, then filled it with hot water and a long squeeze of Dawn. She scratched her nose and left a dollop of suds behind.

"You know, I never have been able to cook for one. After Emily was gone, single portions looked so . . . pointless there on the plate. I really don't eat too much anymore. Your stomach shrinks as you get older, like it knows your body demands less and less, and it's this slow cycle of diminishment. I abhor a poor appetite. It has always confused me, and here I am now—I could eat a biscuit and a nice peach and call it a day. So, I cook for two or more and hope someone invites themselves to supper, which they sometimes do. A nice boy named Caleb comes and collects branches, cleans the gutters, odd jobs I used to love to do but can't do well anymore—he stops by sometimes, keeps me company, eats all I've got, and nothing makes me happier."

"Well, that works out then, because I'm always hungry," Kit said.

Eleanor shook her head and smiled at the dishwater. "I just can't believe you walked up to my door," she said softly.

As kind as Eleanor had been, this life was all so new. Kit understood she should be grateful, and she was. She should stay here as long as she was welcome. But it was hard to trust a good thing that was so foreign to her. She was restless and found herself questioning the value of staying still. If she stayed, she could get bored, or stuck with people she didn't like, or worse—she could get caught. Of course, she could get caught on the run, too. And here she had Eleanor to vouch for her, a nice old white lady nobody had reason to doubt. But the thought that made her tearful and determined to stay: a picture of her smiling child hung up on the wall.

KIT THOUGHT OF MANNY THAT night. When all the signs of this new reality dimmed with the lights, and she lay alone, eyes closed, searching for sleep, she missed the warm shape of him in bed, the narcotic effect of his smell. Defiantly, she remembered only the parts she wanted to. His body, the weight of it, against her; his easy laugh and the puckish look in his eyes when they pulled off a proper con; the way he seemed to read her wants before she'd even allowed herself to know them.

Even now it was impossible to imagine not missing him. He had been her only companion, her protector and friend for nearly as long as she could remember. Choosing the right thing for her baby had been easy, but no logic, not even the truth about Manny's character, would cut him out of her heart.

THE NEXT DAY, ELEANOR WASTED no time in orienting Kit to Pecan Hollow and announced they would attend the spaghetti supper that night. Eleanor hoisted herself into her brown and white Chevy pickup, grunting a little when she landed on the bench seat. Kit slid in next to her. Ten minutes into the drive they came to town. Eleanor parked and idled in front of the grocery store and gave Kit the ten-second tour from inside the truck. This was as close to a central square as the little town had: a post office the size of a roomy outhouse, a modest grocery store, Clete's feed store, the police station, and a twenty-four-hour diner. A defunct railroad section split the central square on the bias and disappeared under a paved crossroad.

"That there's where you get your groceries and your sundries," Eleanor said, pointing to the crumbling, windowless stucco building in front of them. "I like to do my own shopping but I might send you out for the odd something or other." She turned and gestured to a dusty barnlike structure that was covered in corrugated aluminum. "I get my chicken feed from Clete. It's usually all right but I check the bag every time because once it came moldy and sickened my whole little brood. If there was someone else in town I'd take my business there, but in a town this small you can't be choosy."

Kit half-listened and rolled her face around the stream of cool air coming from the vents.

Eleanor prattled on, clearly delighted to play tour guide. She pointed her index finger. "There's the police. Not much need for them here, poor things. They're bored to tears. If you ever get the truck stuck in the mud they'll tow you out. Come to think of it, I did have to call them one time when I found one of these druggie boneheads sleeping in my bushes. I think he tried to break in but nodded off before he got very far. Didn't even budge when I lashed his wrists together with zip ties. Cops came pretty quick and hauled him off, still fast asleep."

Kit smiled in acknowledgment of Eleanor tying up a sleeping intruder, but inside, her guts twisted to see how close they were to police.

"Anyway," Eleanor went on and gestured toward a flamboyant 1950s building with a swooping pitched roof. "If you get sick of my cooking—and you won't—right there is the diner. They make a pretty decent Reuben. I go there for lunch sometimes just to get out and see what's what." The diner looked out of place next to the humble, almost impermanent construction of the other buildings.

They got back on the road and in a few minutes arrived at Friends of Jesus Community Church, a one-room steepled chapel with a neighboring outbuilding. The grounds were neatly kept and teeming with people.

"Here we are," Eleanor said. The lot appeared to be full, so she pulled off the road and parked in the grass. "I've been going to this church since I moved here in 'fifty-two. There's other churches nearby but they're all the weirdo sects. The Jehovah's, the Mormons, the Catholics. A little history for you," Eleanor said and leaned across the bench. "And you're not hearing this from me, but *origially* the Friends was founded by a traveling evangelist, Jimmy D. Buckner. Well, everybody loved him until he was caught *fondling* one of his teenage congregants. Tom Sutter—that's our pastor now—he seized his moment and took over for old Jimmy D., who of course left town utterly disgraced. Tom's a decent man, zealous for Jesus with none of those lurid predilections that got Jimmy D. into trouble."

Kit took note of how Eleanor lit up at the mention of scandal. It was not an interest Kit shared, and she wasn't sure how to respond. She got out of the truck and jogged around to help Eleanor, remembering the effort it had taken her to get in. As they made their way across the grass to the buffet, Kit admired the Christmas lights strung out under the canopy of a pair of oak trees. Long picnic tables covered with butcher paper and paper towel rolls. At the far end, a portly, per-spiring man with a warm expression stood over a steaming stockpot. He clacked his tongs like a crab.

"Ellie! Come, come—I'll trade you the first serving for some of the garlic bread I smell."

Eleanor and Kit carried the half dozen sheet pans of her famous garlic-sesame loaves, made from scratch, to the service table.

"That's all right, Tom, we'll wait our turn," Eleanor said, smiling and angling slightly toward Kit. "I want you to meet my great-niece, Kit Walker."

Tom hesitated for a fraction of a second. Then he took her hand with both of his and shook it in a kindly but overly cozy way. "How do, dear? Are you hungry?"

Kit nodded and quarter-smiled. "I could eat."

More people arrived. Kids tumbled out of the truck beds and went straight for the jungle gym; parents yelled out rote warnings to play safe and hurried to get a good spot in line; little old men helped little old ladies from their seats, making a patient, glacial trip across the lawn to a special line for seniors and handicapped. Kit shrugged back against a tree, gravely aware that she did not be-long. As far as she could tell they all looked white and churchy and straitlaced. They seemed to have roles and rules and some kind of a common understanding of the way things were supposed to go. It was like being dropped in the middle of a foster family again, where everyone knew their place but her. Surely none of them had grown up with a string of strange families, or had robbed people from a young age, or hung out with prostitutes.

When she tried to imagine what it would take to be a part of this group of people, let alone enjoy them, she felt even more alone. She had never been a chameleon. And since she didn't know how to blend in, she just had tried to disappear. Here, she would be introduced around, she was attached to Eleanor. She wondered what would be expected of her. Would she have to start going to church, or dressing nice, or laughing at people's jokes? She didn't know how to be anything other than what she was. Rough, suspicious, quick to anger. She feared it wouldn't be long before she did something to let Eleanor down or even get kicked out. And where would she go then?

Eleanor turned back and squinted. "You look ill, are you morning sick?"

"No, just . . ." Kit took a breath and tried to shed the worry for now. "I never went to anything like this."

Pastor Tom looked at his watch and banged the stockpot lid with a spoon.

"Okay, everyone, let's hold hands and say grace."

The whole lot of them, a couple hundred or more, found someone's hand to hold and bowed their heads in prayer.

"Dear, gracious Lord," he said, his tone conversational and close. "We just thank you for bringing us together tonight and for the blessings of food and shelter, and we just pray that we may be humble and serve you justly, O Lord. In Jesus Christ, Amen."

"Amen."

There was a chorus of rowdy hoots from the crowd and people re-formed their line with military responsiveness.

A woman came by with a chicken enchilada casserole and inserted herself in the conversation.

"You're new," she said to Kit, with unnerving interest. She shifted the casserole to her left hip and held out her right hand, palm facing down. "Sugar Faye Prentiss, but you can call me Sugar." She stood nearly a foot taller than Kit and weighed a hundred pounds more. She had cherubic features with spherical chin and cheeks, a beaming complexion, thick blond hair curled and shaped into a halo the width of her shoulders. Kit would later find out she had once been a successful Avon model. A string of handsome modeling checks had bought her a tidy set of ivory teeth, at which Kit stared baldly. Four sons and an absent husband had nearly doubled her catalog measurements and only enhanced her beauty.

Kit touched what was left of her hair, wished she had a hat to cover herself.

"I'm sorry, but I have to ask," Sugar said, leaning in. "What *happened* to all your *hair*? Was it *cancer* or something?" Kit didn't know how long she could stick around for this scrutiny. She could feel Eleanor straining to hear the answer and realized she hadn't told her aunt anything about the events leading up to her arrival, and her aunt had kindly refrained from prodding.

"No," Kit said. "I guess it keeps my head cool."

Sugar threw back her head and laughed, and all the sumptuous parts of her jiggled. "You are *too much*!" She reached over and touched the side of Kit's face; Kit willed herself not to jerk away and wished Eleanor would bail her out. "You're *so tan*," Sugar said. "Lu-cky. Wish I could get some color on me but I'm just pink as a pig!"

Kit knew a backhanded compliment when she heard one. She knew Sugar and probably everyone else here was going wild wondering how this hairless brown girl could be related to Eleanor. People often thought she was Mexican, and maybe she was, blood-wise. Manny had given them some kind of elevated status on account of his blue eyes and charming demeanor. But she didn't know anything more about being Mexican than they did, except what it felt like on the other end of a white person's upturned nose.

"Those are my kids over there," Sugar Faye said, changing the subject. "We were blessed with four healthy boys." She pointed a trim, bubble gum pink nail at a scrum of three blond boys between the ages of six and ten, and a broad-shouldered man with a toddler on his shoulders standing watch. They were lighting Black Cat firecrackers in an anthill, scattering with the explosions, batting ants dispersed in the blast from their arms and legs.

"I don't know how you do it," Eleanor said.

Sugar Faye looked skyward. "Gracious Lord, please bless me again, but this time won't you let it be a girl?" She sighed and gestured with the casserole. "Well, I better get this on the Sterno before the cheese congeals. If you need anything, *anything*, don't hesitate to just give me a ring, easy to remember, triple three quadruple four, everyone in town knows to call me if they need the slightest thing, or just want to, you know, dish and stuff."

She left in a cloud of her sweet perfume. Kit was already exhausted.

"Let's eat before these javelinas beat us to it!" Eleanor said and took her place in line. Kit was hungry, but the line moved fast and in a few minutes it was their turn to take a plastic tray and place setting each and go through the buffet. Kit heaped the orange spaghetti on her plate, and took a stack of garlic bread slices, skipping the wet green beans. In front of them was a thin, young man with tight curls, a crisp white button-down, and new Wrangler jeans. He seemed to be looking for a place to sit.

"Caleb," Eleanor said, touching his shoulder. He startled as if ripped from a daydream.

"Sorry, didn't mean to alarm you," Eleanor said, laughing. "Would you like to sit with us? That is, if you're not already committed to someone else?" She winked at Kit.

"No, ma'am, I'd like that very much," he said, missing Eleanor's innuendo.

Eleanor held out her hand to present Kit. "I'd like you to meet my niece, Kit. She's new in town."

He faltered a moment, surprised, perhaps, at the news that Eleanor had a niece. Blotches appeared on his neck like he'd been slapped.

"Oh, yes," he said, dusting off the nerves. "Caleb. How do you do?" Kit held out her hand to shake, and he took it. His skin was soft and warm and his grip was strong. His face was nice and plain with squinty eyes, as if he could only take in so much of the world at one time. It was a relief to be near someone who seemed like he didn't fit in either.

Eleanor led the way to a nearby table and they all sat down to eat. Kit started shoveling spaghetti in her mouth. It was hot and good. The garlic bread was heaven, sharp-smelling and pillowy. She noticed Caleb's darting glances. When their eyes met, he smiled for the first time and his whole face opened up, making him suddenly handsome when only a moment ago he had been unremarkable.

"How's Vera doing?" Eleanor said, twirling a shock of noodles onto her fork. "Is she well?"

He nodded. "Some days better than others, ma'am, but today her spirits are good." He looked at Kit, a bit fearful, then scanned the crowd, lifting out of his seat. "She's over there by the beanbag toss. You wanna go say hey?"

He pointed to a thin woman in a melon-colored ruffled dress that looked both expensive and tattered. She wore a shawl around her shoulders, though it must have been eighty degrees, and drew long, cheek-swallowing sips from a tall glass.

"Oh, that's all right," Eleanor said, brows arched high above low eyelids. "She looks like she's having a nice moment to herself." Then she pressed on with her introduction. "You and Kit are about the same age, aren't you?"

"Oh, maybe," he said, his eyes fixed on his plate. "I'm eighteen."

"Wonderful," Eleanor said, looking pleased. She adjusted her glasses and peered up at him, smiling eagerly. "Why don't you tell Kit a little about what you kids do around here?"

His blotches deepened. "Oh, I don't get out much," he said, then sat up a little straighter. He shifted and glanced at Kit, quickly as if he might be burned. "I suppose people meet up at the diner late nights and go to the movies in Katy. At least that's what my brother does."

"You're being modest," Eleanor said. "Caleb's in the police academy over in Richmond. Isn't that nice, Kit?"

Kit's heart hiccupped a little at the word *police*. Harmless though he seemed, she was worried he would find her out, hear something about a strange woman on the run.

"I never thought of police work as nice, I guess."

"Kit!" Eleanor scolded.

"No, she's right, ma'am," he said, straightening his shoulders, his voice just sweeping a lower register. "It's a thankless way to make a living, but someone's got to do it."

A stocky man in his forties wearing a beaver skin cowboy hat sat down next to Kit, so close his thigh pressed against hers. She leaned away.

"Who is this pretty thing, Ellie—she your new maid? *Hab-lah Ing-lish usted?*" he said slowly, lips and breath heavy with alcohol. "I'm a fool for that south-of-the-border look."

Kit ground her molars to keep from lashing out.

"New maid? What's wrong with you, Larry? She's my niece."

Kit clutched her utensils and scooted toward Eleanor to get some room. She didn't like the casual way this man tried to make less of her. Caleb wiped his mouth and pushed his tray aside. He pressed himself halfway up to signal he was ready to step in.

"Pardonay-muah for trying to give a compliment," Larry said, not the least bit contrite.

"Oh, shut it," Eleanor said. "You leave us be."

"Look, I'm just trying to say welcome and hello and nice to meet you. Say, señorita, why'd you chop off all your hair?" he said and pinched a tuft at her neck.

Like a sprung trap she twisted his wrist with one hand and held a fork to his ribs with the other. She stared him down; he didn't struggle, but his eyes swung wildly around the area looking for aid.

"Okay there, haha, simmer down," he said nervously. "Fair enough, fair enough."

She twisted harder.

"Ow! Okay, loud and clear. Uncle, *uncle,* I said!" He looked around again, embarrassed. People had stopped eating and watched. Eleanor stifled a smile. Caleb, who had rushed to Kit's side to help, backed away in recognition that he was not needed. When Kit let him go,

Larry slowly stood up and hitched his leg over the bench. He shook out his wrist and walked away, muttering.

Kit pulsed with adrenaline. She was done with all this. The new faces, the names and comments and making nice. She wanted to go home, burrow into her sheets, and sleep for a year. People started talking and eating again.

Caleb approached her, this time with a bandanna, folded and damp, in his outstretched hand. "Here, it's clean," he said.

"Oh," she said, looking herself over. "Am I hurt?"

"No, it's just you got a little spaghetti on your shirt."

Kit saw the pulpy smear of sauce on her gray T-shirt, the noodle sticking to it. She took the bandanna and met Caleb's friendly eyes. There was a loosening, ever so slight, in her chest.

"He shouldn't have talked to you like that," Caleb said, his face pink with outrage. "He's got no right." Kit was too worked up to respond to him, but she appreciated the show of solidarity. Without mentioning it, Caleb walked them back to the truck and helped Eleanor scale the tall step up into the cab.

"Come see us sometime," Eleanor said, and Caleb nodded.

"You're gonna stay awhile?" he asked in Kit's direction. He looked hopeful.

"Awhile," she said, still too stressed to garnish her words. Eleanor cranked on the engine and stuck her arm out the window as a farewell.

THE DARK, QUIET DRIVE BACK to Eleanor's helped to settle Kit's nerves. She wondered if she ought to be ashamed for acting the way she did, but it wasn't her habit to repent. Manny had told her never to apologize, even to him. He had said that if she went around being sorry all the time people would sniff out her weakness and exploit it. But now she was with nice, straight people, people who lived together and stayed put. She tried to give Larry the benefit of the doubt. Maybe the old cowboy was just being friendly. Or maybe he was still a jackass but just an average jackass. Maybe she didn't need to launch a nuclear response when someone bothered her. More than anything, she worried Eleanor would be disappointed in her.

Eleanor broke the silence. "Well, I can tell you one thing. That isn't the last time ol' Larry is gonna put his foot in his mouth," she said. "But he's gonna think twice before doing it with you."

"I guess I didn't have to stick him with a fork," said Kit.

"He had it coming to him," Eleanor said, shaking her head. "He was way out of line."

Kit laughed, grateful that her aunt didn't fault her.

"Apart from Larry," Eleanor said, turning on her high beams as they crossed over the creek, black and glassy in the dark, "what did you think of the supper?"

Kit wished her honest answer were also positive. She didn't want to hurt Eleanor's feelings, but she had nothing good to say. "I just don't get it," Kit said after a while. "Does everyone really enjoy being together all the time? Don't you run out of things to talk about?"

Eleanor laughed. "To be honest, I find the conversation dull mostly—weather, cattle, so-and-so is late on their payments to such-and-such," she said and leaned in, "but the gossip can be pretty juicy."

Kit just shook her head. "Is that why people get together, to talk about each other?"

"Well, kind of," Eleanor said, "but it's more than that. The back-biting is just a fearful way of saying we care, we're interested. Take Caleb's mama, Vera. She drinks too much. Fact all she does is drink. And she blames it on the death of her husband—tragic, really, had a heart attack in the shower and fell and cracked his skull. Coroner said he woulda survived the heart attack, but it was the fall that killed him." She pursed her lips and shook her head. "Anyhow, the drinking got worse after Bud died, but she had always liked getting drunk more than anything, even more than she liked her kids."

"But what's the use in telling me that?" Kit asked. "It's none of my business."

"Well, I'm getting to that. On account of being nosy, people took it upon themselves to look after Caleb and his brother. You know, offer them rides when his mama was too drunk to drive, or give them after-school jobs to keep them out of her hair. Take them to the movies—you know, fill in the gaps."

Kit felt a slap of jealousy at the thought of so many helpers quietly raising those boys. She crossed her arms and held herself.

"Doesn't it drive you nuts, though? People prying into your personal life?"

Eleanor thought for a bit and sighed. "I think we take the good with the bad because no one *really* wants to be alone. People need other people. That's just how it is."

Kit pressed her forehead against the window and gazed out. The moon, just waning, brushed the treetops in its light. They drove through the center of town, everything closed save the diner, with its steeply slanted roof and neon sign that read QUALITY FOOD. COFFEE. PIE. A beacon in the night. The idea of Eleanor had been a beacon to her, guiding her to better times. And she had been right to follow its light. This baby would need someone like her aunt, someone who was excited about flipping a pancake or naming a chicken. Kit probably needed her, too. But the trade-off, all these people stuck to one spot and her stuck right there with them, was overwhelming.

She had felt more alone in that throng of friendly people than she had on the road so many years ago, kicking through tall grasses, trying to find home. With Manny it had been simple, a planet of two. She realized how much he had shielded her from having to deal with others. He always drew the attention his way, turned on his brilliant charm, while she did her job—picking pockets, lifting jewelry—in his shadow.

She imagined raising this child with him, passing down all the little lessons he had taught her, and felt at once a wistfulness for the order of it and ashamed for having nothing better to give her baby. No religion, no manners, no reliable sense of right and wrong. She had been so sure of herself when she drove away from Manny, choosing what had felt like a better path. She had been so focused on the reasons she had to get away from him, she hadn't known how flimsy she would feel without him and the life they had built together. Right or wrong, she missed him now more than ever.

CHAPTER EIGHTEEN

KIT HAD SPENT THE MORNING PICKING DEWBERRIES ALL UP AND down the farm road that led to the ranch house. She picked and picked until she had filled a kitchen-size garbage bag with berries and brought it home to Eleanor for canning. Eleanor had a giant pot of water on the boil and on every flat surface were dozens of mason jars drying on towels.

"Sweet Lord, that's a lot of fruit," her aunt said and peered inside the bag Kit was holding open for her. "I'm gonna need some more jars." She rummaged around the little makeshift desk she had set up on the counter nearest to the telephone and started sketching equations. "Let's see, that's a thirteen-gallon bag and the jars hold a pint each . . ."

"Is it too much?" Kit asked, suddenly worried she had messed up. "I could eat what you don't can, or—"

"No!" Eleanor said. She flapped her hands as if to tamp down any misunderstanding. "It's marvelous! An embarrassment of riches! I'm just tickled. It's just I've never gotten more than a couple gallons. How far down did you go?"

"Oh, I don't know, nearly up to the bridge."

"Up to the bridge? That's a half a mile of pickin'." She shook her head. "You're a little worker bee, aren't you?" Kit was almost embarrassed by the praise and by how much she liked hearing she had done good.

Her contentment was interrupted by a knock and a shrill but musical voice. "Yoo-hooooo!"

Kit opened the door to see Sugar Faye and another woman looking like they were dressed up for a party. Sugar was wearing high-heeled boots and stylish dark jeans that cinched her waist and flared a little where her stomach stressed the zipper. Her slip of a top was the color and texture of pearl. Kit wondered how many people she had to pay to keep something like that clean. The woman beside her looked country next to her cosmopolitan friend, but not for lack of trying. She wore a floppy brown sun hat over her bouffant and a knee-length mustard vest with matching pants that made her look even shorter than she was.

"Howdy, Kit—hey, Eleanor! How do?" Sugar called out.

"I'm still here," said Eleanor drily. "That's good enough for me."

"Praise Jesus," said Sugar. "Kit, this is Beulah Baker." Beulah waved a little wave from the wrist up, jangling her charm bracelet.

"Nice to meetcha," Beulah said. Her voice was high, like her vocal cords hadn't grown up with the rest of her, and there was a sour twist to her smile. There must have been a can of hairspray between the two of them, and the smell reminded Kit of Red.

"Listen," Sugar said. "Beulah and me were going to hang out at my house, maybe go swimming or do makeup. Nothing fancy, just us girls. I thought you might like to join."

Kit couldn't think of anything at that moment that was less appealing to her. It was friendly of them to have come by, but she figured they were just being nice. That, or Eleanor had put them up to it.

"That's okay," she said and gestured toward the canning operation in the kitchen. "I have a bunch of work to do."

Sugar and Beulah glanced at each other.

"Eleanor," Sugar called through the doorway. "You ever let this girl out of the house?"

"I try," Eleanor said, drying her hands on her apron. "She's a hopeless homebody like me."

Beulah turned to Sugar and whispered not very quietly, "See? I told you she wasn't interested—"

"*Shoosh!*" Sugar snapped, then turned a kinder face to Kit. "Now listen, I *won't* take no for an answer. You can't just show up to a bored little town, looking all exotic and *mysterious,* and not let us size you up. I won't have it." She let out a high-pitched tinkle of laughter.

Kit kind of respected her honesty, though she sure didn't like the idea of being a subject of conversation.

"Get outta here, girl," Eleanor said, taking off her apron. She hung it on a nail and crossed over to Kit. "Everyone needs a friend, even you."

Kit was trapped between the women at the door and Eleanor. "But what about the jars?" she asked hopefully. "Don't you need me to pick up some more?"

Eleanor put up a hand. "That's all right, I'll make do just fine. You go be young," she said, smiling.

"Come *on*, Kit," Sugar said and jangled her keys. "Jump in my car, we'll ride together."

Kit was reluctant to go party with strangers. She flashed Eleanor a look that said *save me,* but her aunt did not seem to get the message. They all appeared to be waiting for her answer.

"Okay," Kit finally said. "But I'll drive myself."

Sugar clapped her hands together like a kid at a circus. "Hot dog! There we go."

"Keys are on the hook," Eleanor said and handed her a rolled-up five-dollar bill from her purse. "Here's a little cash," she said with a gleeful spark, "in case you go out honky-tonkin'."

Kit took the money and said thank you. Then she leaned in and whispered to her aunt, "Are you sure you don't need me here?" But Eleanor turned her toward the door and gave her a gentle push.

KIT TOOK THE BROWN AND white pickup and followed Sugar's jacked-up Bronco over the bumpy farm roads until they hit the nice smooth highway that led to the bigger ranches. Sugar signaled the turn and Kit followed her down a short gravel road lined with poplars and around a circular drive. They parked in front of her house, new construction made to look like a lodge with big barky logs. Inside it was king-size with custom everything, a trophy of a home. There was a menagerie of game on the walls and a collection of firearms on display as if to offer proof of who had shot those animals. The living room was three full-size sofas arranged around a curly buffalo pelt rug. It was at once ostentatious and welcoming, intimidating and comfortable. She couldn't help but want to kick off her boots and stretch out on the leather sofa that was draped in throw blankets, large and plush. Kit couldn't fathom how someone went about paying for a place like this.

A towheaded child with Sugar's angelic face toddled down the hall toward his mother.

"Hiiiiii, baby!" she squealed, so loud Kit could feel her inner ears pulse. "Oooh, come to Mama!" The little boy tripped forward into her arms. She held him close and gave him a little squeeze.

"Do you want to hold Nestor, Kit?" Sugar said, eyeing the bump of Kit's stomach.

Nestor was pudgy and cute and had a sticky brown mess around his mouth, but Kit felt no warmth for the boy. She held him out straight-armed, his legs kicking around. She was shocked at how dense and heavy he was for such a small child. The boy arched his back and whined.

"I swear to God," Sugar said, laughing in disbelief. "I never saw a Mexican that wasn't born knowing how to take care of children."

Kit passed Nestor back to Sugar, irritated by the slight. Sugar took a lolly out of her purse, unwrapped it, and let Nestor suckle it while she stroked his hair.

"Yeah," Beulah chimed in. "Haven't you ever been around babies? Didn't you grow up with a million brothers and sisters and cousins and stuff?" She poured cold white wine into glasses.

"I'm not Mexican," Kit said. Of course, she could have been but couldn't say for sure where her father came from. She didn't see the point in claiming that she was or being the subject of Sugar's opinion about how Mexican or not Kit measured up to be.

Sugar rolled her eyes, frustrated at having to clarify. "Salvadorean, Guatemalan, you know what I mean."

Kit stared at her, wishing she could summon Manny's charms. He'd take charge of the conversation without offending, distract with a flattering question and a wink.

Sugar went on. "Now don't give me that look, I mean that in the best way. I learned everything I know about babies from our live-in. I swear, when Robbie Two was born I didn't know which hole to feed and which one to wipe! She is a *goddamn* hero, that woman. Glory? *Glo-dia!*" Sugar said with an accent meant to sound like Spanish. She kept looking in the direction she expected Gloria to come from until a woman in her fifties did, in fact, appear in the hallway, an older boy, about four years old, with his hands in the back pocket of her jeans. "*Mande?*" she said. She looked tired, and scolded the boy lightly in Spanish.

"Gloria, could you tomar el bebé? We're gonna have some grown-up time."

"Sure thing," Gloria said in a crisp American accent that suggested she'd been in the States a long time, if not all her life. Kit thought it sounded a touch defiant, like she wouldn't be put in her place. Nestor, upon seeing Gloria, pushed himself off of Sugar and toddled happily into his nanny's arms.

"I think she loves them as much as she loves her own kids," Sugar said. "Sometimes I think they love her more than me."

"I *know* they love her more than you," Beulah said. She cocked her head and gave a funny look like she was thinking something over.

"So, now, Kit, if you're not a Mexican, what—" Beulah started to ask *What* are *you,* a question Kit had heard enough times to know when it was coming. But Beulah seemed to stop herself and took a vaguer angle. "What's your deal?"

Kit waited for her to clarify.

"Like who's your parents and whatnot?"

Kit still was not sure how to answer this. She let the question hang, awkward as a fart.

"Like . . . well, Eleanor says your mama was her niece. So, what was your daddy?"

Kit flushed. Why were they so obsessed with knowing "what" she was? It was as if they needed to know her race and country of origin so they could calibrate their opinion of her. The ache of missing her mother was familiar, but it stung in a different way to think of her father, especially here, in the company of these prying women. There was nothing, no trace of him to build on. He could be anyone, a king, a criminal, a poet, a nobody. How had he and her mother met? Had he singled her out in a crowded bar? Maybe her mother had made the first move, slipped her number between his fingers at a concert. Maybe they had one wild night together before parting ways. It must have been a casual encounter, but sometimes she let herself think she was born of love.

"I didn't have parents," Kit said.

Sugar slapped her hand to her heart and drew an audible breath. "Ohhhhh, my word, an *orphan*? That's the saddest thing I've ever heard."

"It was fine, I never knew them so . . ."

"Did you grow up in an orphanage?" Beulah asked. "What was it *like*—were they cruel to you?"

Kit was beginning to buckle under the inquiry and the memories it stirred. The dictionary splitting her cheek; the surprise whippings, the taunts; being left in the car while a foster parent ran errands, no matter how hot it was outside, how she'd roll down the window and fight with herself the whole time about which was more trouble, staying or leaving. Loud, long nights in the group home in between placements; kids who sleepwalked and had night terrors, criers and fighters, and the one boy who talked incessantly to silence the voices in his head. All the nights she had gone to bed wishing she wouldn't wake up in the morning. The constant feeling that she was not wanted, that her very existence was a bother. She had never told anyone about growing up in foster care, and she wasn't about to start with these biddies.

"No, nothing like that," Kit said. "You wouldn't think it, but I had a pretty normal childhood."

The two women exchanged a look, like they knew she was holding out.

"If you never knew your folks," Beulah asked pointedly, "how was it then that you got hooked up with Eleanor?"

Kit tightened the muscles between her shoulders. The question sounded like a trap. She knew from running around with Manny that you never told a lie if you didn't have to.

"My social worker told me about her," Kit said plainly. "So, when I was old enough I came looking."

"You just left everything?" Sugar said, gaping a little to show she needed to be convinced. "Your foster family and your life and came here? To *Pecan Hollow*?"

Beulah scowled at her.

"What?" Sugar said. "It's not like it's a *destination*."

"I'd never had family before, not for real," Kit said, and the truth of it moved her to the edge of tears. She muscled back the emotion, determined not to lose it here. Sugar's hand went back to her heart and Beulah puckered her lips into a pout.

"Hey," Beulah said and sniffed. "Are we gonna do makeup or what? I got my niece watching the kids tonight and she is dumber than a cow. I give her till seven p.m. before I have to come home to fix whatever she screwed up tonight."

"You are bad, Beulah."

"I know, I shouldn't."

"All right," Sugar said, "let's party." She slid a thin pink suitcase with a gold clasp out from under the coffee table and opened it up for them. Inside were dozens of peach-colored bottles, compacts, and pencils, all labeled in cursive. Eye shadows, powders, lipsticks, creams. It smelled like vanilla and was so brazenly girlish, Kit began to sweat.

"Oh, this is like candy to me," Beulah said. "I'll have one of everything." She reached out to touch the lipsticks, but Sugar swatted her hand away.

"Don't touch the merchandise unless you really plan to buy it. Any product that gets damaged or used comes out of my pocket. Here, baby," she said, taking Beulah by the chin. "Ima do your colors."

"Actually, Sugar, why don't you let Kit go first, I would looove to see what you would do with her. She's got so much *po-tential.*"

Sugar clapped her hands together. "You don't mind, do you, Kit? A little makeover? I won't make you buy anything, it's just—" She paused to choose her words, pressing her lips together, looking pained. "I don't know, I'm just dying to pretty you up. Will you let me? Please?"

This was no place for her. All of it was wrong; ever since she got to Pecan Hollow she'd been lying and covering up, pretending to smile, faking a laugh, playing by rules she didn't understand. Kit's throat burned with anger toward the two women. On the surface, they were being friendly, but she knew they had brought her here to take her down a peg. She might be a freak and a criminal, but she was nobody's clown. At least she had her own wheels. Kit got up and crossed the buffalo pelt without a word and let herself out the door.

CHAPTER NINETEEN

BY MID-OCTOBER, THE SEASON HAD CHANGED ALMOST OVERNIGHT from constant unbearable heat to a pleasant cool, with occasional rains that scrubbed and crisped the air. At about six months pregnant, Kit was changing, too. Her wooden face softened, her breasts filled out even more, and the roundness of her belly where the baby was now beginning to kick and squirm was impossible to conceal. As Eleanor had warned, people in town started to talk. At first, there were the long stares from the women in line at the store, or the codgers playing cards with palsied hands in front of the diner. She could feel them assessing and theorizing. When she had been so accustomed to invisibility, being the subject of scrutiny embarrassed her, made her feel like she was living someone else's life.

Sugar Fay, having recently announced her own pregnancy, came by regularly with gifts of food and women's magazines and fresh gossip. Despite Kit's hasty exit from the makeup party, Sugar was determined to stay friends. Kit tolerated her presence as an unavoidable fact of life. She thanked Sugar for the gifts, but she did not stick around for the company.

Eleanor sprang to action with the preparations for the baby. She went to town and raised eyebrows with the volume of groceries she bought. She cooked for hours, freezing casseroles, roasting chickens in threes and using the bones for stock that she had Kit drink like tea.

Collards and turnips, black-eyed peas, Virginia ham with biscuits, sticky pecan pie on Sundays. She knew just what to do for Kit's aches and pains, for food aversions and reflux and cramps.

One chilly Saturday, Kit went to fetch the mail and check the newspaper. At the little post office in town, she opened a small locked box and found the day's mail—a Sears catalog, some bills, and a *Reader's Digest*. Then she crossed the old railroad track that cut through town to the diner with its curved glass façade and shark fin awning. There were two newspaper vending machines out front. One for the *Houston Chronicle*, its plastic window yellowed and cloudy, stacked to the brim. The smaller machine next to it, which held the *Weekly Holler*, was empty. Kit had learned from Eleanor that the *Weekly Holler* was basically a circular with ads from local businesses and a forum where people posted birth announcements, death announcements, garage sales, rodeos, lost animals, and even, from time to time, love letters. People weren't so concerned about national or international news. Even the big-city news from Houston was a little too fast-paced and scintillating. The good stuff was homegrown. Everyone got the *Holler*.

She pushed her dime through the slot and pulled out the *Houston Chronicle*, which was triple the size of the local rag. She flipped to the crime section, something she had done every couple of weeks, hoping and dreading she would find news of Manny. The front page was covered with examples of people acting badly. A man shot in a dispute between his teenage daughters; a six-year-old drowned in the Buffalo Bayou by her stepfather; a woman missing seven years found stuffed in a basement freezer. Heinous crimes she could not imagine committing. Whatever wrong she had done, it was nothing by comparison. But, she thought, that's exactly the kind of justification Manny would come up with. She'd heard a million of them over the years: *They're lucky we only robbed them. Nobody got hurt. It's just money, Kitty Cat. Government steals people's money every damn day. Not my fault I figured out an easy way to get rich. Only difference between me and everybody else is I'm willing to take the risk.* She already felt bad about what she'd done, but now that she was straight, she was just as ashamed of how she had let herself believe that their version of stealing wasn't wrong.

Then, as if he had heard her thoughts, his face appeared on the next page. There was Manny in cuffs, looking directly into the camera, being escorted down a stairwell. The photo was small, maybe two inches by three, next to a brief article below the fold, but there was no mistaking him. Even in black and white, she could see the blue in his eyes. Just above it, a headline in small font: ONE OF TEXACO TWOSOME CONVICTED. Her legs weakened.

Kit spread the *Houston Chronicle* over the flat top of the vending machine and read the article. It was a small piece, perhaps an update on others written before.

Manuel Romero, self-described mastermind of the Texaco Twosome robbery duo, was convicted on all counts, including robbery and un-lawful restraint, following his July 4 arrest. He had held a woman at gunpoint while robbing her barbecue stand, the famed Stoker's BBQ, then took her, briefly, as hostage. Her husband and several custom-ers disarmed and restrained him while his accomplice fled the scene.

The arrest follows a string of robberies mainly at filling sta-tions in remote areas. Mr. Romero's signature style gained some notoriety as Austin County police coined the term "Texaco Two-some" to drum up interest in the case. Police are still searching for his female partner, though an accurate description eludes them. One witness stated she had short, buzzed hair and a dark complex-ion. Another, the owners' daughter, insisted her hair was long. Mr. Romero has declined to provide information on her appearance or whereabouts, stating only that she was "the love of [his] life."

Kit's eyes stung and her face felt hot. This was her first glimpse of what had happened after she drove away, and though she'd wondered what had become of Manny these last three and a half months, this dose of information left her wildly confused. On the one hand she was relieved to know he would be in prison. There had always been the chance that he was hunting her down. The part of her that still loved him was moved, even remorseful, to see that he didn't begrudge her, that even though she had bailed on him he would not betray her. But when she reread the article, she detected something almost theatrical about his quote, like he had known she would be reading it. How was she supposed to take this? Manny was rarely straightforward and sincere. Did he think she would be in his debt?

Just then Beulah Baker passed by, following her husband, who was carrying a stack of packages. Kit slapped the paper shut, then nodded at them, tense and barely breathing, afraid she'd been caught.

"Didn't mean to give you a fright!" Beulah said with a child's laugh.

Kit tried to wave her on, pleasantly enough but without any invitation to stay and chat. They made it to their Wagoneer without stopping and her husband unloaded the packages. Beulah waved again as she climbed up into the car and called out, "You have a blessed day, now!"

Once they were good and gone, Kit looked around as if she were being watched. She knew the police would be looking for her, but the witness description of her buzz cut made her furious. Manny had cut her hair to throw people off the scent, but it had only made her more recognizable. Everyone had seen her roll into town, the freak newcomer with no hair. Someone would only have to read the article and give it a moment's thought. They were already so goddamn suspicious of her, it wouldn't take much imagination.

She pumped another dime in the slot, took the whole stack of papers, including the one in the window, and rushed back to Eleanor's truck.

Kit waited until Eleanor was asleep that night before rolling the grill from the shed out to the driveway. She removed the green lid and dumped in the stack of newspapers. Then she struck a match, threw it on the pile, and watched the papers burn.

Kit knew she owed her aunt the truth; it didn't feel right to be lying to her while living under her roof, eating her food, enjoying her company. This was supposed to be a fresh start, and she didn't see a way to move forward without coming clean to Eleanor. And she couldn't stand the idea of her aunt finding out on her own. On the other hand, she was about three months away from having this baby. If Eleanor had a crisis of conscience and turned her in, her baby might be born in prison, or worse, taken from her. She also didn't want to put Eleanor in the position of knowingly harboring a criminal. If anything happened to her aunt because of Kit's mistakes, she would never forgive herself. Maybe she should leave the state. Her hair had grown over an inch since the robbery at Stokers, and she was pregnant. No one would recognize her if she started over someplace new.

But it was too late to leave. She needed Eleanor. The baby needed her. Making sure her baby had a good home was more important than having a clean conscience. She could live with the guilt. She would have to. Someday she could come out and tell Eleanor that she had stolen honest people's money, that she'd been a party to terror. But not today.

So Kit carried the secret like a promise. She would tell Eleanor when she knew her baby would be safe. In the meantime, she worked overtime to be helpful to Eleanor. She dug trenches for a little irrigation system around the thirsty hydrangeas, welded new latches on the front gate, and, when they finally got a string of sunny days after several days of rain, Kit climbed up on top of the house to mend the roof.

"You're mad! You'll kill yourself and that baby, too!" Eleanor scolded her. "I can't watch this, I'm going inside."

Kit laughed as she scaled the ladder easily and seated herself on the roof. "Don't worry, I'll be careful," she yelled after her aunt. Perched up high, going where she shouldn't, felt as natural as sitting in a lawn chair. She had often pried open the attic window at the Machers' and looked at the stars, the hazy lights of Houston to the east, and to the west, darkness.

Within minutes, Eleanor was back outside again, a sloshing pitcher of iced tea in one hand and in the other a telephone, the tail of its cord winding up the steps and in the front door.

"I decided I should be here ready to call 911 in case you fall."

"Look, if the roof caves in on us from the rain, we won't be any better off. Anyway, I feel good. I'm pregnant, not crippled." Kit began pulling nails with the claw of her hammer and scraping the old, brittle scales to the ground.

"I'm just glad I planted that boxwood around the house," Eleanor said. "It'll break your fall."

They were quiet for a bit while Kit pried up shingles and tossed them aside.

She heard Eleanor clear her throat and looked down at her aunt, who was holding a chicken in her lap and stroking its neck. Kit stopped scraping and caught her breath.

"All right," Eleanor said, sounding stern. "I have something to say. I've been thinking about it a lot. I get the feeling that you don't let much in and you don't let much out. But you're gonna have a little one soon, and you've got to start things off on the right foot. If you have something to tell me, then tell me; and if you wanna know something, well, dammit, you gotta ask me. I don't know how long I have to wait before we have an honest conversation here."

Kit had so far successfully avoided discussing anything from her past in detail. She had said that she left a dead-end relationship in search of real family, that her time in foster care had been shitty and she didn't want to talk about it. She had been expecting and dreading the day when her aunt would press her to say more because she did not think she could bring herself to lie to Eleanor. Why would she want to bring such ugliness into this new life? Surely it was best to keep facing forward. She could not change the past, but she could protect today. And Manny. There was no honest explanation she was willing to share. She searched for something that might satisfy Eleanor's curiosity.

"You can tell me," Eleanor said. "I've lived a long time. You can't scare me. Whatever it is. Just let 'er rip."

"I don't know," Kit said. "A lot of it is fuzzy in my memory. I don't like to go back there if I can help it." Eleanor stopped stroking the hen and was very still, listening.

"I remember being hungry all the time. Even when there was food enough, I was hungry. Bottomless. It was the thing that got me up in the morning. 'What am I gonna eat today?'" She kept her eyes on the shingles. It helped to work while she talked; splitting her attention cut the pain in two. She didn't look at her aunt, didn't think she could keep talking if she saw her face.

"Did you have friends? Anyone you could turn to?" Eleanor asked, hopeful.

Kit thought about it. She had had Miss Rhonda. And Red. The only person from her old life who knew she'd gone to Pecan Hollow. Temporary, stand-in mothers, maybe. And, of course, there was Manny, but she could not call him a friend as she understood the word. She shook her head.

"I wasn't very nice to people," Kit said. "They had no reason to like me. It wears on you, being unwanted over and over. First my mother, then the social workers always trying to get me off their hands, then as soon as I was placed it was like the foster parents were just counting down the days. So, I started to act like I didn't care if I stayed or went. And maybe I even did things that would get me sent back to the group home, just to prove how much I didn't care, to prove I knew what I was."

"Knew what you were?"

"Trash," Kit said, something pooling in her chest, a great sadness at the truth of it.

Eleanor shook her head vigorously. "You are no such thing. Just because people did wrong by you doesn't mean you're worthless. You are a gift. To me you are."

Kit wanted to believe her. Eleanor was tearful and seemed sincere.

But when Kit was all swirled up inside like this, it was impossible to take in the good. She stretched her head to the side, her neck so tight she thought the tendons might snap.

Eleanor covered her mouth and widened her eyes, as if considering something for the first time.

"Did they beat you, dear?"

Kit laughed darkly. "Well, sure," she said, surprised at her aunt's innocence. "That was the easy part."

Eleanor gasped and looked over her shoulder at nothing. When she turned her face up at Kit, her features were pinched together. "I wish you wouldn't make light. I couldn't feel more awful about this, I just couldn't."

Kit felt bitter. She didn't pity Eleanor right now, she resented her.

"You know, I could tell you everything and you wouldn't sleep for a week knowing what I've seen and who looked after me. I'm making light of it because it's too ugly to just talk about. Maybe you're right, and I should be shooting straight with you, but I can't fill you in on years of nothing good over a glass of iced tea. It hurts me to talk about it. I don't want to. I start with one story and the whole mess slides out of me."

Eleanor stomped her foot, sending the hen fluttering off her lap.

"For God's sakes would you come down off that roof! You're too far away, I can't talk to you like this." Kit was startled by her anger and said nothing. Eleanor took a breath and let it out. "Listen, I told you I can take it. Whatever it is, you can tell me. But I can respect your need for privacy. If it ever— If you think it would be helpful to you, I hope you'll come and tell me in your own time." She emptied her pockets of chicken scratch and turned them inside out, shaking out the dust. She walked to the front door, head hung low, pensive. Then she stopped and turned up toward Kit. "You know, that stuff will not go away. It will make you sickly and turn to rot. If not me, *somebody*. You have got to tell somebody."

Both women worked off the stress of their conversation in their own realms. Kit patched the roof until dusk. Eleanor holed up in the kitchen and cooked, and from the smells that wafted up from the open windows, Kit guessed they were having pork chops, grits, and greens, a meal Eleanor knew she loved. She didn't want to be cross with her aunt. If only these things came easy to her, sharing and close conversation. She swatted a late-season mosquito on her neck and wiped it on her shirt. She wasn't ready to detail the cruelties she had suffered, and she couldn't imagine feeling otherwise. Eleanor, she hoped, would forgive her that. She gathered the sandy, rubbery shards of roof and wheeled them to the pickup to dump in the morning. She washed her face and hands at the spigot on the side of the house and tidied the short strands of her hair, something she had begun to do as a small gesture of respect to her aunt, and went inside for dinner.

CHAPTER TWENTY

KIT AWOKE ONE MORNING IN JANUARY, DISTURBED BY THE SILENCE. The creaks underfoot echoed as she pressed cautiously down the stairs. When she saw that the kitchen, which had always been lit and full of sounds and smells by 6:00 a.m., was cold and empty, she readied herself for nothing good. As she turned in to the living room, she saw Eleanor slumped unnaturally into the wing of her high back chair with the *Weekly Holler* spread across her lap like a caftan. Kit cried out, turned, and gagged on an odor, sharp and musty. "No, no, no," she said as if she could undo what she was seeing. She knelt and held Eleanor's frigid hand and stroked it, pressed it between her own, which were warm from sleep and rough as bark. But this cold would not lift.

Alone again, she thought with a familiar pang and cried into Eleanor's hand. *Nothing good can last, nothing good belongs to me.* She was ashamed of the selfishness of these thoughts here next to Eleanor, who had been so decent to her. *It's not fair,* she thought. Eleanor would never get a chance to see the baby. Her aunt had so looked forward to the birth, had filled the drawers of the little chest with soft gowns, socks and hats, diapers, and plush animals she had gone all the way to Houston to buy. It would have been a great gift to have help raising her child; but the thing that she mourned was the way it felt to be around her aunt. Eleanor had paid such close attention, had always known when to move in and when to leave a wide perimeter. Wrapped up in the security of her aunt's home and good care, Kit had let down her guard. And now she was back where she had started.

The numbness began to bloom in her middle, pulsing outward, promising to shield her from the pain, so old and deep it was a part of her.

Alone, alone, alone. Wretched and broken and all alone.

Then, as if in reply, she felt a nudge against her bottom rib. *Not for long*, it seemed to say.

PREGNANT AS SHE WAS, IT took Kit ten minutes to get Eleanor up the stairs. She squatted with her back to her aunt and held her wrists in front of her neck, then stood up. Eleanor's body moved strangely, unnaturally loose in places, stiff in others. She took each step deliberately, managing the balance between the load on her front and the one on her back, until she reached the landing. She shuffled down the hall, laid her aunt gently on the bed, sponged and dried her, and dressed her in a coral knit suit. Though Kit had never worn panty hose herself, she knew Eleanor never went anywhere without them. After struggling to stuff her aunt's rigid legs into a gauzy pair of beige stockings, she finally found a pair of knee-highs balled up in the back of the drawer and snaked them on, making sure the snags were facing down.

There was a little makeup still on Eleanor's soft, powdered face, the shadows of her eyebrows, peach liner marking the vague edges of her lips. With a damp rag, Kit dabbed away the colors from hairline to collarbone, and thought her aunt looked beautiful just so. She attempted to wrap a bun on top of her head, but it wouldn't hold, so she brushed the rusty gray hair smooth over her aunt's shoulders. When she was satisfied that Eleanor would be happy enough with how she looked, Kit lay down next to her aunt and rested, surrounded by the flowers on the wall and the plastic tick of the clock, dosing the moments one by one.

THE CORONER SHOWED UP IN a white van with a raised roof and pulled out a gurney. He was large and fit for his age, late fifties, and nearly bald. He had a cigarette in his mouth, said he had to make sure the doorways and stairs were wide enough. Kit pointed him upstairs and stayed by the front door. She wasn't sure she wanted to see Eleanor again.

When he came back down, two officers arrived wearing black, fleecy uniform coats. The older one had a coffee and chuffed white steam as he sipped. The younger took off his cowboy hat and black leather glove and reached out his hand. Kit recognized him as Caleb, the young man with the shy squint who had been so nice to her at the spaghetti supper. They had crossed paths in town on occasion. He would wave or tip his hat, but she always rushed on by. It didn't matter he was only a cop in training; she was uneasy about his getting a good look at her. Today, though, she had called the police herself. She didn't know what was supposed to happen with the body, but she was at least clearheaded enough to know that *not* calling the police would look shady. She hadn't expected Caleb. He looked so friendly and she was so worn out from crying and carrying Eleanor and missing her, so worried about where she would go next, that she shook his hand and noticed a strange desire to be hugged by him.

"Hi, Kit," he said. "I'm so, so sorry about Miz Eleanor. Officer Jackson gave me a heads-up he was coming to take her away and let me come along."

The older cop nodded to Kit, then went upstairs with the coroner. Caleb stayed downstairs.

"How are you doing?" he asked, real sweet, like he genuinely wanted to know.

She shook her head and felt too sad to answer.

He smiled in an understanding way. "It couldn't have been easy on you, finding her there. I was the one who found my daddy."

Kit remembered Eleanor mentioning his father had died. She kept her eyes on him to show she was listening.

"I don't know if you want to hear about this—"

"I do," Kit said. She was glad for a distraction from her grief.

"He fell in the shower," Caleb said. "I heard the sound. He was a big man, and the weight of him coming down on the bathtub . . . well, I don't have to tell you the rest, but it was something awful."

Kit nodded. "Something so awful you couldn't feel it," she said.

"Exactly," he said, and he lit up. "Like I was watching it on a screen, like I wasn't really a part of it."

There was a pause between them. Kit was comforted to hear him put words to a feeling she had had so many times before.

"Was he a good dad then?" Kit asked.

Caleb let out an uneasy chuckle. "Naw," he said. "He was a sonofabitch."

Kit smiled. She had such a peculiar feeling talking to Caleb. At first, she thought there wasn't much to him, just a nice, simple, white-bread kind of guy. But he was also very steady and reassuring, more than she would expect to look at him. And he had been through hard times, too.

The stairs inside groaned under heavy, cautious steps as the men brought down the gurney. When they got to the bottom of the stairs, the coroner released a latch and extended the gurney's wheeled legs. He handed Kit a clipboard with some paperwork and a pen.

"Here's where you release the remains to me," he said, gruff and detached. "You read it through and sign anywhere you see an X. You can say your goodbyes now." He unzipped the body bag just past Eleanor's face. He pulled out another cigarette, offered one to Officer Jackson, and went back to the van to smoke it. Caleb stepped away to allow Kit a moment with Eleanor.

Kit pulled the sides of the body bag open to get a better look at her aunt. Even in the half hour since Kit had last seen Eleanor's body, it had changed. Her spirit was gone. Her eyelids were sunken and her skin had lost the last of its color. There was nothing of her personality left, only the traces of the life she had lived. Kit stroked Eleanor's fine, long hair to feel her again, and still, nothing. It was a hollow goodbye. She wished she could go back to the night before, when Eleanor, in her long, blue flannel nightgown had poked her head in Kit's room and told her to "take out the damn garbage and tie the bag tighty-tight or the mice will be here to stay." Then she had shuffled in her too-big house slippers and dropped a loud fart and laughed at herself all the way back down the stairs.

THE SLEEPY CEMETERY DIRECTOR ALLOWED it, one less digger to pay, though not without chiding her for the late stage of her pregnancy. It was the very least she could do for Eleanor. The orange clay soil was dense and unyielding, and Kit took plenty of breaks to let the little one rest. But her palms were full of blisters by the time the work was done. Perhaps it was better, she reasoned as she cleaved the earth with her shovel, that Eleanor never knew how wicked she had been. Her aunt had died in peace, she hoped, among family, with the happy promise of a new baby. Wasn't that a good thing?

A great many people showed up, some tearful, some not. Pastor Tom spoke a few words and called her Ellie when he said goodbye. Caleb was there and cried when Beulah went up and sang "I'll Fly Away." Her child's voice, which sounded so silly when she spoke, was angelic in song. The service was simple and elegant, the only hiccup being that Sugar Faye, whose pregnancy was on display in a revealing black dress, wept and snorted and blew her nose in a conspicuous show of grief, her sons in the near distance playing tackle tag among the gravestones. Kit thought Eleanor would have gotten a kick out of it.

When the service was over, Kit took up her shovel and covered the coffin with dirt. Each time she dug her shovel in, her chest tight-

ened, her throat twisted like someone was wringing it. Her hands
began to shake, and she rested on a knee to gather strength and calm
the gale that was stirred up inside her. There was no time to grieve.
Her belly was large and heavy in her hips, and the feeling that she had
to pee just never went away. She had to find a place to live before she
was due. Baby would not bide.

Now that her only connection to this place was gone, Kit couldn't
see any use in staying. Six months in Pecan Hollow and she was
still an outsider. She could feel the stares and whispers at her back
whenever she went to town, and the longer she stayed the more she'd
craved the feeling of a fresh start. About a hundred fifty dollars was
all the money she'd saved, but it was enough to buy a bus ticket and
get a cheap room while she looked for work. It wouldn't last long, but
there was surely something for her in Houston. Yardwork, cleaning.

She was so deep in thought, she hadn't noticed the man standing
behind her. When he said hello she nearly took his head off with the
shovel.

The booze-bloated man in a dated blazer with wide lapels held
a hand to his neck and took a long step backward, cleared his throat.

"C. Lewis Vaughn, Esquire, Miss Walker. I was your aunt's at-
torney."

She leaned on the shovel's handle and let him continue while she
waited for her hackles to go down.

"I'm sorry to catch you at a sensitive time, but your aunt requested
her final wishes be delivered to you." He smiled tightly, showing teeth
with coffee stains of deep amber.

"Now?" she said, feeling cornered.

"No time like the present!" He sat down on a nearby bench and
patted the seat next to him. Kit approached but remained standing.
When he took off his hat there was a band of sweat around his head,
stray hairs glued in curls at his temples. He straightened his bolo tie
and read aloud.

This was the first time she had thought about Eleanor's will or anyone else's for that matter. It felt strange to be included in such an official event.

"*The last will and testament of Eleanor* dah dah dah . . . *prepared by* yours truly . . . et cetera et cetera . . . okay, here we go:

"*To my lost and found niece, Kit Walker, in the unlikely event of my death:*

"*As I write, I am, apart from my little heart thingy, enjoying robust and vigorous health. I have no plans to die, nor have I reckoned myself to this possibility. However, should nature overpower me, the following are my sincerest wishes. I leave the whole of my estate, the specifics of which are listed below, to you, Kit. This is not merely a formality for next of kin, but an expression of my love and affection. It is not much but will ensure you and your child will always have a home.*"

A home. Kit walked away, bracing against a heavy emotion. She leaned her head on a tree trunk and felt the bark press into her forehead and belly. She had been so ready to leave and start over. Now this unimaginable gift. If this was real, how could she leave? How could she stay without Eleanor? Kit tried to tell herself Eleanor had wanted this for her; somewhere in her great, broken heart she'd made room for Kit and the baby to be. It was difficult for Kit to let herself feel how much she might have wanted to stay. Inches from her face, a cicada husk, lifelike and paper-thin, clung to the bark. When she tried to blow it off, it quivered but did not let go.

"Miss Walker, if you don't mind," the lawyer said. He looked impatient and barreled ahead with the specifics of Eleanor's estate. These included title to the house and everything in it, the truck and enough savings to cover the remaining house payments for six months or so. "*Please forgive the pesky note on the house. My payments are small but you'll need a job soon to keep them current. I know you'll figure it out.*"

It was too much. She did not deserve it. She needed time to think this over.

Vaughn shook the papers at her and tapped them with a pen to indicate he needed a signature. She hated him for witnessing this moment, so dear to her, so trivial to him. She wiped her tears on the gray wool sleeve of a coat she'd taken from Eleanor. He looked at her with unveiled suspicion.

"Well, I can't say I haven't seen it before, long-lost relatives coming in to butter up old family members."

Kit narrowed her eyes at him. "What's that supposed to mean?"

"It is strange though, isn't it? Nothing to prove you're really family. Nothing to go on but your word?" He picked his teeth graphically with the cap of his pen. "Ellie told me she didn't know a thing about your background and that she wasn't gonna push the issue. Heart of gold, that woman. Worked out pretty nice for you there, don'tcha think?"

Kit was suddenly hot. "Listen, man. I've got a baby coming and I just buried the only family I've got. You think I wanted this to happen?"

His hands went up in self-defense. "Hey, look, people are talking, it's not just me. You show up, take over her house, few months later she's out of the way. You'd be a fool if you didn't see it."

She wished she could knock this turd of a man into a hole and bury him alive. How could they think she had wanted her aunt dead when Eleanor was the only good thing in her life right now? And not just him, apparently people were *talking*. No way in hell could she stay if people suspected her of hurting Eleanor.

"It's always the old, sick ones, with the long-lost relatives? The *lonely* ones, ain't it?"

Kit stuck her head out. She would not let this smarmy beetle of a man cut her down.

"You're a sorry piece of shit for talking to me like that," she said. "Eleanor was a good woman, and she would fire your ass for coming over here on the day of her funeral, making it seem like I wanted this, any of this."

Vaughn was unperturbed. "Well?" He fluttered the papers at her.

Kit didn't even know what day it was. How could she be expected to make this decision right now? She wanted to cry for how much she wished Eleanor were here. She didn't know how to act right or fall in line. She had gotten used to having an ally and had enjoyed her aunt's protection from the people in town. But whatever doubt she had had about Eleanor's intentions, that she was acting out of guilt, Kit knew now that her aunt had wanted her to stay. That her aunt knew Kit's child deserved an address and a mailbox and chickens to tend. Deserved to go to school and make friends and have neighbors that knew her since she was yea high. Deserved to wake up in the same house every morning with enough to eat and with pictures of her goddamn family on the wall. Eleanor was right. This baby deserved everything Kit never had.

Kit was through with running away.

She grabbed the papers and pen from the lawyer and began to sign.

"Well, congratulations, Miz Walker." He chuckled and tucked the will away in his breast pocket. "You done very good for yourself. I expect you'll be putting the house up for sale? Cashing in and going on your way?"

Not that she owed him an answer, but she felt like putting it on the record.

"No sir, I'll be staying here in Pecan Hollow."

PART III

CHAPTER TWENTY-ONE

PECAN HOLLOW, TX, 1990

WHEN KIT AWOKE SHE LAY FACEUP IN THE GRASS, INTERLACING branches of mature pecans above her. She rested there in a daze, at first not sure where she was, letting the pieces fall slowly together. Muddled memories returned to her, less pungent than before. Pork chops and biscuits and Eleanor humming while she cooked. Hard, cold dirt and blisters on her hands; the echo of her voice in an empty house. A fresh spring of grief bubbled up, and she wished she could see Eleanor one more time, wrap her arms around the dough of her back and see the easy benevolence in her gaze. Eat one perfect meal at her table and ask every question she'd never gotten to ask about her mother.

Then the thought of Manny at her door and with it, more memories. Loud sanitary paper and iodine, a scalpel in the shoulder. Barbecue smoke, gun smoke, baby Ray's cries. The hateful look on Manny's face as he lunged against the men who held him. Her heartbeat quickened. She had been terrified that day, scared enough to leave her partner, her whole life behind. She had been certain that the hate she saw would not pass. It was enough to keep her from looking back.

In the time since she left, she had strived to move on and convinced herself she'd succeeded. And with Charlie born so soon after, there wasn't much room to wallow. There was too much heartache in the looking back, so she had trained her sights on the many demands of now. Keeping Charlie fed and clothed, fixing leaks, patching plaster, minding the hens. She had made a certain peace with being alone—she'd been born that way, after all.

But now, having seen him, tenderized somehow and almost sweet, she wished she could see him again. She could smell him in her pores, her hair; the tang of his sweat and spit on her tongue. The throb of wanting him lingered. She found it impossible to untangle the good feelings from the bad: fright from affection, cunning from caring, loathing from attraction. What Kit couldn't understand was why, after all he had done, his touch still rippled through her. Against all her good sense, she wanted him back like a severed hand. An old worry, felt anew: that she might never feel whole without him.

She was ashamed at the thought of how much she had needed Manny, that her need had almost killed her. Like an infant she had been glued to him, desperate when he dropped out of sight. It felt like a betrayal now, thinking of how she had loved Manny when her whole heart should belong to Charlie. Poor Charlie. How nasty Kit had been to her. She wished she hadn't pushed her down or made her feel like she'd done something wrong. Something in her had burst when her two worlds overlapped. She had lashed out at her daughter, but she was only scared. Scared of the Manny she had left behind.

She pushed herself up stiffly. The chickens had retreated to their hutch for the night, but she could hear them clucking. A smudge of moon behind a passing cloud; a line of white egrets nestled on the fence. Something tickled her left leg and she looked down. In the glow of the front porch light, thousands of ants covered a deep oozing gash on her shin. She hopped up, staggered to the hose, and turned it on her leg. The spray blasted the wound clean and started a fresh bleed, red ribbons trailing down with the gush of water. With the ants and blood flushed out, she could see the depth of the wound. About four inches long, it cut through some of the meat on the outside of her shin and nicked the bone. When she bore weight on it, she could see the bare muscle contract and bleed. If she didn't clean and suture it soon, there might be permanent damage.

"Goddamnit," she said aloud and realized she must have hacked her leg while she was raging on the brambles. She went inside to mend herself.

The house was quiet but for the creaks and sounds of Kit limping across the floor. She stopped to listen for Charlie but heard nothing. She mounted the stairs, using the rail to bear her weight, and peeked in Charlie's room. Books, pencils, and garbage littered the floor; her desk was overturned and her chair broken on its side. Kit could hardly blame her. The sheets, which had been peeled back, sat in a pile at the foot of the bed. On the bare mattress, Charlie lay, knees to chest, staring at her mother shamelessly. Too tired to begin to address the state of the room, or the fight that had inspired it, Kit just sighed. Charlie noticed the bloody leg and lifted her head.

"It's fine," Kit said. "I'm about to fix it up." She turned and hopped to the bathroom. Where others might feel a sickening sting, Kit only felt thumping. She pulled out the tin tackle box filled with baggies of gauze, a bottle of alcohol, ointment, bandages, and a pint of bourbon for nerves. She sat on the edge of the tub and laid out her supplies. The leg throbbed; viscous blood covered the slit of bone. Kit doused the wound, the tools, and her hands in alcohol, then threaded a hooked needle she had pinched from Doc's supplies. She took a nip of bourbon and a deep breath.

The door opened and Charlie peered in, a swish of black hair and worried eyes.

"You might as well help me," Kit said, and Charlie sat down beside her. Kit took the alcohol and disinfected Charlie's hands, too. "Here," Kit said, pushing the sides of the gash closed to form a neat line. "Hold this steady while I stitch." Charlie did as she was told, wincing when Kit first pierced the skin. When she was finished suturing, Charlie wrapped the leg in thick, clean gauze. Together they scrubbed the bathroom and wiped away the blood Kit had tracked up the stairs.

After the grisly excitement of their evening, they recessed to the living room and Charlie turned on the TV. A cooling breeze passed through the transom windows. Kit propped her bum leg on a chair and lowered herself next to Charlie on the sagging floral sofa Aunt Eleanor had bought a half a century ago. Sitting there in the dark room, Charlie breathing hotly by her side, Kit looked at her daughter, half his, and knew she should tell her something about this man who had appeared out of thin air. She owed it to her. But to reveal the truth about Manny would be to incriminate herself. One question would lead to another and the whole mess would be laid bare, hideous in the light. How could she explain choosing to live with a man she didn't know, helping him rip people off and living on money that wasn't theirs? The thought of explaining to Charlie where she came from and why Charlie had never met her father brought up a shame that Kit could not stomach.

She pulled her girl closer to her and squeezed so hard, Charlie shrugged her off. Kit didn't know why Manny had come, or how long he would stay. Maybe he was changed, maybe he came in peace. She didn't know how to sort through the mystery of her feelings for him. But there was a warning in the instinct that had overwhelmed her at the sight of him, to protect Charlie, and that's what she resolved to do.

CHAPTER TWENTY-TWO

AFTER HE LEFT KIT'S HOUSE, MANNY WALKED THE HUNDRED YARDS or so to the main farm road renewed. There was a rightness to this moment. How surprised Kit had been, how her throat had pulsed, her pupils gaped wide open. He liked the changes he saw, the funny pageboy hair and the heft in her arms, the toasted color of her skin. She'd been working, hard labor by the looks of it. The smell of it, too. By God's grace he had refrained from pinning her to the door and taking fourteen years of touch in a lump sum. Now, the urge to return to her—to pry her open with questions, to grope her all over—was so acute he felt himself listing forward, as if into a strong gale, to resist it. There would be time for catching up another day; he couldn't rush her. If he was going to stay, he would have to find work—honest work. No mischief to mar the clean surface of his slate. With all these little ranches, someone was bound to need his help. He felt infinite patience surround him and walked toward town. His town. *Their* town.

Far ahead he saw the steeple of a small church reaching above the tops of a cluster of live oak. How fitting. He said a prayer of thanks and continued down his path. At the crest of a small hill, a silvery lump shimmered on the hot asphalt. As he got closer, he could see it was fresh roadkill, a possum turned inside out, its face intact and grinning. *Tough luck*, he thought. He squatted to look at the thing, now a mass of pulp and fur. "Boo!" he said and grimaced back at the stinking creature, overrun with flies. He dragged the possum by its ratty tail and laid it to rest in the grassy ditch.

A paunchy man in his fifties edged the church house path with a weed whacker. He wheezed with exertion and focused so intensely on his task that he didn't see Manny standing in front of him. Manny waited. The man wore a clerical collar on a sleeveless shirt, and when he looked up and saw Manny, he yelled.

"Holy shit!"

Manny hadn't meant to startle the man, but as a boy he had loved to hide behind corners and jump out at people as they passed by. Loved seeing the horror on their faces, the panicked breath, the animal twitch. It was a thrill to see the masks of politeness fall away. Nothing was more honest or lovable than terror. These were the times when he felt closest to them.

Manny chuckled and removed his hat in easy reverence. The man killed the motor.

"Didn't mean to catch you off guard, there, Father."

"You can call me Pastor Tom. How do?" They shook hands. Pastor Tom seemed friendly but circumspect.

"Raised Catholic, Pastor, old habits die hard. My name is Manny Romero."

"How can I help you, sir?" the pastor asked, wiping grass clippings stuck to the sweat on his arms.

"I'm looking to work."

"Okay, where you coming from?" Tom asked. Manny knew most people could sense a lie, and he'd found the more truthful he was, the more people trusted him.

"I just served over a decade in state prison and am hoping for a new start."

"I see," Tom said soberly. He rested his folded hands atop his belly. "What were your crimes?"

"Armed robbery and aggravated assault. Guilty as charged. I'm not proud of what I done, but I served my time and hope to make it up."

"Make it up to who, son?"

Manny laughed humbly. "I guess I don't know yet. There is a girl . . . But I don't think she'll have me."

"You're to reckon with God before any woman or man. Hard work is a good enough place to start. Can you clean?"

"I could make a prison toilet sparkle."

"Are you a drinking man?"

"I was prone, yes. But not since prison. I much prefer a warm woman, to be honest."

"You are honest, I'll say that." Pastor Tom buffed his head with a hankie and seemed to consider the request. Cicadas chattered in the lull between the two men. Manny waited patiently.

"Well, unless there's something else you want to tell me, I'm happy to have you. I can't pay you enough to live on, so you'll need another job, but my wife can feed you. Lord knows I could spare a second helping," he said and swatted his gut. Pastor Tom handed Manny the weed whacker.

"Welcome."

"Thank you, sir. Thank you much." Manny put his hand on Pastor Tom's shoulder. "Pastor Tom, could we pray?"

Surprise verging on alarm colored Tom's face, but he nodded and bowed his head. By initiating a prayer, Manny knew he was encroaching on the pastor's role as spiritual leader. He couldn't help toying with the man's ego, but he made a note to back off until their rapport was more secure. If he could win over the pastor, he'd have the good graces of all of Pecan Hollow.

That Sunday, Manny went to the church and stood outside the open doors, assessing, as always, the exits and variables within. The thin windows of the church house vibrated with the hymns of a motley choir in shiny purple gowns, passably in tune, invigorated by the

Holy Spirit. The pious congregation swayed and clapped, singing by heart a song of Jesus' boundless love. A little girl in big glasses cried into her elbow, confused and overwhelmed by charismatic fervor. Pastor Tom presided with pinched brow, keeping time by patting the side of his thigh as he paced in front of the narrow pulpit. Manny buffed the dust off his boots on the backs of his calves and walked through the doors.

The eyes of the congregation swept across him, and heads turned to consult with their seat mates. He wondered what they must think, these plain country folks, of his striking features, his kingly carriage. He had always savored the way his looks ruffled people like a kind of magic. He tried to connect with Pastor Tom, but the pastor was at the pulpit collecting his thoughts. Manny tucked himself into a pew in the middle of the sanctuary. An elderly couple in front of him craned their heads around and stared, yellow-eyed and unfriendly. When a woman with a starchy-looking beehive saw him sit next to her, she cast an ugly little glare, crimped her purse, and slid her giant rump down the pew.

It occurred to Manny that the woman was giving him berth not out of deference, but out of fear. He scanned the room, hoping this response was an anomaly, but could see from the slant-eyes and pursed mouths that they were all, to a man, suspicious of him. Manny was as shaken by his inability to read the situation as he was by the rejection itself. And in this holy place. He felt compelled to revise their wrong impression of him but was too unnerved. He had had so little experience with rejection, he found it nearly impossible to bear. He opened the hymnal, hot at the neck, not seeing the printed word.

In the middle of the first reading, the double doors opened, letting in a harsh light, and Sandy scurried in with a woman who appeared to be her mother. She looked embarrassed, and her mother trembled. The older woman seemed freshly high. They took seats in the last row of pews, near the aisle. Sandy had pulled her stringy hair back tight, showing pink rows of scalp. She wore what appeared to be a secondhand dress, her nicest one no doubt, which was better suited for a bar than for a church. Her mother had a Sunday hat high on the crown of her head and slightly askew. She stuck her bedroom-slippered feet into the aisle and slumped into a morbid, asthmatic sleep.

Manny ducked out of his pew and went to sit between them, relieved to see a kindly face.

"What are you doing here?" Sandy whispered, delighted.

"I never miss a Sunday service," he said.

She blushed and tucked down her chin. "You sure look nice," she said.

Manny looked over the spandex dress and glitter rubbed across her breasts. "Thanks," he said. When her face sagged a little, he added, as a token, "You too."

The song ended and Pastor Tom raised his hands aloft and people hushed as they waited for the sermon. A teenager stood and ushered a squirmy flock of children to Bible School in the adjacent building. Sandy nestled against Manny and he slipped his hand down the back of her dress. She raised her lips to his ear and whispered humidly, "You're *bad,* Mr. Manny."

Sandy's mother had been snoring arrhythmically since they first sat down, but now she stopped and rolled forward on herself, kind of slithering into the aisle. Sandy called out for her mother and lunged across Manny's lap.

"Sit down," he said. "I'll take care of this." He swiped a short pencil from the pew in front of him and knelt at her mother's side. He sensed the eyes upon him again. He heard one woman shriek, "What's he done to her?" and another shot back, "Oh, you know what's bothering her as much as I do." Pastor Tom called for order. Manny felt the woman's pulse, which was very slow, but steady, and her breath barely perceptible. He'd roused enough people out of dope-induced stupors to know she'd be fine, but it occurred to him to use this unfortunate scene to his advantage. He waved away a few people who had gathered around.

"Please stay back," he said. "This woman's heart has stopped. Someone call an ambulance. I'm gonna try to bring her back." He straddled her, stacked his hands at the base of her sternum, and pressed five times, but not so hard as to wake her. He repositioned, pinched her nose, and breathed into her mouth. He felt her lips move inside his and hoped she didn't wake too soon. The longer she stayed passed out, the better the effect would be when he revived her.

He could hear the murmur rise and fall across the crowd. Prayers and speculations, even tears. Sandy chewed on the end of her braid, whimpering as tears ran down her cheeks. He continued the CPR for three cycles, then four, until finally he heard the woman making sounds and knew it was time. He jabbed the blunt end of the pencil into her ribs, and she shot up as if from a nightmare and howled. The congregants were silent for a moment. Ms. Blanchet panted and swayed. He held her hand gallantly and helped her lie back down. Then Sandy collapsed next to her mother.

"Oh, Mama," she said, weeping, then jumped up and threw her arms around Manny.

Pastor Tom shouted, "Praise God!" and there erupted a vibrant chorus of "Hallelujah!" and "Sweet Jesus!"

"Come up here, son, and let us take a look at you," Pastor Tom said with his arms spread wide.

Manny knew not to take center stage. "Sir," he said, "might I stay by her side till the medics get here? It just doesn't feel right to leave her alone."

Pastor Tom stepped off the dais and strode toward him, embraced him with a great slap on the back. "Bless you, son," he said.

"Only God is responsible and only He deserves your thanks," Manny said loudly enough for the others to hear. Heroism had caught their attention, and humility would secure their loyalty. Country people ate that shit up with a spoon. "I hate to have disrupted the service, now let's all get back to worshipping the Lord."

"Everyone, this is Manuel Romero. He's new in town. I hope

you'll make him feel real welcome." To Manny's deep satisfaction, they all began to clap. They filed past him shaking his hand. Women who had looked upon him as if he were a virulent leper now noticed the blue of his eyes and shyly offered their hands in greeting. Manny thanked God for sending Sandy's mama to his aid.

CHAPTER TWENTY-THREE

KIT SET OUT TO WALKING, UNSURE WHERE SHE WOULD GO BUT COM-
pelled to leave the little house until the shimmy in her legs was gone.
She could feel the hard, black scab on her shin rubbing against her
jeans. It had been two weeks since Manny had shown up and Kit had
managed to avoid him but not the rumors of his heroism at church.
Something about it stank of old Manny, how conveniently he made
such a splash when he rolled into town. Not knowing why he was
there or what he was up to was eating at her like acid.

She had an urge to tear across the fields, faster than her legs could
go. She ended up at Doc's. Doc bumped the door open with her hip,
in her hands a giant lop-eared rabbit.

"I need Warbucks for a bit."

"You wanna get up on that nut?" Doc said, looking like she was
holding in a list of follow-up questions. The rabbit kicked its legs
and twisted, almost slipping out of Doc's grasp. She snatched it
by the loose skin behind its ears. "Baby, if you can catch eem, you
can ride eem," she said. "Throw him some food, whydontcha, while
you're at it."

Kit tried Charlie's alfalfa lure, and Warbucks came right to her,
dipped his head low for a scratch and a nuzzle, and took the halter
without a fight. He didn't make getting on as easy for her. As she
heaved the saddle up over his withers, he skirted away and she nearly

fell over from the forward motion of forty pounds of leather. Once the saddle was on, he blew out his gut to keep her from cinching the girth too tight. She had to canter him on a lead rope and cinch it twice before it fit snug enough that she wouldn't slide right underneath him. She was too short, her hamstrings too tight, to get on him using the stirrup, so she held the reins and saddle horn in one hand and pulled as she swung her right leg up and over. Her seat was still lopsided when he began to buck, more a flirtation than an earnest pitch. She knew that if he had wanted her off, she'd be pasture-bound and breathless in one two-legged kick.

They clopped the asphalt road through town and passed the diner, a few people lit up in the window, no doubt swapping stories about nothing in particular. The smell of fryer grease lingered long after they left the paved road for softer footing. This path ran past the bigger ranches—the Haggertys, the Fultons, and the Kingstons—wealthy folks, oilmen and cattle barons, too big to dwell full-time in Pecan Hollow. Having ridden without incident for some time, she felt emboldened to go faster and urged Warbucks with a squeeze of her thighs. As if he had been waiting for his cue all evening, he reared a little and surged ahead in an instant gallop. The rush of air cooled the damp on her face and neck and under her arms. The speed and the danger of losing her seat frightened her, lashed her attention to the task of staying balanced and hanging on. A fistful of coarse mane in one hand, the horn in the other, she recovered the flailing stirrups with her toes, sank her weight back into her heels, and found herself more secure. As she settled, she sensed the horse unwinding and drumming a steady rhythm.

Up ahead, she saw the chapel. The marquee read BIBLE STUDY 5PM, LED BY MANUEL.

"You gotta be kidding me," she muttered. "It couldn't be."

She pulled back on the reins and strained to peer inside, but she couldn't get close enough on Warbucks without giving herself away. She parked him by the hitching post, a carved statue of Jesus holding out a brass ring. As she approached the multipurpose room, its doors open for a cross-breeze, she heard Manny reading a passage.

"At that point Peter got up the nerve to ask, 'Master, how many times do I forgive a brother or sister who hurts me? Seven?' Jesus replied, 'Seven! Hardly. Try seventy times seven.'"

So it *was* him. Manny, reading stories to the Bible thumpers of Pecan Hollow? Never in her life would she have guessed it. It was unnerving, this change of character, and the quickness to settle in her town. Flagrant even. An affront. But soon, the rounded murmur of his voice, both familiar and, in this context, foreign and out of place, began to have a sedative effect. For a moment, she felt childlike and open. Then she heard a rising chatter and scooting of chairs, signaling the end of the meeting. She rose quietly, crossed over to Warbucks, and started untying his tether.

"When did you get here?" Manny said, suddenly at her side.

She backed up and tripped over the gutter that ran from the side of the building. He reached out to steady her.

"Whoa, there, Kitty Cat!" He held out his hands to show he meant no harm.

She pushed him off. The shame of being discovered scorched her face. He smiled in a doting, parental way, as if Kit could do no wrong. She had melted under that look as a kid, but today it felt condescending. She took two long steps away from him.

"Hey, what are you doing lurking around back here?" he said. "You could have come in, you know." There was a small Bible, feathered with paper notes, sticking out of his pocket.

"I was out for a ride. I didn't know you'd be here." She found it difficult to meet his eyes. "Since when do you read the Bible?"

"Since prison," he said with a little shrug. "First, I read it because I was bored. Then I came to hate it, because it showed me a side of myself I didn't want to see. Now, of course, I treasure it, because I see now that God accepts me just as I am."

She chafed at his bald piousness, not just the fact of it, but the feeling that she didn't know him anymore.

"So you're just clean now or something? No more cons, no more crime?" She got madder as she spoke. "What do you do for money if you're not stealing it out of someone's pocket?"

He smiled and passed over the dig. "Who's this handsome fella?" He approached the horse, knuckles up. Warbucks pushed back and shied away, but Manny gripped him by the bridle and stroked the bow of his neck.

"Leave him," she said.

"Easy, easy there," he said. Warbucks yielded but did not relax.

"Listen, I don't get what you're up to, why you're here," Kit said. "But I don't need you making trouble in my life."

"I'm making trouble?" he said. "You're the one out here spying on me."

He could always turn it back on her. Kit wanted to evaporate. She punched the side of the church and yelled. Warbucks nickered and snatched a spray of weeds by the gutter.

"Don't mess this up for me," she said, ignoring his taunt. "I like my life. I've been just fine here without you." She leaned against the wall and took a breath. "What do you want from me?"

Manny looked down at his boots and kicked up a divot in the grass.

"Look, the last thing I want is to cause you trouble. I spent the last decade praying for you, wishing you good things, feeling sorry for what I did to you."

"Sorry? Ha!" She heard the waver in her voice. "Since when are you sorry for anything?" She wanted to hate him and fear him.

"Kit, I'm here because I want to earn your forgiveness."

Forgiveness. Something in her crumbled at this word.

"Oh, yeah?" she said. "What for?"

"Let me count the ways," he said. "For starters, I blew it that last day. Shouldn't have been drinkin' and going off script. Stupid."

"What was all that about anyway?"

He moved slightly toward her. "Kitty Cat, you really wanna hash this out here? Let's go somewhere and talk."

She shook her head and stepped back. There was too much to atone for. She couldn't shake the image of those two cooks knocked out on the floor or the look of terror on Mrs. Stoker's. He didn't deserve to be here or to see Charlie, whom he hadn't even wanted. She should chew him out, or fight him, but all she could think to do was run. She tugged the loose end of the lead rope and in one swift movement had hoisted herself onto Warbucks's back and was tearing off.

CHAPTER TWENTY-FOUR

IT WAS MOSQUITO HOUR, WHEN THE INSECTS EMERGED IN A LOW-lying fog against the green haze of dusk. The smell of warm moss and manure hung in the humid air. Charlie hurried up the steps and smacked a blood-swollen mosquito at the back of her neck. She felt like she was starving. Since she hit puberty (oh, how she despised the word), she had fits of hunger that came on like a riot.

Charlie opened the refrigerator door and let it clunk against the cabinets—something Kit hated—in pointless protest. Even though they had, in their way, made up after the scuffle in the front yard, Charlie was still sore. That man was the first ever person from Kit's past, the first proof that her mother hadn't just materialized as an adult the same time Charlie was born. She was so thirsty for a story, to know about her mom, that she was tempted to hunt down the man and ask him herself. She supposed Kit loved her, the way a mom has to love a child by definition. But she had a feeling that Kit, like a racehorse prancing in its stall, would bolt if anything released her from that duty.

The fridge was typically sparse. A glass bottle of buttermilk, a filmy packet of bologna, a jar of pickled okra. She emptied the bottle in one long swig, then wrenched open the jar, fished out a spear of okra, and wrapped it in bologna to tide her over while she decided what to do for dinner. She looked for change in the coffee can under the sink and found just enough to eat out.

The stench of bug spray, the hard stuff, hung around her as she approached the diner. After she entered she stood in the blast of air-conditioning for a moment before straddling a swivel chair at the counter and double-checking the coins in her pocket—$3.16. Her old babysitter, Sandy, came by to take her order.

"Oh, hey, Charlie. How you?" she said, looking glad to have company.

"Pretty good. Pretty hungry."

Sandy shimmied the skirt of her uniform down from where it had ridden up at the widest part of her hips and flipped to a fresh page on her notepad. "All right, whatcha having?"

"Can I have a peanut butter malt and a side of buttered toast for three bucks?"

"Sure," Sandy said with a snap of her gum. "What do you say?"

"Puh-leeze." Charlie played along with Sandy's little game. She was a nice person, Sandy. There was a time when she had felt like a big sister, but ever since Charlie had been nine or ten she'd known she was smarter than Sandy, which made her feel sorry for the waitress. Sandy was the kind of person that got pushed around by life and everyone in it. Realizing this about Sandy, Charlie had resolved to always be in charge of herself and never take shit from anyone.

Sandy returned with a stack of buttered toast and a frosty stainless-steel cup. She set the toast in front of Charlie and poured the peanut butter malt into a tall, fluted glass. There was a little malt left in the steel cup, which she held out for Charlie.

"You can have it," Charlie said.

"Aw, ain't you sweet?" Sandy said and downed the melted malt, tapping the side to get the last of the slush. She thumbed the malt from the corners of her mouth. "Wanna know a secret?" She looked around with twinkling eyes. Without waiting for a response, she said, "I'm in love."

Charlie cringed at her openness. She imagined the sorts of guys who could win Sandy's easy heart. A toothless crackhead, maybe, or a horny married man or, more likely, some barely decent-looking trucker passing through town, who would only use her and leave her on his way out. Sandy had left a sizable and diverse population of exes in and around Pecan Hollow, old and young, dozens of truckers, farmers, hired hands. Once she slept with her second cousin on accident and a pair of brothers—not hers—on purpose. Last year she had gone after Bill Marcus after his wife died and, when he broke it off, she went after his fifteen-year-old son. Sadly, Sandy's type was anyone who would pay her attention. Charlie scolded herself for thinking so ill of Sandy, but she knew she was right. She cut her toast into strips and dipped them in the malt.

"Dang, that's a good malt," she said.

Sandy smiled. "I know. I put just a pinch of salt in it. Makes all the difference." She filled the metal cup, left it in the sink, and came back over to Charlie.

"What's he like, or whatever?" Charlie asked, her best attempt at interest. Sandy's fair lashes fluttered, eyes bright.

"I'm not even kidding, he's the hottest guy you have ever seen. He's *real* exotic, and smart as a whip, like he never stops thinkin', you can just *tell*." Sandy drifted for a bit and then reengaged like she'd just remembered something. "Plus, he's a man of God."

"Oh, Christ," Charlie said too quietly for Sandy to hear. It really pissed her off how shitty Sandy's life was. She could give her a lecture about spending less time on boys and more time reading books or learning a skill or something. But maybe the kinder thing was to allow the girl her fantasies.

"You know," Charlie said, wiping her mouth with a paper napkin, "if there were a competition for best malt, you would win first place."

Sandy blushed at the compliment. "Everyone's good at something," she said softly and turned and left Charlie to her meal.

Charlie honed in on her supper. She savored every buttery mouthful of her humble supper, sipped her malt slowly. She had a vague impression that someone had sat next to her but was so engrossed in eating that when the man pressed his hand against her midback she nearly fell off her seat with surprise.

Charlie grabbed the counter to keep from falling. Someone reached out a hand to help her. It was Dirk, the boy she had seen outside Doc's stable. Charlie refused the hand and struggled to right herself.

"Sorry to startle you," he said. Charlie scowled, but Dirk just smiled wider. "Okay if I sit next to you?"

She saw Sandy move away as if to give them room but could feel her watching.

"Free country," Charlie said, hoping she didn't look as embarrassed as she felt, like a cat who had sprung up and failed to land on its feet.

"What are you doing here?" he asked.

"This is pretty much the only place to eat, and I wanted some supper so I came here. Lord," she huffed.

He shook his head in disbelief. "What's it like to get so worked up over nothing all the time, missy?"

The question only made her feel more worked up. It was strange how he was neither bothered nor intimidated by her attitude. She didn't know what to do but pick a fight.

"Why are you so curious about me, wantin' to know every little thing?" she asked. "Do you *like* me or something?" She made it sound like an accusation, but once she asked, she realized she wanted to know the answer. Dirk let the question hang and stirred his coffee.

After a minute, he said, "I don't think I know you well enough to like you."

Charlie felt her stomach drop and tried not to let it show. Dirk went on, "But what little I see makes me want to know more." She let her long hair fall like a curtain between them so she could blush and smile in private.

It was as if her feelings were attached to him by a leash that he could pull in any direction he wanted. She suddenly became aware of herself. Had she bathed today? What did she smell like? She knew she hadn't combed her hair. Looking at her lap she saw a smear of peanut butter malt in the fringe of her jean cutoffs. How could she be such a slob? She unfolded a pointlessly thin paper napkin and tried to cover the spot.

This was new to her. She had noticed boys before, but vaguely and superficially. Tim Pritchard for his blue-green eyes; the Brunell twins for being not-bad-looking and twins; Gil what's-his-name for his shoulder-length hair he kept tucked behind his ears. And even so, the interest was passing and low voltage. With Dirk she felt like a Tesla coil. She liked his looks, but there was something about the way he was, guileless, totally open and curious, that confused and excited her.

They sat in silence for a few minutes while Charlie got over herself and Dirk glanced at the menu.

"I don't know why I bother to look at this thing," he said and slapped the menu shut. "I always order biscuits and gravy."

Charlie still didn't know what to say. Why was she all locked up?

Dirk leaned in. "Say, why do you think Sandy's taking so long to come over here and take my order?" Charlie looked and saw Sandy idly drying a coffee cup, her ear cocked toward the two. Her open demeanor seemed to have soured. He leaned in closer to Charlie's ear, sending a rolling charge down her spine.

"Looks to me like she's eavesdropping."

As if on cue, Sandy came over, still drying the very dry cup, and asked Dirk curtly for his order.

"Biscuits and gravy, and don't be shy with the gravy."

"Ain't you trying to lose weight, Dirkin?" Sandy said, one brow arched.

Dirk smiled a big fake smile back at her. "Drown 'em to hell."

Sandy warmed up his coffee and returned to her station, checking them out through the side of her eyes.

DIRK SET CHARLIE'S BIKE IN the bed of his silver Toyota truck.

"You don't see many foreign cars around here," Charlie said.

Dirk laughed. "Yeah, I get a lotta shit for this one. You'd think I was a communist or something just cause I drive Japanese." He cleared the baggies and beer bottles off the seat; a horse blanket covered coiled springs that had popped through the upholstery underneath. She sat down and took in the wheaty, dust, and diesel smell. She put her feet up on the dash.

"Where to, miss?"

She was glad he asked because she wasn't ready to go home yet. She shrugged.

"I have an idea," he said. She was content to let him lead and lay her head against the seat back, belly full of milkshake and butterflies.

They pulled through a rusting gate and approached a clearing. At the far reach of the headlights was Mockingbird Lake. She tensed. Had she seen this in a horror film? Maybe she shouldn't have gone with him so easily. She glanced around, noting a hunting knife in the caddy by the dash. When he parked at the bank, he got out and left her in the car. She watched him rummage for something in the back of the truck and she took the knife, slipping it down her boot just in case. Just like her mom had taught her.

Dirk left the headlights on, and the moths and night bugs all descended on the area; the catfish could be heard bubbling and grunting over Charley Pride on the radio. He pulled a tube of catfish bait and squeezed the ochre paste out into a capsule the size of a grub. It stank of rot and shit and something else. Liver maybe.

After rinsing his fingers in the shallows, he set two bent-up lawn chairs on the shore and gestured for her to sit. "You first," she said.

Dirk chuckled a little under his breath and gave her a sarcastic salute. He sat and cast his line and held it out to Charlie. "Here, hold this a sec," he said.

She sat down next to him and took the rod.

He shoved his hand in his pocket and pulled out a lighter and a joint.

"What the hell is that?" Charlie asked, though she knew exactly what it was.

The joint between his lips, Dirk mumbled, "It's a marijuana cigarette."

"What do you want that for?" She told herself to shut up and be cool, but she had never been this close to drugs before.

"Welp," he said. "I guess it feels good. So does a hot shower, so does a hamburger, so does sex. Just like those things, it's a nice thing to share with someone. Why, is it weirding you out?"

"I don't know . . . maybe you're just trying to take advantage of me." She wasn't sure she believed that, but she felt the need to push back.

Dirk smiled. He held the flame to the twisted end, took a smooth mouthful, and inhaled, holding it a beat before letting it go. "Whatever, dude," he said.

Charlie reached out to take the joint, but Dirk pulled it back slightly.

"Hey, seriously, no pressure. It's not such a big fucking deal, just another way to relax."

Charlie took the joint from him and tugged a snort of smoke straight into her lungs. She hacked violently. Dirk laughed and collapsed forward, not even trying to hold himself up. The feeling came on almost instantly, like she was being dipped into warm sand, her head airy, a natural grin forming on her face. She swayed (or thought she was swaying) as if to a ballad, and finally found her center. *Oh, this is what he meant*, she thought. *It just feels good.*

"Sure does," Dirk said, and Charlie realized she had spoken out loud. She handed over the joint and Dirk toked, thin-lipped.

"So, what's your story?" he asked through billows of smoke.

"My *story*?"

"I mean, what's the deal, it's just you and your mom, right?" She must have signaled her discomfort with the question because he quickly followed up. "Sorry, I get a little nosy when I'm high. No shame, honest. My dad took off when I was six or something. I didn't mean to make it weird, I was just thinking. People around here talk, you know, how the Walker ladies are a bit of a mystery."

She would not normally indulge such personal questions, but something about the way he asked and the magic running through her body caused the thick wall between her thoughts and her mouth to crumble.

"I don't know," she said between residual coughs. "My mom is pretty stingy on details. I think all her family is gone but she doesn't like to talk about them. I get this feeling like something terrible happened. Maybe I'm afraid to ask. And whoever my dad was was just some guy she went out with when she was younger. She said he was handsome, smart, not much else. Except when I was little, she would say he was the most generous man she had ever met because he let her have me all to herself."

Dirk humphed. "That's sweet. My mom calls my dad a motherfucker." Charlie's explosive laugh blew snot out her nose. Too high to be embarrassed, she wiped her nose with the tail of her shirt.

She was not the only kid in town who didn't know her father, but she might have been the only one who never had a man at home at all. She was glad, at least, she did not have to deal with stepdads and temporary "uncles" like some of the girls she knew. As she sat there close enough to Dirk to feel him breathe, she admitted to herself she wanted him.

Charlie changed the subject. "God, Sandy was being a freak tonight."

"Yeah, she was probably just jealous. We hooked up a while back."

"You did?" Charlie felt weird but laughed to show she didn't care.

"I mean, if we're being honest, who *hasn't* hooked up with her?"

She snarfed and covered her face with her hands, letting the fishing pole fall to the ground. She picked it up again and jerked on the line. "Poor Sandy."

"I shouldn't poke fun, because it's really sad. Her mom's a junkie, her dad never came around. She's just this bottomless pit and she fills it with"—he paused as if searching for the right word—"with dicks!" They both laughed like high people, helplessly.

"You're horrible. Now I know how you talk about women, we'll never be an item," she said, a flirty smile on her lips.

"Who said anything about being an item?" he said, grinning right back at her.

Charlie found herself studying the broad yoke of his shoulders built for bearing heavy loads; the haze of blond stubble across his cheeks and chin; his hands, nearly twice the breadth of hers. She wanted to prod and squeeze him to know his density and the feel of his skin. She had to stop herself from handling the firm fatty layer around his middle. A force drew her toward him, not just curiosity or attraction, something more like appetite. She settled into her seat, jerking the line from time to time, not caring that the fish weren't biting.

CHAPTER TWENTY-FIVE

KIT APPROACHED THE HOUSE ONLY HALF-SETTLED AND UNSURE how she would talk to Charlie. It was past dinnertime and her daughter might be worried or, more likely, pissed. The kitchen light was on. There was a mess of bologna and an open jar of okra on the counter. She noted the stillness in the house at once and hollered up the stairs. No response. She checked Charlie's room, but it was empty. Downstairs, she found a note on the kitchen counter.

Out. —Ch.

"Spell out your goddamn name, girl," Kit said, crumpling the paper in her hand. Even the handwriting—hard strokes of sloppy print—had a bad attitude. Kit wondered where Charlie would have gone. She didn't have any friends, really. Charlie was too headstrong, wouldn't share, and took her feelings out on others. She could make friends sometimes, but she could not keep them.

Kit thought about the people she'd seen Charlie with lately, and then remembered the look on that Jim Dirkin's face when Charlie was flirting with him at Doc's. An uneasy chill crept over her. He was far too old, seventeen, eighteen maybe. And he had a past. She had played dumb with Charlie but had known exactly who he was. Two years ago, Dirk had been dropping acid with some friends behind the

Truxtop and one of them had freaked out and run for a quarter mile down the interstate until she got run over by a dozy trucker. She had lived, but barely, and had a feeding tube, and her family had to move to Houston to be near the hospital. Since he had given her the drugs, her parents blamed him.

Kit had about five different reasons to kick some ass tonight, but she only needed one.

THE ORCHARD TRAILER COMMUNITY HOUSED fifty-odd trailers on twenty-five acres of mushy clay. Kit nearly sank her back wheels in a patch of deep mud and just barely finessed her way out. She left her truck at the chain fence entrance and let herself in.

A man in a fake lizard cowboy hat stopped her. "What are you doing here, miss?" he said.

Kit considered whether to blow him off or make nice. Though it pained her, she figured things would go more quickly if she tried the latter.

"I'm here to fetch my daughter, Charlotte. I think she's over at Mrs. Dirkin's place."

The man seemed bothered but pointed to the other end of the park. "Corner trailer, back row." Kit nodded in thanks and moved quickly.

She barged into the double-wide, using far too much force to pull open the flimsy screen door, causing it to smack the outside of the trailer. Dirk's mother was frying sausage patties at the kitchenette stove, a cigarette between her teeth and spiky curlers in her hair.

"Where's my daughter?" Kit said.

"Get out of my house, you maniac," his mother snarled, waving her spatula. Kit blew past her to the closed door in back. She tried the bedroom door—stuck—and kicked it in, the cheap lock easily giving way.

Nothing but a twist of dingy sheets, a stack of books, and an anemic mutt who acknowledged the intrusion with a lazy growl. Just then, from behind her, Kit heard the unmistakable *chk-CHK* of a pump-action shotgun.

"Here's another idea," said Mrs. Dirkin. "You take your sorry ass out of here, and I won't shoot you in the puss." With the gun on her, Kit cooled off enough to understand the woman was serious.

"Goddamnit," she grumbled and backed out of the trailer.

Mrs. Dirkin flicked her ciggie out and locked the door behind her.

Kit wove through the trailer homes, sick from waning adrenaline, a numbness starting its crawl from her belly outward. She wanted to hurt someone, but the truth was, she was scared. Scared of losing Charlie, of being left behind, of the sucking cold and blue that followed her around so much of her life.

KIT DROVE HER TIRES HOT, twenty miles out full speed. When she reached the county line, she parked and let her engine idle. Afraid if she crossed it she'd never come back, she turned around and sped home. She did this over and over until her tank ran low, like a manic dog running laps in a pen. Halfway home she heard a twangy country song and saw the neon blue sign of the Roll-In honky-tonk.

Kit parked and stepped inside the dim and smoky bar. She edged her way through a moderate crowd, looking through randy bikers and cowboys like they were made of glass. She found a stool and ordered a shot of tequila and a chaser. She took them both down in seconds. With a swirl of her finger, she signaled the bartender for another round. A cowboy slid up next to her.

"Next round is on me," he said and threw down a twenty.

Without looking, she said, "That's okay, I got it."

"I insist," he said, a courtly hand laid over his heart.

Kit glanced up. He was cocky, pretty, and lean. She could tell by the heavy calluses on his palms that the cowboy getup wasn't just for show. *What the hell,* she thought.

"Bulls?" she asked.

"Broncs," he said. "Name's Trip."

"Kit."

"Pleasure," he said, his green eyes lively.

Bartender pushed two tequilas and two beers in front of them. They clinked and drank.

"How come you look so cranky?" He dipped his finger in the shot glass and sucked on it.

"Excuse me?" She was already beginning to regret giving this guy an opening.

"No offense, but you just look like you've got a lot on your mind. Thought you might like to tell someone about it . . ."

"Oh, like you?" she said. The warm feel of her drink was pouring into her lips, cheeks, thighs.

Trip shrugged.

Kit polished off her beer. She held the brown bottle up to her eyes and saw the bar swirl through the thick glass. She rolled the bottle toward Trip.

"You really wanna know, huh?"

"Yes'm."

"When I was younger I got into some trouble with a fella."

"What kind of trouble?" he asked.

"None of your business," she said, though there was a sliver of her that wanted to tell all, broadcast every detail and be done with it. Untold, her crimes were no less shameful, but they were contained. She couldn't just stop now and confess to this guy, some accidental priest, and set in motion the undoing of her constant, diligent silence.

"Was he an ex?" he asked.

"Never really thought of it that way," she said. Was there a name for what Manny was to her? "I guess you could say that. Anyhow, I thought I'd left him behind, but he's come back."

"Well, shit." Trip rested his chin on his hand sympathetically. Even though she thought she was finished talking, Kit noticed her mouth kept moving.

"On top of that," she said, "my thirteen-year-old daughter is probably fucking some inbreed under a bridge right now."

Trip said nothing and pulled at his beer. "Well," he said after a while. "Should we go kick his ass?"

This was the right thing to say. She felt a surge of beer-driven camaraderie.

"Ha! If I knew where he was I'd say yes." Her voice belted out louder than she intended. She could feel herself unwinding too fast, like the spool of a kite caught up in a strong wind.

"His mama put a shotgun on me and drove me out. He'd be hog food by now if I could find him." She laughed loosely and realized she hadn't heard the sound in a long time. She thought of Charlie. *Poor child,* she thought. *Born to a mama who never laughs.*

Kit felt swimmy all of a sudden. She flushed pink and began to fan herself. She was overheating and fully drunk.

"Fresh air?" Trip offered.

"God yes." Kit scooted off the stool and went outside fast as she could get there.

A drowsy country song plucked away in the background as Kit cooled off and Trip lit a smoke. He pulled her by the arm and began to dance real slow. She laughed and complied stiffly before falling in step with him. *A mama who doesn't dance.*

He nuzzled her neck and tugged her close. He kissed her. Maybe it was the alcohol, but his touch did not burn. She felt sexy in a drunk, loose-limbed way and kissed back. This closeness felt so sweet, she wondered why she couldn't have it all the time. There had been only three since Manny, all one-night stands, all drunk and anonymous and far from home. She would not want the blowback of sleeping with someone from Pecan Hollow, someone she would have to see again, talk to, someone who might ask questions she didn't want to answer.

They swayed together, kissing more hungrily. Then Trip clutched her ass with both hands and lifted her up. She wrapped her legs around his waist. He walked her to the back of his truck and set her down on the open gate.

Kit pulled away. She didn't want to just screw in a dark parking lot.

"Oh, I don't think so," she said.

"No?" he said, nibbling her collarbone.

"I have to go," she said, less forcefully. She did want him, just not here.

"Aw, stay a little while," he cooed and kissed her more gently.

Kit surrendered to the warm feeling of being with him. She kissed his neck and squeezed him with her thighs. As she did, she sensed something change in Trip. His movements stopped responding to hers and started to follow their own rough rhythm. He dragged his teeth on her bottom lip and bit down. She tasted blood.

"Hey! Watch it!"

"It's just a little love bite," he mumbled. He groped her hungrily, and Kit stiffened, pushing back.

Trip ripped her snap-button shirt wide open and grabbed her breast like a cut of meat. Kit began to thrash.

"Relax, baby . . ." He sounded like he was breaking a yearling.

"No! NO!! Stop it!" She scanned what little she could see from the bed of the truck and saw no one, heard nothing but the music, now blaring some shit-kicking AC/DC song that drowned out her voice.

Trip tugged his jeans down in front and pushed her farther back in the bed of the truck. He pinned one of her wrists down with one knee and the other with his hand. With his free hand he yanked at her jeans. She tried to knee him, but his cowboy thighs, forged by clinging to bucking horses, were too strong to pry open. She screamed again, this time not for help. It was that old feeling of being held down, forced to fight when she wanted to be loved. Something surged through her bones and reared up, stronger, and she knew. She could win this fight.

She spotted a crowbar by the spare tire. She pulled a deep breath between screams and the numb feeling took over. She waited for her moment. Soon, he let one hand free to pull her jeans past her knees. She reached for the crowbar but it was too far. She pulled his head toward her and crunched down on the cartilage of his nose. Trip howled and drew his arm back to punch her, but she kneed him in the groin. He curled and fell over. Kit pulled up her jeans, knelt over him, and slugged him in the face. Blood gushed out his nose and into his ears. She pounded him again and then kicked him in the ribs.

She grabbed the crowbar in case there was any fight left in him and hovered over the unmoving body. Then, from behind, someone circled her waist and wrenched the weapon from her. She flailed, confused and weakened from the beating. Far off, she heard a familiar voice but could not understand the words. The man put her down and turned her, and she saw that it was Caleb, his face lit blue by the neon light of the Roll-In sign. Her legs gave out, so she sat down, and he sat next to her.

"Hey, hey there, c'mon now . . ." He put an arm around her shoulder tentatively, and when she did not shrug it off, he pulled her gently to him. She inched toward him in notches, until, amid the stench of the dumpster and the greased-up asphalt, his own smell of milk soap drew her near and to her great surprise she began to weep.

Caleb swaddled her in his arms. Kit's cries slowed down and she began to breathe. It was a strange sensation, to be held like this, and she felt suddenly young and small. There was a great throbbing inside, and if she didn't know better she might say that her wounds were beginning to hurt. As soon as she had the thought, the throbbing went away. She touched her lip where Trip had bitten her and looked at the blood.

"Kit, did he . . ." He looked up at the charcoal sky. "Did he get to you?"

She took a minute to understand his question. "Uh . . . no," she said, when she realized he was asking if the cowboy had raped her. Seeing her pants undone, she fastened them. "No, I don't think so."

He looked over at the battered man, who was beginning to groan.

"Well, you sure got to him," he said. "He's probably been trampled by two-ton bulls that didn't mark him up like that."

Caleb gingerly moved her off him and went to the battered cowboy. Kit shuddered at the loss of warmth and wished he wouldn't go. He checked the man's pulse at the jugular, slipped a money clip from the man's front pocket, and angled his ID toward the neon light.

"Trip Kendrick. Figures. This fool makes trouble every time he rides into town." He radioed an EMT from the police car with a casual authority not typical of Caleb, which tickled something in Kit, some primitive need to know that she was in able hands.

"He okay?" she asked.

"Oh, sure," Caleb said. "Don't you worry about him. You gotta go to the hospital, too, you know."

"Hell no," she said and struggled to get off the ground, using the bumper of a car to pull herself up, and walked toward her truck.

"I'm not going and you're not making me," she insisted. If she did go to the hospital, she would have to suffer the indignities of a rape kit, the paper gown, the countless explanations that no, it really didn't hurt, *nothing* did. The puzzled and helpless looks as they discharged her without fixing a goddamn thing.

"Can you be reasonable, please? You're hurt," he said, imploring her to agree to get checked out.

"I'm not hurt," she said, leaning against the car. "It's nothing."

His demeanor shifted in recognition. "Kit, sometimes when you've been through something really awful, your body kind of shuts down. You know, you don't feel pain so you can get out of trouble quick. It's a useful thing," he said. "But the pain always comes, sooner or later." She felt embarrassed at this, like he was saying something true, something for which she had no response. She didn't like to think about the pain, waiting in the wings for its moment to return. It was nice to see him worried for her, but she had been to enough hospitals over the years to know going to one now would only make things worse.

"You think they're gonna put me in a nice room, tuck me into bed, and ask me how I feel? Shit, they're just gonna throw me in the hallway with all the other people who look like me, make me wait seven hours just to slap on a Band-Aid, and send me on my way."

He pinched his brow at her, like he couldn't believe her but didn't want to argue. Then he sighed loudly and said, "I'm going to at least stay with you for a bit."

Kit relaxed a little at this. "Can you patch me up before Charlie gets back?" She could still taste iron from where Trip had bitten her lip, and her knuckles were split from the punching.

"I can take care of you," he said, and Kit was surprised when he didn't blush but held her in his gaze. She nodded and hobbled slowly toward the passenger seat with Caleb close enough to touch.

An ashy light began to show as Caleb pulled up the gravel drive to his house. A giant orange tabby left his bed in the azaleas to greet them, wove between his owner's legs. Caleb shooed him off and walked around to Kit. He offered an arm to help her out of the car, but she refused, hoisted herself forward, and stiff-legged, made her way to his door. He went in ahead of her and clattered around in a cabinet for his first aid supplies, laid them out on a tray lined with a clean towel. She lingered at the doorway, waiting for direction.

"Your house is neat as shit," she said and could hear from the fatty sound of her voice that she was still drunk. "Where am I supposed to sit? I'm filthy." He held his hand out to her.

"Sit here," he said and led her to the taut and tidy couch. She collapsed onto it and he lifted her feet and propped up her head with a pillow. Caleb gloved his hands and loaded a cotton ball with alcohol. She blinked her eyes against the fumes. As he dabbed the oozy cuts on her lips, he seemed to maintain a clinical distance. His face calm, removed. His touch careful and efficient. But Kit could tell by the blush across his neck that he was embarrassed, or enlivened, by their closeness. When he was finished, he handed her a glass of water. She drank it all at once, coughing at the last gulp.

"I have to test you for a concussion now." He shone a penlight in her eyes. "What's your name?"

"Tom Selleck."

A hedging laugh. "Do you feel nauseated?"

"No."

"That's good," he said. "Can you hold out your arms and touch your fingers to your nose?"

She reached out straight and as she touched her nose she snarfed, a spasm of a laugh.

"I don't think I've ever heard you laugh before," he said. He looked guarded, but amused.

"Sorry," she said and covered a smile.

"Now I know there's something wrong with you," he jabbed. She smiled again, this time letting it show.

He exhaled deeply. "Well, should I take you home?" The thin morning sun shone through the curtains, lighting up his face. Kit nodded. Caleb headed to the door, but Kit stopped him.

"Hey." She reached toward him for a lift off the sofa. He took her hand—those pretty nails of his—and helped her to stand.

"You saved a life today," she said and clapped him on the back. "I was gonna kill that motherfucker." He smoothed back his hair, the creases gone from his brow, and for a moment they shared a smile, uncomplicated, between two people who might be friends.

CHAPTER TWENTY-SIX

CHARLIE AWOKE IN THE BACK OF A TRUCK TO THE NASAL *crick-crack* of egrets on the lake. The weed had knocked her out and she had fallen asleep next to Dirk, who was sighing peacefully, an arm thrown over his eyes. Dew had glazed the truck and everything in it, soaked her clothes and shoes. She pushed herself up, careful not to jostle Dirk, and looked for something to drink. She was thirsty as hell. Nothing in the back, nothing in the cab. She could wake Dirk up and ask him to take her to the gas station for a Coke, but she was feeling funny about having spent the night with him. Not that she thought he had done anything to her, it was just that she had never slept with anyone like that, no one but her mom. She didn't know what he would expect of her, or what he thought it meant that she had gotten high and slept with him—*next to* him.

She lifted her bike by the handlebar and lowered it off the side of the truck to the ground. She sat on the edge and hopped off, the truck swaying a little with the shift in weight. Dirk snoozed on. The grass was thick for riding, so she walked the bike until there was road enough to ride into town.

When she got to the gas station, she left her bike out front and threw open the door. She didn't have a cent on her, but grabbed a bottle from the fridge anyway and walked it up to the register. There was Wanda at her post behind the counter, watching the news on a little black-and-white set mounted on the wall; to her right, gathered beside the coffeepot, were Beulah Baker and the man who had come calling a couple weeks back. The man who had thrown her mom into a frenzy. She hadn't gotten a good look at him before, but here in the white fluorescent light he was striking. Beulah must have thought so, too. She stood on one leg, the other hitched up, her foot wrapped coyly around her ankle. She wore head-to-toe spandex with little Velcro weights strapped to her wrists and ankles.

"I can't *tell* you how impressed I was with your take on Samson and Delilah," she said to the man. "I don't think I've ever heard it told so . . . *sensual*. You make the Bible positively *thrilling*."

"It's not me," Manny said. "It's in the scripture. The Good Book is only boring for people who lack imagination."

Charlie marveled at his smoothness. She laughed at Beulah twirling her hair and biting her lip, her leotard riding up in the back. Beulah tugged it down with a swipe of her thumb.

"Now where are you off to looking so fit?" Manny asked, tugging the pink strap at her shoulder.

"Oh, I'm fixin' to go to Jazzercise? Over in Waller?"

"Is that right?" he said, eyes locked on Beulah like she was fascinating beyond belief. Charlie couldn't decide whether this was the most odious or the most hilarious conversation she had ever witnessed.

"Well, I just *have* to exercise, I'm too fond of my chips and queso!" She slapped him on the shoulder to punctuate her joke. "Anyhoo, much as I'd like to stay and chat . . . I better not be late."

"Not on account of me," he said. She squinted, like what he had said was too cute.

"Well, bye then," she said, sweet as corn syrup.

The man nodded farewell, and Beulah sashayed down the snack aisle in her white high-tops, a secret smile on her face until she saw Charlie. "What are you looking at, missy?" she said in a nasty way. Charlie waited till she had turned and left before she mimed gagging herself in Beulah's direction. Ever since the pencil incident, Beulah and her crew, the well-to-do ladies of Pecan Hollow, went out of their way to be rude to Charlie. Not that she had ever been in their good favor, but now they openly scowled.

Wanda wiped down the cash register with a spray bottle of Windex and a rag. She wore an oversize T-shirt and shorts with big pockets. The gray hair she parted down the middle was in dire need of a comb.

"Say, Wanda," Charlie said, sidling up to the counter all casual-like. "I left my money at home. How's about you let me drink a Coke now and pay for it later?"

"You're fulla shit, Walker. I got no Cokes for beggars."

Charlie huffed. "Come on! I'll ride right back and pay you once I find some money at my house. Just this once, man. I'm thirsty."

"Go home and drink something at your house then," said Wanda, who was perpetually crabby. "I'm not giving nothing out for free." She even drew back the "leave a penny, take a penny" saucer in case Charlie was inclined to avail herself of it.

"I'm sick of that nasty well water, I just want a Coke. Come on, Wanda."

Wanda wasn't having it. She folded her big arms on top of her stomach and set her bottom lip to show she would not budge. Charlie was too thirsty to keep pressing. She might as well ride home and drink the stinking well water. Maybe a miracle had happened and her mom had picked up a liter of Big Red or something.

"Bye, Wanda, I'll remember your kindness next time you need a favor from me!" Charlie said as she walked out the door. Wanda flipped her off.

She was astride her bike and ready to head home, to face whatever shitstorm awaited her, when the handsome man came out after her.

"Hey, you're Kit's girl, right?" the man said, a few feet behind her. She turned to face him. He seemed taller now that he stood so close to her. Beautiful, if beautiful had been chewed up, spit out, and sun-dried. And his eyes, boy, did they shine. He unwrapped a lemon candy and popped it in his mouth.

"Yeah, you came by the other day," she said. "I remember."

"Manny," he said, holding out a hand to shake. "I think I glimpsed you in the window. You're the spitting image of your mother."

She felt she owed it to him to be pleasant, but something about meeting a man she didn't know outside a gas station gave her pause. He must have seen her hesitate because he withdrew his hand. Then he reached behind him and pulled a pair of Cokes out of his back pockets.

"Did you buy those?" she asked.

He shook his head no and smiled, with mischief on his eyebrows.

"Well, shit," she said. "You really didn't have to do that."

"It was the principle of the thing," he said. "She was being unreasonable."

Charlie laughed. "You've got a funny set of principles." She thought her comment was fair, but Manny withdrew his head and made a face as if snubbed. Did he really think he was doing the right thing by stealing?

She remembered her rasping thirst and felt she couldn't get the drink down her throat quick enough. The sweet, cold liquid flooded her mouth, fizzing into her nostrils. She pinched her nose and scrunched her face, then drank again.

"You're welcome," he said.

"Shit, sorry, thanks," she said, wiping her mouth with the back of her arm. "Nice of you."

He flipped the top off his bottle and held it out to toast.

"To getting what you want," he said.

She tipped her bottle toward him without touching. She was inclined to interview the guy and find out why Kit was so sore at him, why he'd shown up out of the blue.

"Say, none of my business, but aren't you a little young to be riding around early morning by yourself?"

"Is thirteen too young?" she said, a little annoyed by his gall. "I've been getting around on my own since forever."

Manny put up his hands, bowed his head. "Fair enough, I guess you country girls know how to look out for yourselves."

"I gotta go," she said. "Nice to meet you proper."

"Tell your mama I said hi," he said.

"I'd better not," Charlie said, remembering the fight that had followed his arrival. "She seemed pretty pissed after you left."

"You don't say," Manny said, frowning as if in thought. "In that case, you're probably right. I don't want to get either one of us in trouble."

"Well, too late for me," she said, walking her bike to the road. "But for your sake I won't mention seeing you. You really don't want to get on her bad side."

Charlie pedaled toward home on a nice sugar high. Between hanging out with Dirk and meeting this mystery man, this was about the most excitement she had maybe ever had. If only she could run home to Kit, flop down in her lap, and tell her everything.

CHAPTER TWENTY-SEVEN

AS THE GIRL BIKED AWAY FROM HIM, MANNY WANTED TO RUN AFTER her and make her stay. He had so much to ask her, this girl who must certainly be his daughter. He puzzled through the pieces of what he knew: the girl was the right age to have been born within a year of the last time he and Kit had been together. But he had walked Kit to the abortion, and paid the doctor, and done everything but cut it out himself. She had bled all over two sets of sheets, an awful mess. But maybe, somehow, the doctor had botched the procedure. It would have to be a miracle, but this great swelling in his chest and the love he was feeling for the kid told him he was not wrong. This girl was his.

She was her mother in her toughness, the arrogant cheekbones, the dark-eyed squint. Blunt, too. But she had more charisma, more vitality. Confidence even. Kit was all fang, yet she lacked the sense to know when to let down her guard. But the overall look of the girl was Manny, through and through. And she'd gotten his long legs, too, thank God. There was no guile in Charlie that he could see, but that could be taught. He started to imagine the possibilities. He had come to Pecan Hollow for Kit, not knowing she was hiding something even better: his own flesh and blood.

He considered how to broach the topic of Charlie without sending Kit into a tizzy. He had given her a wide berth these past two weeks, but wondered about testing her, seeing if she'd become more malleable. He sensed Kit's attraction to him was still there, he'd always been able to spot it. If she'd let him in, just a bit, he could make a case for spending more time with her, catching up, righting the wrongs they'd done to each other. How quickly would she fess up about having the baby? Had she meant to? Or when she realized she was still pregnant, simply run? He would have to appear indifferent about the girl though. Kit would be cautious if not hostile on that issue, he was sure.

In an hour he'd be expected at a volunteer job he had created for himself, running errands for an old widow named Jobeth Crabtree, who lived all alone on a ranch. She had been salty and suspicious at first, made him stand at a distance while she sized him up. When she found out Pastor Tom had sent him, she uttered a stiff apology and told him she wouldn't pay a cent, but if he was doing the Lord's work, she wouldn't turn him away. How he hated the elderly, those walking corpses, all bones and liver spots and cloudy eyes.

Once he had ingratiated himself, she allowed him considerable access to her home. He sat with her on the porch and fluffed her pillows, brought her iced tea with mint when she got thirsty, and dosed her medicine, the print on the labels being too tiny for Jobeth to decipher. He read the Bible to her, fetched her groceries, fed her cats and a teacup Chihuahua named Churro. A few hours a week, he gave her his time and didn't charge her for anything. Given all the value he was bringing to her, he thought it only fair to deduct a tiny tax for his troubles. For example, when he shopped for groceries, he added a few things for himself to the cart. He always offered her the receipt as a show of honesty, but she couldn't make out the numbers. And while she napped in her easy chair he slipped a few bills from the stacks of cash she tucked under the linens, never enough to notice just by looking. This way she got to think he was there out of the goodness of his heart and for the pleasure of her company. Win-win.

Manny took in the molasses stink of the asphalt and began to walk. He would need wheels eventually, but for now didn't mind the miles underfoot, the hellish heat. How long he had dreamed of stretching his legs like this, covering distance, when he was in prison. Free to roam, anonymous and safe. There he had jogged in place in his cell, working hard, going nowhere. A small corner of the yard, which was bare cement surrounded by thirty feet of fence and barbed wire, had been his only territory, and even those privileges were regularly stripped. They had tried to break him down, make him small. But here he was expanding. He was making his mark in this little town.

AFTER HE'D SPENT AN HOUR or so doing odds and ends for Jobeth, Sandy picked him up and drove him to Kit's, parking along the split-log fence outside her property. The wind picked up as the afternoon sun lurked behind the trees. Sandy stuffed her stale gum in the ash-tray and replaced it with a fresh pink strip, then tucked her bare feet beneath her. As Manny looked at Kit's house, he could feel Sandy looking at him.

"What do you know about those two?" he said, cranking down the window.

She pulled at her chewing gum and wrapped it around her finger. "They used to get along okay. Seems like they've been growing apart. That kind of thing happens to mother and daughter, I guess."

"How do you figure?" Manny asked.

"Well, around the time a girl gets her cycle, I guess. Hormones and whatnot . . ." She tucked her chin with an embarrassed flush.

He leaned in, curious, played with the natty hem of her synthetic skirt.

Eager to help, she mustered a matter-of-fact tone and went on. "This is a small town, you know. And there aren't a lot of men to go around. I know Miz Kit ain't the dating type, but I think it's just human nature for a lady to be jealous when there's someone prettier and younger around." She snatched a breath. "At least that's when the trouble started with my mama. I wasn't looking for it, swear to God."

He looked at Sandy intently. She continued, seeming to know what he wanted.

"But I developed early, and her boyfriends . . . noticed me. I was still playing with dolls when my boobs came in. I didn't care about men, not being with them. But she didn't know that. She expected the worst of me. I guess I was flattered, maybe I egged 'em on. That's right around the time she started using." Sandy scratched a mosquito bite with a purple drugstore press-on nail.

"Manny?" She paused, as if unsure of whether to ask the question. "What is it that you see in her?" He didn't like being baited. She probed. "She's so rough and boyish. And, no offense, but it don't seem like she's interested."

Manny lashed her with a look. "Oh, she's more than interested. She's bound to me. She puts up such a fight but inside, deep inside, she knows I'm all she ever needed." He felt himself puff up with a righteous sort of feeling. "I'm the someone who sees the black thorns around her heart, who knows the wrong in her and likes her better that way. I'm the only one who won't try to make her something she's not."

Sandy seemed to buckle under the load of his sentiment. Her eyes lost focus, her lips disappeared between her teeth. She began to pry the false nail from her thumb.

"Seems like a lot of work," she said, petulantly.

"Work? The work is the reason. Once you stop having to work for it," he said, "well, you might as well blow off your fucking head."

Sandy seemed to take this in and changed tack. "She must mean an awful lot to you," she said. "I forget you knew each other, back when."

"We were a team," Manny said, half-calmed by her approach. "She knows as well as I do that there's no running from it." Manny took Sandy's sweaty hands in his and held them, felt her tug just slightly away. "See, Kit's not a woman but a feral creature. She bites and scratches and draws blood. I saw that fierceness in her eyes the first day I met her. She and I took each other close to death and lived right there on the edge of it. We took a piss on the rules and lived free and wild like God made us. I never thought I needed anyone till I met her."

Sandy gave him a bemused look, like she was lost in a maze groping for an opening. "I could do that for you, Manny." She simpered. "I could make you bleed." The words tumbled out of her mouth like foreign objects. Manny laughed and stroked her cheek with the back of his hand.

"My dear, you're much too sweet to do harm. You're a flower, lovely, fragile."

He got out of the car and closed the door. "Thanks for the ride," he called, slapping the rear end of the Caprice. Tears in her eyes, she drove away.

Manny crossed the stagnant waters of the ditch and made his way to a thicket of pecan saplings overgrown with wild grapevines. Here he could sit and enjoy the shade and check on Kit. He wanted to be near her, to know her rhythms and her habits. Was she an early riser? When did she go to work? What did she like to eat? Then, a sickening thought. Were there men?

CHAPTER TWENTY-EIGHT

KIT ROLLED OVER IN BED AND SAT HERSELF UP. THE MATTRESS slumped on the side where she had slept the past five or so hours. She'd gotten back to the house as the sun was coming up, collapsed into bed, and slept deeply. Now it was noon and her muscles and joints had stiffened so much that when she went downstairs, it felt like trudging through mud. She made it to the sink and brought back a cup full of ice water, then turned on the ceiling fan and returned to her bed, her bare feet propped on the brass footboard. How strange it felt to rest. A warm feeling had lingered after she left Caleb's home. To the tick of the fan she let her mind wander. She could not explain this feeling of peace. After a night like that, she should be off somewhere digging a trench or burning brush; there would be rage, a violent act against nature. But there in his house with its ridiculous curtains, he had handled her like a fallen wren. She couldn't remember the last time she'd felt so cared for, maybe not since Eleanor.

She was just about to start worrying again about Charlie when the girl traipsed through the front door and up to her room as if a day hadn't passed since they'd seen each other.

"Where have you been?" Kit barked, though she wanted to hug her daughter tight till she yelled. Charlie stopped in front of Kit's door.

"Smoking weed with Dirk," she said, direct and barefaced. On another day, Kit would have come down harder on her. Far as she knew, Charlie had never done drugs before, and she sure as hell shouldn't have been out with a boy all night. But Kit was so relieved to see her safe, so weary of fighting, she called a silent truce.

"What happened to you?" Charlie said, her tone less flippant, and Kit realized she must have seen her busted lip.

She didn't like lying, especially not after Charlie's latest show of honesty, but she wasn't ready to get into any of what happened last night.

"I took Warbucks out for a ride," Kit said. "Got pitched off and kissed a fence post on my way down."

"Shit," Charlie said, apparently satisfied. "Okay, well, I'm gonna cram for my tests tomorrow. Do not disturb." And with a flourish of her sleep-tousled hair, she disappeared into her room. How Kit missed the days when Charlie had looked up to her, how she would run up to her after school clutching a drawing she had made, some scribble resembling nothing. The pride in Charlie's voice as she described the drawing to her mom. She felt the pang in her heart even now, at Charlie's capacity for wonder. Charlie would push and push, "Look at this, Mommy! Did you see?" until Kit could muster the desired amount of praise. How could she have wasted those days, so squeamish about the demands of motherhood that she couldn't absorb how beautiful it was to be needed? Worse still, she hadn't seen how much Charlie had given to her.

Now she shuddered at how close she'd come to taking off last night, running laps in and out of town, flirting with escape. She hoped to God Charlie never found out. As she replayed the tape of the evening before, it was like watching someone else's movie. The trailer park, the drinking, ignoring her instinct that Trip was trouble—in the light of day it all seemed so dramatic.

Ever since Manny came back, she'd recognized that she had been weird as shit. Off-balance. Like he had suddenly appeared on the bridge she and Charlie had been walking, a bridge that was only wide enough for two. She was so accustomed to dealing with things alone, in the swirling darkness of her own mind, that the idea of sharing Charlie with someone—with Manny—was paralyzing. And how could they just pick up where they left off, after all that had happened?

The three of them, a happy TV family, roast in the oven, a stiff drink in his hand? She almost laughed. His presence confused and frightened her, and she was sure last night's tussle with Trip would never have happened if she hadn't run into Manny. And now it was like he was everywhere. It hadn't been long before news of the dashing reformed convict, Manuel, was all over town. Kit heard tell of his kindly deeds: at the grocery store between gushing housewives, "Did you ever meet a straight man that was so . . . so sensitive?" or at the diner, "I swear he hadn't even touched his sandwich, but when he saw poor old Levi counting his pennies for a bowl of soup, Manny slid his lunch right on down the counter and went hungry." She had heard of his theatrics in church with Ms. Blanchet several times, each more embellished than the last. When Beulah Baker had called him "positively Christlike," Kit left her shopping cart in the middle of the canned foods aisle and walked out. He was conning the whole damn town—*her* goddamn town. She knew the whole charade was somehow directed at her. But to what end? He had said he wanted her forgiveness, but the Manny she knew wanted more.

He'd had the sense to stay away from her, at least. She had had only one encounter with him aside from seeing him at the church with Warbucks. She had just come out of the post office with a huge box of flea collars for Doc, and he had a handful of letters to mail. She stopped cold and let the door swat her behind. He wore a T-shirt from the church softball league and his old jeans, his hair still long, now threaded with gray. Hadn't she noticed it before, this mortal change? She reminded herself of the last time she saw him, drunk and hateful, and held it up to the man in front of her. He *was* different. In his downcast eyes, his tentative manner. He was hum-

bled. Maybe it wasn't his fault the town was so lusty for a hero. Maybe
it wasn't a con, but contrition. She didn't know which feelings to trust,
the ones she felt now, which shimmered with the possibility that the
good she had known was not gone; or the bruise he'd left behind, dark
and deep, the canny voice that whispered *beware*? She took a lozenge
of ice from the glass by her bed and slipped it inside her cheek. The
cold deepened, then numbed until she could feel the nerves under her
teeth beat. She'd be a fool to take his act at face value. Manny *always*
had an angle, and he never left without getting what he came for.

Kit got up, walked to the bathroom, and turned on the shower.
As she waited for the old boiler to get going, she shed her soiled and
bloodied clothes and looked at the damage. Her fat, bitten lip, glossy
with ointment, made her look sultry; new bruising was beginning to
show, five maroon smudges where the cowboy had grabbed her scant
handful of breast. She turned and craned her neck around to see her
back reflected in the mirror. Nearly half of its surface was purpled
and scuffed from being shoved in the bed of the truck. Between this
and the old machete gash on her shin, she looked barely better than
dog food.

She lingered as the steam billowed around her, then stood under
the shower and closed her eyes. Her thoughts flashed to Trip's teeth
in her lip, the vicious change in his voice. The metallic smell of his
truck as she skidded deeper into its bed. And the strength in her arms
as she beat him. Now she was fifteen years back, rolling over a messy
bed with Manny after a job, at once dodging his grasp and fighting
to be held. Icy air-conditioning, the Doors on the radio, whiskey and
lemon drops on his breath.

CHAPTER TWENTY-NINE

CHARLIE WOKE UP EARLY THE NEXT MORNING, FRIED AN EGG, AND rode her bike to the school to take her tests. Kit had been so distracted the last few days she had completely forgotten about the suspension. Charlie's show of responsibility was either promising or suspicious, but Kit chose to reward her daughter's initiative by allowing her to get to and from school unchaperoned. This was partly out of guilt for being neglectful and partly because she just wanted to have a good day, free from strife. It seemed like every time she tried to come down hard on Charlie, it pushed her away. Maybe Kit needed to trust her a little more. Maybe it wasn't the end of the world if she shared a joint with a crush. She went to Doc's and put in a half day of work so she could be home when Charlie returned. Kit mucked the stalls and refreshed the floors with sawdust and hay, watered and fed every living thing in the place. Then she prepped a tray of sterilized tools and assisted while Doc gelded a pretty cremello colt.

When she got back she was hot, tired, and hungry but restored from having been useful. She was in such fine fettle she decided to cook up some frozen tamales for her and Charlie. While the tamales steamed, she waited idly, looking at the family photos that were gathered above the dresser. There were her great-grandparents, severe and clad in black, her great-grandmother holding the Bible in her lap. The wedding photo of Eleanor and Amos. And young Eleanor, a vixen dancer, piercing the camera with sass. Kit missed having her aunt there, a living link to these moments in time. Still, it meant something to have this visual reminder that they came from real people. She had not materialized from nothing, even if it felt that way sometimes.

She wanted to mark a spot on the wall for Charlie. Though they had never owned a camera, Kit had purchased photos from the school when she could afford them. She opened the dresser and rummaged through knitting needles and yarn, old receipts, and batteries caked in crystallized acid until she found a bent sheet of eight small photos. Sweet Charlie, thick braids resting on her shoulders, her eyes wide open.

Kit brought the photos into the kitchen, where the bitter smell of burnt fat was strong. She grabbed the top off the pot, releasing billows of steam and smoke, and lifted the colander of tamales onto the counter. Her hands pinkened from the steam, so she hit the tap to slow the burn. As she ran her hands under the faucet, she heard a knock at the door. She turned off the water and listened, heard movement on the porch. There was no car visible from the window. She wiped her hands on her jeans, and cracked open the door.

Manny stood there, smelling of soap and mint, dressed up for a date. Long hair combed back and neat, secondhand slacks, a vigorous shine on his boots. She kept the door cracked and propped her toe behind it, a glance at the gun in case she needed it. After a quick assessment she decided he seemed not apt to start any trouble, at least not now. His eyebrows pinched a look of concern and Kit remembered what a mess she must be.

"Forgive me for showing up uninvited," he said. "But I heard you got roughed up and had to see you were okay."

"*Me* roughed up?"

He laughed. "Fair enough. I guess I don't have to worry about you. The guy must look like a piñata at the end of the party."

She felt a hint of pleasure at how well she had fought. A younger version of Kit would have basked in his pride. Still, she didn't like him knowing her business. "How did you hear about that?"

"Pastor Tom told me, heard they took the guy to county hospital because his internal injuries were too much for our doctor out here. That a woman had done it." He looked her up and down as if checking for something. "Now, who else would I think of but you?"

A woman had done it. Kit wondered what this new Manny would do if he heard the cowboy had tried to rape her.

Manny slid one hand in his pocket, took a step back, and said, "I'll get out of your hair."

As he stood there before her, something old and stronger than she cared to struggle with took over. She told herself that she was just curious about him, that he seemed changed, that she only wanted to talk. That she wanted to know what was going through his mind that day, why he'd changed tack and held up that poor woman at the barbecue joint. *Lonely* was not a word she wanted to use, but that was the feeling that arose when he shifted back on his heels and turned to go. Like it or not, he was the only person that connected her to her past, the only one, besides Charlie, who knew her at all.

"No," she said, turning to the side to make way. "Come on in."

Manny hesitated, then scuffed his boots on the welcome mat, ducked his head, and crossed the threshold.

Kit one-handed a pair of beers from the fridge and popped the caps. Manny waited for her to sit at the kitchen table before he seated himself. He kept his eyes soft and slightly downward, and all the while she watched him intently. He did not drink any, but Kit slopped hers back.

Manny nodded his head toward the mess on the counter. "Sorry, did I interrupt your dinner?"

Kit was dying to eat, but not here with him. She wanted to gorge, standing up, with no witnesses. She swallowed the better part of her beer to feel full.

"Look, I don't have a lot of time, so you can just say what you wanted to say."

"I'm sorry, I just can't believe I'm sitting here right now. You've been on my mind for a long time, and now I find I don't know what to say."

"That's a first," Kit said.

Manny shrugged, smiled.

A rain started up, soft, then so hard it squirted through the screen on the open window. Manny got up to pull the window closed, took a dish towel that was wadded in a ball on the counter to mop up the moisture on the sill. Kit was antsy and didn't like his stall tactics, shit he would pull to buy time when they were conning.

"Did I ever tell you anything about my folks?" he asked.

Kit was irritated by the opening. Of all the things they had to hash out, his family was not first on her list.

"No, you never told me much of anything about yourself," she said. "Which is funny because it seemed like you were always bragging about something or trying to teach me a lesson, running your mouth like a carnival barker." She felt a tumbling of old anger. "You never fuckin' shut up."

Manny smiled apologetically. "I was pretty selfish back then," he said and held the towel under a hot tap, rinsing and squeezing rhythmically. "You know," he said, "my father was an immigrant, he came over here as a teenager from Cuba on an actual raft with his uncle. When he got to Miami, he wouldn't take just any job in a kitchen like all the other guys he knew. He was trying to be somebody." He folded the towel symmetrically in half and squared it to the edge of the counter. "My mother's family was *rich* rich, not that any of it ever came my way, and she spoke that standard English like they did in the movies. She was as American as Jane goddamn Russell. Even Cubans couldn't tell she was one of their own. And he worshipped her. I remember he was always taking classes to lose his accent. Always trying to cover up the fact that he was foreign. When I was born, they would tell me, my eyes were so blue the nurse crossed herself, and my father got on his knees and prayed, like I was some kind of gift from God."

Kit was torn between her genuine interest in the story and her reluctance to reveal this to him. The tension between the two was making her surly.

"What's your fuckin' point?" she said.

"Nobody in my family had blue eyes. They were all brown, brown, and brown. How did I get blue eyes? Some little drop of conquistador blood from five hundred years ago just waiting for its moment to shine? To them, it was a God-given blessing. They treated me like I was the center of the universe. They spoiled me. And my little brother hated me for it. You'd think I would be so full of their love and kindnesses that I'd have to turn out good. But all it did, all that fuss, was make me feel invincible. And the more people fawned all over me, the more I hated them. I was bad, okay? That's my point. I want you to know that I *know* I was a shit."

Kit waited for more to determine if this was for real, aware that beneath the flowery speech he could be gaming her. "Okay?" she said.

"Kitty, I'm telling you," he said, his eyes direct and warm, "because I want to make amends. What do I need to do to get you to forgive me?"

Again, the mention of forgiveness set something alight in her. To forgive was frightening, and yet she sensed how much she needed to let down her arms. It had hardened her to begrudge him, and others, for so long. His eyes, a warmer blue, reached out to her, and she was blinded, for a moment, to why she could not trust this new Manny, the kind and modest incarnation of the rat she once knew. He seemed reformed, and everyone else thought so, too. He wasn't hiding his old ways; in fact, he wore them plainly.

But the force of her memories pushed back against the Manny in front of her. She tried to hold down the images as if drowning them, but they broke the surface and sputtered to life. The creak of the glider and the painless cut; the stolen bouquet begging on the pillow; the casual expression on his face as he held a family in terror; the way freedom sang through her on that highway without him.

She bolted upright, toppling the chair on its side.

"This was a bad idea. You need to get out of here." She began to tremble. "Now-now-now!"

Manny looked confused, hurt even.

Her breaths were quick and short, the jolt of last night still in her blood.

Manny reached his hand over toward her. "Hey, now. I'm not mad at you for ditching me." He grabbed her eyes with his. "I'm not. You were always free to leave. From day one. You know that."

She bit the side of her tongue to taste her blood. "You're a bad man."

"Yes, I was," he said. "The worst kind."

He took her hand. She jerked it away, but he held tight and looked her in the eyes.

"Hey, if I were you, I'd have left, too."

She turned away, blistering under his gaze, hating the way he disarmed her.

"You know they asked me about you when they took me in, questioned me about my partner, who you were, what you'd done. I told them I had forced you into it."

"Why though?" she asked, hoping she hadn't given away that she had seen how he was quoted in the paper.

"You're all I thought about in there. I couldn't let you get locked up. I needed to know you would be there when I got out. Even if it meant I had to come find you myself." He ran his thumb along the vein that snaked over her wrist and across the back of her hand. "The thought of seeing you again was what kept me from hanging myself on my sheets."

The image of him dangling by the neck in a prison cell shook her, but she steeled herself. "I would have left you even if you hadn't done what you did." She sniffed and held his gaze.

She could tell by the way he sat back in his chair and tilted his head to the side that she had gotten his attention.

"Don't act like you don't know. You wanted me to— You made me kill our baby," she said, as heartbroken as if it were actually true.

"The abortion?" he said and squinted, disbelieving. "You left me because of that?"

Kit nodded, trying not to let the hurt show. "There were other things, too."

"I just had no idea," he said and shook his head, like he was sifting through the implications of this turn. "If you could have seen your face when you told me you were keeping it, all full of bluster. But you were scared, just a baby yourself. It was the only way."

She paced the length of the braided kitchen rug.

"Listen, I don't regret a thing. God's wisdom is infinite and we are just where we should be. Turns out you were right, after all." He paused, as if waiting to let a revelation sink in. She let the pieces lay and did not put them together.

"I know Charlie is mine," he said.

Kit's ears rang. She ran his words over in her mind to make sure she had heard right. *Mine.* She couldn't seem to get enough air in her lungs and the collar of her shirt felt like it was cinched around her neck. She was hot and cold, the slimy way she felt when she was about to puke. He was saying something but she couldn't make out the garbled, foreign sounds.

She went for the door and tore out into the warm rain. When she reached the fence, she bent herself in half. No. No, he couldn't have Charlie. He couldn't have a piece of the only person in her life she cherished. Why couldn't even this secret belong to her? The trees dripped heavily on her back. Baritone bullfrogs croaked in the distance. Manny showed up behind her. She turned and shoved him back a few paces. He held out his palms like an offering.

"Hey, hey," he said gently, as if approaching a spooked horse. "You don't have to worry. I don't mean you harm. She's yours, really. You raised her, you loved her all this time. I know what that's like," he said, "because of how I felt for you. All I ask, with your blessing, is to get to know her. I want her to know I wouldn't have left on purpose." His voice seemed to catch on a feeling, a shimmer passed across his eyes. "And if I had known, that you were still pregnant, that you really wanted to keep her, I never would have taken you out that day. I never woulda done what I did."

Kit heard him, though his voice sounded faint and far as an echo. As she made room for this new possibility, the thrashing in her chest settled. She shook her head, not knowing where to land, tired of fighting it. Under the camouflage of rain, she released a few long tears. She hung there a good while before turning to him.

"How did you know?" she asked.

Manny laughed a big one. "Kitty Cat, come on." He looked at her like she was joking. "She looks just like me."

It hurt to admit it was true. Charlie had many elegant and striking features, none of which had come from Kit, but she had always considered those essential—and not heritable—traits. God-given features that belonged to Charlie.

He kept his distance but gestured with his jaw toward the house. "Can I beg your forgiveness where it's nice and dry? Maybe share some of that Mexican food?"

"I don't know how," she said, not even wanting to utter the words *to forgive*, but even in admitting this was surprised to feel a slender ray of warmth, an opening in her breath.

CHAPTER THIRTY

WHEN CHARLIE TRAMPED INSIDE, SOAKED TO HER SCALP, KIT FROZE like she'd been caught stealing. Manny stood up and put his hand on Kit's shoulder. They passed a weighted thing between them, she and Manny, back and forth like a stone, until finally Kit cleared her throat. She held the words back, rolling them around in her mouth before she let them go, once and forever. As if preparing herself to jump from a great height, she imagined the possible outcomes. Would they hug and cry? Would Charlie run away, would they chase her down and hold her till she calmed? She couldn't know until she said the thing she thought she'd never say.

"Go on and say hello," she said. Her voice was dusky and tight. "This is Manny. This is your father."

Charlie's features were slow to register. She only stared as rainwater ran from the twists of her hair down her arm. Kit couldn't get a read on what Charlie was feeling, or if she even understood. There was an off-center look that Kit couldn't quite understand. Then, as if vomiting, Charlie hurled out laughter, a stream of uncontrollable gusts of sound, gasping for air. She held on to the banister and swung around, plopping down on the base of the staircase, stricken by hilarity that was only known to her.

"That's it," Kit said. "This was a mistake." Then she turned to Manny and growled, "Get on out."

Manny pressed the tension down with his hands. "Now, hang on a second. We just turned her world upside down." More softly, he said, "Let me talk to her."

Charlie was trying to speak but kept laughing over her words, wheezing. She dragged herself up from the step and came over to the kitchen table. She looked at Manny, checking him out. "*You're* my dad?" she said. "Manny, huh?" Then she turned to Kit and pointed at her. "I *thought* you were acting crazy when he came by."

Kit shook her head, willing herself not to turn this into a fight.

"Look, let me make this right," Manny said, lifting a set of keys off their hook by the door. "Kitty, I'm taking your truck. Me and Charlie are gonna go get acquainted. I'll have her back in an hour." He went over and laid a hand on Charlie's back and swept her toward the door, not by force, but as if she were already headed that way. She glanced back at Kit, as if expecting her to kick this guy's ass down the steps, but Kit just stood there, frozen, unnatural as a scarecrow. Then, on a ten-second delay, she went after them.

"Wait!" she yelled and jogged out into the rain and down the front steps. "Where y'all going? I'm coming with you!"

Manny was already starting up the truck.

"I'm not gonna kidnap her or anything," he said and winked. "I just got out of prison, Kitty. Not trying to go back there anytime soon." He looked around and stuck his hand out the window. "Hey, look, stopped raining."

As Manny drove away with Charlie, Kit ran the length of the driveway, cleared the cattle guard, and continued onto the main road for a ways until they were too far gone. When she lost sight of them, she bent at the waist, her hands propped on her knees, and caught her breath. Huffing, spent, she felt the blood fill her face and ears and fingertips, her tongue fat against her teeth, and wished she hadn't let Charlie go. She stood up and got light-headed, her vision silvered and faded.

"They're coming back, they're coming back, they're coming back," she said to quiet her terrified heart.

THE SUMMER RAIN HAD FALLEN hard, and anything that wasn't paved was mud. Charlie and Manny sat in the truck in an empty field, a humid mist just visible rising around them. Charlie ached with the shock of it, like a bone-deep flu. It was still unclear how she came to be sitting here with this man, her father. *Father.* When she first heard the word, Charlie had shuffled the pieces around until she arranged something that made sense. She'd stood there stupidly, letting those words fall to the floor, and could hear only the grind and squeak of toads and a hot gale rustling the leaves, envoy of a second rain. Then she had seen the storm in his brow, the way his lip cut across his teeth, and she knew.

Father. Maybe it sounded strange because there had not been a slot waiting for him to fill. There had been no trace of him to miss, no photo, no anecdotes, no fuzzy memories. It had always been simply Kit and Charlie, the End. She remembered what Mrs. Fowler had said about needing a man in the house, that kids needed discipline. Was that what he would be like? Spankings and groundings and stern words? Or touch football in the yard and frosty hunting trips at dawn?

"I can't believe Mom let you drive the truck," she said, hoping to puncture the silence. She recalled their conversation in the parking lot. The stolen Cokes, the friendly way he had called after her, had seemed concerned about her traveling alone. The way she had felt when he spoke to her in the parking lot, both curious and wary. In light of this new information, his actions made more sense. He must have known, then, who she was. But if so, why hadn't he said something?

"She kind of owes me one," he said, with a tone that rang sullen. "Hey, you like doughnuts?"

"Sure I do," she said.

He leaned over and buckled the seat belt across her lap, tugging the loose end until it was snug. Then he lay hard on the gas and the wheels spun a few rounds before gripping a dry patch and sending them lurching forward, ripping up a circle in the soggy pasture, bits of turf flying by and landing in their wake. She squealed, rode that truck like a roller coaster, arms stretched out the window, letting the sudden shifts in speed and direction tug her body where they would.

He brought the truck to a stop and turned to Charlie. They were breathless and mottled with mud splatter, eyes bright. "No," she said, giggling. "I mean the doughnuts you can eat."

"Ohhh," he said, smacking his forehead with his palm. "I knew that."

They drove twenty miles west to the Do-Nut Hole off the interstate, sandwiched between a Western Union and an aerobics studio in a drab strip mall. The light in the window was blinking, which meant they were frying up a fresh batch.

"Follow my lead and keep cool," Manny instructed. He glided up to the counter and got the cashier's attention. "I'll have a baker's dozen, half glazed, half jelly, half chocolate." Charlie, beset by sudden shyness, reached up toward his ear and whispered, "Sprinkles."

"Half sprinkles."

The cashier bit her lip. "So . . . three of each."

"She's smart, ain't she, Charlie?"

The cashier arranged the doughnuts in rows, taking her time. She returned with the box and rang them up.

"'L be four dollars, please," she said, her gaze blatantly fixed on the swath of chest that showed at the collar of his shirt.

"That's a steal," Manny said. He reached in his pocket, then put his hands back on the counter. "You know what? One more box just like it, please and thank you." When the cashier turned around, so did Manny, carrying the box of doughnuts, and he cruised right out without paying. Charlie followed him and played it cool. By the time the woman turned around they were back in the truck.

They parked under a billboard on the way back to Pecan Hollow and ate, the box between them. The air hung heavy and damp except when a passing car sent an occasional breeze their way.

"That was crazy," Charlie said halfway through a sprinkles doughnut. She wanted to ask him why he kept stealing these little things they could easily have paid for, but she didn't want to offend him. "Aren't you afraid of getting caught?"

Manny looked at her, amused. "What? You never slipped a pack of gum in your pocket? Never took a dollar out of your mama's wallet?"

She smiled behind her hair. "No, I mean, you know how you were saying to my mom that you weren't trying to go back to prison?"

"Ah," he said, mid-chew, nodding. "Look, I'm not trying to hide it, I was in prison all that time. Since before you were born probably."

Charlie's eyes popped open. "No shit?" she said, thinking his crimes might have been more serious than walking out with a box of doughnuts. "What for?"

Manny chuckled. "Armed robbery."

"Wow . . ." Charlie said, uneasy. "Well, shouldn't you be a little more careful?" She held the remains of her doughnut.

"Nah," he said. "I do the small stuff because it doesn't matter. Who's gonna bust me for a Coke?" He stuffed half a plain glazed into his mouth. He chewed for a bit and swallowed. "I just want you to know, I would have been here for you if I could."

As Charlie took this in, she studied his features. His skin, lashes, hair were each a different shade of brown, like hers. But his eyes were blue like there was sky behind them, and she liked the way the creases at his eyes stretched down to his jaw, even when he wasn't smiling. She looked at her large hands, with their long tapered fingers, and saw they were his.

She imagined herself with eyes like his and wondered if the world looked different through them. She had certainly noticed being treated differently than her light-eyed, fair-haired classmates. People used slurs in that stupid way that was supposed to be friendly, as if to prove how not a big deal it was to call you that. There were a few openly hateful people in town, but most everyone was that kind of rude that made it hard to pinpoint. The way her teachers expected less of her, and yet she never could seem to please them, no matter how hard she tried. The way she would find out about parties a week after they happened, that her invitation had "gotten lost in the mail." Sadly, she had no group to identify with when the slurs came. She imagined if she had actually been Mexican (or known who the hell she was), these names might hurt a lot more, but she would have the solidarity of a culture behind her, too. When he caught her looking she turned away.

"So, like, are we Mexican, or . . . what are we?" she asked.

"Ah," he said as he finished off a jellied and sucked the goo from his fingers. "I can't speak for your mama; she's some kind of orphan mongrel, but being from Texas, she's bound to have some Mexican somewhere." He licked his lips and wiped them sort of primly with a hankie. "But me and you, we're Cuban."

She tried to remember what she knew about Cuba from social studies class: Cuban missile crisis, Cuban cigars, Fidel Castro. But they were vague impressions that had no personal impact, just two-dimensional images culled from what little information had made its way to her in Pecan Hollow. Black beans and plantains, salsa dancing, rusty cars from the fifties. She felt ashamed of her small life.

"Is that where you're from?"

"No, no. I don't even speak much Spanish to tell you the truth. I grew up in Florida. My father—your grandfather—came over and wanted us to fit in, so they spoke English at home. He wanted so badly to be American he kind of scribbled over the Cuban parts of him and pretended they weren't there."

Charlie noticed there was something canned about the way he spoke, as if he'd said these things in just this way a dozen times before, but she brushed it aside. When he described her grandparents, it didn't seem real. She thought of the photos on her wall at home, the ancient people she never knew. At least she had stories of Eleanor.

"Do you have any pictures of them?" she asked Manny. He seemed taken aback.

"Why would I have something like that on me?" he said. This time she detected not smoke screen but an unpleasant truth. Again, she tucked it aside.

"So what was she like?" she said, changing the subject.

He jerked his head back a little, squinted at her. "My mother?"

"No," she said. "Mine."

"Hmmm," he said and tapped his top lip. She saw how it curled up at the ridge like hers. "Stubborn. Secretive. All clammed up most of the time. Not pretty, but you couldn't take your eyes off her." He smiled. "What's she like now?"

The question made her choke up a little. "Pretty much the same, I guess. She's hard, in every way possible. Hard to be around, hard to please, hard to like. She's not a happy person, that's for sure. For my whole life, it's just been the two of us, and when she gets on my nerves there's no place to go. I got no one to talk to, not really." It was nice to be able to tell someone who got it. There was so much she wanted him to decode for her. In another world, she would have loved to sit and chat with her mom like this, to tell her what was on her mind, to ask her questions about her life before. She longed for these little luxuries, but they felt as vague and remote as Cuba.

"That's kind of how it was for us, too," Manny said. "She never was a talker, was she? We just had each other. It was pretty great for a long time but . . ." He sniffed.

"What happened?" She was thirsty to know what had caused them to split. She was sure it had been her mom's fault. He must have gotten sick of her strong-and-silent BS. Or maybe Kit had been the one to leave, allergic as she was to a good thing.

"Oh, that's boring grown-up stuff," he said. "Don't you fret about such things."

"Come on," she pushed. "I can take it."

"How old did you say you were again . . . ?" he said and squinted. "About nine?"

He was razzing her. "Thirteen and a half," she said. "Going on Old Enough for Grown-up Stuff." He laughed for real at that one.

"Ahh, I don't know," he said, a little more seriously. "The thing about your mama," he went on, and looked off at the dome of an oak tree, searching. "She's kind of like beef jerky. She's tough and it takes a lot of work for a little reward, but for some reason you keep going back for more."

Charlie rolled back laughing, giddy to know he understood.

"Hang on, I got one," she said. "She's kind of like a badger wearing Tony Lamas. She's short, she's mean, and she looks silly in boots." She laughed so hard she snorted a globule of wet doughnut into her sinuses. She coughed and laughed and Manny whacked her across the back, laughing with her. She curled her legs up underneath her and tilted her head toward him. He lifted his arm to make room, and she rested her cheek against his ribs.

MANNY PULLED UP TO THE house. She got out and leaned through his window. She smelled the wax in his hair, the lemon drops on his breath.

"Don't you want to come back in?" she asked.

He took a deep breath and whistled it through his front teeth. "I don't think so, sweetheart. Let's do this one step at a time."

A pull at her throat. She realized she had expected him to stay around until she was ready for him to go.

"Okay." She pushed back from the window, trying to look blasé, and walked toward the house. Without turning she shouted, "And thanks for the doughnuts!"

Manny tooted the horn at her in response and got out of the truck. Charlie turned around and watched him go, wishing she could follow.

CHAPTER THIRTY-ONE

THE NEXT MORNING, CHARLIE WOKE UP BRIGHT AND HAPPY. SHE went over the previous day like a dream, tracking each moment. The muddy truck, the doughnuts, Cuba. She plunked down the stairs like it was Christmas morning, ate some Fig Newtons, and ran back to her room to get dressed. She could barely contain the news that her father had come back to be with her. And while she was acutely aware that Pecan Hollow was not ready for this twist, she was anxious to talk about it with somebody, somebody other than Kit. Although she had never said a word to Dirk before two weeks ago, he was the first and only person she wanted to tell. She got a little light in the middle thinking of their time by the lake, a crackling joint between them. She left another, more detailed, note for Kit.

Out. Diner. DONT WORRY. —Ch.

She pedaled her bike as fast as she could into town. It would be too obvious of her to go poking around the trailers, but she was hoping he'd show up at the diner, or near it, soon enough.

With the breakfast rush done by nine, the place was nearly empty save for the cook, who was scraping and greasing the griddle in back, and Sandy, who was rolling place settings for the lunch crowd. Charlie became aware that in reuniting with her father, she had suddenly changed status. This ranking system was all but explicit in Pecan Hollow. At the top were the girls from intact homes; then there were the ones from divorced homes; lower still, the offspring of unmarried parents who stayed together; then girls from single mom homes where the father had run off; then, at the bottom, were the ones like Charlie, where the father had never been known at all. Sandy, with her loose ways and tragic mother, was often referenced in hushed tones as what could become of fatherless girls.

"Hey, Sandy, you seen Dirk around here?"

Sandy blushed like she'd been caught doing something wicked. "Dirk Dirkin? Huh." She put her hand on her hip. "No, babe, don't think I have . . . why, you two have a ron-day-voo?"

Sandy got busy making a peanut butter malt without being asked. She wiped the melting drip of malt from the side of the heavy glass, squirted a pile of whipped cream on top, and finished it with a straw. "This one's on the house."

Charlie thanked her and sipped it, sweet and frothy, her agenda briefly halted by the treat.

"I had a feeling there was a love connection between you two," Sandy said, spidering her fingers across the counter toward Charlie. Charlie recoiled.

"Oh, don't be shy. It's fun to be in love. I do it all the time."

"Don't be weird, man, we're just friends," Charlie said, aware that even in the act of resisting the accusation she was confirming it.

Charlie tried to think where else she could wait around for Dirk to show up without getting interrogated by Sandy, but it was hot out and the malt was damn good.

"You're getting so grown up. You know, I used to change your diapers," Sandy said, like she was bragging.

Charlie gave a begrudging "You don't say."

"Sure did. You know I probably changed more than your mama did." Sandy deftly rolled a fork, knife, and spoon in a paper napkin. "She didn't bother herself much."

Charlie was irritated at being reminded—by Sandy of all people—of her mother's shortcomings.

"Yeah, well, we all know she's not the motherly type, I guess."

"It wasn't her fault, bless her heart, she just didn't know about those things."

Something about Sandy's tone made Charlie stop drinking and push the glass away. She dug in her pocket to pay. On the house or not, she didn't want to owe Sandy for shit.

"Guess you must be pretty pissed at her," Sandy said, slyly.

Charlie tossed three bucks on the counter. "Sandy Blanchet, are you deliberately trying to get under my skin?"

Sandy returned to her napkin rolling, carrying some secret like a banner. "For what she did to your dad and all."

Charlie stood up, confused anger sweeping over her, breaking across her skin like hives. "You know I have a half a million nasty things I could say to you but won't because it ain't worth it. But I'm not gonna stand here and listen to you manufacture gossip because you've got nothing better to do than swing your braid and moon over anything with a pecker."

Sandy pantomimed zipping her lips. "Geez, forget I said anything," she said. "It's just, if I were you, I'd want to know."

Charlie pivoted to face the door but didn't advance. She realized not knowing would be worse.

"I don't have a dad, and you know that as well as I do," Charlie said.

Sandy gave her a pitying sort of look. "Listen, Charlie, I know, okay? About Manny?"

"How the hell—" Charlie started. Something collapsed in her middle. She felt like the news about her father had been cheapened by Sandy knowing, too.

"All right," Charlie said without turning. "I'll bite. What all did she do to my so-called dad, *allegedly*?"

Sandy leaned forward, seemingly delighted to bear the news.

"She went and kidnapped you from him," she said and pursed her sliver-thin lips in smug triumph.

Charlie laughed, a horn blown, to show that she wouldn't fall so easily for such drivel. It was just like Sandy to insert herself in the middle of a juicy drama. What irked her almost as much as the possibility that the news was true was the hungry smile on Sandy's face when she was telling it. And yet a germ of doubt took hold at the base of Charlie's gut.

"And where are you getting this from? You been smoking some of your mama's crack?" She winced at the ugliness of her own words. She felt even worse when Sandy brushed off the insult like she'd heard it a thousand times before.

"Honest to God," Sandy said, hand raised like a pledge. "Manny told me. He didn't want you to know. He didn't want to turn you against your mama. But he told me the whole story. It's a cryin' shame. Says they were young and hungry, and she ripped off a gas station or something, and when she came back with the money, he wouldn't have it. Says he ripped the bag outta her hands and marched that money inside to give it right back to the people what she stole it from. But by then the police had put him in cuffs and your mama had up and gone, took his car and his baby and disappeared into thin air." Sandy flushed and panted with the thrill of it and pulled the braid off her neck, swirled it into a bun, and let it fall back down. "Manny didn't want to shame her around town, so he's never told anyone else the true story. But he told it to me. And I thought you should hear it, too."

Charlie held Sandy's gaze as the story sped past her, the questions flying up before her like startled birds. What was Sandy doing talking to Manny? Why was Sandy the first to know that Manny was her father? Could her mother really have done those awful things? Her head felt like it was splitting with the pressure of all these revelations.

For now, she had to get the fuck out of this diner. She spat on the floor at Sandy's feet and walked a straight line out the door.

CHARLIE KEPT HER EYES PINNED to the ground in front of her, tears making swirls of the pavement. Though she intended to keep walking until her mind cleared up, she hadn't picked a direction and found herself marching a wide loop around the cluster of buildings at the town's center. As she completed the circle around the back of the diner she got the feeling she was being watched. Then there was the sound of comments under breath, snickering. She knew before she turned toward the sound that someone was making fun of her.

There was a three-man huddle by a stack of milk crates. One had hog-pink skin, reddish hair that stuck to his forehead, and reddish fuzz over his lip. Another was skinny and so hunched he was C-shaped, as if he were draped over a barrel. He wore a knit cap pulled over his ears, though it was hot and humid as an armpit, and drank a tallboy from a paper bag. The third man had his back to her, but she could tell from the fatty hips and his butcher's hands that it was Dirk. Dirk, who she'd been looking for, who she'd sought out to share the unimaginable news of her father, who she hoped could help her feel better about Sandy's ugly rumor.

Charlie had so hoped to see Dirk that she did not immediately jump to the conclusion that he was making fun of her. Maybe they hadn't seen her. Maybe they were yukking about something else. She stuck out her hand and waved.

"Hey you," she said loudly enough to cut through the sounds of their mumbling. "I was just thinking about you." *I was just thinking about you?* She could have punched herself for how desperate that sounded. And when Dirk looked over his shoulder and raised his eyebrows without saying anything back, she could have punched him, too.

The guy in the cap whistled a lewd sound. The redhead was looking at her with a snaggletoothed grin; Dirk's eyes were on his feet. It stank back here, a fishy smell of old fry oil and garbage juice that dripped from the cracks in the dumpster. Nothing good was going on.

"What's your damage, dude?" she said. "Too cool to say hello?"

"What's up, Walker?" he said, still not meeting her eyes. He was shifty as hell. Was he high? She had never seen these creeps before, definitely not from town. Dirk took a swig of beer, crumpled the can in his fist, and tossed it in the dumpster. The redhead pulled another tallboy from a backpack that was slumped against the milk crates, cracked it open, took a long foamy slurp, and handed it to Dirk.

"So are these your fucking dealers or are you just giving out blow jobs?" she said, pissed. Dirk shook his head and rolled his eyes. The C-shaped guy took it personally and puffed out his chest.

"What you fucking say, bitch?" he said. He talked like he was street, but he didn't look that tough.

The redhead bit his lip and cocked his head. "What do you know about giving head, li'l mama?"

"I know your mom gives it up for free," she said. The two guys stepped toward her. She was ready to run or fight.

Dirk looked uneasy. He pushed the guys back and left the circle, taking Charlie by the arm. He led her around the corner of the diner. "Look," he said. He glanced left and right like he was making sure no one was listening. "I had fun with you the other night. Okay? But we can't hang out anymore."

"Why not?" she said, already feeling like she could cry, willing herself not to.

"Do you seriously not know?" he said. He scratched his blond hair sideways. "Your mom busted in my trailer like a goddamn hurricane looking for you the other night. Mama said she looked ready to kill somebody. Pretty sure that somebody was me."

"She fuckin' what?" Charlie snapped. She didn't need another reason to be mortified by her mom.

"Yeah. She was acting like I was gonna deflower you or something.

And maybe I've been guilty of that in the past," he said, "but we both know I didn't lay a hand on you."

She blushed so hard she wanted to pull the neck of her shirt over her face. He'd seen it for sure, because he seemed less angry at her.

"Screw her," Charlie said. "Why should she stop us?"

"I'm sorry, man," he said. "You keep your crazy. I've got enough of my own."

She didn't know what to say, and all of this was making her miserable. She was getting the feeling this might be the last time she talked to Dirk.

"Why didn't you, then?" she asked.

"Why didn't I what?" Dirk said, all perplexed, and again she had the urge to punch him.

"Kiss me, you idiot. Why didn't you make a move? My breath smell like dog shit or something?"

Dirk shook his head and took a step back toward his goober friends. "You're just a kid, Walker," he said. "Go home."

Charlie wanted to say something cruel to him, but she was out of juice. The thing she had with Dirk had been so fleeting, she never really got a hold on it. He'd wandered by and slipped through her fingers. Yet she felt such loss. Maybe she had hoped for too much too soon.

The strikes against her mom kept piling up, and her disappointment was turning into hatred. Just when Charlie was on the verge of feeling like a half-normal teenager her mom went and blasted it to bits. The fact that Dirk had been such an asshole to her was the shit icing on a garbage cake. She hadn't even gotten a chance to kiss him, she thought bitterly, though she knew the real loss was that feeling she'd come here with: the lift in her heart when she thought about jumping in his truck, driving off somewhere, and forgetting how much she hated her life.

CHAPTER THIRTY-TWO

KIT CHURNED OVER THE EVENING WITH MANNY AS SHE DROVE A shipment of supplies from the post office to Doc's place. Ever since she'd told Charlie about Manny, it was like she had dropped the weight of an unbearable load, but now its contents were scattered asunder. Though the secret had plagued her, she had enjoyed the protection of control. She wondered what Manny had told Charlie, how he had cast their relationship. Would he know to protect their daughter from the whole truth? Would he reveal things just to spite her? Still, there was, in the telling, a restoration of Charlie's dignity, the dignity of knowing where she came from. There was humanity in knowing. Kit had not been granted the same, and because of it, she might never feel whole. What scraps she had been given, she had clung to—the note, her mother's name, the few stories of cattlemen and dancers and hurricanes. But they were only scraps. Charlie could have more.

She felt for Charlie, wished she could see inside and know what her daughter's heart was doing. Kit couldn't help but worry that the knowledge of her father would drive Charlie further away from her. Would Charlie feel cheated? Would she hate Kit for leaving a hole where her father had been? She had envied how sweetly Charlie had smiled up at him; Kit knew better than anyone how alluring Manny could be. With a sickening twinge, she considered that he might want Charlie all to himself, that she might want to go with him.

She was approaching Doc's when a possum family crossed the road, a fat mama with three miniatures clinging to her back. To avoid hitting them, Kit turned wide into the shallow end of a ditch. The back of her truck clipped a culvert and dislodged something, which now dragged behind her making an awful racket. She cursed, slowed and stopped, but in truth was glad to have a diversion. Whatever had happened to the truck, she was sure she could fix it.

She walked around and clawed through the odds and ends in the bed of the truck. Rubber boots, a poncho, a shovel. She opened a cooler and found a couple of short bungee cords that just might work. Kit got on her back and wriggled under the truck. The muffler and tailpipe were almost completely disconnected from the body, all but one bracket having been destroyed. She started to dismantle the rig but remembered to put on gloves so her fingers wouldn't blister. When she shimmied back out from under the shade of the truck, she startled to see Manny standing there.

"Goddamnit!" she said.

Manny laughed. "Whoa there, easy, girl. I just got here, I swear." He helped her up. "Can you use a hand?"

Kit shook her head. Manny was wearing his old jeans and a tissue-thin western shirt. He looked so much like his old self that she half-expected to see the Mustang parked nearby. "What are you doing here?" she asked.

"I was headed back to church from the vet. Dropped off Jobeth's little dropkick dog for some shots and stuff."

"Yeah, I heard you've been do-gooding all over town," she said. "Hang on, I just gotta strap this thing down." She didn't like that he had been by Doc's. It seemed he was working his way into every corner of her life. She lay back on the ground, shifting sideways under the truck, and snaked the bungees around the exhaust pipe and through what remained of the brackets. She just needed a quick fix to get her to Doc's and back home and could weld everything into place at the house.

"What did you do to your leg?" he said. She looked down and squinted. The heat and the movement had caused the scabbed-over gash on her shin to split open again and blood was soaking through her jeans.

"It's nothing, just a cut." Her voice was a cramped echo off the undercarriage. Without asking, he gently pulled the cuff up over her shin. She let him look. He pressed on the center of the gash.

"What are you doing?" she asked, bothered by his touch.

"I'll never get over that," he said, rubbing the jam of her blood between his fingers. "It's such a blessing."

"It's a damn curse," she said. "It keeps me from knowing when to stop getting hurt."

She secured the last section of the bungee and tugged the muffler to see if it would hold. "That'll do it."

Before she could get out herself, Manny took her by the boots and dragged her from under the truck, the gravel scratching her back and collecting under her shirt. He took her beneath the arms and lifted her up to stand, batted away the dust and the grit. She felt immobilized, like a pup taken by the scruff of its neck. He searched her face, then moved closer, a hair's breadth between them. She felt an old, familiar wanting, a heady flush fanning across her cheeks and down her chest, a weakness in the muscles of her legs. The smell of his sweat and shampoo and a candied fragrance she recognized but couldn't place. She could feel Manny wanting her, too, in the way he stood so still as if waiting for a shy bird to light.

A black car approached—was it police? As it neared, she thought she saw Caleb. She felt embarrassed, even after she saw it was no one, a stranger passing through. The man lifted his open hand off the wheel, a country greeting, and passed them by. Something locked up inside and she pulled back, stuffing her fists in her pockets.

"I gotta go now," she said, taking two steps backward.

Manny's eyes blacked over. He breathed low and slow and

forced a taut smile. "Hang on, can I get a ride to the church? I'll be late if I walk."

Kit saw he was hurt and felt a need to appease him, unclear whether she was protecting his feelings or protecting herself. She nodded and threw the gloves in back.

They bounced along in silence for a while, a hot wind riffling their shirts and hair. Kit went slow to keep from stressing the bungees that held up her muffler.

"Who's that fat kid hanging out with Charlie?" Manny asked.

"That'd be Jim Dirkin." Kit wondered how and when he had known they had been spending time together.

"Looks to me like he's moving in on our daughter," he said.

The phrase *our daughter* bothered Kit. Just yesterday she had longed for family, had resolved to make things right with Charlie after keeping her in the dark for so long. She thought she could figure out a way to let the girl know her father. But he hadn't earned the right to claim her as his own. Kit was the one who had carried Charlie, birthed her, kept her safe and fed and schooled when she hadn't even known how to do these things for herself. If he wanted to know Charlie, it would be on Kit's terms. She wanted to back him off but knew to keep quiet, not to draw out the venom behind his eyes.

"Dirk's not so bad," she said. "Not my first choice, I'll admit, but if I put a stop to it, she'll just run toward him."

Manny shook his head. "I never thought you'd be so naïve."

Kit scooped up a pair of pecans from her cupholder and cracked them in her fist. She picked out the brain-like meats, dropping the sharp shells to the wind.

"Listen, Charlie's tough. She can look out for herself. Let it be, okay?" She had never been good at telling Manny off. She ate one half of a pecan, green and bitter, and spat it out the window.

"No good?" Manny asked.

"Too young."

Manny took the other half for himself and ate it. "I don't know," he said. "Tastes just right to me."

Kit looked at Manny, his skin creased and seasoned with time, the whole of him still stunning. She knew she should be cautious, but the fetters that bound her to him were stronger than her common sense.

She reached across and pushed her fingers through his hair, felt the damp on his scalp, the cool silk of his hair. He tensed beneath her hand and the back of his neck went red under the copper tan. The space between them sizzled, needs welled up inside her, pressing out at her breasts, hips. Like always, a sick elixir of hunger and hate. To strike was to seduce, to want was to fear, to love was to hoard. She took her foot off the gas and let the car drift to the shoulder, where it idled and stalled. He tipped back in the seat, unbelieving. Out of breath and insane with anger and wanting him, she clutched the back of his neck and straddled him, pressed her forehead to his, and closed her hands around his throat. She could bite him, rip out his lip with her teeth and chew. She wanted every inch of him pressing into her. His face calm, grateful, too, and so beautiful. When the vessels began to burst in the whites of his eyes and his blues went purple, she let go. He coughed and rubbed his neck, turned his weight over on her, and pinned her to the seat.

"I came back for you, Kitty Cat," he rasped and leaned in and whispered a call into her ear. "I came back. Even though you left me, I came to find you. You don't belong stuck in this place. These people don't understand you. Tell me this: When did you feel more perfect than you did with me? Fucked up and free?" Tears eked from the corners of his eyes and slipped down those deep creases. "You've been hollow without me," he said. "Look at you. No one to care for you, no one to touch you. I can see it," he said against her neck. "How hungry you are. I know you want me back. Leave with me. Let's go. Let's go."

Kit wanted to slip away, no note, no goodbyes. Like water down a drain, she would just disappear. Under the spell of this invitation, she even forgot about Charlie. She was a nameless runaway, stalking her next meal, waiting for someone to tell her who she was. She was starving, and with him she would never be hungry again. She closed her eyes and felt something pull her toward him, a beautiful undertow.

She lost herself in an eddy of movement and touch. Their bodies slipped into one another, a fusion of similar substances. Lemon drops and the smell of swamp filled the truck and she was sixteen again, then thirteen, then just born, grasping at the breast, rooting for milk to fill her belly. She could curl up and be fed by him. She would never be alone.

Then something, a spring or bare shaft of metal, dug into her spine. She tasted salt and rust and her skin chilled. "Easy," Manny said and heaved his body against her again, the metal thing gouging her deeper. A probe, unwelcome. An injury.

"I don't want this," she said, but he pressed on more feverishly, as if he sensed a window closing. "Get off!" she said.

"Okay, all right, I understand," he said, pacifying, but his hands were in her hair, his body glued to hers. She was flung back on the bed of that cowboy's truck, cold metal at her spine, and then years before, to a hard motel mattress, more scared of loneliness than of physical harm. His breath hot and damp at her ear. *This is not love.* She pushed him off, noticing how much stronger she was, how he had lost his advantage over her. Then her feet were on his chest and she hurled him against the half-open window. She kicked the door latch and he tumbled into the dust, and before he could get to his feet, she peeled out like the ground was collapsing away.

CHAPTER THIRTY-THREE

MANNY STOOD THERE CHOKING ON THE DUST KICKED UP BY KIT'S tires and was catapulted back to the day when he first lost her. He had watched her cut a path in that black Mustang, and even after she disappeared, after the cuffs were clamped to his wrists, he pinned his eyes to the horizon, certain she'd circle back. Then, the years in prison waiting for her to appear, a bashful apology on her lips, perhaps a small, hard tool stowed somewhere indecent where the guards wouldn't look.

His careful calm gave way to a bulldozing rage. He squeezed shut his eyes and saw himself torching the town, house by house, field by field, stopping only to watch the blazing figures dance in their yards and listen to their smoke-muffled screams. The specific violence of this fantasy startled even him, as if these thoughts and inclinations had been crocked and fermented in the dark somewhere, waiting for the lid to be lifted. This drive to destroy was so ambitious and true that he wondered if the source was divine, and so he watched and waited for a sign. Since his time in prison, Manny recognized the force of God in him as so powerful, sometimes it overtook him. He needed to siphon its strength to keep it contained, to stay focused.

Then, a holy nudge from the darkness. *Deliver me a sacrifice.*

His iceberg eyes opened and sharpened like picks on a plump mare, nibbling on a fence post and shivering off flies. A horse. His turmoil was now organized by the narrow focus of a predator. With a jealous flare, he remembered the preening stallion Kit had been riding the night he discovered her outside Bible study, the way she'd caressed the length of the horse's body, ears to rump, had held him between her thighs and flown, swiftly away from Manny, just as she had done now. The same horse he'd just seen at the vet's, rolling in a shitty pile of hay.

WHEN NIGHT FELL, MANNY RETURNED in darkness to the vet's stable. The buckskin appeared in the window of its stall, ears tilted forward in sudden vigilance, slivers of white around his eyes as he scanned for danger.

"Ho, boy," Manny said and offered a bruised apple to the animal. The horse, torn by the desire for sweetness and the fear of the unknown, took two steps back and stretched out his neck, teeth grasping at the fruit. Manny kept the apple just out of reach until the horse inched close enough. He let the animal eat, juice and pulp running out the loose corners of his mouth, and clutched his halter tight. Then, with a sure swipe of his deer knife, Manny severed the jugular. A hot spray of blood and a scream. The horse reared back his head, the knife embedded in his throat, outraged for a moment, before falling into wide-eyed surrender. In his perfect vulnerability, the dying animal allowed Manny to feel a oneness, a gentle caring. The downy hollow behind his chin, the trickle of snot from his nostril, like a child. *Grace*, Manny thought. Then there was only the gurgling and gush of a waning heartbeat. The horse fell to his knobby knees and stayed there a moment before the full weight of his body threw him sideways and he was dead.

He had been a handsome beast, maybe a bit like him, Manny thought. Cocky and gorgeous and strong. But with all its swagger and the formidable size of its dick, it was just prey at its core. Organized around fear, those powerful legs made for running fast and far; the side-seeing eyes, the swivelly ears, the bowels that can shit on the move. In the end, there was no fight in that animal.

Knife in hand, Manny dipped his blood-sticky arm in the horse trough up to his elbow and swished it around, the green water whirling to brownish red. He splashed water on his face and cleaned his neck and hair, removed his shirt and dunked it, wringing out the blood. Now cleansed, he sheathed the blade in his belt and walked down the road in peace, his brow soft and spirit light, uplifted by the sacrifice.

CHAPTER THIRTY-FOUR

THAT NIGHT, KIT WAS IN A HEAVY SLEEP WHEN SHE WAS AWOKEN BY the phone ringing. She followed the sound with a hand to the wall and went down the stairs to the kitchen. She did not let herself worry because Charlie was home and well. But she could not imagine that, at this hour, the caller could have good news.

She held the receiver to her ear and Doc spoke.

"You need to come over here, babe," she said. Her voice was thick with sorrow. "Someone's killed my Warbucks."

The horror in Doc's voice jostled Kit out of her thoughts. She jumped into her clothes, whispered goodbye to Charlie, and locked the front door behind her.

DOC WAS SITTING ON THE ground in Warbucks's stall in an area purpled with blood. She lit a pipe of something pungent; its blue wisps wrapped around her in the stillness. Without turning, Doc seemed to know that Kit had arrived.

"I was in bed when it happened," Doc said, dazed and distant. "Laying there a bit drunk on my valerian root vodka. Just as I was slipping off into a good sleep, I felt it, my spine twanged with a knowing, child, and I could hardly croak out a spell before I heard it." She crumpled then, a skirt of tears below her eyes. "A gruesome scream." Her hand darted to her throat like a frightened bird. "Then silence. I knew sure as I was born that evil had come and taken the good and left. I lit a candle to light the way for a soul and went outside to see which one of my darlings was dead."

Kit was barely breathing as Doc spoke. She recalled the strength, the enormous power of Warbucks beneath her, the thrill of galloping and not knowing, or caring, about what was ahead of them. She was a poor friend in moments like these, wished she could say one helpful thing. She sat silent in the sawdust next to her friend. The smell of iron from Warbucks's spilt blood was overwhelming.

"If I had a backhoe I'd bury him here," Doc said. She pulled a long one off the pipe and spoke as she exhaled, her words muffled. "We'll have to call the county to haul him out. They'll sell him to the glue factory, no doubt. Well, ashes to ashes . . . he's just soft matter now." She reached out to touch the stallion's forelock but pulled her hand away.

"I'll dig," Kit said. There was something she could do.

Puffy-faced and charmless, Doc turned to Kit.

"No need. All that's good is gone. His soul fled quick, even before his body died. Something scared him, Kit. Something dark and noxious."

A dull choking feeling, like a child grabbing her by the throat, urged her to cry out, but she held back. Though her legs wanted to run, she stayed put. The realization struck her like a plank, squarely and out of nowhere.

That night, the coyotes. The memory was as vivid as the day it happened. She saw them huddled and wiggling, smelled the new rot on their mother. Pulling the trigger was easy. Easy because it was right. She had killed them out of mercy, to spare them the unbearable feeling of being alone in the world before they were ready; she thought he had seen that. In the car the next day he had said she was special. *We're the same,* he had said. *We do the hard thing that must be done,* she had understood.

A sickly, guilty feeling started in her stomach. She had underestimated how much she had embarrassed him earlier that day, how wronged he would feel. Now, thinking back on the other times she had let him down—the proposal and the day she left him at Stoker's— she was sure this was Manny's work. But what did it mean? Was this some sort of a message? Or a threat? Or was he so hurt he had to take it out on something weaker than he was?

Doc must have noticed the look on her face and leaned forward intently. Kit could smell the cocoa butter in her curls. "You know something," Doc said. Kit paused, unsure how to talk about it or admit that she was indirectly responsible for Warbucks's death. She wanted to tell Doc, but what if she was wrong?

"Tell me now, dammit," Doc said, suddenly alive, pink around the neck. "Now is no time for your little wounded bird BS. I won't have it. Tell me what you know."

Kit looked down. She wanted to speak but her lips wouldn't move. Whether out of loyalty or out of fear, she couldn't say the thing she knew. She was unable to name him, to acknowledge how her lives had merged and that it had come to this. She could not claim the past that was surely, mercilessly, catching up to her.

THE SUN HAD NOT YET risen by the time Kit made it home, and Charlie was twisted into a pillow, one leg dangling off the bed. Kit hovered at her side for a moment and longed to sleep next to her, absorb her warmth and easy rest. It shouldn't be so hard for a mother to hold her daughter, but it was.

She shook Charlie awake.

"Get yourself together, we're going to help Doc." She went over to the closet, pulled down a canvas bag, and tossed it at Charlie. "Might pack a few things just in case she needs us to stay the night."

"Jesus," Charlie said, squinting, and covered her eyes. "What the hell for?"

Kit wasn't prepared to explain herself. "Someone did something awful to Warbucks," she said. "She needs us."

Charlie sat up. "Warbucks? Oh my god." She pulled her arms inside her T-shirt and stretched it over her bent knees, just waking up to what Kit had told her. "What kind of a sicko would hurt a horse?"

Kit just shook her head, hoping she was wrong about Manny, certain that she wasn't.

"Doc must be really messed up about it," Charlie said, clearly looking for the rest of the story. "But why would we stay over there? Doc doesn't need a babysitter. She's got bigger balls than any man in town."

Kit ignored her, wishing for once Charlie would just go with the flow. She trotted down the stairs and put a few things in a duffel—a flashlight, some ammo, her shotgun. Charlie appeared at the top of the stairs.

"You're bringing the gun?" she said. "This is insane. How about a toothbrush? Why won't you just tell me what the shit is going on? Why do you always act cagey all the time? Maybe you got something to hide."

"The fuck do you mean by that?" Kit snapped, climbing the stairs. Her daughter seemed to be trying to connect dots that didn't go, and Kit didn't appreciate the scrutiny in this particular moment. Charlie retreated to her bedroom.

"Nothing, I don't know," Charlie mumbled. She picked her jeans off the floor, sat on the bed and pulled them over her feet, then jimmied them up to her waist.

"Are we talking about something that ain't being said?" Kit asked.

Charlie smoldered. "I've been hearing all sorts of things about you."

Kit waited for her to go on. It wouldn't be the first time that people in town had talked about her. But there was a bruised quality to her daughter's voice that worried Kit.

"It's garbage, really," Charlie said. "Sandy likes to think she knows stuff but she's a liar. I fuckin' hate her."

"Sandy?" Kit said, impatient to get moving. She cared none too much for Sandy's opinion of her. She took Charlie by the arm. "What did Sandy say? Why are you being so mysterious?"

Charlie backed against the wall and shook her head, disbelieving. "Me, mysterious? *You're* mysterious. You're a fuckin' puzzle wrapped up in chains and padlocked and dropped in the middle of the ocean! Why didn't you tell me about Manny until he came a-knocking on our door? I shouldn'ta had to wonder who my father was or where you came from or any of it. I should get to take that shit for granted but I can't! If you were any kind of mother, you'd know that kids shouldn't have to question *Did my mom really kidnap me from my dad? Is my mom a criminal?* because that's fuckin' ridiculous, but that's exactly what's on my mind right now."

Kit let go of her arm, leaving a yellow cuff where her hand had been.

"Yeah, that's what I'm wondering right now," Charlie said, her eyes full of tears, "and by the look on your face maybe I don't have to wonder anymore."

Kit felt her guts collapse. She shuffled words around searching for a way to explain. How could she tell Charlie any of it? "I didn't kidnap you, exactly," she said.

This seemed to make Charlie even more angry.

"*Exactly?* Roughly, then? You basically sort of kind of kidnapped me but not exactly?"

"You were mine—" Kit reached for her. Charlie dodged.

"*Yours?* I'm not property, yours or anyone's. You can't just cheat me out of having a father, I don't care why you did it."

"That's not what I meant—I thought I was doing the right thing."

Kit could see that Charlie was trying to understand, but she couldn't figure out a way to connect. It was as if Kit were on a rope, swinging toward and away from her daughter, and she couldn't stop the motion, all she could do was hang on.

"Manny's been here for two weeks and the whole town loves him. We've been here since I was born and what do we have to show for it?

You're the town nut and I'm the town nut's freak daughter. My life is so messed up. Because of you *no one* wants to come near me." Charlie started to cry into her hands. "Maybe you want to be alone," she said. "But I don't."

What really hurt was that Kit knew her daughter was right. She had always wished for more for Charlie. Friends, hobbies, family, a proper childhood. But Kit always got in the way. She was guilty and she should make it right. Maybe all she needed to do was go to Charlie, hold her, tell her everything would be okay. Red's words from long ago came to her like a commandment: *Be there for her little spirit.*

But how was she supposed to start being a different person all of a sudden? She didn't know how to make Charlie feel better or give her advice or listen to her feelings. She couldn't tell her about the doctor in the trailer, or the day she came running into Pecan Hollow. There wasn't a way to make any of this right. All she could do was keep her daughter safe. Kit pinned Charlie's wrist behind her back.

"Maybe you're right," Kit said, as cool as she could. "Maybe I'm terrible and everything's fucked. But right now, you're coming with me."

Charlie broke away and tried to throw the bedroom door between her and Kit. Kit wedged herself in the jamb and pushed her way back in. She took Charlie by the waist, flipped her upside down over her shoulder, and carried her down the stairs.

"Let go a me! Let go!" Charlie screamed too close to Kit's ear. Kit clenched her teeth and kept a hold of Charlie's thrashing legs. Charlie gripped the banister and nearly toppled them both, but Kit managed to jerk loose and bring them safely to the truck. She opened the passenger door with her free hand, dumped Charlie in the truck, and slammed the door behind her.

At least Charlie knew when to stop fighting. She stayed sullen all the way to Doc's. Even though little had been resolved, she had said more to her mother than ever before. Now that it was out, all she could do was wait to see what Kit would do. Charlie was afraid of the most likely outcome: that her mom would do nothing.

She was so absorbed in thinking about the dustup with Kit that she hadn't prepared herself for the scene at Doc's. When she saw what had happened, the ragged second mouth under Warbucks's jaw, the sticky lake of blood, she was nearly sick. Kit hosed away the gore while Doc curried the stallion's coat. When they finished, Charlie helped dry him with towels, then cover him with a large tarp to keep the bugs off him. County came by with a flatbed and a crane and dragged the body slowly up the ramp and onto the truck. Doc cried into a hankie, said a prayer, and kissed him on the muzzle before they hauled him off.

Charlie took up chores without being asked, eager to have something to do, to feel that she was being helpful. Hardly anyone spoke a word until dinner. A thick gumbo of chicken and venison sausage simmered on the stove, filling the room with steam and spice. Kit, detached and brooding, pumped great scalding spoonfuls of the stew into her mouth. Doc cleared her throat to puncture the silence. Charlie was exhausted and hungry but couldn't bring herself to eat meat today, not after sending Warbucks to become dog food.

"What's the plan, exactly?" Charlie said. "Why are we really staying here?"

From a glass bottle Doc sipped some peaty spirit, then tucked it away in the pocket of her overalls. She heaved herself up and shuffled around the table, gathering the dishes. She must have known better than to jump between fighting dogs.

Kit looked at Charlie but did not answer.

Charlie wanted to pluck out Kit's eyes and squash them. She shoved the table toward her mom, got up, and left through the kitchen door.

Outside, the air still smelled of warm dirt and manure. She turned over a feed bucket and sat, smoldering like an ember in a haystack. *Damn that crazy bitch to hell.* She flicked the loose edge of a scab on her elbow and thought about Manny, how closely he listened to her, how interested he was. How he was smart, like smarter than the whole town put together, and she wondered what it would be like if she could have grown up with him instead of Kit. Or what they could have been like as a family. When he first came around she'd made a secret wish that Kit would fall for him. She got the feeling that Kit was into him, even before she knew who he was. Now that Kit was acting more and more deranged, Charlie just wished he could take her away, from her mom, from Dirk and Sandy and Leigh Prentiss, from the whole goddamn town and every backward idiot in it.

From a cluster of shrubs, she heard a slight, stealthy noise. The sound of someone trying to be quiet. At first, she froze, listening and scanning the dim arena. A duet of June bugs hurled themselves at the light by the kitchen door. After a moment, she heard the sound again, whatever it was, moving more boldly. She picked up a dusty horseshoe from a bucket near her feet and backed up to the wall of the barn, waiting. She could call for help if she needed to, but she didn't want to draw attention just yet. There was more sulking to do.

A form appeared, a sinister face. She chucked the U-shaped weapon reflexively, poorly, a couple of yards from its target. A creature, fat and furry, scurried into the faint light cast from the kitchen, and hissed. A possum, toothy and smiling like a demon. She threw another horseshoe at it, aiming carefully, this one just glancing off the hump of the creature's back. The possum stiffened and fell to the ground.

Charlie felt a vise grip on the back of her neck.

"Stop that, you," Doc said.

Charlie slouched away and rubbed the sore spot. "What's the big deal?" she said.

"You can't punish an innocent animal just because you're quarreling with your mama," Doc said and marched her over to where the animal lay curled, mouth agape. "It's low character."

"Oh please," Charlie said, a little stung by Doc's reprimand. "Possums are devils. They're pests. You should have let me kill it."

"You don't mean that, sha," Doc said and waved her arms around Charlie as if clearing the air of stink. "You've got the wrong idea about them. Possums are more than that, don't you know?" She squatted and stroked the possum from head to tail. "They're shy creatures, never harmed a single human being. And they're scavengers, you know, nature's sanitation workers. But they're better than buzzards at cleaning carcasses because possums, they eat the bones. I think people take one look at 'em and think they're evil, just cause they're ugly—what would that make me then?" She wheezed a laugh and slapped Charlie on the back.

Charlie looked at the house and saw her mom cleaning, her crazy-ass haircut, that jagged fringe in the middle of her forehead, like a kid had found a sharp set of scissors. And all those battle scars. Charlie was both determined to distinguish herself as nothing like her mother and deeply troubled by their sameness.

"You know the best thing about possums?" Doc asked. "They take care of their young."

Charlie considered this and nudged the animal with her boot. "Why do they just freeze up like that?"

"Look here, and listen. All God's little critters do something different when a threat comes upon 'em. Some fight. The ones with the long claws and teeth, your big felines and your canines. Some of 'em, like horses, they run away."

Doc leaned down and pressed her ear to the possum's belly. Charlie swayed back, as if the animal would spring to life any moment.

Doc pulled Charlie by the hand. "Listen to the heartbeat, see?"

Charlie knelt and put her ear to the fur, softer than she had expected. The heart pumped at less than a beat per second.

"It's not pretending; this creature is preparing to die. The brain shuts off all their feelings and they go to sleep so that if they get eaten, they don't feel the teeth sinking into them. Good thing is predators don't usually like dead meat, so they pass on by. Isn't it beautiful? Nature is forgiving, always looking out for us, always finding a way to do the best thing."

Charlie looked at the empty stall and felt sad for Doc. "I'm sorry about Warbucks."

Doc took a cleansing breath. She squeezed Charlie on the neck again, gently this time, and went inside.

AN HOUR AFTER LIGHTS-OUT CHARLIE could hear the long, slow breaths of deep sleep. Doc snored laboriously on her bed; Kit was coiled on top of the sleeping bag next to hers, the shotgun inches from an outstretched hand. Charlie thought of her parents like Manny had described, young and tearing around Texas in his Mustang. It hurt her to think of Kit like that, like she had missed out on the fun, on all the best parts of her mother. It seemed like Manny could slice the world down its middle and open it up to her, whereas Kit had only made it smaller.

The embers in her chest had cooled, but Charlie had made up her mind. She had to know what it was like to be with her dad, and she didn't see how she could do it with Kit around. Kit would come after her, and she'd be mad. She remembered what Dirk had said, how Kit had busted into the trailer looking for Charlie with murder in her eyes. She picked up the gun. Lifted it slowly by its slim, oily barrel, careful not to brush Kit with the strap. It was heavy in her hand, unwieldy, but when she hung it on one shoulder she felt strong.

Charlie crossed the room to leave, wincing with every creak of the floorboards, but no one stirred. She lowered herself down the steep stairs from the loft to the ground floor. About halfway, she lost her footing and slid down three steps before she caught herself. Kit called out her name and Charlie's stomach flopped.

"Are you okay?" Kit asked.

Charlie wrestled with her breath as her heart pounded. "I'm going to take a dump, geez." She went downstairs, stayed in the bathroom a long time, and washed her hands in case her mom was still up. Then she stood at the base of the stairs and listened. When she was

convinced her mom and Doc were both asleep, she found her shoes
by the front door and slipped quietly away.

As she approached the front gate, an inconvenient memory
surfaced. Not a memory exactly, but the sensation of crawling into
bed with Kit in the middle of the night. Though fully asleep, Kit
would shift to make room for Charlie. How perfectly warm she
felt tucked into the little harbor of her mother's side-lying lap.
Tears slid down her cheeks and hung suspended from her jaw. It
wasn't enough, merely to remember. She had to see what it would
be like not to be disappointed all the time. She wiped her face dry
and turned left away from town. The first day Manny had come to
visit, he had told Kit he was staying at the Big Sky Motel, and she
was pretty sure she knew the one. It would take over an hour, she
guessed, to make it there on foot.

CHAPTER THIRTY-FIVE

HE HAD ONLY GONE BY TO WATCH. HE LOVED TO TRACK THE SHAD-
ows stretching over pulled shades, to see which lights stayed on and
which went out. To know what time Kit went to bed and what Charlie did after her mother was down. Sandy had invited herself, armed,
this time, with the bribe that she could give him a copy of Kit's key
if he let her come. He hadn't known they would be gone, lights out,
driveway empty. Sandy found the spare key taped slyly under the top
step and let him in the back door. As he went in, a bramble snagged
the skin of his tricep and broke off, embedded like a tick.

Just being in this house, with her smells all around him, turned
him on. He hustled Sandy toward the kitchen sink, lifted her up, and
plunged her mouth with his tongue. Strawberry gum. Sweet junk sex,
this one, plentiful and cheap, a bottomless soda. She gripped his hips
tightly with her knees, locked her ankles behind him.

"When do you think she's coming back?" she whispered, finger-
ing his hair.

"Could be anytime."

"What if she catches us?" she said, not cautious, but thrilled.
"What'll we do?"

"That's why I need you on the lookout," he said and kissed each
eye, steered her out the door, and patted her on her broad, flat behind.
She stalked back to the car in pouty obedience. He was tiring of her

soft petulance, her scent—the chemical tell of her imitation perfume, and how it followed him around—the way she rouged her cheeks to carve out cheekbones where there were none. She only made him crave Kit more. Manny wanted to slip Kit on like skin, feel what she felt, pad around in her footsteps. He had been so dutiful, so restrained with her, not letting his hunger show. He had veered off track with the horse, and the virulence of his jealousy had surprised him. But it was a necessary detour. A purge. Now that he was here, in her private place, his obsession was baited, and he was salivating. He had never been able to penetrate her, see her guts, the way he wanted. They were the same stuff, but she always kept part of herself out of reach. Here, perhaps, he could stick his hand in and take it. He needed a talisman. More than that he craved a sign, something to let him know Kit still needed him.

With Sandy perched at the car window like a spaniel, he ventured upstairs and found, at the end of the hall, Kit's room. He walked toward it deliberately, as if approaching a holy place. When he felt clods of dirt crunch underfoot, he knew he was treading on the same soil Kit had. A fussy lampshade on the bedside table, old lady wallpaper, and an antique brass bed. The smell of dust, old paper, cedar sap—none of it was hers. And yet, to have let it be, after all this time, to have lived tracelessly, was classic Kit.

"I know you," he said with such fondness.

He opened the closet door, rummaged through a few things stowed in a box on the floor. Nothing of use to him. Some crude drawings and a framed photo, her dead aunt's will, a recipe for garlic bread.

He knelt and nestled his head in the rivulets she'd left in the unmade bed, overwhelmed by feelings both vicious and tender. "Together or apart, you could never hide from me." He slid his hands under the mattress as if he could find her there, fingers groping, face pressed into the seam. Why could he have anyone he wanted but her? How could she reject him when he had given her all of him, everything she could need? He had been contrite, he had humbled himself. Didn't she know what that meant to him? He lurched forward screaming and pushed the mattress halfway off the bed.

Something clattered to the floor. He crouched and tucked his head under the bed. Dust balls and tissues and a shadowy clump. He reached out and held it like a small animal in his hand, brushed off the dust and held it to the light. It was a trinket, a tiny chandelier made of pink shells. *Galveston.*

She had held on to it all these years.

As he gazed at the bauble, which was no more than six strands of pink shells, the shape of conchs and the size of pearls, attached to a rack of spokes, which were encrusted in the same shells, he remembered the dare, how she had balked, only briefly, and accepted the challenge. He knew then that he could trust her. That she had saved the souvenir was all the sign he needed.

Then he sensed a leering presence in the doorway.

He turned to see Sandy, nude and transformed. At her side, she dangled three feet of braid like a dead snake, limp and headless. Her once long hair was now choppy and short around her face. Like Kit. Without speaking she went to the dirty clothes on the floor and put on plain underwear, men's jeans, and a work-soiled white T-shirt. She approached Manny and stopped in front of him, a grotesque facsimile of his one true love. In the dim light of the lamp he saw that she had wiped away her makeup. In her eyes, the mad look of last resort. She tugged him by the belt and punched him across the nose. Something warm and wet trickled over his lip. He tasted blood.

Entranced by the brazen move, he lifted her under the thighs and plowed her against the wall. He forced his mouth across her face like he could swallow her whole. She bit at him furiously and yanked his head back, denying him, and he flipped her around, arms pinned at the small of her back. "Face me like a man," she seethed, and even now her voice came out like that of a wild thing, like Kit's.

He pulled down the jeans, too tight around her hips, but she took his hands and wrapped them around her neck. "Hurt me," she said. "Break my bones." And she blinked, her eyes glossed over with tears, and dissolved the spell. She whimpered, and all of a sudden Manny saw her as she was. A feeble, sallow waif in masquerade. She kept nothing to herself, left it all in the open, emotionally pornographic. He hated her face, her poor teeth, her fawning regard. Her vulnerability made him ill.

The mounting desires and hateful twitch that churned beneath his skin since Kit had left him today, and fourteen years ago, and even before Kit, since his mother had favored his faggy brother over him, and taken him to bed and caressed him like her one and only, since his father had tucked his dick between his legs and hunched away, cuckolded by his own son—all of it rained down like many whips at this monster. Hair like Kit, bags for breasts like Mother, wilting spine like Papa. He wrapped the braid around her neck and pulled it tight. She looked back more directly, searching his eyes for connection. After a minute, when lack of air tripped her instincts, fear overtook her. She thrashed.

"Yes," Manny said. "Fight it."

He held her by her throat while the rest of her flailed. Soon, she fell limp into resigned, fatal sadness. He tightened the noose, her only vanity, years of her small life wrapped around her neck, punishing her weakness. And as she faded out of this world that had failed her so terribly, even to the end, her eyebrows furrowed and her eyes met Manny's with what looked like disdain. Her lips puckered, and with all the strength she had left, she spat.

"Good girl," Manny said, and he held her until the last heartbeat. He admired the fierceness she had shown there at the end, albeit too late to save her. And as soon as she was gone he was overwhelmed by a sense of peace and rightness, even a fondness for this docile creature in his arms. He thanked God for his mercy and for showing him the way. All this time he had squandered his gift on manipulation, charm, libidinous excesses. Cheap, sordid, disposable. Here, now, he had tapped the purest source, the power to take a life.

He regarded her now like a miracle. She was warm to touch, still, so much so that he wouldn't have believed she was dead, if it weren't for the look on her face. All life had been cast out, the eyes vacant and askew. He pulled the T-shirt she was wearing up and over her face, a partial shroud.

Just then he heard a car pull up and could see from the window that it was police. His heart picked up. Had someone seen him come here? Or maybe had called about the horse, came to ask Kit about it? Manny wasn't armed. He might be able to slip away unnoticed, or hide until they left. Surely the cop wouldn't bust in. Wasn't that kind of town.

The cop slammed his car door and stepped into the light of the front porch so Manny could get a look at him. A baby face. A boy with a gun. He had seen him at church once, nothing special. Too curious to leave, Manny went downstairs and crouched next to the door, listening. The cop marched up the steps and knocked, three decisive raps. A tedious minute passed.

"It's Caleb," the cop called out. *First name basis, are we?* Manny thought with a jealous punch. He peered through one of the tall, curtained windows flanking the door in time to see the guy puff into the hollow of his hand and sniff. He was checking his breath.

"I'm sorry to bother you so late," the cop said. "I hope I didn't spook you. I was headed home for the night and got to thinking . . ." The words came out mushy, like he'd been drinking. "I decided . . ." the cop said and took a breath. "I decided I should check on you. Make sure you're all right after the other night at the Roll-In." Caleb's voice broke like that of a teenager, and he coughed to clear it.

This goofus do-gooder was head over heels. Manny felt bad for him, really. The cop and Sandy were cut from the same cloth. Victims both. *Edible things for animals like us.*

Manny smothered a laugh with the back of his hand and froze. The cop stopped moving and cocked his ear. Manny scanned the room for weapons. No gun above the door. Maybe there was a knife in the kitchen, or a good, heavy pot. But the bitch didn't cook, and there was no counting on anything being where it ought to be. A kitchen chair brought down on the head would have to suffice.

Manny stood to the side where the door would open and raised the chair above his head. He'd begun to sweat now, his heart giddy as he waited for the right moment. But the cop didn't bust in, or even bother to look around the house.

"Oh, okay," the cop said. "Um, yeah, sorry to bother you." He drooped like a cut flower and slunk away to his car, dejected from the looks of it. Ashamed. And then Manny understood. The cop had heard Manny laughing and thought it was Kit.

AS HE CARRIED SANDY OUT like a bride, Manny hummed his favorite hymn.

> *There is power, power, wonder-working power,*
> *In the blood of the lamb.*
> *There is power, power, wonder-working power,*
> *In the precious blood of the lamb.*

He contemplated her in a bashful sort of way. After all, she had been his first. Dear Sandy, not fit for this world, not even for a town as humble as this. Meek and mild, shat upon by all. Perhaps he was guilty of abusing her, too, but at least he had given her his attention, had filled her heart with the love she felt for him. He could be proud for having shepherded a soul in pain back into the Lord's generous arms.

He loaded her remains in the deep trunk of her Caprice. It took some doing, as she was a densely packed woman, ever more so now that she was dead. When she was nicely arranged, he shut the trunk and headed back to the house to clean up after himself. He wanted to wipe the last traces of his little peccadillo from the scene. A few loose ends, nothing glaring, but he liked to be tidy.

The sound of someone walking over gravel stopped him in his tracks. This was an unpleasant interruption.

In the blacks and grays up ahead he caught sight of the lanky silhouette with Kit's determination and his swagger marching a straight line down the middle of the driveway, a shotgun slung across her back. Then, awestruck, he understood.

God had delivered her to him.

He had been missing the signs. Now that his eyes were open, it all made sense. It was so clear he felt stupid he hadn't seen it before. The prize was Charlie all along. It must be. Could it be that even Kit's rejection was part of the plan? Kit was never going to take him back; she had a new love, the love he knew all too well. The love of a parent. All this time his focus had been Kit, but he hadn't wanted to admit how much she had changed, how she had lost her edge, been clipped by small town comforts, her scent unfresh with stasis. He had a chance to start over with this new child, forge new adventures. He could raise his pup even better than he'd raised Kit because the girl was half him. Unblemished. Superior. *Praise God.*

TWENTY MINUTES INTO HER WALK to the Big Sky Motel, Charlie passed her home and saw a set of headlights pointed away from the house. She thought, at first, that her mother must have woken up and beaten her there. But why hadn't Kit passed her on the way? She turned down the rough road, crossed the rusting cattle guard on tiptoe. The hens burbled in their hutch as she passed by. Now that she was closer she could see the lights were low, not a truck but a car. Her chest tightened up and she stopped to locate whoever was waiting at her house. She reached around to flip the safety off her mother's gun. She was trying to make out the car's color through the glare when a man appeared and clucked his tongue.

"Your mama let you run around at all hours of the morning?"

It was Manny. She grinned and laughed a little, feeling mighty glad to see him. Her luck, it seemed, was turning.

"You scared the crap out of me," she said, letting out a nervous laugh. "What are you doing here so early?"

She thought Manny looked irritated at first, though it was hard to tell in the dark. But when he spoke she could hear she'd been mistaken.

"You ever get a wrong feeling?" he said. "Like something's going south? I woke up an hour ago and couldn't shake the worry that something had happened to you and your mama. When I knocked and you didn't answer . . . well, I admit I feared the worst."

She thought it strange he'd go to all that trouble on a feeling, but then maybe that was what family did for each other. How would she know?

"Well, what are you doing wandering around in the dark?"

Now that he was here in front of her, her plan seemed flimsy and childish.

"It's okay, sweetheart, I won't tell," he said, nice as can be, enough to relax her a little.

"Um," she said, hoping her nerves didn't show. "Actually, I was looking for you. I was thinking . . . maybe I could stay with you for a while. If you don't mind."

He grinned and tilted his head to the side. "You do what you want, don't you?" he said. "You know, the right thing to do is call up your mother and discuss this with her. I gather by the early hour she doesn't know you're here."

"No," Charlie said. "No, we can't tell Kit, not yet. I need to get away from her. Look, I know what happened. I know she took me from you. Before I was born." She kicked a cake of dried mud off the hubcap. "I could just kill her for it."

"Ah," he said. "I hoped we could discuss it all together. But it's a touchy topic with your mama." His tone didn't quite match his words, like he was thinking of something else as he spoke.

"I *know*," she said. "I tried to talk to her about it and she shut it down."

He was quiet, long enough that she was about to say something just to break the silence.

"Lookee here," he finally said. "How about this? Let's get out of here. We'll go do something, just for fun. In a few hours, we'll call up your mama so she doesn't worry her head off, and then we'll make a plan. All of us. Together."

The thought of talking to Kit right now made Charlie sick to her stomach. But she liked the sound of hanging out with Manny for the day. He swung open the car door for her to get in.

"Hey, I just want to get some of my things from upstairs," Charlie said.

Manny seemed to tense at this. "Why don't we shove off? Kit could be back any minute. Don't you think?"

He wasn't wrong, but she wanted her shit. "Won't be a minute."

As she walked up the swaybacked steps to the front door Charlie brushed down the hairs on the back of her neck. Inside, she detected a dank smell, not of home. An armadillo, perhaps, had burrowed and died under the baseboards. She found her muddy boots where she'd last kicked them off by the stairs. She went around back to the laundry shed and found her favorite jeans in a pile by the washer. There was a wet load in there, so, out of some rote courtesy, she gathered the clean clothes to put in the dryer. In the stiff tangle, she noticed something odd, an article of clothing she didn't recognize. A miniskirt. She shook it out and with it a skimpy top, a manner of dress that had no business being in this house. *Kit would never wear garbage like this*, Charlie thought. Unless she had completely lost her mind. It couldn't be her mom's, but if it was, all the more reason for her to get the fuck out of whatever nervous breakdown was about to happen.

Still, Charlie found it difficult to leave the house, as if it might be the last time she would see it in a long while. She brushed her teeth and scrubbed her pits, flopped down on her bed and stared out the faded chintz curtains she'd looked at every day of her life. Of course

she'd be back. She could come home whenever she liked. Manny issued a short toot from the car horn outside. She went downstairs and
locked up. Then, as she left the house, she slammed the old screen
door behind her, a gesture that made leaving feel more ordinary.

As she approached the car she noticed there was something
different about Manny today. He was beginning to look like a dad.
A little concerned and tired around the eyes, his shirt misbuttoned
and collar half up like he hadn't bothered to look in the mirror this
morning. It was sweet. Why did Kit have to be so hard to love when
Manny had shown her it could be so easy? She felt wicked for choosing him, but right now she was sick of the struggle, sick of being
tough and working so hard to matter. Maybe some time apart would
do everyone good.

CHAPTER THIRTY-SIX

KIT COULD FEEL IT BEFORE SHE SAW IT. THE FIGURE-EIGHT MOTION of her hips on a galloping horse, perfectly in sync. Then, a ditch ahead of her, so deep she couldn't see the bottom, so wide there was no way around. She tensed and lost her seat, felt the horse stutter-step and slow beneath her while her body kept hurtling forward. She flailed and wrapped her arms around the horse's neck. But as the full force of her weight flew past him, she felt the neck snap in her hands and turn to mush. She began to cry and tried in vain to put him together, fix what she had done. Then his hoof became a claw and as it moved toward her she felt relieved that it was alive and maybe everything would be okay. When the claw plunged into her abdomen and pulled out a mess of her innards, it left a hole clean through the back of her. She felt tremendous pain and startled, gasping, awake.

She could tell from the cold and the quiet at her side that Charlie was gone, but reached out for her nonetheless. The gun was missing, too.

She shook Doc violently. "She's gone," she said, her voice tight with panic.

Doc's face looked dead in the violet predawn light. "Whatcha going on about, babe?" she said drowsily, the shit smell of her dry mouth hitting Kit's nostrils. Doc fumbled for the pull on her lamp and with a click filled the room with amber light.

Kit started to turn over the room. She crouched and looked under the bed, not sure what she was looking for.

"Charlie's gone," she said. "She left in the night. Maybe she just went home, but I have a bad feeling about it." She hesitated to voice the suspicion out loud. "I think she went to find Manny—her father."

Doc swung her legs and felt for her slippers, still trying to understand. "She what now? Manny hoo?"

"I'm sorry, I didn't want to say before. Charlie's father got out of prison and came here to meet her and now I think she's run away. Or else he's come and taken her."

"Sonofabitch." Doc wiggled out of bed and pulled overalls over her nightshirt. "There was a rumor going around. Never paid it any mind. Is he the handsome devil—"

Kit could scream for how tedious it was to explain things now.

"I don't have time to talk this through, man, we gotta go," she said.

"Okay, but how come you so sure?" Doc said.

Kit suddenly felt ashamed and afraid and had to look away.

"I think it was him that killed Warbucks."

Doc bit down on her cheek, her green eyes filling with tears.

Kit had no time for apologies. "You search the clinic and the stables," she said.

"What about the trailer park?" Doc offered. "Maybe she's hanging out with Dirk?"

It could be worth ruling out, but Kit didn't think Mrs. Dirkin would abide another visit from her.

"You go," Kit said. She tugged her boots half on and stamped her feet. "I'm going home." In four long strides, she was downstairs and, seconds later, speeding down the road.

She lost minutes at a time, her trip elliptical moments between stretches of black. As she pulled up to the house she thought she saw Charlie through the window, but it was just a curtain flicking in the wind. She rushed up the stairs and found the front door locked. In a panic, she pounded the door. "Charlie! Open up!" Had she been the one to lock up? She couldn't remember, didn't know if it mattered or not. She ran back to the truck to grab the keys and let herself in. Again, she called her daughter's name, not knowing whether she would find her dead or alive or not at all. She went upstairs and paused in front of Charlie's room. At first, she was afraid to go in, could only listen through the crack. The house was mum. She toed open the door to a crushing emptiness, the room, the house, her heart. There was only Charlie's bed, unmade, as usual, and the very few things she had kept around her: some books, a table and chair. In her closet, a few empty hangers, a lone sock, and a *MAD* magazine folded up the middle. What she would have given for a smart-ass note on the kitchen table.

On her way down the stairs, she saw the dresser underneath the family photo wall and remembered the sheet of pictures from Charlie's school. A photo of Charlie might come in handy, in case they had left town. She pulled the bent grid of photos, eight smiling Charlies, from the dresser and pressed them to her face. Her breath came quickly now, a sign of fresh panic. It felt like there was a cage around her lungs preventing her from taking a full breath. *Stay calm, stay calm. If you want to find her, you have to stay calm.*

She sat down next to the dresser, folded forward, and let her feelings slide out the soles of her feet and through the floorboards until she felt nothing but a low-frequency hum. Tears ran down her cheeks and her breath returned. Then she remembered what Manny had told her when he first arrived. He'd been staying at a motel off the interstate, five miles away. What the hell was it called? There were a handful of places on that stretch, and she would check them all if she had to, but only one seemed decent enough for Manny. She folded the photos and tucked them into her front pocket. Then she left without bothering to close the front door, without noticing how her own bed had been carefully made.

CHAPTER THIRTY-SEVEN

MANNY HAD TO RUSH TO FINISH BEFORE THE SUN CAME UP, QUICKLY washing his hands in lake water to replace the smell of her with the funk of algae and fish. He was pleased with his work. Some light biblical symbolism, nothing too heavy-handed. And he'd been gentle with Sandy, even kissed her before he left, a chaste peck on the cheek in case her spirit was looking on. How long before someone found her? If only he could linger and catch the look on their face. A part of him wished Charlie would wander out of her sleep and find him at work. How would she react to his little project? Would it be instant horror, or perhaps a flash of curiosity, even intrigue? It would be a harsh but swift way to know if she had the mettle to join him.

When he got back to the car, Charlie was still asleep in the passenger seat. He decided not to wake her until he had cleared the area, so he left the door slightly ajar and coasted as far as it would go down the slope before starting the engine. Charlie rubbed her eyes as they jittered over the uneven gravel.

"Where are we?" she said, looking around.

Manny let out a breath, thrilled at how narrowly he had escaped discovery.

"About to head out," he said. "Just had to make a little pit stop."

He wondered if she was groggy enough to let it slip past, the strange location, the sweat and stink about him. She tipped her head against the headrest and stared off at the horizon, so he drove on. Twenty minutes or so passed before she spoke again.

"I'm thirsty," she said. She smacked and frowned slightly, as though she tasted something foul.

"Let's make a little more headway before we stop," he said. "I know a place on the way."

Charlie rolled her head over toward him. "On the way *where?*" She looked curious, he thought, but not suspicious.

"On the way to the best day of your life," he said and winked.

She snorted a little and rolled her head back toward the window, grinning. "Yeehaw."

"There's something you need to know," he said, his tone somber. "You'll be hearing about it in town. Just heard it myself at the gas station while you were asleep."

Charlie yawned and stretched her long arms and pressed them against the ceiling. "Oh yeah?"

"A girl in town was killed last night."

She looked at him fast. "What girl?"

There was alarm in her eyes. A pulse at her throat.

"No one knows yet," he said. "But they tell me it was monstrous."

"Oh my god," she said and slumped back into her seat. "Damn. What else did they say? Was she a little kid, or . . . ?"

"They didn't say, just a girl, strangled to death."

Charlie's hand went to her neck. She shook her head, anxious. "We should go back, don't you think? It feels wrong to go out at a time like this."

"Hell no," he said. "That's exactly why we should get outta Dodge. I'm keeping you close until they catch him—or her."

CHAPTER THIRTY-EIGHT

AN ELECTRONIC COW MOOED AS KIT OPENED THE DOOR TO THE RE-
ception office of the Big Sky Motel. In the dark and dusty space,
the smell of microwaved popcorn and canine flatulence was so thick
she had to breathe through her mouth. The managers had the same
salt-and-pepper hair cut short, same soft cookie shape with thick
necks and sloped shoulders. They stood side by side, so close they
looked connected at the arms. The woman's main distinction was a
heavily made-up face, with peacock shadow swiped over her lids and
coral gloss on her lips. A balding, geriatric poodle on a dingy cushion
wheezed in its sleep.

"Welcome to the Big Sky Motel," she said in a monotone. Between them sat a nameplate, which read BERT AND MABEL SCHUL-
WEISER, OWNERS.

"Hi there, I need some help," Kit said. "Either of you seen a
Manny Romero?" Her voice was dry around his name.

They stared at her, still as a painting.

For once, she wished she were more of a people person. Manny,
she thought, darkly, would have these two eating out of his hand.

"I'm looking for a missing person. I think she's been kidnapped."

Mabel shifted slightly away from Bert and pouted her lips out as
she considered this request. "Missing person, eh?" she asked, betray-

ing her curiosity. Her painted eyebrows pushed toward her scalp. She elbowed Bert. "Did you hear that, Bertie? A *kidnapping*."

Bert indulged no one with a response.

Kit unfolded the sheet of Charlie's school pictures and pushed it across the counter. "Ever seen this girl?"

Bert kept his eyes on Kit. Mabel lifted the glasses hanging around her neck and inspected the photos.

"No, I don't believe I have. Is she the kidnapped girl?"

Kit bristled at Charlie being talked about, even though she knew she needed these people's help. "Can I just look at your registry for a second?"

Mabel glanced at her husband, who had not varied his position in the slightest.

"No'm," he said. "Those records is private." Mabel looked around the room as if searching for a way to help, keep her hands in the intrigue. Kit knew if there was a way in, it would be through Mabel.

"Curious if y'all had any drifters coming through," Kit said. "Maybe someone didn't seem quite right?"

"Ma'am, we're a roadside motel," Mabel said. "All of 'em are drifters, no one seems quite right."

"Ever see a guy come in here with bright blue eyes, tall—"

Mabel clapped her hands together and looked like she had just won something.

"Oh, yes! The handsome fella, oh, he was—"

Bert hissed a reproach, stepped in front of his wife and crossed his arms. "We don't know nothing, and if we did, we wouldn't tell ya without a signed warrant." His voice was surprisingly deep. Mabel mashed her sticky lips together and squinted, as if it pained her not to divulge what she knew.

"Look, it's my daughter," Kit said, pissed as hell and ready to drag him outside by the scruff.

"We ain't seen her," Bert said and set his shotgun on the counter.

Mabel let herself come around the desk and handed Kit a pen and paper. "Will you leave a number in case we do?"

Angry tears came as Kit scribbled her phone number, not that she'd be home to answer a call.

She blew out the reception door and tucked around the corner until she was sure the owners weren't watching her. Then she went to the long train of rooms and pressed her ear to the first of twelve doors, straining for a voice, some sound of people stirring. At each room she listened and tried to see between the curtains, most of which were drawn shut. Inside one, a woman with curly red hair lay sleeping under a pile of sheets; in another a man sat on the edge of the bed in an undershirt, drinking from a can and smoking a butt. When she got to the eleventh room, she saw on the ground in front of the door a smudge of yellow. She knelt down and dragged her finger through the crystalline powder and shards of yellow candy. It looked like Manny's favorite lemon drops crushed underfoot. She licked her finger. Intensely sour and sweet.

Kit hurled herself against the door three times until she felt the frame begin to splinter, then kicked as hard as she could and stumbled into the dark, cold room. She spun around, disoriented and unarmed. It smelled of him, not fresh, but it was there. Lemon and the unnamable scent that was just Manny. The room was neat the way he liked it. Hospital corners on the bed and windows polished to a sheen. She went to the bathroom, opened the closet. There were no clothes or toiletries, and no sign of Charlie. He'd checked out.

As her body shook with wasted adrenaline, her mind filled with unwanted images of Charlie, gasping against the weight of those hands, her thin arms and legs flailing until they fell around her. She began to feel dizzy and her chest knotted. She sucked at a full breath, but her airway had shut, as if it were she who was being strangled. She staggered toward the door and opened it, and in the expanse, she was able to inhale. She could not abide this helpless feeling, like her hands were tied to her feet. What was she supposed to do? She couldn't do this alone. Even with Doc on the hunt, it wasn't enough. She needed more bodies looking for Charlie.

KIT HAD NEVER BEEN INSIDE the police station, never wanted to. The law, for her, had retained its repellent charge after all these years, and she was conditioned to keep a safe distance. Today, she pulled open the heavy glass door and found Caleb sleeping at his desk like a kid in school. The other officers she knew of—Jackson, Alvarez, and the old-timer whose name she forgot—were either out on a call or getting ready to start a shift. She cleared her throat. Caleb slept on, and she could smell the bourbon in his sweat. She brought her hand down on the table like a mallet. He startled, wiped the spittle from his cheek.

"Oh, hey there," he said. He looked embarrassed and smiled up at her. But the smile was quickly replaced with a different look, like he'd remembered something sad, and went cool. He stood up, tucked in his shirt, and cleared the sleep from his throat.

"What can I do for you?" he asked, more formally.

All the momentum she'd sailed in on just dropped away and she found it difficult to speak. She stood there on the edge of asking, as if gathering courage to step in an icy river.

"I need your help," she said, her voice dusty and dry. The sound of the word *help*, a plea, opened a tender place, as if the act of asking itself intensified her need.

"I can't find"—her throat tightened and she had to wrestle it open before she could finish—"my daughter."

Concern appeared between his upturned brows then washed away. "When was the last time you saw her?" he asked. He seemed bruised and aloof in the way he wouldn't make eye contact, the downbeat in his voice. The part of her that had grown to care for him was curious about what was making him act this way.

"Last night when we went to bed," she said.

"That's really not long enough for us to start worrying yet," he said, again, so removed. "We can't declare her a missing person until

it's been twenty-four hours. Then we can send out an alert and orga-
nize a search party. Give it some more time, I'm sure it's fine."

"She's in trouble, I just know it. You have to do something," she
said, her breath shortening. "Ple—"

Kit's plea was interrupted by the sound of a horn honking as a
pickup parked astride the station's entrance ramp. Judd Pruitt tumbled out and burst inside, all raspy and out of breath.

"I need to make a report or something," he said. "There's a body,
a dead one."

Caleb left Kit and waved his hands out in front of him.

"No need to get all worked up, Judd," Caleb said. "You know you
can call the county to pick it up—is it oversize? Livestock?"

"No, no, no." The man was too flustered to talk.

Caleb looked around and whispered, "Is it a cattle mutilation?"

Judd's face reddened, the veins on his temples bulging.

"Man, it's a *person*!" he said and wrung his hat like a wet rag. "It's
a girl, Lord Jesus. It's a human *being*!"

Caleb went still. Kit's stomach flipped and her mouth went dry.
She charged Judd and got in his face. "What do you mean? Who is it?
Was it Charlie?" All of her senses were clogged up, like her head had
been dipped in wax. She saw flashes of Charlie shot up with bullets,
facedown in a bathtub, smothered under a pillow.

Judd hunkered like he was about to be hit. "No! No, ma'am, I
don't believe so."

"What do you mean? How do you know?" She had him against
the door by now. "How can you be so sure?"

Judd flinched and talked away from her.

"Charlie's just a slight little thing, right?"

"She's five foot four, a hundred and five pounds, hair black, eyes
brown—"

"This was a f-full-bodied person," Judd said, his hands cupped out
as if holding something soft and round.

"Are you sure?" she shrieked, and he nodded furiously. She let go of Judd's shirt and nearly wept with relief. Her breath returned. "It's not her," she whispered.

"Okay, there," Caleb said, pushing his way between the two to give Judd some air. "That's good. Glad we could sort that out. Now, Judd, I need to get a full statement from you. Let's sit down here," he said and led the man over to a chair next to his desk. Caleb poured him a cup of water and pulled out the padded rolling chair for him.

Kit leaned against a wall for support, then slid down and held her shins. She couldn't be sure Charlie was safe, but perhaps she was not dead.

"Here," Caleb said to Judd. "Have a cookie." He opened a plastic tub of gingersnaps, took two for himself, and handed the rest to Pruitt. He folded back the top pages of a yellow notepad and wrote the date in the upper margin. "Tell me everything, and take it slow."

Judd ate a cookie, dribbling crumbs all over the hump of his belly, then drank the water noisily.

"Now before I get into it, you have to understand, I been trespassing on Arlo Skinner's property to go fishing for sixteen years and I ain't about to stop, so . . ." He looked to Caleb for some assurance that his fishing would not be affected.

"Fine, okay, get on with it," Caleb said.

"I will, but just so you know, he's got a lake full of fish and no one controlling its numbers. They'd eat themselves alive if I didn't come and thin them out."

"Got it," Caleb said, losing his patience. "Loud and clear."

"Well, I mention it because from time to time, there'd be carcasses washed up and rotting on the edges of the lake, so I didn't take note of the stench other than it was more *pungent* than usual." He ate another cookie, washed it down. "It wasn't until I had about sixty pounds of angry fish around my ankles that I noticed something yonder sticking out of the manger. A gray foot, kinda slender. I was thinkin' maybe it was a doe or a coyote, crawled in the manger to eat and got trapped? But I got this feeling, right in my gut, that told me it wasn't any such thing. Too much flesh upon it. I paddled ashore and banked the boat in the mud. I didn't want to look, but I went ahead toward the manger, every step wishing I could turn back and forget I saw anything. When I got high enough on the hill I saw the rest of her. She was messed up, man." He started to cry and took another minute with a tissue, pinching the tears from his eyes. "Maybe I should have gone to her, but all I could do was run."

Kit grew heavy as she heard the details of Judd's story. She had thought the death would be accidental, natural causes perhaps. A heart attack in an empty field. But this was malice. It was wicked. She gathered herself off the floor and interrupted the interview.

"Hey," she said. "I need an answer, we're wasting time."

Caleb looked irritated.

"I'll send out some feelers, but that's the best I can do at this point," he said, hands open as if to show they were empty, helpless. "Look, I mean it's not the first time she's run off, right?"

Kit's eyes widened then narrowed, face flushed.

"Look, this girl's dead," she said. "You can't save her now. But Charlie's alive. You have to help her."

Caleb looked away and shook his head.

"I have to see about this body. It can't wait. I'm sorry."

Her shoulder and elbow dipped back, like she was winding up to punch him, but then all the color and emotion drained from her face and her arms went limp. Nothing she could do to him would bring Charlie back. Again, she felt a void, as if she had been cored.

As Kit drove away from the station, everything behind her turned to black. All this time, fending for herself, and the one time she needed help from the guy whose job was to help people, he said no. This was exactly why she had never opened up, or told anyone about Manny or any of it, because she was rightly convinced that no one would listen. She could only press on. She sped over to Doc's and pushed down the hope that Charlie would be standing there when she threw open the door. Before she was out of the truck, Doc had run out to greet her.

"Just got off the phone there," Doc said all out of breath. "A girl's dead."

"I heard," Kit said. "Did they say who?" She was hanging on to what Judd had said, that the dead girl wasn't Charlie. Doc caught her look and shook her head and waved her hands like she was clearing away cobwebs. "Don't you go there, sha, it's not your Charlie, not a chance. Listen, there's a town meeting at Friends of Jesus in a half hour," Doc said and slapped the hood of Kit's truck. "For now, we keep looking. We stick together, okay? And then we stop by the church, see who knows what."

CHAPTER THIRTY-NINE

WHEN KIT AND DOC ARRIVED AT FRIENDS OF JESUS, THE SUN stretched long and low and lit up the church like fire. Doc went for the door but Kit held her back.

"Wait, Doc. I don't wanna go in there yet," she said. "Let's just listen for a minute." She rested her arms on the sill of a small stained glass window of a dove holding an olive branch against a blue sky. The window was open wide to let in the late afternoon air.

Inside, Pastor Tom walked up and down the aisle, shushing the anxious crowd that was gathered there until he stood behind the pulpit and waved his hands about his head.

"Quiet! Everybody, hush!"

The citizens of Pecan Hollow settled into their seats, finished their sentences, and turned toward the front.

"I have called everyone here today to address what has happened, to discuss the death of one of our girls. We've just learned they were able to identify the body as Miss Sandy Blanchet." He paused as people let out cries, some of horror, some of relief. "And to pray her soul makes its way to God." He smoothed a damp strand away from his temple.

Sandy. Kit held her heart as if to slow its beating. Doc crossed herself and kissed her amulet. There was a frenzy of concern from the crowd.

Vernon Brewster, an old cattle rancher, stood up and set his hat on the pew. A palsy rattled his hands, which he then clasped behind his back. "What was the . . . nature of the crime?"

Pastor Tom shuddered. "The police are not discussing details," he said. "But I am told it was a most disturbing scene."

There were gasps and then a sober pause as the information sank in.

"I mean this in the best way possible," said Beulah Baker, lifting a finger. "And I'm not saying she deserved it, but I think Sandy lived in a world of sin and you know—"

"Oh shut up, Beulah," said Dorelle Chapman. "You're a sinner like the worst of us. You're a flirt and a gossip. Why don't you just leave that poor girl alone?"

Beulah gaped dramatically and tightened the floral kerchief around her neck.

Tilly Warner, who was sitting behind Beulah, lay a supportive hand on her shoulder. "Here comes my two cents: I never did like the way that Kit Walker came into town all those years ago, all stealthy and whatnot, and just squatted at old Miss Eleanor's, God rest her soul. I didn't like it one bit. And then—what was it—just a few months later? Eleanor winds up dead?"

Pastor Tom held up a hand of moderation. "Now, Tilly, you know Eleanor had heart troubles. Coroner confirmed it was heart failure."

Tilly closed her eyes and set her face like she wasn't changing her mind. "I'm just sayin' is all."

"What are the police doing about it? What am I supposed to do with my kids?" asked Gail Peters, who had a child on each knee and one in a stroller to her right.

"I spoke to Officer Nabors just now. He's enforcing a curfew of nine p.m. Anyone out after that will be arrested. Now, this may be a wanderer, but we cannot rule out the possibility that the evildoer . . . that Satan is guiding the hand of someone among us. That his pawn is here in town. Maybe even here in this room."

The crowd fell silent and heads turned left and right in tense assessment.

Kit felt a thunderclap of panic in her chest as her suspicion grew more certain. Manny had slathered his charm all over the town. He had been running around with Sandy, no doubt stringing her along. He had played nice with the church people, wormed his way in with Charlie. She had to say it out loud or it would make her ill.

"Doc," she said softly. Doc's attention was fixed on the meeting inside. Kit tugged on her arm and she turned to Kit.

"What is it?" she said.

"Doc, I think it was Manny. It was him that killed Sandy. It was him that—" She choked on the words that would follow. Doc gathered her up and patted her back, like she could slap out the bad.

"Hush, now. Don't you go there, hear me? Don't let that despair come near. We got one thing to do and it's find your Charlie." She let Kit go and pointed inside the church. "Now let's get in there and see what we can learn."

Pastor Tom's voice boomed. "Now, I want everyone to cooperate with the investigation and to report anything suspicious, even if it's someone you know."

"Well, I'd feel pretty suspicious of anyone who's not here right now, if you want my opinion," said Glennis Purdue, who ran a hair salon out of her kitchen. Reflexively she pulled a cigarette out of its pack and held it to her lips, then stuffed it back and clasped her purse primly.

Beulah piped up again. "Let's not forget that Charlie Walker stabbed Leigh Prentiss in the face like a *psycho*." Some nodded, others stayed silent. "And you know what else I heard? After she did it, she just laughed and laughed." Beulah pressed a manicured finger to her lips as if holding in a dangerous secret. "I hate to say it, but you know, violence begets violence."

Principal Fowler grunted in agreement.

Kit pushed away from the window and stalked out across the lawn. Doc followed.

"They're not gonna fuckin' help me," she said and wrenched a dry branch off the tree overhead. "Those bumpkins are pointing the finger at Charlie? And she's the one that needs their help! Uh-uh, I'm on my own."

"*Nom de Dieu,* would you shut up for a minute?" Doc snapped. "It's just talk, it's what they do. I know they're cranky and full of doubt, but they're human beings. And they've got children and families too and if you talk to them like you're a person and not a wild animal they might just help you out."

"Shit no," Kit said. She twisted the smaller twigs off the main branch and pitched them into the field. "We're wasting time. I gotta get back out there."

"Lemme butter 'em up, then, babe. Maybe they listen to me. You gotta find out what they know, could save lots of time if you give 'em a chance."

Kit went back to the window to listen.

"Now, as you know," said Tom, "Miz Blanchet can't afford much in the way of a funeral, so I'm passing around a collection for a casket. We'll have a sign-up sheet in back for pallbearers and flower donations, anything you can think of to help." Tom held either side of the pulpit and dropped his head between his arms. "Now let's pray. Lord, our Father, hear us. Sister Sandy has been taken from this world, and we just ask you take her in kindly and gently and give her a nice spot in heaven. We fear she was in the hands of Satan, O Lord. We beg you to wrest her from his evil grips and carry her soul to you, God. And we just ask you to watch over us now. In your sweet name, O Lord, Christ Jesus, we pray. Amen."

Kit watched the people of the town dig into their pockets and purses and give all they had. The baskets filled quickly and were passed hand over shoulder to the front. Tom took the collection and bowed in thanks. Kit didn't think they were as good at heart as they claimed, but maybe they were good enough. The old wooden door groaned as she pushed her way in, and every head in the church turned to look. She stood there in the aisle, flanked by the souls of Pecan Hollow. She dared not meet their eyes, but swept her gaze above their heads and gathered the courage to speak.

A sharp hoot slipped out of the organ. The organist popped up and waved her hands in nervous apology, played a few chords to clear the air, then sat quietly and listened.

"Charlie's missing," Kit said. No one spoke. Someone coughed. Gail Peters's middle child said, "What you say, Mama?" and was quickly shushed. Kit began to lose her nerve and took a step backward. Then Doc appeared beside her.

"Y'all hear her out now," Doc said and stepped aside. Kit looked down before she spoke. She couldn't focus with all these eyes.

"My daughter, Charlie. You all know her," she said. "I need your help in finding her."

A man with floppy gray hair and a bandanna around his neck said, "When did you see her last, dear?"

"Last time I saw her was about nine o'clock last night." She remembered how furious Charlie had been, how she hadn't touched her food. How there was no more snarl in her voice. Now she wondered if she had stopped fighting because she had already decided to leave.

"I think she's with her father," Kit said. People exchanged whispers. She paused, not quite ready to share this last piece. "I think Manny took her."

A collection of gasps and words of surprise.

"What do you mean, Manny's her father?"

"Manny who, now?"

"He's that looker been hanging around lately."

"Oh, *Manuel*. From Bible study? *That's* your girl's daddy?"

Kit realized she was still holding the branch she had pulled off the tree outside and rubbed the bark with her thumb.

Alonzo Martinez, the griddle cook at the diner, cleared his throat. "I don't know if this helps, but, uh, I saw the two of them, Charlie and Sandy, up at the diner the other day? Seemed to me like they were having a tiff. Sandy must've gotten under her skin, cause your girl stormed off."

Glennis raised her eyebrows and mouthed the word *motive* to the woman next to her. Kit rushed up to her and brought the stick down right next to her with a crack. Glennis jumped and turned away, her face shriveled up in fear. Doc yanked Kit back by her shirt and sat her down on the dais.

"Listen, Charlie didn't do shit, and you know it!" She lit up with an anger so bright she could scarcely see. "You've got to listen to me! I think Manny killed Sandy, and now he has Charlie—"

"That's ridiculous."

"He wouldn't! He saved her mama's life!"

"Maybe if you'd kept a closer eye on her you'd know where she was."

"If he's her father, he's got a right to be with her, doesn't he?"

"Quiet!" Tom said and slammed his palm on the pulpit. Everyone hushed. Then Tom turned to Kit. "Look, Kit. You come to us asking for help. That's fine. Now, we will send up our prayers and keep our eyes peeled for your daughter. But, we have a bigger problem here. How can we even trust you're being up front with us? I'm sorry to say it, but we don't know you from Adam. You don't fear God, you don't fear no one. I've been waiting for you to walk through those doors since the day you set foot in Pecan Hollow, and today you finally came." He was preaching, and his tone became more folksy as the spirit moved him. "You come in here, throwing accusations, stirring up my flock. Your girl Charlie's always run wild, she'll find her way home. And if she is with Mr. Romero like you're saying, she'll be safe enough. Whatever you got against him, he ain't no killer." His voice slowed and became grave. "I seen him carry Jobeth Crabtree from her pew to her car when her hip was buggin' her."

Jobeth nodded from her pew.

Pastor Tom continued. "I seen him *weep* reading scripture. I seen him prayin' when ain't *nobody* was lookin' cause that's the kind of man he is. He's the godly kind. He didn't kill Sandy Blanchet any more'n he killed JFK. Miz Walker," he said and pointed toward the door. "You can take your accusations and your violent heathen ways right outta my church and let the good people of Pecan Hollow grieve."

The congregation was nodding and yessing and turning their eyes toward the ceiling.

Kit shook her head and covered her ears. She had known they would turn their backs on her. It was worse than if she hadn't asked at all.

"Shame on all of you," Doc said. "Imagine if it were your child."

Pastor Tom pointed at Doc now. "You, too, with your black magic. Outta my church! Out!"

Kit prickled all over. She stalked down the aisle, fuming, and, just before leaving, raised her branch high and smashed the colored glass window.

CHAPTER FORTY

AS THEY CRUISED PAST THE PECAN ORCHARDS AND HAY FARMS THAT surrounded Pecan Hollow, long fields with miles of fences, some new, some mended, Charlie gathered the courage to finally ask about Sandy's car. She'd nurtured a solid grudge against the girl, and she wished nothing good for her, but it didn't sit well with her to be in Sandy's space without her permission.

"Well, it's a long story," Manny said a little loudly, and he turned down the radio so low she could only hear the hard consonant sounds from the speaker. "But the short of it is, she wanted me to have it."

"She what?" Charlie said. "This piece of shit is the only thing of any value she has ever had. Why would she give it away?"

"Well, not *give*, exactly. She loaned it to me. I told her I was trying to see you more, but it was hard walking everywhere, and so on, and I guess she felt bad for me. She was nice enough to lend it to me for a few days."

Charlie worried if she poked at his explanation it would not hold, so she let it be, for now. She knew Manny and Sandy had been chummy, since he had apparently been confiding in her about how Kit had kidnapped Charlie as a baby. Knowing Sandy, she thought with a shudder, they were probably more than chummy.

About a half hour after they'd left Pecan Hollow, Manny stopped at a gas station, a log-cabin-style building painted red. "Need a pit stop?" he asked.

"I'm good," Charlie said. Manny disappeared inside the convenience store and when he came out a few minutes later, he was smiling like he'd won a prize.

He grabbed his bag and Kit's gun from the back and gestured with his head for Charlie to come with him. She wondered, with a nervous chill, why he was bringing the gun.

"Quick change of plans," he said, hot magic in his eyes. "Come on, it'll be fun."

Charlie followed him, a whole flock of wings flapping around her stomach, to a zippy tomato-colored sports car with a T-top and fleecy seat covers. He tossed their things in the back and opened the door gallantly.

"We're not taking this," she said, frightened and thrilled.

Manny pinched his brow to a hard line above his eyes that told her she should listen. She sat down in the cramped passenger seat, her long legs folded and pressed to the dash. Manny laughed and hopped in, started her up with a brilliant roar.

"We can't," she said and whipped her head around to see if anyone was looking.

"Just a little joyride," he said.

"What about Sandy's car?" She felt genuinely distraught that he would be so careless with something so dear to Sandy.

"We'll be back for it later," he said. "It'll be fine!" He looked toward the station and cut a swift C backward before sliding out onto the main road. Charlie's gut was roller-coaster high. The wind spun her hair into a net around her face, and she clawed it and tied it back.

"How the shit did you get the keys for this?" she asked, trying her best not to sound like a sourpuss.

"Just a little sleight of hand while I was waiting in line in there," he said proudly. "There were three guys in line, but only one of them wore cologne. Expensive, smelled like orange. I knew that was our mark. When he bought a magazine and asked for the key to the john, I figured he'd be in there long enough for us to pull it off."

Charlie couldn't settle on a feeling. She was excited and scared, and also guilty. Guilty for leaving Sandy's car behind, and for having this adventure without her mom. But there was such freedom in jumping in and letting go, being driven away into the unknown. She buried her face in her hands and screamed, and the sound of it blended with the screams of the engine and the highway sweeping by.

MANNY AND CHARLIE SPENT THE day at a jumbo arcade and roller rink. Manny pulled out a hundred-dollar bill, smooth and unreal, the first she had ever seen. He slid it in the change machine, which spewed a seemingly endless shower of quarters. Manny caught them all in a plastic bag and laughed at the look on Charlie's face. She thought of the change jar at home, and how her mom would notice if she'd taken even one quarter for a Popsicle or a pack of gum. A glimmer of conscience, a question—*Where did he get that money?*—appeared and vanished.

They played every game twice and spent the rest of the quarters on foot-long hot dogs and soft serve and buckets of soda. Charlie could feel his attention and his care, in the way he slipped a fresh stack of quarters in her hand as soon as she ran out, or how the moment she began to feel overwhelmed by the lights and pinging sounds of the arcade, he led her outside to watch the sun drop into the horizon like a big brass coin. When they left, she felt goofy and happy and slipped her arms around Manny as they walked to the car. She loved him for bringing her here and treating her to this big adventure. This was, she imagined, what it felt like to be spoiled. She thought with bitterness about Kit's idea of fun. Beating Charlie at cards after supper, gunning it over the hump at the railroad crossing, lighting a bonfire after they'd cleared the pasture of branches. Charlie had cherished those times, because they were all she had, but now Manny was showing her how to live.

After the arcade, he made a point of stopping at a Town n' Country mall. Charlie stayed in the car and listened to AM radio while he went in to pick up something. When he got back fifteen minutes later, he said he wanted to treat her to dinner. She was full from the soda and junk food and didn't feel like eating any more, but it didn't seem decent to turn him down.

They pulled up to the restaurant at dusk. Mosquitoes trolled outside the windows like little ghosts. Charlie kept repeating scenes from the day in hopes she could etch them forever in her memory. Manny turned and pulled from the backseat a white paper shopping bag.

"I gotcha something," he said, pushing away the hair from his brow. "Go ahead and slip this on. Don't worry, I won't look."

Charlie wasn't used to getting presents. All her life she had watched the girls from school get dresses, stuffed animals, puppies, and even ponies from their dads. What little Kit had given her had never even been wrapped. She reached in and held up a plain striped T-shirt. She was a little surprised because it wasn't anything special, not that it was bad. She smiled and put it in her lap and reached in the bag again. This time it was a plain pair of dark jeans.

"Wow," she said. "Thank you." She was fearful of breaching the peace between them. "It's always good to have extra clothes."

"Well, go on," he said. "Put 'em on. Trust me, it's a perfect fit."

She didn't know if he meant to change here, in the car, or in the restaurant. Either way it was starting to feel weird.

"That's okay," she said. "I'm comfortable in the clothes I'm wearing, if you don't mind."

Manny looked annoyed. He cocked his head.

"Why are you being difficult? Just put 'em on, I want to see what you look like."

Something sick in her belly told her not to push back.

"Here?" she said.

"Geez, what a prude. Don't worry, I'm not gonna look." He covered his eyes with his hands and made a show of turning around. His greased hair, dark and wavy like hers, had parted in back to expose a bald spot the size of a poker chip.

She put the new shirt over her head and shoulders and wiggled her arms through the shirt underneath, then worked it over her head, pushed her arms through the armholes, and pulled the old shirt off through the neckhole. The pants would be more difficult to change modestly. They were in this goddamn convertible and there were people around, going in and coming from the restaurant. She nearly cried, wishing she were back at Doc's house, her mom asleep beside her.

"Do you need a hand?" he asked, making a quarter-turn.

"No! No, I got it," she said. She would just have to be quick. "Just please don't turn around."

She yanked the pants she was wearing down to her ankles and kicked them off, then wiggled her feet into the new jeans and tugged upward, shimmying to get them on as fast as she could. They were stiff and stuck around her hips, which she lifted high to get the pants the rest of the way up. When they were finally up, she zipped and buttoned them and caught her breath.

"I'm done," she said and hugged herself.

Manny turned around. "My God," he said and looked at her a moment. His eyes went soft and dewy. "It could be her."

Charlie knew what he meant, and she didn't like it.

"All right," she said, antsy to get out of the car. "Can we go in now?"

He looked at her like a painter checking a canvas. She curled under his gaze, couldn't wait another minute. She put on her boots and opened the little door. At this, Manny seemed to snap out of it. He folded her old things squarely and stowed them in the paper bag, then followed her inside.

The steak house was one of a chain she'd seen in passing, but Kit could never have afforded to eat there. She stepped inside and her skin goosed against the crash of air-conditioning. The hostess led a winding path through the burnished wooden tables to a short booth with green vinyl seats, a light fixture of stained glass hanging between them. The napkins were cloth, the menus tall and leather-bound, not laminated like the ones from the diner.

"This is real nice," she said. "But I would have been happy with KFC."

"But you're my best girl," he said. "And this is a very special occasion."

Manny didn't explain what he meant and Charlie didn't ask.

After the waiter came and took their drink orders, Manny excused himself to go to the restroom and left the keys on the table.

"Don't run off now," he said, and disappeared into the back of the house. Why did he leave the keys? she wondered. Was it a test? Why mention her running off? The waitress came by with a four-part caddy of chopped things: chives, cheese, sour cream, and bacon bits. Thinking it some kind of appetizer, she spun the caddy around and spooned some cheese and bacon into her mouth.

"Geez, ya dummy," said a young voice, bossy and snide. "That's for the baked potatoes. It's *toppings*." It was Leigh Prentiss, all dressed up in a plaid jumper with a ruffled collar and patent leather shoes. Her speech was thickened by the healing hole in her cheek, now unbandaged. It looked like a bullet wound all scabbed over.

"I didn't know you ate here," said Leigh, looking down at Charlie. "We come here every time we visit my cousins in Yoakum. It's our family tradition. I get the *fillette MIG-non*."

"It's my first time," Charlie said. "It's nice." There was a tense pause where Leigh seemed to be waiting for an apology. It would be simple enough to give, but Charlie was reluctant to bring it up out of nowhere. Then she remembered what Manny had told her in the car.

"Did you hear about—"

"The *murder*?" Leigh said. "Oh yes, everyone's talking about it. That's why we're here so early, we gotta be back before the curfew. You know about the curfew, right? Daddy says they'll throw you in jail if you're out past nine."

"Geez. That's so crazy." Charlie wondered when she would even be back in Pecan Hollow.

Maybe it was because she was far from home, but she was beginning to feel friendly toward Leigh. All in all, Charlie could see how she had overreacted, and how scared and hurt Leigh must have been to get wounded like that. She felt ashamed for what she'd done and offered an olive branch.

"I'm sorry I stuck you and fucked up your face," Charlie said. "It looks like it really hurt."

"It did," Leigh said and held her cheek in remembrance. Several tables away, in a big circular booth, her parents and four brothers broke into laughter that filled the room.

"My mama said it will strengthen my character, like Barbra Streisand's nose." She drew a comically large nose in the air with her index finger. "She said distinctive women have more power than beautiful ones. I'm pretty sure she's just trying to make me feel better, but who knows." The girls were silent. Leigh eyed the toppings and smoothed her pinafore. "I'm sorry for looking at your answers. It wasn't very Christian of me. You're so good at math is all."

Charlie smiled back at Leigh in her stupid dress. She wasn't so bad. Maybe, she thought, they could hang out sometime. Then she remembered Manny. She craned her head around to the back of the restaurant.

"Hey, my dad'll be back from the bathroom soon. I probably shouldn't be talking to you."

"Wait, that was your *dad*?" Leigh squatted by the table to get closer. "But he's so *hot*," she said, as if it were a forbidden word.

"Ew, no!" Charlie said. "Look, can you just go back to your table? I'm sorry. I just don't want to get in trouble."

"Okay, fine, but why shouldn't I be talking to you? Is he superprotective of you?" Leigh twirled a ringlet under her ear. "I wish my dad was like that."

"I don't know, it's just a feeling I get." Charlie was starting to get anxious that Manny would see them. Why was she so worried? It was kind of weird that he'd bought her a new outfit, but maybe that was a normal Dad thing. Or maybe her clothes were dirty and he hadn't wanted to embarrass her. It occurred to her that maybe she should try to call her mom and tell her where they were. Now that she was so far from home, she didn't really want to stay with Manny anymore, but neither did she want Manny to be mad. They had only just begun to get to know each other, and she was mortally afraid of screwing things up.

"Leigh, listen. Can you do something for me? Can you let my mom know I'm okay?"

"She doesn't know you're here?" Leigh gaped like she had just struck the motherlode of gossip.

"It's kind of hard to explain, but it's fine. Just tell her, okay?" Charlie squeezed Leigh's wrist to cement the message. "Will you, please?"

She nodded eagerly. "Yeah, I'll tell her. You can count on me."

"Thanks, buddy," Charlie said, resolving to talk to Manny about going back to Pecan Hollow after the meal. "See ya."

"See ya," said Leigh, grinning, and she wove through the tables to the front door, where her family was waiting.

CHAPTER FORTY-ONE

KIT STRUGGLED TO BREATHE AS SHE RAN FROM THE CHURCH HOUSE. A current gathered in her throat and she screamed, a dusty wind sweeping the sound across a grove of pecans. She dropped to her knees and pressed her forehead against the warm asphalt. It was shameful of those people to turn down her pleas. They had always attached strings to their kindness. She wished Doc could put a hex on them. And yet, what else did she expect? Shame on her for thinking she could be treated with any kind of fairness. As soon as she found Charlie they would pack up and leave. There was something batting in her chest, like a bird thrashing around in a cardboard box. If only she could touch Charlie, to tangle that hair in her hands and draw her close.

When the numbing came on, it was unwanted.

"*No, please, no,*" she whispered. The feeling started in her face and rolled down her insides like wet paint. Her hands tingled and cramped before she ceased to feel them at all. She pressed her nails in her cheeks, clawed for a feeling as if she could dig it up. Soon, she felt nothing but a void.

When Doc caught up to her, Kit had no idea how long she'd been on the road. Her mind was stunned still, she moved slowly, automatically. The passenger door of Doc's van groaned open and Doc helped her in, gently manipulating each limb as if she were made of glass.

"I can't take it," Kit suddenly said, her voice sounding as if she were at the bottom of a well. And once her mouth started moving she found she couldn't stop. "I can't not know where she is. He can't have her, he can't take her from me, oh God, I want to die, please let me die before I see him lay a hand on her—"

"Hush, now, hush," Doc said, her green eyes worried and big. "She'll be okay, we'll find her, babe."

"You don't know that!" Kit shouted. To hope was too painful. She couldn't feel her arms and feet. She was crazed with a need to move. "I let him in. I was weak, and I missed him. I let her meet him, even though I knew he could be dangerous, even though I knew she would love him."

The guilt was too much. She screamed so hard her eardrums popped, and Doc clapped her ears to block the noise. Kit couldn't get a full breath and began gulping at the air. "Oh my god, the coyotes, those little pups. It wasn't mercy, he helped me kill them to see if I was *wicked*, to see if I could kill. And then Warbucks." She winced as she recalled the great heap of the stallion covered in blood. "That was murder. He did that to punish me. Or to *warn* me."

Doc took her arms, but Kit shoved her back, clawed at the door handle. "Get back, now, Doc. I don't want to hurt you. You got to let me go."

Doc pulled Kit into her arms, her strength completely over-whelming. Kit lashed out and flailed and bit at Doc's hand. She hadn't felt this small since she was a girl. Doc held tight, her arms thick and strong as thighs. Kit thrashed until she was sapped and hung limp in Doc's embrace. Doc turned her around and draped Kit over her shoulder like she was burping a baby. She stroked her back and hummed a sad song.

Kit's skin burned where Doc touched her, but with every pass of her hand the hurt felt more like warmth, and there began a melting within. She hung across the soft, broad shoulder and felt her breath align with Doc's, her heart slowed to a gentle rhythm. She lost all sense of being separate. A memory burbled up, springlike, and enveloped her.

It had been the end of a hard freeze, the first day of thaw. A scattering of birdsong cheered the air that had hung silent and dour for a week. The grasses, once furry with frost, now hung wet and limp; the sun had burned a hole in the cloud cover, dispersing the frigid fog.

Kit had been clearing fallen branches from the yard for firewood. Some were as thick as her waist and ten feet long, but she'd hoist them over her shoulder and lean forward to drag them to a bonfire in a clearing. Aunt Eleanor had said the labor would come on slowly, feel like gas pains or cramps. She wondered, what with her condition, if she would notice the contractions at all. Instead, they came on like a hot summer storm, suddenly and violently with thunderclaps and lightning. Pain in her body was new to her, a sobering shock, but instead of bracing against it, she followed it, knowing through some timeless medium that this was good for her, it was the pain of creation.

She staggered inside, falling to her hands and knees every time a surge came on, and climbed on the bed. After several hours of spasms, she began to quake. She vomited and collapsed, shivering and stripped of all her strength. She felt for the first time that she could not do this alone. Then her baby drove forward and when she reached down she could feel the slick top of its head. One last surge of strength helped her rise and try again, fearing if she could not deliver now they both might die. She squatted and held on to the brass footboard for balance, feeling her hips split by unimaginable pressure and pushed, and a spreading force like the hands of God drew her open. The baby came faceup and still ensconced in the caul, like a new foal. She cupped the head in her hands and pushed again with a wild growl and pulled her baby to her chest. She lay back and wept, such relief and sweetness enveloped her and all she could see was the child in her arms. She peeled away the membrane and wiped the muck from her baby's eyes and cut the cord with some sewing shears. She lay upon the baby a soft blanket to keep her warm. All on her own, the baby found her breast and began to nurse. They fell asleep together on the bed, breathing as one. She woke up to contractions and saw she was delivering the placenta, just like Aunt Eleanor had said would happen. In the moments after, when she lay the baby in the Moses basket and got up to wash her hands and between her legs, she missed the baby so much she was weeping. She found a pitcher and a cup on the dresser and filled them both with water and set them on the nightstand. *Drink as much water as you can hold*, Eleanor had said. When she was clean, she wiped the baby with a damp cloth and dried her well so she didn't catch a chill. She wrapped her in a thin blue blanket that had belonged to Eleanor's daughter, Emily, and lay down with her in the old brass bed. The baby was tired, and Kit was, too, and they slept there all night and into the next afternoon, waking only to feed.

Kit ached from the memory of that sweetness, the way every worry, every memory vanished and all she could experience happened in the short distance between that baby and her. Giving birth to Charlie had felt like joining the human race. She had finally known love, and it was nothing like what she had felt with Manny. It was awe at seemingly nothing at all, it was what she felt when she was giving, when she heard her baby cry; it was dependence, heartbreak, a kind of rapture. She felt uplifted and bettered for having loved this baby. It all felt like a gift she didn't deserve, but she was happy to have stolen.

Why had she smothered these memories, why had she not bathed in them and let them hold her over through hard times, let her be better to Charlie? How could she have let her daughter convince her that they were on opposite sides, when they were the very same? Why had she not told Charlie the story of her birth, how she came into the world and brought Kit with her?

She felt as if sucked into a violent current of sadness, bandied about, sobbing, swimming, her tears like a fluid she could breathe. She was scared at first, but then let the salty solution quiet her. The static cleared and every cell vibrated, liquid vibration all around and within her to her very core.

She could see herself then as a child, younger than Charlie and not clever or tough as she had always thought she had been, but as helpless as a motherless pup. When Manny found her, she had been a walking void, gutted and scraped clean. He entered the void and filled it with his perfect smile and made her feel like kin. His attention had warmed her through and through, his ideas had expanded her sense of possibility. He had taught her his trade and let her in on his secrets. She had been so grateful she wasn't going back to foster care, she hadn't realized that he was worse, far worse. Having never known the lasting affection of others, she had not known better than to call it love. Her throat closed up and she held her hands to her eyes as she remembered, even now, how sweet it was to have someone care for her. She had not been wrong to want those things. So lost and alone she thought she had found family in a criminal like Manny. She was not his family, or his lover; until this very moment, she was, and always had been, his prisoner.

Only now was it dawning on her that she had been his biggest con of all. With an elegant sleight of hand, he had taken her life, her body, her innocence. He had thrust himself into her bloodstream, put life inside her. And now that he had found her and Charlie, he would claim—or kill—them both.

CHAPTER FORTY-TWO

CHARLIE FOUGHT BACK DROWSINESS FROM HER LONG DAY OF EXCESS.

"We're almost to the motel," Manny said.

She looked at the clock, after 9:00 p.m. "It's so late though, do you think we should just call my mom and head back home? I can see your place another time," she said. She had had her fill of adventure and wanted to end the day in her own bed. Maybe, she thought, her mom would be so glad to see her she wouldn't ream the shit out of her when she got back.

He kept driving, squinting into the headlights of a passing car. He checked the rearview.

"I still have plans for us, cutie, but don't worry, we're not too far away."

"Far from what?" she asked. She felt uneasy when he didn't answer. "Kit's gonna lose her shit, you know how she is."

Manny flicked open a canister of lemon drops with his thumb. "Did she ever tell you about how we met?" He parted the wax paper, took two and pushed them into his mouth, then tipped the canister toward her.

Charlie sucked on the candy, its sour sweetness wetting her mouth. "She never tells me anything."

The lemon drops crackled against his teeth as he rolled them around with his tongue.

"It wasn't too far from here, I was filling up my car and went in to use the bathroom. When I'm getting ready to go, out of nowhere comes your mama, arms full of shit she'd stolen from the gas station, just booking it."

"What? She was stealing?"

"I just watched, I couldn't believe what I was seeing. She headed for my car and dove in my window to take my lunch, but she got stuck. I had to laugh, it was too funny and so strange. I tried to help by lifting her out of there, but she fought me. She was fierce. I knew right then we'd be good friends."

"Weren't you mad? She was stealing from you. Did you call the cops?"

"Mad? No way. I admired her. Still do. There's something wild about her, I knew I'd never get bored."

"That's so crazy," she said. "How old were you guys?"

"She must have been your age. Well, a little younger."

Younger than me? Charlie thought. She had imagined them at twenty, fit and messy and beautiful. Why was Kit alone if she was so young? Who was watching her? Tears pushed at her eyes as she remembered how little she knew about her mother.

"But you were driving . . ." she whispered, trying to sort through the pieces that didn't quite fit. "So you were like sixteen when you met her?"

"Me? No, I was in my late twenties, at least." He looked over with a half grin, his face taking on the glow from the dash. "Well, don't look so scandalized, silly. It's not like we were lovers right then. I waited until she was of age, I'm not a pedo."

Charlie flushed at this last, ugly word. The treats, the new clothes, the dinner, these scraps of information were beginning to take shape, but it was so grotesque, so shockingly dark, it could only be seen indirectly as a blurred monster lurking on the periphery, an alligator in the swamp. She sank into the seat and pulled her knees to her chest.

CHAPTER FORTY-THREE

A WILD PANIC CLAWED ITS WAY UP KIT'S THROAT. SHE FOUGHT IT back and leaned on the accelerator, hands gripping the steering wheel so tight she could barely feel them. Doc had tried to tackle her to keep her from leaving, telling Kit that she needed more time to get aligned, or some shit. Kit had fought her off and climbed out of the van and into her truck, tearing blindly into the night for Charlie.

The old truck rattled as she pushed it to its natural limits, peeling around dark and dangerous curves. She moved moment to moment because to advance even one inch ahead of herself could invite terror, collapse. She rolled down her window to catch a hard breeze. A gusty smell of manure and ant killer whipped into the cabin. She barely noticed the headlights approach and pass her by; only when the car stopped, changed direction, and sped directly behind her did she shift her focus. The driver lay on the horn, swerving dangerously close, then accelerated and pulled up beside her. Kit braked slightly to drop back and look at the other vehicle, a black Suburban. It veered into her lane and nearly blew off her side mirror.

Kit punched her horn and yelled at her truck to go faster, but it maxed out at eighty. The Suburban easily matched her speed. Finally, a woman leaned out the window, banging on the door.

"Hhhheeeeyyy!!!! Hey, Kit!" It was Sugar Faye, her hairsprayed bubble barely disturbed by the rushing wind. She pointed to the side of the road. "Hey, pull over, will ya?"

Sugar. Goddamn her. Kit shook off the sting of fear in her skin and coasted to a stop. She got out and met Sugar at her door. The kids were piled in the back rows and Rob manned the wheel.

"Eeek, sorry about that! I must have given you a fright," Sugar said.

"You almost ran me off the damn road," Kit said. "I can't stay here, I have to go. Charlie's missing."

Sugar Faye held her throat. "Oh god, oh no. Well, that's what I was—"

Kit grabbed her by the shoulders. "Do you know something? What's this about?"

Sugar waved her hands around. "Yes, okay, hear me out, sorry, I'm just flustered. Listen, we were down in Yoakum visiting my cousin—she just had her gallbladder or her appendix or sump'm taken out so I set with her and brought up some of my kolaches—anyway, after we left we stopped for supper at our favorite steak house—"

"Sugar Faye, would you get to the damn point?"

"Yes, okay, so Leigh saw Charlie over there—"

"She did? Wait, where? At the steak house?"

"Ole Steak Taverne, hang on—" Sugar fished around the glove box for a map and pointed to the spot with a long pink nail. "Look, it's oh, about eighty miles southwest of here. You could make it in an hour if you really book it."

Kit took the map and traced the route from Pecan Hollow. A woozy feeling lapped against her, an echo of a memory, dispersed and vague.

"Anyway," Sugar said. "Leigh says something just didn't look right. Said Charlie was there with her dad, but that she didn't want him to see her talking to Leigh. And of course, she doesn't have a dad, so I felt pretty suspicious about that. But then Leigh said Charlie said to tell you she was okay, but of course that makes me even more suspicious, and I was gonna call you when we got home, but then I saw your truck and flagged you down and here we are."

Kit leaned against her truck to take in what she'd heard. Charlie's okay, for now at least. And she was with Manny, but why? If they were eating out in a restaurant, they weren't exactly on the run, were they? Unless he had nothing to lose. With an awful start, she remembered the restaurant in Galveston with the giant crab. Maybe he didn't want to hurt Charlie, maybe he was *training* her.

Sugar Faye seemed excited to have something useful for Kit. "Did that help?"

"Yes, thank you, thank you. I have to go now," Kit said, swiveling toward the truck. Sugar turned her back around and pulled her into a soft, perfumed hug. Kit stiffened at first, but Sugar held on to her, and spoke into her ear.

"Girl, don't you worry, okay?" she said sweetly. Sugar pulled back and wiped a tear, black with mascara, from under her eye. "I'm sorry about all that in church. Folks were just scared. We are gonna find your baby. I'm gonna get on the horn, call everyone I know to get their asses outside and start looking. Curfew be damned."

Kit sighed, not wanting to waste any more time explaining that the people of Pecan Hollow would no sooner help her find her daughter than they would skip church on Sunday. Instead, she nodded and got in the truck. If the town did somehow pull together for her, then hallelujah, but she sure as shit wasn't counting on it.

CHAPTER FORTY-FOUR

KIT FOLLOWED THE MAP TO THE RESTAURANT WHERE CHARLIE WAS last seen, her foot never leaving the gas pedal as the night slurred past her. A steady rain of insects slapped the windshield, and the over-worked engine groaned. At her feet, straw papers and loose napkins tumbled and bobbed in the stale air that curled through the half-open windows. She could feel the soft weight of her child against her breast, smell the clean scent of her new skin, hear her burble and coo. Even at this distance, she spoke to her with the full conviction the sound would carry. *Hang on, baby. I'm coming.*

When Kit approached Yoakum, the stench of rotten eggs became so intense she had to roll up the window. As she reached for the crank, it occurred to her, clear as a chime, where Manny had taken her girl. The smell of sulfur. The oil fields. He was taking Charlie back to the place where they had made her.

All the billboards had been taken down, no Mae or Elvis or Little Richard to lead the way. But she couldn't miss Clifford's Hollywood Palace. Though abandoned and dark, its sign still loomed over the highway. At this hour, the roads were nearly empty save for a few eighteen-wheelers punching through the night. She exited, parked by the entrance. There was a spry little hot rod pulled up closest to the stairs. A toy for Manny, she thought. She had been right to come here. She left her keys in the ignition and let down the tailgate as quietly as she could. Then she drew the machete from the bed of her truck and tapped it against her calf, a cold comfort.

An abrupt gust of wind cut a high pitch through the cracks in the sign behind her; all manner of vermin were rustling around in the weeds and the walls. Some yahoo had scrawled PRIVIT RESIDENSE on a bowed sheet of plywood covering a downstairs window. As she approached the dusty, abandoned building, she kept her eye on the purple door with its hand-painted sign. No lights, no sounds. *Please, let it not be too late.*

Memories of the last time she had been here rose up around her like a stench. How he had ambushed her on bended knee, deserted her when she turned him down. How she had withered without him, rolled in her own mess, and begged for his return. She was ashamed to revisit that time with a wise mind. And when he finally slipped back into her life, as if he had never left, the way he held himself to her hips and forced himself, his genes, his very makeup inside of her. Here now, a new fear emerged. That he had taken Charlie not to hurt Kit, but to replace her.

The windows had been boarded up, but poorly. Kit peered through a gap in the plywood. There was a worried sound, and Kit held her breath to hear it. A rustling of wings—it was only the cooing of pigeons. She emptied a crate full of sooty spray bottles and rags and stood on it to see through a long bar of exposed window high above her head. The purple shag carpet had been ripped out to the subflooring. Someone had burned the mattress to its coils and there was a charred hole in the ceiling above it. In the closet, the cutout of Dolly Parton, now battered and defiled. A camping lantern cast a small artificial light on the far side of the room. There perched on the giant purple bathtub sat Charlie, her thin legs folded over the edge. Dressed in a striped shirt and starchy new jeans, she looked like a willowy version of young Kit. Manny, seated next to her, had his fingers in her hair, like he was sussing out the tangles. At his feet was Kit's shotgun.

SHADOWS OF PECAN HOLLOW

Kit went straight for the door and busted in. Charlie turned toward the noise, a ray of recognition passing over her face. She wanted Charlie to run to her, but she just turned her eyes away, flat and unfocused. Was she drugged? Didn't seem like Manny's style. His charm was the only intoxicant he needed. Maybe, she thought with a start, Charlie didn't want to be saved. Maybe he simply had her in his thrall, a force Kit knew too well. The idea that Charlie was there of her own free will scared Kit even more than him holding her captive.

Kit's heart rapped so loudly she could feel it in her ears and eyeballs and all the nails in her hands and feet. She could not lose herself to this fright. She called upon the numbing, and the fear settled like silt in a lake after a rain, her breath now smooth and steady, and she could hear every sound in the room. The calm cleared the way for a single thought. Charlie needed her mother.

"Charlie," Kit said. "I'm here, Charlie. Are you okay?"

Manny still had not turned to look at her. He fanned Charlie's hair across her back. "Well, aren't you the clever cat? How did you find us?"

Kit tried to keep her voice level. "Now don't act like you didn't mean to lead me here," Kit said. "Clifford's? The Dolly room? If I found you, it's because you wanted me to."

"It's not about what I want," he said. "It's what she wants." Charlie met his eyes and he put a soft hand on her back. "It's okay, go ahead."

Charlie clasped her hands together. "I've been thinking," she said. "We don't get along anymore. You and me, we're like . . ." She drifted and looked at Manny, then continued, "Siamese twins. We been stuck together too long." She wouldn't look at Kit directly. "I been thinking it's best I go live with Dad."

The words came out of her like cardboard, the words were not her own. Even so, hearing them weakened Kit at the joints. She could not let him win. He would expect her to unravel, to rage, to take Charlie back by force. But he would not let her go unharmed.

Then Charlie glanced at her, sharply, briefly, and Kit could see in her features a presence and a cunning she had not detected before. Charlie was not drugged or brainwashed. She was playing along. *Atta girl*, she thought with a swell of pride for her daughter. *I couldn't see through him, but you can.* Kit set her machete on the floor and stepped over it as an offering of peace. She, too, would have to play along to get closer to Charlie.

"I didn't come to take her away," she said. "I came here because I thought about what you said, about us being together, us three." She winced on the inside. Lying wasn't her thing, and the words didn't sound convincing. "I want to see if we can try to be a family."

Manny's eyes widened unnaturally, feigning irritation.

"Don't you see? You're the third wheel. No one invited you here; go on home."

There was a wounded, flustered quality to his voice, like he had made up his mind and now she was complicating things. She probed his eyes, those brilliant blues, ever shifting, and found something in his face, a wanting she would handle deftly. He seemed to want her to beg. She sat down next to him and put her hand on his thigh. He didn't pull away.

"I'm sorry," she said, her voice hoarse and mellow, like that of a child about to fall asleep. "I shouldn't have pretended you didn't matter to me. That was my pride. Truth is, I looked for you coming down the drive every day since I left, hoping you'd come for us." She tightened her grip on his leg. "Now that you're here, I don't want to let you go."

Manny pulled Charlie to his chest and squeezed Kit's hand so hard it buckled.

Charlie froze, her eyes wet at the corners. Kit caught her gaze and subtly shook her head, as if to say, *Don't react, keep calm. I've got this.*

SOMETHING GLIMMERED IN MANNY'S HEART, the place where Kit had lived. It moved him to feel her come close. He wanted to believe his partner, his muse, was back. How long since she had cozied up to him like that? Had lowered her defenses and let him take over? How long since she belonged to him? His child, his mistress, his slave. A lifetime. And yet he knew he could not trust this Kit. She was biding her time. Trying to get close enough to take Charlie and run. She'd say anything for the girl. He stroked the ragged surface of her knuckles, scars he knew, one of them cut from his own teeth, a right hook landed just so. He prayed. He waited. Nothing. Then he turned to his once partner in crime, his only lasting love. Dark dashes for eyes, that sullen mouth, the barely there tits. Skin coffee-toned like his own, but chewed up like an old bull hide. Sure, he had worshipped her once, but her life was over now. Charlie's had just begun.

"Stand up," he said. She obeyed. Then he saw her steal a glance at Charlie, a signal. She would make her move any second. Soon he would have to kill Kit. And as he imagined holding her throat, squeezing the life from her, he was overwhelmed with fury and love.

Bye, old friend.

He reached out for her with his left hand, the one that wasn't holding on to Charlie, and even as he did he was not sure if he would caress or kill her. Kit kneed him in the gut, and he doubled over, bringing Charlie down with him. Kit tried to pull Charlie from his grasp but he held on. The girl bleated for her mother. Manny rose and flung Kit with one arm across the room, shattering the picture window. A stirring show of strength, he thought. She collapsed onto a pile of glass on the ground. Then stunned, but steady, she rose. A viper, coiled, welcoming a trigger to strike.

KIT COULD NOT FEEL THE wound but could see it was bad. There was a shard of glass the size of a hatchet head sticking out of her hip. Blood soaked her jeans and pooled in her boot. She wasn't sure if she could walk, but Manny didn't know that yet. She had to get Charlie back before she bled out.

"She's not like us, Manny," Kit said, leaning on her strong leg. "She's good. She'd never hurt a soul."

Manny clicked his tongue. "That's not what I heard. I heard she did a vicious thing. I heard she knows how to fight and win."

"You heard wrong," Kit said. "She'll never do your dirty work, not like me."

"I already know her better than you do," he said. He pulled Charlie close to him, his hand so tight around her arm that the skin where he held her dimpled and turned yellow. "You had your chance. Now it's my turn."

"Now it's your turn to what?" she cried, trembling. "To rape her? To make her your slave? To take what's good in her and poison it?" Kit took a step closer, a warm gush on her hip. She was dizzy and wouldn't last much longer.

"I wanted you, I *cherished* you," he said, furious. "Everything you have I gave you."

A thousand feelings, long unspoken, rose to the surface, gasping for air. "You *ruined* me," she said, losing hold of herself. For a moment, she couldn't see through the tears, or hear anything but her own crushing sobs.

"You should have let me starve," she said, and felt a bright anguish, fresh as a clean cut. "Please, just let her go."

"There is no letting her go. I'm a part of her. She *is* me," he said, wild eyed. "Look at her." He held Charlie by the jaws like a prize hound. "She is *us*, Kitty Cat. You and me, together. A miracle and a sin." At this Charlie began to cry.

Manny took Charlie by the arm and shook her. "Stop it, stop crying."

Kit wiped away her own tears and looked hard at Charlie. There wasn't much time.

"Don't listen to him," she said. "You're my baby," and as her mouth formed the word the vibrations unlocked tremendous strength and vulnerability, at once mother and child, shepherd and lamb. "Always. But you belong to *no one*."

Manny seemed incensed by Kit's words, perhaps by their tenderness, or the love that would never belong to him. He rushed at Kit and clamped his hands around her throat. "Shut up, shut up, shut up!"

In that instant, Charlie hoisted up the shotgun, its strap unhooked and dangling, and pointed it at Manny's head. She trembled, but her grip was strong. Her eyes were narrow and dark beneath her brow.

"See?" he said, aiming those vivid blue eyes back at her like pistols. "See that sleight of hand? That's my girl," he said. He let go of Kit's neck and she coughed and breathed deeply. He pinned Kit's hands behind her, twisting them up toward her shoulder blades. She struggled against him.

"Let her go, or I'll shoot," Charlie said.

"She'll do it, too," Kit said. "Don't put that on her conscience, Manny. If you love her let me go."

"You wouldn't shoot your dear old daddy, though, would you?" Manny smiled a smile that had fed and clothed them, stolen countless hearts, gotten them out of trouble as soon as they had gotten in it. That smile, long and friendly, with a little mischief in the curl of his upper lip, had always worked. But it wouldn't work today.

Charlie stared at him, panting, and checked the safety with her thumb.

"I don't have a daddy," Charlie said and clenched her eyes shut. Then she pulled the trigger.

Silence.

She hadn't pulled hard enough to release the round.

Manny laughed and took a step toward her. She panicked and tried squeezing harder but lost her aim, stumbled backward, and fired a shot through the popcorn ceiling. She slid the gun to Kit just as Manny grabbed her.

"You let her go!" Kit yelled and staggered forward on her left leg, the other dragging behind her. A gush of blood from her hip kept time with her heart.

Manny held Charlie up under her arms, her long legs dangling like a marionette's.

Kit pointed her gun at Manny, but there was no shot without hitting Charlie. She would have to maim him. There should be three shells in there, but she might only get one chance to take him down. She aimed low and pulled off a round that peppered the meat of his calf with buckshot. Manny roared and dropped Charlie. With her target clear, Kit reloaded and fired a second round straight at his gut. There was no complexity to the moment, only action, swift and clean. Manny curled around the wound.

"Run!" Kit screamed and aimed again at Manny. Charlie clambered to her feet and sprang for the door. Manny got to his knees and lunged at Kit. She aimed at his face, his ugliness laid bare as if his skin had peeled away from muscle and bone, and said a quiet goodbye.

But before she could take the shot, he fell on her with his full weight, her head cracking on the floor, seeing white, stunned still. Her gun pinwheeled across the floor and out of reach. Before her vision cleared, he had his knees on her wrists down by her waist. She had never seen him like this, unhinged, wild, desperate, and needy.

There was nothing she could do to overpower him, so she closed her eyes and let the calm roll in. Her heartbeat slowed. The sting of adrenaline subsided, and her muscle tone softened. She found Manny's eyes, blue as death, half-hidden under his brow. As she went supple, he leaned down, as if to kiss her, weight shifting slightly off her right wrist, and for a moment loosened his hold.

She quickly freed her hand and shoved her thumb in the wound in his abdomen, his flesh all hot, wet, and soft. He twisted away from the jab and she rolled over and scrambled toward the door. Manny staggered toward her, crying. She had to glance away from him to see what she was looking for. The machete, its fresh edge glinting even in the dim light. Before she could grab it, Manny had her by the neck again, his huge hands pinching off her air. Had he seen it? He pressed his face, wet and rough, against hers and tried again to kiss her, his tongue groping, his teeth clashing against hers. He sucked the air from her, like he would snuff her out, and she felt an allover dimming as her strength ran thin and she slipped out of herself. She noticed, strangely, the faded twist of lemon drops on his breath and his same old smell. The numbing like a drug now, soporific, a call to rest. She could drift away, she could sleep, and let go.

Then she heard a sound as if broadcast from the end of a long corridor. Someone calling, a baby crying. The sound grew clearer, closer, the way an infant's cries would sound if you were running toward her in the night. As if dunked in icy water, she came to. Her face engorged, her hands prickled, Manny sucking on her, leech-like. She squinted, bracing, and bashed his forehead with hers, hard enough to ring her ears. He pulled back, enough of a beat for her to snatch up the machete and slash. A stripe opened up underneath his collarbone and filled with blood. He looked down at it, aghast, touched it with two fingers, and looked back at Kit. All rage again, he swiped a grizzly paw at her. She recoiled and swung again and the blade landed in his neck, stopping at bone. She held the machete there, Manny looking askance at the blade, gullies of blood spilling from his mouth, burbling around the steel. He uttered a strange wet sound. He fumbled around for some invisible thing and passed his eyes over Kit, not seeing her. Then his legs gave way and his body hit the floor.

Kit dropped to her knees, shivering, sapped, and let the machete fall. She tried to call out for Charlie—had she made it out?—but even her voice had given up. She slumped to the side and rolled on her back, the popcorn ceiling like a level mass of clouds above her.

As she sank out of consciousness, there was a sound from the darkness outside. A voice, small and scared, the sweetest she had ever heard.

"Mama?"

Then Charlie appeared in the dim light and knelt next to her mother. Kit opened her mouth, reaching for her daughter, longing to hold her, and again, no sound. As the room spun swiftly away from her, Kit thought, *She's safe, she's safe, she's safe.*

CHAPTER FORTY-FIVE

THE FIRST THING KIT NOTICED WHEN SHE WOKE UP WAS PAIN. A radiating pain from the back of her head, a sharp sickly pain from the gash in her hip, and deep, muscular ache all over her body, like she was being crushed in the fist of some giant. There were tubes in her nose and hand, a catheter from between her legs, and a thicker one coming out of a bandage around her hip. She moaned, which seemed to make more of the pain, but also less.

Charlie was wrapped in a hospital blanket in a chair next to the bed. When she saw Kit stirring, her eyes got big. She jumped and went to the door, the blanket trailing behind her. Instead of her clothes, she wore a pair of baggy green scrubs.

"Hey, somebody!" she called, halfway into the hall. "She's awake!" Then she turned around and smiled at Kit. "Holy shit, you're awake!" As she started back toward Kit, her feet got caught in the blanket and she tripped and fell, sliding across the floor, arms outstretched. Kit tried to reach for her and was hit by a wall of pain. She cried out. It hurt so bad she felt sickness rise up and turned her head to vomit. She retched, her stomach empty, and collapsed back on the pillow. Charlie appeared next to her, chewing on a thumbnail.

"I want to hug you," Charlie said. "But I'm afraid I'll fuck you up or something."

Kit lifted her fingers to show her she wanted to be touched. Her throat and her mouth were dry, and she wasn't sure if she could speak. Charlie covered Kit's hand with hers, lightly, so as not to hurt her. There was blood beneath Charlie's nails and in the curves of her cuticles. She came close and lay her head next to her mother's. Kit drank in the feeling of her daughter, smelled the gun smoke in her hair, tasted her saltwater tears. All this and the vivid burn of a lifetime of hurt. She cried out again.

Charlie stepped back, wiped her tears with the soft side of her wrist, looking incredulous. "Wait a sec," she said, looking stunned. "You're hurting?"

Kit herself could not understand, but the numbness she had known nearly her whole life was indeed gone.

She nodded slightly, wincing. She tried to clear her throat and gagged on the paste of her spit. On a rolling table behind Charlie, there was a large plastic mug with a straw leaning out of it. Kit gestured with her head that she wanted some water.

"Oh!" Charlie said. "You're thirsty. Okay, hang on, sorry I drank it all." She went to the sink and filled up the mug, then she brought the water to Kit and bent the straw toward her split and bloodied lips. Kit sipped the cool water, let it fill her mouth and run down her throat.

There was a cursory knock at the door, and a short, spry nurse in colorful scrubs bustled in with a clipboard. She washed her hands briskly at the sink and snapped on a pair of rubber gloves.

"'Scuse me, hon, coming through," she said, brushing past Charlie. "I need you to stand over there so I can work, mkay?" Charlie obeyed.

With a practiced efficiency, she checked and squeezed a bag of fluids that was dripping down a tube into Kit's hand, wrote something down on her clipboard. Then she took Kit's vitals and looked in her eyes. She smelled like coffee and iodine.

"You got pretty beat up, missy," she said. "How's your pain?" Her voice was a brassy trumpet in Kit's ear. Kit shook her head to say she felt like shit.

"One to five, five's the worst."

Kit held up five fingers. She wanted to explain that all this was new to her. "Is it supposed to hurt this bad?" she croaked.

The nurse laughed sympathetically. "Well, of course it should! You got cut up to ribbons, you poor thing. Oughta hurt like the dickens! I'm awfully sorry you're feeling so bad."

Kit nodded, a little choked up at the kind way the nurse was talking to her.

"Bless your heart," she said and put a little button attached to a wire in Kit's hand. "This is your morphine pump. Hit it now and anytime the pain gets to three." Kit fingered the button but didn't press it. The pain was terrible, but she wanted to see how long she could stand it.

The nurse pulled a watch out of her pocket and, seeing the time, shook her head. "The doctor's behind schedule today so I'm gonna explain a few things to you, mkay?" Kit nodded. She could see Charlie straighten up at attention, as if ready to commit what the nurse had to say to memory.

"You sustained a laceration to your right femoral artery. That's this big one right here," she said pointing to the front of her right hip. "You were taken right into surgery, where they sutured you up and took you to recovery. You lost a lot of blood, so we had to give you a transfusion of donor blood and kept you on fluids and electrolytes." Kit remembered being thrust into the window, the sound of shattered glass.

"You could have died, but this little lady," she said, pointing to Charlie, "she saved your life. Brave li'l sister you got there. Police said they found her leaning all her weight on the wound, trying to stem the blood." Charlie fiddled with the drawstring on her scrubs.

"Aaanyhoo," the nurse said and dropped her clipboard in a clear plastic box hanging by the door. "That's all I got. Take small sips of water and Doctor will be by in a few hours."

Charlie returned to her station and held the straw up for Kit again.

She sipped and swallowed.

"How did you know to do that?" Kit finally spoke, her voice raspy. "Stop the bleeding, I mean?"

Charlie shrugged. A lull fell between them. Kit had little memory of anything that happened after she killed Manny, and even that was devoid of imagery, just a spray of sensation and sound.

"Did you—did you see me do it?" Kit asked.

Charlie looked around the room, as if searching for distraction.

"Yeah," she said. "I couldn't just leave you with him. After he went down I ran to a pay phone I noticed on our way to the motel. There was some change on the floor of that car Manny stole."

Kit shuddered at the many ways she had failed to protect Charlie that night. She could hardly stand the thought of her daughter, all alone, pressing her beautiful hands on a gushing wound, not knowing if her mother would make it.

"I don't deserve you," she said to Charlie, who, in her oversize scrubs, looked like a much younger child playing dress-up.

"Not gonna lie," Charlie said. "It's gonna be pretty tough to wipe that one out of my memory." She stared loosely at the wall behind Kit. "I mean, you pretty much lopped his fuckin' head off."

Kit winced again. It was ghastly, and yet Charlie saying it aloud made it slightly less so.

Charlie got quiet. She began to cry, held the butts of her hands to her eyes, her ribs fluttering with sobs, her voice full and mournful.

Kit reached out her hand. "I'm so sorry," she said, holding back tears for Charlie.

"No, it's not that," Charlie said. "I'm not crying about what I saw. I just—I know he's bad, and I'm not sorry he's dead. You know, after he took me to that place, I knew he was a creepy fucker. But like—" She looked up at the ceiling. "I was kind of excited to have a dad, and

I'm just so sad that he's gone. You know, not Manny exactly, but the person I thought was my dad."

Kit half-smiled, aching with the truth of it and loving her daughter so much it became a new pain. She thumbed away the tears around Charlie's eyes, then drew her near, so their foreheads touched. "I think maybe what you're missing is a parent that doesn't treat you like shit," she said. Charlie let out a sniffly laugh. "I'd say I did my best, but my best was most people's worst. I thought the best thing I could teach you was how to be tough."

Charlie tucked her chin to her chest and turned away.

"Little kids aren't supposed to be tough, though, are they?" Kit said.

Charlie's whole face turned upside down, and she sobbed like she'd been holding it in all her life. Kit pulled her into her arms and held her daughter tight, squeezed her with all the love in her heart. The pain soon overwhelmed her so that she had to let Charlie go and lie back down. All at once, the pain subsided, and a heavy, peaceful feeling coursed through her body.

"The nurse said hit it when you get to three," Charlie said, the morphine drip button in her hand. "She said it was okay. You'll feel better soon."

Kit nodded minutely, eyes closed. "I'm just going to rest for a bit," she said.

"Okay," Charlie said, her eyes blotchy and swollen from tears. "I'll be here."

Charlie pulled the chair closer to the bed. Before she drifted off, Kit pulled back the blanket and patted the space next to her. Charlie climbed in, ever so carefully, and curled up in the warm bay of her mother's lap.

CHAPTER FORTY-SIX

LATER THAT DAY, KIT CRACKED HER EYES, RUBBED AWAY A MORTAR of goop, and found Caleb in the armchair next to her, perfectly upright, eyes closed. She could tell by the slow drag of his breath that he was sleeping. Her heartbeat sped up, and she wasn't sure if it was from injury or because of how oddly endearing he looked there, dozing like a horse.

"Where's Charlie?" she asked.

His eyes flitted open. "Hi," he said and smiled. "I think she went to get some lunch."

Then Kit remembered his reaction when she had asked him to help her look for Charlie. She rolled her head away from him. There was a load of anger inside her, rearing and ready to buck. It was so big she feared it might hurt her. She groped around for the morphine button.

"I got nothin' to say to you," she said, hoping her scorn would push him backward and out the door.

"I'm sorry, Kit," he said, like he could read her mind. "I felt so bad about turning you away that I went looking for you as soon as I was done with Sandy's crime scene, but you weren't home. They'd seen you at the church and said you'd left in a huff. Doc told me what really happened. I'm just so sorry."

All his talking only made her more angry, a bitter brew of old hurt and new.

"You be mad at me all you want, Kit," he said. "I deserve it. I can't believe I didn't listen to you."

She shook her head slightly and fixed her gaze on a dry-erase board that tracked her meals, pees, and shits.

"I'm a terrible cop!" he said, and she could hear he was smiling. *Smiling.* What did he think was so funny about all this? "I have terrible instincts!" he said.

She turned toward him, his friendly, goofy face just gazing at her like she was a newborn baby.

"If you feel so terrible, why do you look so happy?" she asked.

"Well, dang it," he said. "I'm just so relieved to see you. After Sandy . . . and when I heard Charlie had been seen out in the boonies with that . . ." He exhaled and slapped his hands on his thighs. "Well, I've never been so glad to see you give me a dirty look."

She tried to sit herself up, but a new colossal pain shot through her. She went to hit the morphine button then changed her mind and waited for the searing waves to ebb. Though her eyes were closed, she sensed him move to her side. She wanted to come around. Couldn't she remember the good that came before he let her down?

When she opened her eyes he was right there, kind and concerned.

"Look, I'll change the subject, okay, no pressure," he said, pulled a pen from his shirt pocket, and clicked it open. "Don't suppose you'd be up for giving me a statement," he said, gauging her reaction.

She wasn't tracking. "I know it's bad timing and maybe bad taste, but you know, technically I am still on this case—" He stopped, likely noticing her confusion. "Sandy's murder?" There was a little dip of disappointment in her middle as she wondered if that was why he had come today and not to see her. "We sure don't have to do it right now if you're not up for it," he said.

The prospect of putting something down on official record gave her pause. She had killed a man last night, and there would be specific questions about how long she knew Manny, the nature of their relationship, and possibly even why she had come to Pecan Hollow. A simple lining up of the date she came to town and the day Manny was arrested would be damning. She needed time to think this through.

"I'm not up for it." The guilt hung heavy around her.

He clicked the pen closed. "Fair enough," he said. "Good excuse to come back tomorrow." He looked like he was thinking something over. "Look, I know you've never been real enthused about us, but just so you know, you've got a lot of fans back in Pecan Hollow."

"Ha," she said. "What's the punch line?"

"No, seriously. You're a hero. Charlie, too."

She was no hero, she was an outlaw. Even *outlaw* was too grand a name for what she was. She was a crook. And a coward. She'd been hiding from the wrong she'd done for too long. She had to come clean to him.

"Look, don't call me that," she said. "I'm a criminal."

He pulled his chair up to the bed. "You're not. What you did, that was self-defense," he said, all worked up. "That was an act of courage."

"No, no, I'm not talking about that," she said. "Listen, please. Before I came here, I was with Manny. We were together, kind of, and we did bad things. I did bad things. I never worked for anything, just went around scaring people and taking their hard-earned money. I never wanted you—or anyone—to know because I thought they'd take Charlie away from me. But now, with what just happened, people will be looking into things, and . . ." She trailed off. He was fumbling in his back pocket for something. She flashed angry eyes at him.

"The hell are you doing?" she said. "I'm making my goddamn confession here."

Caleb let out a nervous laugh. "Listen, sorry, I just— If you give me a quick second." He opened his wallet and pulled out a square not much larger than a postage stamp and placed it in the palm of his hand.

Kit strained to focus on the grainy scrap in black and white. He held it closer and she took it, wincing against the pain of moving. It was cut from a copy of a photo, cropped around the image of a young woman, her eyes reflected in a rearview mirror, her ponytail thrashing in the wind.

"That's me," she whispered, frightened at what this could mean. "How did you find this?"

Caleb tugged at the collar of his shirt, his throat blotchy.

"Right after you came to town, when I was at the academy," he said, "I was on a ride-along with the Richmond PD, and the cop I was shadowing had this flyer printed and taped to the dash. They'd sent out an APB on the lookout for a young woman about five foot tall, hair dark, driving a Mustang. They said hair length could be long or buzzed. When I saw you there at the spaghetti supper, I knew it was you. It wasn't just your hair. It was your eyes, like you could knife somebody with them. Your eyes were the giveaway."

"You knew all this time?" she asked, feeling so exposed, robbed of her armor. She hadn't realized how much her secrets had been a part of her.

"I guess I did."

She lay back to rest, eyes closed, splicing this new information into the last fourteen years. "And you just let me be?"

"I was never going to turn you in," he said, his cheeks looking hot to touch. "Especially not after I saw you were gonna have a baby."

She wanted to say something to Caleb, about how she'd felt him loving her all these years. How she didn't think she deserved someone so friendly and decent. How she had thought she might break him. She remembered the curly-haired gosling standing in line at the spaghetti supper, so earnest and new. How she had spent all these years swerving around him like he was a small thing she could crush.

"You should have arrested me," she said, feeling sleepy. "I did wrong, I should go to jail." His fingers found her hand now. He dragged them from the tips of her nails to the crease in her elbow and back again, a swirl around her palm. It did not burn. It was a gesture

SHADOWS OF PECAN HOLLOW

both bold and comforting. She closed her eyes and felt the pain flow out of her.

"Aren't you going to take a statement?" she asked, wondering as she said it why she just couldn't let a good moment be.

"I guess not," he said and tucked the covers behind her shoulders, flipped off the lights. He settled back into his seat, folded his hands across his chest, and shut his eyes. His hands were larger than she had remembered, the backs of them fleeced with blond. And his nails, while trim, could have used a good cleaning.

The setting sun appeared through a part in the curtains and warmed her face. She could hear a pair of chickadees squabbling outside the window. She closed her eyes again and felt at once the ache in her hip and the warmth that was settling around her heart.

A FEW DAYS BEFORE KIT was set to leave the hospital, there was a quick rap on her door. "Anyone home?" somebody said. Then in came a woman wearing an iridescent aqua unitard with stirrups and white patent leather heels. Her platinum hair was fluffed and sprayed in a fancy mullet. Under the heavy makeup, the familiar face was thin and haggard.

"Red, is that you?" Kit said, dumbstruck. She hadn't seen her since the night fourteen years ago when she'd come by, newly pregnant and scared. "You look . . ." Kit swung around in search of an accurate but inoffensive description.

"Rode hard and put up wet? Lord, don't I know it. But we've all been through some shit, now, ain't we?" she said. "Look at yew! All battle scarred and victorious and whatnot. I read about you in the paper is how I knew to come. Oh, Kit," she said and looked troubled, like she was digging up something uncomfortable.

Kit was trying to figure out what Red was doing here. She was happy to see her, but it was painful, too. With Manny dead, Red was the only one who had known Kit back then.

"Well, you know I could chew the cud with you all day long, and *dang* is it nice to see ya, but I might as well cut to the chase. I've come to beg your pardon."

"Pardon for what?" Kit asked.

"Well, baby," Red said, catching a deep preparatory breath. "It's like this. Manny and I, we kept in touch when he was in prison. I'd come for his conjugals and such, just to keep his spirits up. He really seemed changed, all biblical and right with the Lord. When he got out I picked him up, and right off the bat he dug into me trying to find out where you were. At first, I played dumb, cause it seemed to me you didn't want to be found, but he didn't buy it. He made threats I knew he'd make good on, so I—" She stopped and covered her mouth with her hand like she didn't want to say the next part. "I told him where you might have gone to."

Kit felt heavy in her gut and so tired. She dropped her head to the pillow and closed her eyes. Manny had found her because of Red.

Red's voice began to waver and she stopped talking to rummage in her purse.

"Goddamn, I'm *not* about to cry. I got my full face on and wouldn't you know my touch-up bag is at home?" She looked at the ceiling, her thick, coated lashes batting, little inky pools gathering at the rims of her eyes. She groped around for something, snapped her fingers. "Quee-ick! Someone hand me a hankie, dammit!" Kit passed her the box next to her bed and Red pulled three tissues and folded them and held them under her eyes to draw out the tears.

"Anyhow, I felt so bad, and I was worried for you. I tried calling you, but you didn't answer. I left you a message, did you get it? Doesn't matter. When I couldn't reach you, I shot myself so full of smack I nearly died. Good thing I got nosy neighbors. Lois Tennenbaum, god bless her vicious little heart, been causing me trouble for the twenty years I've lived on Mesquite Lane. That night, she barged in my house to complain about my music being loud and found me unconscious and facedown in my own sick. That old bitch straddled me and gave me mouth to mouth and pumped my chest till I started breathing again. Spent a few days in the hospital, called my folks, and got my-self straight in a rehab thingy. I honestly don't know how I got into that hard stuff, used to be Dr Pepper was my only fix, but I just let my guard down with one of those guys, got caught at the wrong time. Only had to do it once."

Red blew her nose loudly, then seemed to notice Charlie for the first time.

"Oh, my lord in heaven, is this—?" She pointed at Charlie. "Did you keep it? This your baby?"

Kit nodded. Red clicked over to Charlie and threw her arms around her.

"Oh, sweet baby," she said and took Charlie by the face. "Your mama almost had to get rid of you, but she *didn't*. She wanted you, you hear?" Charlie nodded, a little stunned. "Goddamn," Red said. "I didn't expect that. Whew!" Charlie giggled.

Red pulled up her chair to Kit's bedside and brushed the jagged layers away from her face. "You sure do have goofy-looking hair . . . What have you been cutting it with, a fork and knife?" Kit laughed a little and Red sighed. "Hon, I tried looking out for you. I hope it felt like something to you, but it sure wasn't enough. You were a kid, I turned the other way. I should have called the cops on him. I should have taken you by the hand and led you out of there myself." She pulled a cigarette out of a rhinestone-encrusted case and went to light it, then put it away. "My drug counselor says, 'Winifred, you're shoulding all over yourself,' but fact is, I owe you an amends."

Kit's eyes clouded up and she felt faint. Red was right. She had been the only person in a position to help her and she'd let her stay with Manny. Maybe Red hadn't known how bad he was. She must have known something wasn't right, though.

"Don't you hate me?" Red said with eyes brimming. "I sure would feel better if you did."

Kit cooled as she considered her old friend. She took a full breath and tried to let go of the ugly feeling that had passed over her. Red was here in good faith. She didn't want to push Red away. Kit could feel forgiveness coming on, and she wanted her old friend to know it.

"Look, Manny's the one who hurt me," Kit said, "and no one's responsible but him. I appreciate your telling me in person like this. And I missed you. I did. I hope you don't feel too bad, because you were there for me when I called." Kit looked down at her scarred and calloused hands. "But I think it might be too painful to see you anymore, cause of everything you said. Knowing you knew and didn't help. I'm glad you came, though, Red. Thank you."

Red kept her eyes on Kit and squeezed her hand.

"I gotcha, babe," she said. Then she tipped her head toward Charlie. "You did good." Kit nodded.

"Welp, I got a hot date tonight. I better mosey." Red hoisted herself up, hovered over Kit, and smeared her forehead with a glossy kiss. Then she picked up her purse, fluffed her hairdo in the chrome of a cabinet, and jiggled out the door.

"THE HELL WAS THAT?" CHARLIE said, emerging from her corner of the room. "That . . . woman was your friend?" Charlie didn't think she'd forget her as long as she lived.

"I didn't mean for you to hear all of that," Kit said, a touch shameful, fragile, almost.

"It's okay," Charlie said, softening her tone. "It was kind of interesting to hear a little more about you. I can't believe you know someone like her."

Kit kept her eyes closed and waved for Charlie to sit down next to her. She looked like a ragged doll lying there, her strange bob a mess around her face, the covers pulled up to her armpits.

"I'm sorry," Kit said. "I guess I kept you in the dark about a lot of stuff. Some of it you should know about." She took a deep breath and let it go. "I'm not so good at looking backward. It pains me to do it. But I want you to know where I've been in case . . ."

Charlie leaned in. "In case what?"

Her eyes met Charlie's for a moment and then fluttered closed.

"I don't know," Kit said. "In case it helps you make sense of why I'm so hard to love."

Charlie was very still, as if the wrong move or word would break her mother's moment of honesty.

"When I was born," Kit said, "my mother left me and never came back."

Charlie's throat filled up with emotion.

And then Kit told her everything—about the foster families and running away and meeting Manny. She told her about the stealing and robberies, how Manny had taken advantage of her, and what happened the day Kit fled to Pecan Hollow. After she got it all out, she was quiet for a while, maybe thinking things over.

"I worry sometimes I made you suspicious of everyone, cause I never learned who was kindly and who was not. And I think that's made it hard for you to have friends. And I'm really sorry for that. But you have to know it's because I was trying to keep you safe. If I done right or wrong, it was always for you."

Charlie didn't realize she was crying until she felt the tears splash on her arms. She wiped them away but they came and came. She pitied her mom, so lonesome for so long. And she understood, maybe a sliver, of how her mother had felt. Charlie, too, had felt motherless sometimes. But hearing her story now, told straight, it didn't matter how awful the truth was. It was just such a relief to shine a light in the shadow.

CHAPTER FORTY-SEVEN

THE DAY KIT WAS SET TO LEAVE THE HOSPITAL, SHE WAITED FOR Charlie and Doc to pick her up. She'd been cleared by doctors and said goodbye to her nurses and the physical therapist who had been helping her use her leg again. The doctors had urged her to take her pain meds, but she did not want to numb anymore. She was afraid of losing feeling, because the feeling, whatever it was, let her know she was still there. The doctors warned her the limp might not go away, and if that wasn't bad enough, they'd served her up a hospital bill the size of Texas. It was the kind of debt that she'd spend the rest of her life repaying unless she won the lottery or robbed a bank. The only thing she owned of any value was Eleanor's house.

She had already started to consider selling when she found out from Caleb that Sandy had been killed in her room, that the clothes Sandy had worn were found in the dryer. It was hard to imagine getting a full night's sleep in the house knowing all that. She wondered bitterly if Manny had known he was ruining the place for her. She figured she could get enough out of it to pay down the bulk of her bill and maybe buy a trailer, a home you could move. She felt lighter when she imagined a fresh start, but only when she didn't think about what it would do to Charlie.

It wasn't just the house she dreaded, though, it was the town. She couldn't forget how they had looked back at her that night at the church, rows of judging eyes and scolding lips. She couldn't face them again, not after they had turned their backs on her and Charlie. There were a couple dozen greeting cards she hadn't opened stacked on the counter next to the cotton balls and hand soap. She didn't need sympathy from them. What she needed did not fit on a card.

She thought of Eleanor, how much she had loved that house and left it to Kit, and wondered what she would have said. If her great-aunt had known what happened at the church, would she still have told Kit to stick with it, make nice with everyone? Or would she have been outraged and given her blessing to sell the house and make a home somewhere new? Kit hated the thought of someone else coming in and stripping the wallpaper, painting the walls, adding their personal touch to a home in which four generations of her family had now lived.

AROUND TEN IN THE MORNING, Charlie and Doc showed up with a fistful of ugly balloons and a pink teddy bear.

"Get rid of that shit," Kit said, and they laughed at her. Doc let the balloons bob upward, scatter on the ceiling, and Charlie tossed the bear in the linens basket. They moved in to hug her, and she let them, even hugged them back, though reluctance was still her habit.

"Here, I brought you some clothes from home," Charlie said, holding out a big plastic Walmart bag.

Kit took the bag and held it open, looked inside. "Thanks."

Charlie paused, chewed on her lip. "I figured you probably didn't want to wear your frickin' murder clothes."

Kit laughed and winced at the pain of laughter. "Good thinking," she said. "Whatever I was wearing they cut right off of me. This'll be just fine."

The effort of dressing and getting into Doc's van and being friendly to Doc and Charlie knocked her out as soon as they got on the road. Kit relaxed to the sounds of Doc's bayou vowels and Charlie's hoarse interjections, the rush of the wind through the windows, and drifted in and out of sleep.

The thrum of the cattle guard awoke her, and as she took in the sight of the little ranch house, Kit scarcely recognized it. Once a shabby, flaking gray, the clapboard had been stripped and painted a gorgeous cream, with moss green windows and doors. Someone had filled the holes in the drive, which was now cushy with fresh gravel. And there were people—dozens of them—milling about, holding drinks, shooting the shit.

"What the hell is going on?" Kit said, feeling unsteady.

"Surprise, babe, this is for you!" Doc said and parked the van.

Charlie beamed and clapped her hands. "Mom! Can you believe it?" she said. Kit hadn't seen Charlie so excited in years. "Mom, get out! Everyone's waiting!" Charlie bounded out of the van, ran a few steps and waited, then ran back to the van to help Kit out. There was a squeamish rumble in Kit's stomach as she stuck both legs out the door and slid to her feet. She got the nerve to look at the crowd, the faces she recognized but had never bothered to understand. The people of Pecan Hollow were smiling and applauding.

"Mom, you're a frickin' hero," Charlie said. "Everybody knows what you did, how you saved us from him. People kept calling and stopping by, asking me what they could do to make things right. I said I didn't know but could someone clear out the brambles from the back door? So, they pooled together and cleared the brambles and then some. They've been working these last couple weeks to fancy up the house. Isn't it awesome?"

The sounds of hoots and cattle calls, many hands clapping, morphed into one sound, like water in her ears. The look on Charlie's face, ecstatic and impatient, begged for a reaction. Kit was embarrassed and confused. She didn't know how to act or what to say. Were they mocking her? She tensed up thinking about people creeping around the house without her knowing. The one place where she had felt safe, crawling with strangers. But they hadn't been creeping, had they? They had been helping. Even if it wasn't the kind of help she asked for, it was something. And here they all were with sorry in their eyes. This resentment she'd been carrying had been so comfortable, much easier to bear than forgiveness.

"You did this for me?" she asked, too quietly for them to hear.

Doc slid the van door behind her, as if to cue her to move forward.

"Well," Charlie said, laughing. "What the hell do you think?" For the first time she noticed how nice Charlie looked, her thick hair brushed and braided, a clean white blouse that was new to Kit, tucked into her jeans. And so tall.

She cleared her throat, reached out for Charlie's hand, and shuffled toward the steps, now patched and painted the same mossy green as the front door. As she scanned the faces there was one, in particular, she hoped to see. But there were so many, and she could not make Caleb out among all the cowboy hats. She tested the first step with her foot and it was strong and did not creak. There was a full-bodied, expectant silence behind her. She could smell the paint, and the young thyme they'd planted in the window boxes. When she stepped inside, she was relieved to see that most of the interior had been cleaned, but unchanged. It comforted her to be among Eleanor's things, maybe now more than ever.

Charlie tugged her, too hard, toward the kitchen. A burst of pain.

"Look in the fridge," she said. "Just look!"

There was a basket full of green apples, a block of cheese and butter, three loaves of bread, two dozen eggs, and homemade pickles and jams. There was a gooey pecan pie and a gallon of milk, a ham, two rolls of ready-made biscuits, and breakfast sausage in a tube. People had crowded around the house, and a few started to poke their heads in.

Sugar Faye pushed her way inside with a cooler rolling behind her, high heels muddy, gold bracelets jangling.

"Welcome hoooome," she said. "Do you like it? Did it just blow your mind? I chaired the food committee, of course," she said proudly. "Lookee here in the freezer." Her nails clicked on the freezer handle as she pulled the door open. Behind a gust of chilly mist were stacks of glass dishes covered in foil. "There's spaghetti casserole and chicken tetrazzini, King Ranch casserole and enchiladas and two trays of cornbread."

Her fridge hadn't been so full or so tempting since Eleanor. Still, Kit was too resentful to thank them.

"And here, I got us some hot tamales and pimento cheese sandwiches and a thermos of lemonade spiked with my cousin's homemade hooch," Sugar said, and she winked conspicuously at Kit before pulling her into a warm, perfumed hug. "You know, for the pain."

Kit just stood there, stony, until Sugar backed off. The anger flared up, snatched away her breath. She grabbed the back of the chair, swayed by the sudden spike of emotion. She felt a heaviness she knew would only lift if she faced the waiting crowd, the same people who had shouted her out of the church like a flea-bitten stray.

"You ran me off," she said aloud, her voice cracking. She heard someone gasp, another coughed. People outside craned toward the windows to hear. Everyone's eyes were on her.

"I needed your help," she said and pointed at Charlie. "She needed you."

Apart from the small sounds of many people gathered together, all was silent. The faces she saw were long and sorry, some ashamed.

"She's right," someone said. It was Pastor Tom, leaning against the banister. She waited for something long-winded, but that was it. A few people murmured in agreement.

"I didn't want to do what I did," she said. "I shouldn'ta had to. I didn't need any of this," she said, swinging her arm around. "A coat of paint isn't gonna help me forget how you shut us out. Not gonna help her forget watching me—" She stopped, breathless, and closed her eyes. Was it any use explaining? "We don't need your fair-weather friendship." When she opened her eyes again they were all still there, solemn and sorry.

"For what it's worth, sweetie," Sugar Faye said. "I made good on my promise to you. We were a couple hundred strong that night, looking for Charlie. I raised hell until I had an army out there combing the pastures, knocking on doors. You never seen so many flashlights in one place."

Kit hadn't known that. The image of all those people banding together to help made her want to cry, but she couldn't, not here. She wanted to hold on to this anger. It was hers.

"So you'll listen to Sugar but not to me?" Kit said bitterly. "If you had helped me sooner, maybe I wouldn't have had to do what I did." They had wronged her so deeply, she couldn't see how she could ever feel any different. "I'm sorry, but I'm through being where I'm not wanted."

Sugar Faye looked pained. Doc swooped in and started muscling the crowd.

"This woman is exhausted. Let's give her some room now, y'all. Let's leave her be." She waved her arms around, shooing them toward the door.

"Now hang on a sec, there, everybody stop!" Caleb emerged, pressing against the exiting throng. He was livid and blew a shrill whistle between his teeth. "Kit, you listen here." He took off his hat and frisbeed it onto the kitchen table and stood so that he had Kit on his right, and a dozen or so people to his left, with the rest pressed around the house and crammed on the porch. Kit nearly smiled to see him, his cheeks flushed, a little wildflower in his buttonhole. He cleared his throat and wavered, for a moment, as if he were just now realizing he would have to deliver on the expectations he'd only now set.

"Now, Kit, we all"—he swooped his arm across the crowd— "we *all* owe you an apology. We did the unforgivable. We left you to search for your child, left you to reckon with a cruel and dangerous man, all on your own. Hell, some of us trusted *him* even more than we trusted you." He cast a glance at Pastor Tom, who bowed his head in recognition.

"You're right to hold a grudge. We can be a clannish and suspicious people, and we let you down." A few people nodded as Caleb's speech took on a preachy rhythm. Kit had never seen him this forceful. "And you never gave a rip what we thought." At this he smiled and shook his head. "You couldn't care less if the ladies talked about your haircut or your misbehaving daughter, you wouldn't mind how many heads you turned. But some of us have been waiting for you to see that we are here for you. And you have to see here, Kit, that if you want the good you gotta get with the bad. We're a family here, and family doesn't get to sign out. Family stays. Family forgives." A scattering of "that's it!" and "uh-huh" and "preach!" issued from the listening crowd. Kit burned under this direct and public appeal. And she burned with a feeling so fond and wishful, she began to sweat and dabbed the moisture from her temples with her sleeve. And it wasn't clear if it was fondness for Caleb or a reluctant closeness with these people gathered around her.

"Now we have come here to apologize to you and Charlie," he said, reaching into Sugar Faye's cooler, "to welcome you home, and to eat some goshdang pimento cheese." He pulled out a stack of tea-size sandwiches with orange filling, slapped them on a paper plate, and set them down in front of Kit. He let his message hang a beat to sink in. "So, what do you say?"

Kit looked out at the faces smiling and urging her on. There was prim and pretty Beulah and Principal Fowler looking chastened; all she could see of Glennis was her beehive; and there were the two old widows who lived together, whose names escaped her, but whose wrinkled faces reminded her of Eleanor, powdery and kind. Eleanor. She wished her great-aunt were here now. Kit thought maybe Manny wouldn't have gotten past the front door if Eleanor had been there. She imagined Eleanor would have smelled a rat, driven him out, and told everybody in town not to trust him. She'd have protected her family.

All at once, the anger rose, wrapped around her like a swarm of bees, and stung. And she shook her head as if she could shake herself free of this hurt and buried her face in the rough folds of her hands. She had a thousand reasons to hate these people, and only a handful of reasons not to. Her body ached, her heart throbbed, and she was tired, so tired she felt the labor of holding her eyes shut. She was tired of trying, tired of being wronged, tired of being disappointed in everyone and in herself.

Then, there was Charlie, two warm arms skimming her shoulders, squeezing her tight, and tighter. Strong arms. Arms like Kit's, but free from scars. This child. This child was not doomed to roam. She had an address and enough to eat and she woke up in the same house every morning. She had neighbors who knew her name and family pictures on the wall. This child had a mother. This child was something special.

Tears dripped from her eyes and wet her hands and the bees dispersed. Her chest opened up and there arose in her a warm and grinding hunger, useful and good. She took a soft sandwich and passed it to Charlie, then another to Caleb and took one for herself. She ate it, salty and creamy with a pop of cayenne and a clear memory of the first day she came to this house fourteen years ago and ate this same sandwich at this table. There was a lightening in the room, a collective exhale, and people began filing in. Sugar dealt out paper plates, Doc served the sandwiches, and Charlie dispensed Dixie cups of hooch lemonade. When the house had filled up, people sat on the porch and in the beds of their trucks, on overturned buckets and crates and cross-legged on the grass. Kit was not ready to move among them, but she listened to them tell stories of how she had slain the dragon and saved the town, and how proud they were to know her.

CHAPTER FORTY-EIGHT

ONCE SHE WAS ABLE TO WALK ON HER OWN, KIT CALLED CALEB TO meet for coffee at the diner. He wore a pressed denim shirt and jeans, and his badge was hooked onto his pocket. Of course, he looked nicer than she did, she thought. And she had even tried to look half-decent by combing her hair and wearing her clean jeans. As she looked at Caleb, she noticed things she hadn't seen before. A scar cutting through the honey blond hair of his eyebrows; a little chip in his front tooth; one deep dimple in his right cheek when he smiled, and he smiled broadly when he saw her. He seemed different in the way he carried himself, more confident, not so cautious. It made her less afraid of damaging him.

They sat down, and the new waitress, Sandy's replacement, a cheerleader type with a high ponytail and a store-bought tan, brought them two coffees.

Caleb looked like he had a million things to say. "So, how are you?"

"How am I?" she said, feeling anxious all of a sudden. It was strange to be here on a date, at last, with this gentle man, who had waited years for her to give her heart freely. No lures, no manipulations, just the patience of a monk and a heart overflowing.

"Better every day," she said. "How are you?"

Caleb smiled, then, realizing something, he smacked the table.

"I almost forgot!" He reached in his back pocket and pulled out something red and plastic. When he laid it on the table she could see it was a biohazard bag.

"I know this might be a little sensitive," he said. "But I thought you'd want it back. I pulled it from the . . . from where I found you. And, well, just to warn you, there's some blood on it. Yours, I think."

Kit took the bag. She tried ripping it open, but the plastic was thick and her hands were flimsy these days. Caleb tore it open for her, stretching the plastic, and shook out what was inside.

It was the sheet of school photos, folded into quarters, caked in blood. Brown, dry blood absorbed into the photo paper, smeared over the smiling Charlies. She pulled it by the corners and laid it on the table, smoothed out its rigid bends. Some of the dried blood flaked off. She brushed it aside. Bleary images returned to her, blood in her eyes, glass sticking out of her hip, Charlie appearing in the doorway before everything turned to black. She was heavy with the thought of what Charlie had seen. Too much ugliness, too much blood.

A waitress passed by.

"Hey, can you get me some scissors?" Kit said.

"Sure!" the cheerleader chirped. She found a pair in a catchall can by the register and brought it to Kit. There was one photo at the center that was nearly clean. She clipped away at the photos on the outside and singled out the good one. She wet her napkin in her water glass and dabbed a little rusty spot from the corner of the picture, then slid it in her back pocket. The rest of the photos she stuffed back in the red bag and pushed it to the side.

She noticed Caleb waiting patiently as always. "Thank you for getting this to me," she said. "As soon as I get home I'm gonna put this up on the wall."

They drank their coffee and ordered some pie to go with it. As they ate, they talked about the goings-on in town. About the trouble in Beulah's marriage, how Sugar's youngest son got a girl pregnant, Dirk's latest DWI and how he might face jail time. Kit shared that

Charlie's test results had come in, and though they were just short of passing, the school had agreed to graduate her to the eighth grade, given the summer she had had.

Kit found herself relaxing and enjoying the pleasure of a little chitchat to pass the time—just like Aunt Eleanor would have. After an hour or so, Caleb took out a couple of fives from his wallet and lay them on the check. He smiled.

"Time for me to go back to work."

Kit did not want to lose the warmth of being near him. She did not want him to go.

"Hang on," she said. "I'll walk there with you." She hoisted herself out of the booth and took his slim and steady arm, leaning generously into his side for balance, loving the feel of him next to her.

EPILOGUE

KIT KEPT THINKING THAT, WITH MANNY GONE FOR GOOD, SHE MIGHT finally feel safe, but she still faced each morning uneasy, ever looking into darkness. Perhaps it was the shock of killing him, the feel of it locked into her bones. She couldn't swing an ax or clear brush without releasing that grisly sensation. Meat, bone, blood. A slammed door would throttle her back to the motel with its dirty pigeon smell, and she would remember not the relief of seeing Charlie safe, but always the terror that preceded it, when she hadn't known which one of them would die first.

She knew she should be grateful they had made it out alive. And things were better than ever with Charlie. They now talked with an honesty Kit had never dreamed possible. Charlie came to her with her worries, however small, and Kit had learned to listen. Charlie told Kit about Dirk, how he had stopped talking to her and why. How she still liked him even though she knew she shouldn't. Kit only said she understood, and that had been enough for Charlie. It had been painful to let her daughter in on the sins of her past, but she learned they were not quite so ugly as she had always thought. And there was freedom in letting Charlie know more about where she came from. Now, when Charlie asked her questions, even the hard ones, she answered. Still, she knew it was only a matter of time before Charlie moved on and started a life of her own. And when she did, Kit would be left to reckon with the darkness again.

When she realized Manny's death would not end her worry, she felt freshly lost. He had loomed so large, for so long, that she could not see that the gaping sadness at her center was not caused by him. He had climbed into the hole and lived there, stretching and warping it, making her think it had been filled. But its source, the great sadness of her life, was never knowing her mother.

Caleb looked into it for her. It took him a few weeks, but he found Marie de Clair. There was a minor rap sheet—shoplifting, drug possession, public nudity—and a joint bank account she shared with an old boyfriend, a rich landman, whom Caleb was able to get on the phone. He said she had been living in a rest home in Corpus Christi since a heart attack left her feeble and shaken. He had loved her so much he paid for her convalescence. He said she wasn't a kind woman, or even a good one, but that there was magic about her.

The day Kit found out, the news had sickened her, like a meal she had eaten too quickly. She had not expected to find her mother, just a trail of crumbs she could savor, just enough to move forward without the shock of meeting her in person. The woman she had dreamed of all her life, in beds cold and lonely, could always remain a watery figure, a myth.

After a month of stomachaches and sleepless nights, she dug a map out of her glove compartment. She carefully traced the route with a pencil, two hundred miles southwest, then she fueled the truck and filled up its tires.

In three hours, she arrived in Corpus with its salty air and seagulls and a long seawall that reminded her, chillingly, of Galveston. She parked the truck in front of the old folks' home where her mother lived and kept it running. The plain stucco building was fronted by a porte cochere with a wheelchair ramp leading up to the automatic glass doors. Bushy hibiscus and palmetto filled the planters and distracted from the exterior, which was salt-stripped and gray. She could walk through those doors right now and see the woman who had given birth to her. She wondered if Marie would know, just by looking at her, that Kit was her daughter. Was there something in the genes that let you remember, no matter how long had passed, who your children were? She lost her breath thinking about all the questions she had been holding inside. *Why did you leave me? How can you go on living without your child? If you could do it again, would you keep me?*

It was then that she realized there would be no answer good enough to explain the damage her mother had wrought by leaving her. It was true that Marie had been abandoned when her own mother died, that her father, in his way, had left her, too. But how could she explain leaving an infant with nothing but a blanket and a note, short and ambiguous. How could she correct the lesson Kit would spend the rest of her life trying to unlearn? That an unwanted child must take what she can get. Kit knew she herself had been, at times, a terrible mother. She had fought with Charlie when her daughter needed holding. She'd gone silent when Charlie needed encouragement. She'd acted like a child when Charlie needed an adult. Maybe Kit had no right to judge, but raising a child was the only thing that let her broken heart keep beating.

She remembered how, right after her birth, Charlie crept up to Kit's breast like a little squirrel and started nursing all by herself. Her eyes were swollen shut, and she was all turned around in a strange and scary world with nothing but the warmth of her mother's skin and the taste of her milk to comfort her. All Kit had to do was hold her. Though it required nothing of her, it was everything Charlie needed. She ached now, as she wondered if Marie had ever given her that, a moment of comfort before she was left in the cold.

She dragged her sleeve across her eyes, then pulled a pen and a baggie from her pocket. The note she had held and read so many times had become a proxy for her mother. Her throat knotted as she wrote her own message on the back of the original.

For Marie de Clair.
I was something special.

She left the note at the front desk and returned to her truck feeling both lightness and loss. She wept, battered hands held to her face, muffling the sobs, wishing there were someone who could hold her. And then, she remembered. Warm arms skimming her shoulders, her stormy dark hair. Charlie. Whose childhood was nearly over, those moments faded in the wash of much to do and too little time. Who had thrown her weight onto Kit's wound to save her life. Who still curled up to sleep with her mama. Kit shifted her truck into gear and drove full speed back to Pecan Hollow. Home to her daughter, her wet-cat, claws out, foulmouthed Charlie, her heart unbearably alive and hurting with the gossamer quality of a wound beginning to mend.

ACKNOWLEDGMENTS

TO MY MIGHTY AGENT, LIZ WINICK RUBINSTEIN, THANK YOU FOR OPEN-
ing the door. And to my gentle, brilliant editor, Liz Stein, thanks for
inviting me in. I could not be more grateful to everyone at William Morrow, without whom this book would be a big, sprawling document in a
file titled "PUBLISH??" To Kaitlin Harri in marketing, and my pub-
licist, Alison Hinchcliffe: thank you for making sure *Shadows of Pecan
Hollow* finds its audience. For the beautiful cover art, thanks to designer
Yeon Kim. To production editor, Rachel Weinick, and copy editor, Susan
Brown, for their attention to detail. Much gratitude to Zoe Bodzas for
her peek-a-boo interjections of praise, and Ariana Sinclair for cheerily
keeping me on schedule.

To my readers, Julia Langbein, JJ Strong, Erin Cantelo, Ross
McNamara, and Adam Countee, and the Revisionaries writing
group, Jay Fernandez, Anne Barnett, Tatiana MacGillivray, Luis
Romero. Thanks for helping me make the sausage.

To the staff and participants of Community of Writers, thank
you for your devotion to the creative life and for reminding me that I
want to be an author.

Thanks to my teachers, especially: Janet Fitch, whose long hair I
covet, and whose advice on the craft of writing has stuck with me for
fifteen years; Ruth Bellows, for letting me rewrite that Nabokov

paper because she knew I could do better; and Toni Attwell, for her support and her implausible enthusiasm for Sir Gawain and the Green Knight. To my cousin Katherine Center, for her hard-earned wisdom and encouragement.

To my therapists, Judi, Allison, and Sam, for asking and for listening.

My moral support committee: Annski, Sara, Sarah, Colleen, Mel, Mollie, Dan, Julia, Nangs, and cousin John. Everyone should be so fortunate to have lifelong friends like you.

To my parents: Lucy, for surrounding me with books and for calling me a "great writer" since the moment I learned my letters; Robert, for following his creative compass, and for sharing his love of country living; and Synda, for her world famous pecan pralines and for showing me what a tough-ass Texas woman is made of.

A million thanks to Paty, for caring for my kids (during a pandemic) so I could meet my deadlines.

To my three children, who are all younger than this book: thank you for ignoring my "Do Not Disturb" sign, climbing into my lap, and making me play with you. You taught me that I can always write after you go to bed.

To my sweetheart, Jake: Thank you for doing what you love for a living and taking for granted that I should, too.